Tangled Power

TANGLED POWER

COMPASS POINTS
BOOK TWO

JILLIAN WITT

This book is a work of fiction. Names, characters, and events in this book are the products of the author's imagination or are fictitious. Any similarity to real persons living or dead is coincidental.

Published by Myth and Magic Book Club Publishing
Copyright © 2024 by Jillian Witt

All rights reserved. No part of this book may be reproduced in any form or by any electronic or mechanical means, including information storage and retrieval systems, without written permission from the author, except for the use of brief quotations in a book review.

Cover Artwork & Map by Holly Dunn
Developmental Editing by Rebecca Faith Editorial
Line Editing by Paper Poppy Editorial
Proofreading by Isla Elrick

ALSO BY JILLIAN WITT

Compass Points (Compass Points #1)
Tangled Power (Compass Points #2)

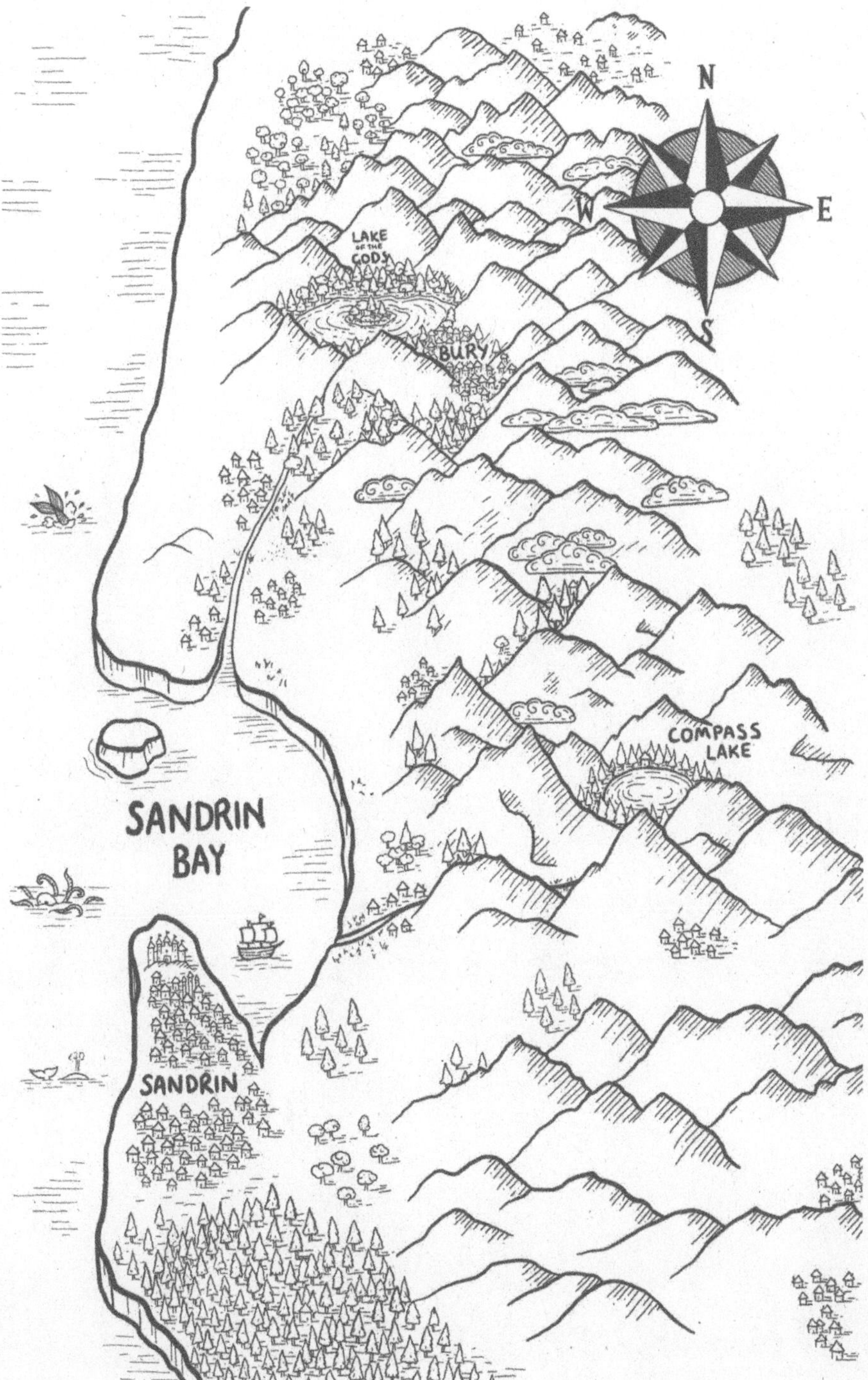
N
W
E
S
LAKE OF THE GODS
BURY
COMPASS LAKE
SANDRIN BAY
SANDRIN

To anyone who has tried to carry the weight of the world on their shoulders—
you don't have to do it alone.

BOOK 1 RECAP

Tangled Power takes place after the events of *Compass Points*. I know its hard to remember all the details of books you may have read weeks or months ago, so I wanted to offer a summary page.

Visit here for a recap of the events of *Compass Points*: https://www.jillianwitt.com/compass-points-summary

I hope you enjoy the continuation of Rose's story!

PROLOGUE

500 years ago

Arie's pace quickened. A loud rattling sound interrupted his casual walk into the grand entry hall of the temple at the top of Mount Bury. He broke into a jog, hastening to the open circular room with the four gods' altars when the noise grew louder. He was early to meet Zrak and hadn't expected to encounter anyone else. Arie paused to survey the room he entered. Offering plates before four statues decorated its interior, one set at each cardinal point. The path he'd come down placed him at an ordinal point. Above, the open sky decorated the roofless temple, designed to make the worshiper feel withdrawn from the continent. Nothing seemed out of place.

Arie was always impressed with the offerings here. The mountain trail was a challenge. He always flew. He couldn't picture the human—or now, fae—that could endure the hike to the top. His gaze caught on an opening in the floor in the center of the room.

Tilting his head, he walked toward the unexpected hole and looked down. A gilded, spiral staircase unfolded below him into the heart of the mountain.

This must have been the source of the noise. How had it opened? Down, down, down it circled. He couldn't make out what lay at the bottom. Arie spun on the spot, searching again to see if anyone else was in the room. This stairway hadn't been here previously, and as one of the gods honored here, he considered himself an expert on the temple. Confirming he was alone, he shrugged and began his descent.

Each step took him deeper into the mountain. His pace slowed as he realized this was no quick walk. Whatever lay below was still out of sight. Meaning he would be going down these stairs for a long time. Suddenly remembering he was a shapeshifting god, Arie transformed into a large, black bird and glided toward the bottom.

Ever since the Flood, the disaster that overtook the continent the last time the gods sought selfish gain over protecting those under their care, Mount Bury had boasted more wild magic than most. He wasn't sure what it meant, but his feathers tingled as he got closer to the floor of the cavern. Finally, the shape of a figure in the middle of the open room came into view.

Zrak was directing his wind to shape a cavern rock into a table. Arie's eyes lit up as Zrak repeated the process twice more and then placed a small glass vial on each of the three tables he'd created. Arie's gaze locked on the table in the center. The vial called to him. Intrigued by what Zrak was up to, Arie prepared to make himself known.

"About time you showed up," Zrak said without turning to look at the bird.

Arie shifted into his human form, and the wild magic hit him harder, his skin aflame as if his fire magic had been set free to dance beneath it. "What are you doing down here? What is this place?" Arie asked.

"I'm glad you followed me. This is why I asked to meet—what I wanted to show you." He turned and gave Arie a pointed look, his face cast in shadow. "You will need to know about this when I'm gone."

Arie sucked in a breath. He still hoped to find a way to stop Zrak from going through with the sacrifice. They could find another way to maintain the balance.

"There is no other way," Zrak said, answering Arie's unspoken question. "Wipe that sad look off your face. We all agreed, and I intend to go through with it."

Massaging his temples, Arie buried his objections and gestured to Zrak. "By all means then, please tell me what I'm looking at and why we'll need it."

Zrak's lips quirked up at the corner, trying to hold back a smile. "That's more like it," he replied flatly.

How dare he take this so lightly? How dare he be so cavalier about removing himself from the continent? Arie wanted to shake him. Fire danced under Arie's skin again as the wild magic amplified his power, inflaming his rising anger. "What is this place?"

"I can see the wild magic is already having its way with your fluctuating emotions." Zrak's gaze raked over Arie as he tried to shake off the magic.

"Is it not affecting you?"

"It seems to choose only one power at a time," Zrak said, his hands resting on his hips.

Arie shook his head. It was so typical. Zrak always had to know how things worked. "You're trying to distract me," Arie replied, balling his hands into fists.

Zrak stepped forward, a sliver of light in the cavern falling across his face. He looked his age—which wasn't a compliment to an immortal god. His usually vibrant skin seemed dull, and the laugh lines around his eyes and mouth were downturned. He was still breathtaking. Not even a bad day could ruin Zrak's otherworldly beauty. It was a small comfort to Arie. No matter the front Zrak put on, this decision, this direction from Aurora's compass, was clearly wearing on him.

He raised his hands in a gesture of peace. "I didn't mean to. I've found wild magic in a few places across the continent, and I'm simply intrigued by it." He paused, remembering what Arie asked him. "But to your question—yes—I believe in our plan." He gestured to the tables behind him. "I also believe in contingency plans."

Arie couldn't hide his smirk. Of course he did. Zrak had more plans and backup plans than a fire had embers. "And what, may I ask, is this particular plan we're working on?" Arie stepped forward to inspect the center vial—the one that called to him.

"Be careful with that," Zrak chided. "Each contains a remnant of yours, Aurora's, and Aterra's magic."

Arie wrapped his fingers around the glass tighter as he felt the essence of his magic within. He held it to the light and saw flame dancing within. Anger bubbled inside him. He wanted to smash it. "You took some of our magic when we created the fae courts?" Arie asked.

"I siphoned a tiny amount for this trial," Zrak said offhandedly as he gestured to the tabletops before him.

Arie wanted to scream or laugh at how casually Zrak had violated their trust during the Creation. He let out a long breath. His trust in Zrak was absolute. Though the others would likely not agree. "And what is this trial? What is it for?" Arie set the vial back down.

"It's for when things go wrong."

Well, that was reassuring. "Are you expecting things to go wrong?" Arie asked.

"We already failed once, and look where that got us." Zrak gestured around them. The cavern, this meeting, and Zrak's appearance were all reminders of the cost of their failure. Zrak would pay the price for their selfishness. "This time," he continued, "we must plan for everything, even if we don't want to look too closely at what events would lead to certain paths."

That felt like a condemnation to Arie, but he couldn't figure out what it was for. He walked slowly around the three tables. The only reason to need samples of their magic would be to compare against a future, flawed iteration.

"So, this particular hypothetical path..." he started, his hands slipping into his pockets. "We're assuming one of the remaining gods' magic has been corrupted...and this test would identify which one?" he mused. "You're expecting one of us to do something to upset the delicate balance we're sacrificing so much to preserve?" Zrak didn't interrupt. He just held Arie's gaze as he completed his thought. "Isn't that why we created the fae courts? Shouldn't they be able to restrain us?"

"How are the fae courts to know one of the gods has upset the balance?" Zrak asked. "By the time they see signs of corruption on the continent, it may be too late." Zrak shook his head. "No. You three must be the first line of defense."

That was fair. It's not like the gods had to present themselves to the fae leaders with any regularity.

"So, we test each other and then notify the Compass Points? And they unify to take care of it?" Arie laughed to himself. It was a dark laugh, though, devoid of humor. Maybe this plan did have holes in it. "Have you checked in on the fae courts and their leaders? It's been only weeks since Creation, and already, they isolate themselves. I'm sure they would have fled to the four corners of the continent, putting as much distance between themselves as possible, if we hadn't made their seats of power at Compass Lake."

Zrak shrugged as if he had not a care in the world, instead of days left of existence. "They need time to adjust to their power. We can't expect them to be benevolent from day one. Think about what we did with ours."

When he put it that way, Arie realized his point. The Compass Points only had a fraction of the gods' power, but the gods had also done much worse with theirs. The fae would go through phases. First, hoarding and protecting their power, then hopefully figuring out how to use it for the good of the continent.

"Fine." Arie waved his hand at the vials. "So, your assumption is"—he started listing items off his fingers—"first, we create the fae, giving the continent the means to unite and overpower a god should we abuse our position again. Second, you sacrifice yourself to correct the balance." He flicked out a third finger. "Third, one of the remaining gods ignores said sacrifice and continues to pursue self-interest and power, sending the continent careening toward untold devastation...again." He looked around the cavern. "When that happens, you want me to bring Aterra and Aurora down here for a little get-together, so we can find whose magic has been corrupted. Do I have that right?" The pitch of his voice rose in exasperation with his speech.

"That sums it up nicely. Very astute," Zrak said. His lips were pushed together in a flat line, like he was desperately trying to fight another smile.

"This isn't funny!" Arie shouted. "How could you think we'd be dumb enough to need this test when you're literally giving your existence to prevent something like this from happening?" Arie's voice echoed through the mountain cavern around them. "Forget about the fae for a moment. Why would one of the gods risk it? We just saw what our selfishness caused."

Zrak moved to take Arie's shoulders, his long fingers digging into the muscle. He gripped tight until Arie raised his eyes to meet Zrak's. "I don't think this is funny, Arie, but it is necessary. I want to believe this plan won't be needed, but as you said, I'm sacrificing my existence on this plane. I will not leave it to chance."

Arie nodded. He supposed that was Zrak's right. His shoulders strained to sag in Zrak's hold, but Zrak's fingers dug in, forcing him to maintain eye contact for a little longer.

"How do you know it won't be me then?" Arie asked quietly.

"Oh, Arie." His smile was soft. "I'm not sure you'll be capable once I'm gone."

Arie wondered at that. It spoke to a depth of understanding between him and Zrak. Arie liked to play flippant but felt his friend's impending sacrifice like a wild animal gnawing in his stomach. There was no way he'd continue on their selfish path once Zrak was gone. Part of him was glad that Zrak knew it too. "But you're not sure about Aurora and Aterra?" Arie couldn't help but ask.

"I know what Aurora means to you and I'm glad you two finally found each other. This isn't a moral judgment on her or Aterra. It would simply be remiss not to have contingencies in place."

Zrak's gaze drifted from Arie's. The thousand-yard stare he'd perfected usually meant that he knew more than he was saying.

Arie squeezed his eyes shut as if wishing the conversation to end but knowing he should prepare for the worst. "What do you need me to do?"

"Bring them here when the time is right. Ensure the test is taken by all three of you at the same time."

"And how exactly do we take this test?" Arie asked, looking at the vials again.

"All three of you stand together over there." Zrak gestured toward the staircase. "Call your magic. The one unable to do so will be the one who's corrupted."

"How do you know that?" Arie asked.

"The wild magic you've felt here? That amplification of your power? It's a remnant of our misuse of magic. It can't be controlled, and it is selective in how it affects us. It is born of instability, and is thus drawn to volatile magic." A look of concern crossed Zrak's face as he continued. "It's, of course, dangerous to use in this way. It will be difficult to control should it find corruption, but it's all we've got." Zrak gave Arie a stern look. "Make sure no one is in the temple or on the mountain should you take the test."

Arie nodded. After feeling the fire beneath his skin, he didn't doubt Zrak's words. Over their existence together, Arie had learned Zrak's knowledge of magic was greater than most.

"What will the Compass Points do with the god or goddess who has disrespected your sacrifice? How will they stop them?" Arie asked.

"We've given them the ability." Zrak looked tired, finally releasing Arie's shoulders from his hold. "The execution is something they will need to figure out together."

CHAPTER ONE

"You really think now is the time to make a weapon?" Luc's voice was still groggy while pulling a shirt over his head and entering the Suden workshop.

Rose already had the fire going. She'd been at it for hours. In some recent past, she'd hoped to drift off to sleep for one more night without the responsibilities of a Compass Point, but that was beyond her grasp. At least Luc had given her a few hours of bliss—their relationship so new and begging to be explored. Her magic strained toward him as he walked in. There was a *wanting* between their magic she'd never experienced before. Hiding her power for the last ten years gave her no indication of whether this was normal between fae lovers. She attempted to refocus on her task, with her mind racing through the next steps to save the continent.

"Yes," she said, glaring at him. "I obviously do." Well in the midst of forging, she gestured to the work before her. "When else will we have time to make you a weapon?"

Dawn approached, the darkness on the lake fading. The pair had promised to return to Norden house early to fill in the many blanks they left after the Refilling Ceremony the day prior, but they still had hours.

Luc tapped his finger to his chin playfully. "I thought you didn't want to make weapons for the Suden Point."

"That was ten problems ago," Rose replied, adding the eye-roll his comment deserved.

Slow, careful steps brought Luc across the room. She pretended to ignore his approach, focusing on the blade she was crafting instead. Hammering at her anxieties usually worked for her. Luc was standing dangerously close before she acknowledged him. Pine and cinnamon filled her nose as his magic enveloped them. It was a presence all its own—demanding to be acknowledged. Her back to Luc, the slow smile that curved her lips was hidden. He was releasing his power from the tight hold he typically kept over it. Since acknowledging this thing between them was real, it seemed to strain for her when they were close. Whether it was a conscious decision or not, it was a heady thing to have his power so singularly focused on her.

Part of her wanted him to unleash it.

"You may want to give me some space," she said. Her words came out breathier than intended as she relaxed into his magic. It was thick in the air around them, tendrils circling and spiraling in all directions. His magic dared her to lean back into it, but she already knew it wouldn't let her fall.

Raising his hands in surrender, Luc halted his progress, his magic slipping away from her. "Tell me what you need."

She regretted her request, missing the insistent feel of his magic as it returned to its owner. She took a deep breath before voicing her fears. "I need you to be safe when we go after Aterra and Aiden. I know we can't guarantee that. So a magical weapon is one advantage I can give you."

"Okay." The curve of his lip was soft as Rose glanced over her shoulder at his too-easy concession.

"This isn't funny!" She set her forging hammer down and ran her fingers through her dark, shoulder-length hair. Her pale skin was covered in streaks of ash and dirt from the hours she had already worked.

She really should have stayed in bed.

"It's a little funny," he offered. The tone of his voice coaxing her to relax. "You're making me a weapon in the middle of the night. Don't you need me for part of this process?"

Rose wiped the sweat from her face with too much vigor, hating that he was right. With only an hour or two of sleep, she had snuck out to the forge and started working. Certainty drove her here. The certainty that they wouldn't have time after telling the Compass Points what they faced—who they faced.

Once the Compass Points knew Aterra, the Suden god, was pulling Aiden's strings, they would want to act quickly to fulfill their duty. Maintaining the balance was their reason for existence. And the balance was in shambles; the mist plague coating the continent proved it.

A thought kept swirling in Rose's mind. Did the Compass Points even know how to do such a thing? This may be why the fae courts were created, but had they ever been tested?

They were about to find out.

"I do need you," Rose said a little too quickly. Luc caught the dual meaning in her words, and his soft smile turned into one of her favorite smirks. She rolled her eyes. "I need to feel your magic to finish the weapon. I'm not ready to merge your magic into the blade, but the sooner I know the heart of your magic, the better the weapon will turn out."

The weapon-making process would be tricky with him. It wasn't physical, but it was inherently intimate. A wielder and their magic were so connected that knowing one meant knowing things about the other. Things some would preferred were left private. That was part of why she was picky about who she made weapons for. Given the nature of her relationship with Luc, she couldn't separate the process from her feelings for the Suden Point. She was sure she'd uncover things about him they hadn't discussed yet, though he seemed unconcerned when she said as much.

"I'm an open book for you, Rose. I'd prefer we have the leisure of time to learn each other, but that hasn't been our path."

Turning from the forge and stepping over to the worktable, she crooked her finger, calling him back to her. They would find out together how their relationship would shape this process. There was no one she would rather experiment with.

Luc stepped forward, caging her in, his lithe body unyielding as it framed her. He pushed up his sleeves and his powerful forearms stole her attention, reaching around on either side of her, careful not to lean into the forge's heat.

"You're going to be a distraction, aren't you?" She pulled her gaze from his exposed skin to meet his eyes. The heat in them told her the answer before he responded.

"Only if you ask nicely," he said, his voice smooth and deep as his hands moved to her hips, lining up their bodies as he pulled closer.

"I'm armed," Rose noted as she held the metal of the blade she'd been working on between them.

"Threatening me with my own blade?" His smirk was back, and his eyebrow raised.

She shrugged while wrapping it in her wind so as not to actually burn them.

"You're always a little dangerous," he said. "That's what makes it interesting." He dipped his head around the blade and nipped her neck.

She didn't stand a chance, and they both knew it. The blade was set aside before things escalated. Soaking in his attention, she let her head fall slowly back. Hands free of the weapon, she propped against the table behind her. Her weight rested against it as she gave him all the access his lips demanded.

He trailed kisses down the column of her neck, nipping her shoulder as he moved. His expert tongue seemed intent on tasting the sweat there. A shiver of anticipation shot through her. His hands explored the skin beneath her tunic as his mouth ventured lower.

JILLIAN WITT

"Luc," came her half-hearted whisper. She didn't want him to stop. Her body ached for him to learn its every dip and curve. And yet—she needed to focus on making his sword. Even as she eagerly responded to the pleasure he stoked, her mind wouldn't release the fears about what came next. She lifted her hand, caressing his cheek and settling under his chin, returning his face to hers. "We have work to do."

"That we do," he said, holding her gaze. His eyes danced with a wicked gleam in the firelight. Straightening, he asked, "What do you need from me? I admit I don't know how this works. The other weapons masters I worked with barely needed me for the process."

"Well, you didn't get very good weapons from them, did you?" she responded. She hadn't had enough time to learn how other magical weapons masters were trained. She only knew the technique her mother had taught her, and the strength of her weapons vouched for it.

Revealing the technique would also be new. She had never explained her process to anyone. Rose thought about how Luc had torn down every wall she erected. He learned her secrets and protected them as his own. She could trust him with this.

"I need you to stand by the forge while I work this a little more. Having something small to exercise your magic while you're there would be helpful."

He picked up a rock from the ground as he moved where she pointed. Holding out his hand, he set the rock levitating above it. "Will this suffice?"

"Yes." Rose let his magic twist around her as she returned to the forge. "Give me a little while. The more I lose myself in the rhythm of forging, the more my senses open to the magic." She shrugged as she continued, trying to lessen the immensity of explaining this process to another. Her gaze darted over her shoulder to check on Luc. Their eyes met, and she knew she wasn't fooling anyone with the attempt at a calm veneer. His face held nothing but patience, though, as she considered her next words. "At some point, my magic will start to test yours. It interacts differently with each magic it evaluates, so I can't tell you exactly what it will do." She raised her eyes to meet his. "I can tell you that it will push until it gets to the heart of your magic—whatever that looks like."

She glanced at him again. His lips pressed together. He seemed at war with whether to reassure her or let her continue her explanation uninterrupted. "Do whatever you need to, Rose," he whispered.

Warmth shot through her as his need to reassure won out. "When I get to the heart of your power, I'll see things, usually flashes of emotion, places, those you care about, beliefs that you hold dear." She considered how to explain. "It should be similar to when you showed me a taste of your mind shadow magic."

He nodded.

"I admit, I don't know if your mind shadow will change how this works—you inherently have the ability to show others scenes from your life. I'm sure that will make itself known somehow in this evaluation." She turned back to the forge. "I also feel like I have to mention that I've never made a weapon for someone I'm so...emotionally entangled with."

"Is that what we're calling it?" Luc didn't miss a beat. The need to confirm his raised eyebrow matching his wry tone was too great. She couldn't contain her smirk as reality perfectly matched her imagination.

He winked at her. "You can experiment with me."

He was teasing her, but heat shot straight to her lower belly nonetheless. She rolled her neck out, trying to refocus. "Alright, I'm going to get started. Keep your magic a little bit active, like I said."

His element continued to hover the rock above his hand. This display was more than a little activity. Most Suden were unable to use the earth to push objects from it. More commonly they dug or broke the land apart beneath them. But Luc's magic was different. Further proven by the fact that another line of his power wrapped around her as she lost herself in her work.

He was powerful, of course. He was the Suden Point. It still impressed her that he could maintain the two separate actions. Doing both for any length of time should tire him. Rose snuck glances at him as she worked, unable to see signs of stress or fatigue.

Her weapons master magic streaked toward him. An inheritance from her mother and a unique flavor of the talent due to her dual fae lines, it was ethereal compared to the heft of Luc's magic. That didn't mean hers couldn't hold its own. He shivered as it reached him. A thread of her power spun around his outstretched palm.

His magic, cocooning her by the forge, fell back to weave with hers as it investigated. Their magics teased and twisted together. She let them, taking the opportunity to press and search his power as they entwined.

Completing a circle, her power paused as his returned to him —taunting—sinking into his skin and daring her to follow. Luc's face was impassive. His gaze focused on the rock levitating above his palm.

Eyes fluttering closed, she felt the edges of her power as it enveloped him. Her control slipped as it searched him, skipping across his skin. Her magic wanted him—more so than the usual requirement to make a weapon. And the amount of raw power available to him was its own siren song. She sucked in a breath. Her magic was intent on this next step.

Trying to gauge this experience from his perspective, her gaze raked over him. His eyes tracked hers, but he appeared otherwise unphased. He raised his eyebrow again as her magic snuck deeper into him. He looked down at the exposed skin of his arm where her magic's touch would be most felt. Intrigue and—was that arousal?—flicked over his features.

She might have called it off with anyone else, but Luc wasn't just anyone. Her anxiety about their future battles was heavy in her chest, outweighing the unknown of her magic's *need* to explore him. If a weapon was the only safety she could offer, she would ensure he had one.

"This next part might be a little more invasive," she said, giving him one more chance to say no.

Luc nodded his consent. Gazes locked, she let her magic go. It chased the power that had been loosed in the workshop, rushing into Luc and down a dark tunnel after it. Her magic followed his toward the heart of his power. The makeshift walls flew by as her magic pressed forward. They held moving images, voices, and full memories coming to life. She sped forward too quickly to investigate each one. A tunnel made sense for a Suden, she thought as she fell through it, like the pits in the earth they were well known for making.

The images and scenes on the walls were unexpected. She never saw complete scenes or replayed memories from someone's life. Usually it was snapshots, scents, and feelings. Taking a calming breath, she let herself continue to fall. She knew this would be different. His mind shadow alone would change this process. But his magic was also different. There was so much about it—about him—to learn. The immensity of how badly she wanted to know everything slammed into her.

The rapid descent slowed as her plan took shape. She only needed to learn a little today and could learn a little more in their next session. His power could overwhelm her if she took in too much of it at once. Reaching out to the moving images lining the passage, she plucked one to study closer, holding the corner carefully between two fingers.

The image held a short scene—Luc's hands in his pockets, head hung in defeat, as he walked toward a door. A female stood in the opening, fists on hips, glaring daggers at him. Something about the image called to her, and Rose's other hand reached to touch Luc's face in the image itself.

The image rippled as soon as her magic touched it. Her brow furrowed as she tried to pull away. But she was in too deep. A sharp gasp slipped from her lips as the image came alive around her, pulling her into it.

CHAPTER TWO

"What did you do this time?" the female called from the door the child version of Luc was walking toward. She was short and lean, her dark hair knotted atop her head.

"I didn't do it on purpose," Luc replied. He looked so young to Rose. He couldn't have been more than eight. His shoulders sagged, carrying much more weight than his small frame should have to support.

"That's not what I asked," she pressed. Her hands crossed at her chest as she waited for the answer.

"I shook the schoolyard," he replied, getting close enough to her that he didn't have to shout. His voice was soft, uninterested in disseminating news of his failure.

"Luc." She scratched her head as she looked at him, considering how to proceed. Rose could tell from her interloping view of the scene that the female was disappointed—maybe even angry. Wrinkles lined her face, and gray flecked her dark brown bun. She looked tired. It led Rose to believe this might not be a first occurrence.

"We talked about this," she said, reinforcing Rose's suspicion.

"You have to keep control of your power. None of the other children are having these outbursts."

"Richard says his dad taught him how to keep his magic level," Luc said as he finally looked up at the female.

Her intake of breath was sharp. Rose noticed it then, the similarity in their noses and the set of their mouths. This was Luc's mother. Given what Rose knew about his absent father, his words must have hit her like a slap in the face.

"I taught you what you needed to know about earth magic. Are you saying that wasn't good enough?" Her stern tone couldn't mask the disappointment, though Rose couldn't read its intention.

"I don't know." Luc shrugged. "I keep trying to clench it tight and bind it deep inside me, like you said." His eyes pleading, he looked helpless, an expression Rose was unused to seeing on the feared Suden Point of the present. "There is just this dark tunnel inside me that power erupts from sometimes, and I can't hold on."

Luc's mother looked at the sky. "Was anyone hurt?" she asked as her gaze returned to the child before her.

"Anthony fell in the earth shake..." Luc said. His hand scratched through the hair at the back of his head. "It split parts of the schoolyard, and he fell into one of the smaller crevices." His voice sped up to reassure her. "They got him out, though."

Before Luc's mother could express further frustration, another smaller child with dark brown skin came barreling down the street. "He was defending me!" the child barely got out before he started coughing to catch his breath.

Even at this age, Rose could see this was Luc's younger brother, Aaron. He was ganglier as a child than the broad-shouldered fae she knew now. But the look of concern on his face for Luc was a dead giveaway—one she'd seen before.

A male who could only be Aaron's father joined Luc's mother at the doorway. Luc spoke fondly of his stepfather. He raised Luc as his own, even though the town never ceased pointing out the unnatural tendencies of Luc's power. And the kids he grew up with had no shortage of taunts for him about his birth father's abandonment. The fae surveyed the two children on the doorstep, Aaron still breathing heavily from his run home.

"What's all this?" he asked. "You're both home early." His voice held nothing but patience—a stark contrast to the tone of the conversation between Luc and his mother.

"Anthony was picking on me again," Aaron said. "He told me I'd never learn how to read."

Rose found that an interesting statement given that Aaron's current position at Suden house was librarian and researcher. She was inwardly glad that Aaron had proved this Anthony kid so wrong. Aaron's father crossed his arms over his chest and waited for his son to continue.

"Luc heard him picking on me, and I swear, he tried to take the deep breaths that Mother recommends. But his hands still started to shake. He tried to grip them into tighter fists. I promise he worked to push the magic down." Aaron was out of breath again as he rushed to defend his brother. "His knuckles were white, and I think he almost held it!" He sighed. "Then Anthony told me I was too stupid to learn..." Aaron hesitated, unwilling to condemn his brother with the final words.

Luc stepped in to finish the story. "And I lost control," he said in a monotone.

Luc's mother and stepfather shared a resigned glance. His stepfather opened his mouth, about to speak, but his mother spoke first.

"That doesn't excuse attacking someone," she said firmly. "No matter the reason."

"Yes, Mother," Luc answered softly. "They've asked me not to return until I can control myself." His head fell as he and Aaron scampered inside, leaving the adults on the doorstep. Luc must have continued to eavesdrop from inside the house because the scene continued.

"Other kids have trouble controlling their element," Luc's

stepfather whispered. "How can they justify taking such an extreme approach to him?" He sounded genuinely bewildered, running his fingers through his short black hair.

"You know the devastation one of his lapses in control causes, Jack. Remember last time?" She sighed. "I'm sure it will require a more powerful Suden than any of the teachers to move things back into place."

"And...you can't do it?" Jack asked carefully. He wrapped his arm around her shoulder as he spoke the words.

Rose understood the meaning of the question. He wondered if all of Luc's power came from his birth father or if she could counter any of it.

She shook her head, her gaze searching the street as if to confirm it empty before leaning back into his embrace and continuing. "I told you; his father's magic was...unique."

Jack grunted.

"I can't help him." She shivered, and Jack's arms tightened around her. Her voice grew softer. "I'm afraid. I'm afraid this isn't *just* Suden strength. And it's still growing. He needs to suppress it," she said as if trying to convince herself. "If he's too strong when tested, they'll have questions about his line. Questions I can't answer."

Her eyes widened as she spoke. The fear for her child was very real. Rose struggled to understand what questions about the father would be so challenging.

"He could be the next Suden Point, Rebecca. That's not to be feared. It's an honor," Jack said.

"Will they let him be Suden Point if I can't assure them of his paternal lineage? I fear for him as word of his power spreads. The village already talks about his magic being an aberration. I can't imagine he'd fare any better at Compass Lake."

Rose could hear how tired she sounded as Jack leaned in to continue talking. The words ran together, and the world blurred around her as she was thrown from the scene.

※

GASPING FOR AIR, she found herself back in the starting tunnel. Well, that was new. Her mind spun as she found her feet. Luc's power made this exploration wholly unique. Her heart rate slowed, and her breathing leveled out. What had watching the scene cost her? She was tired. She may be out of practice, working with such immense power, but it had been magically draining to even observe that slice of Luc's life. The memory she'd fallen out of was once again a picture on the wall. Her fingers stretched to reach for it again, but she paused. She needed to be smart about this, especially if each viewing would exhaust her power further.

Questions bubbled to her lips, and she had no one to ask them of. The scene left her wanting more. How many schoolyard incidents like this had been part of Luc's childhood? When had he learned the absolute control for which he was now known? He became Suden Point anyway, no matter his mother's wishes—what had changed? The wall was lined with more images. Her magic itched to explore them all. Did each one represent a moment in Luc's life?

She could feel the tug of common sense telling her to call it for today. She was pushing herself further than she had in a long time. The Suden Point's power was a lot to grasp. These were all good points. But she and her magic *wanted* more. This was like the opening chapter of her favorite book—she needed to devour every page.

"One more," she whispered to herself. The same way she'd whispered, "one more chapter," a thousand times before, while reading when she should be sleeping. Now certainly wasn't the time to exercise restraint, she thought, as her hand moved to another image on her left.

Michael, the Suden Point before Luc, was in the frame with him, his hand outstretched in introduction. Her finger grazed the corners of the memory as she plucked it from the wall. The edges blurred—then she sank into blackness and felt nothing.

CHAPTER THREE

Removing the damp, cool towel covering her face, Rose opened her eyes. She was in a large, open space, the soft yellow of the sun's emerging light peeking through a second-floor window. The soft cushion beneath her indicated she was on the long chair in Suden house's grand entry room. Luc's brother, Aaron, walked into the room with a replacement cloth. He sat in the empty wooden chair next to where she lay and handed it to her. Folding his muscular arms across his broad chest, he seemed too big for the seat. Or maybe it was that she'd recently seen him as such a small child. The pieces knit together in her mind.

She had been evaluating Luc's magic. And then—what? Had she passed out?

"Where is Luc?" Rose asked, her voice groggier than expected. How long had she been lying there?

"Fetching a healer," Aaron said. His tone was even, but the firm line of his mouth told her he wasn't saying everything he wanted to.

She remembered sinking into Luc's skin, a tunnel leading to the heart of his power. There were images—memories. It came back in flashes. Watching one, reaching for another, then darkness. Had she really exhausted herself so fully? When had that last happened? As a child, training with Mom? She shook her head. Cutting herself a break, she chided that this was the first time she had evaluated a Compass Point's magic at the source. Maybe her weapons-master magic wasn't strong enough. "Do you know what happened?" she asked.

Aaron's patient look reminded her of the one his father wore in the memory. He shook his head in response to her question. "Not quite, though I gather from Luc's rant that he feels responsible for breaking you." His words were a statement, but his gaze held only questions.

"I was evaluating his magic," she said. "I want to make him a weapon for the journey we'll have to take."

Aaron nodded, unsurprised by the news.

She searched his features, hoping to find a semblance of understanding. "I was trying to give him protection, the only way I know how."

The lines of his face softened. While he wasn't yet overly fond of Rose, protecting his brother was something he knew well.

"So, what? It didn't work? You passed out?" He leaned forward in his chair.

"It was working." Rose hesitated. She should talk to Luc about this first, but if anyone else knew about Luc's past, it would be Aaron. "I saw a scene from your childhood—something about Luc shaking the schoolyard?"

"You'll have to be more specific," Aaron said, his tone wry and lip twitching, trying desperately not to curl into a smile.

"He said he was asked to leave school after this one... And you said he was defending you?" Rose added, recalling the details.

Aaron nodded. He tilted his head to each side, an odd mix of stretching and indecision. Finally, he came to some conclusion as his gaze locked with hers. "Luc didn't have an easy childhood."

"I gathered."

"He wasn't bad. He was, in fact, wonderful. The best older brother I could ask for." Aaron paused, searching for words. "You know, many fae have issues controlling their element when they're young."

Rose nodded. It was common.

"The impacts of those lapses aren't usually broadly felt, though." Aaron's gaze begged Rose to put the pieces together, wanting her to finish a sentence for him so he wouldn't have to spill his brother's secrets.

Rose put him out of his misery. "I understand. Not many eight-year-olds can break apart the schoolyard." She tried to sit up, to better invest in this conversation. "Luc could, though. His slips had higher stakes due to the nature of his power."

Aaron nodded. "Made worse because Mother couldn't help him with it." Aaron glanced at the door nervously, as if expecting Luc to walk through it.

"He told me he doesn't know his father, Aaron. You're not betraying him."

Aaron let out a breath, and his shoulders sagged. Her comment freed him to tell the rest of his story. "It was just such a big part of his life growing up. Everyone cared about his magic and where it came from. I always hoped he could leave it behind. Like when he became Suden Point, maybe others would no longer question his fae lines."

Rose gave Aaron a gentle smile. It was incredibly naive to think that the center of fae politics wouldn't care about lineage, especially when someone so unknown with such strength appeared. She appreciated Aaron's sentiment, though. Luc didn't deserve the baggage.

Rose rolled her neck and stretched her arms. Her body felt fine. It must have been a temporary burnout of her magic. A pang of grief hit her unexpectedly as she wished Mom were around to explain the situation. She had evaluated other Nordens at Compass Lake when she worked with Mom—though never the Norden Point. Or maybe Suden magic was different at the source? She'd been doing fine as a reclusive weapons master, but her overly selective process meant she didn't have a wealth of experience from which to draw conclusions.

Her feet hit the floor as she attempted to stand. She needed to figure this out. Not just for Luc, but for all the Compass Points. She would need to arm them all with her magical weapons. Anything to improve their chances in the fight against Aterra.

"Aaron, could I ask a favor of you?"

He nodded slowly, his face partially pinched in worry as she stood, likely anticipating how Luc would yell if she injured herself getting up too fast.

"Could I evaluate your magic?" she tacked on more information before Aaron could respond. "I haven't evaluated any other Sudens at their seat of power. I started with the Suden Point." Rose stumbled over her words. "I need to know how an average Suden compares."

Aaron's lip twitched again. She could have sworn he fought a smile as she awkwardly attempted to describe his magic relative to Luc's. She winced and kept rushing through, to get to the part Aaron would understand. "I need to know before Luc blames himself and his magic for whatever happened. I think I just went too far, too fast, with his power. I want to be able to tell him my magic was simply...exhausted."

Aaron only considered for a moment before nodding. She suspected she'd hooked him with Luc blaming himself. It was apparent Aaron would do anything for his brother.

※

IT TOOK Rose only moments to find her place again in the rhythm of her swings, the forge fire still warm. Not that she was actually making a weapon for Aaron, but the same rules she explained to Luc applied. Her evaluation was more thorough when she lost herself in the familiar movements of making a weapon.

Aaron did his part. He stood where Luc had been and played

with his magic. The difference in their power was evident even in the activity Aaron chose. While Luc had balanced a rock above his palm, pushing his element away from itself, Aaron drew lines in the dirt floor of the workshop—a more passive motion.

Glancing at the Suden over her shoulder and seeing his nod, Rose settled into the process. Her power pressed forward. Magically, he bore nearly no resemblance to Luc. That, right there, might have been enough information, but she wanted to be sure. Her power wound around Aaron and seeped into his skin.

It wasn't an endless plummeting down a dark tunnel. The path to Aaron's power had her skating across a plateau. A wide expanse unfolded before her. Halting, she sat on the ground, reaching for the connection to the earth magic he wielded. Emotions flashed through her mind: contentment, peace, and a gnawing anxiety with a particular focus. No full scenes, or moving images. This was more in line with her expectations of the process. Experiencing feelings, beliefs, and snapshots of those the evaluated held dear was what she usually saw.

This was enough. She knew what Aaron's weapon would be. It would need to be defensive. Something to protect his family should danger arrive. He wouldn't go out and chase it. Rose suspected the focused anxiety was for someone Aaron cared about, who did tackle problems by chasing them down: Luc.

The safety of Compass Lake calmed Aaron, but danger didn't just follow Luc, he actively sought it. Him leading the investigations on the mist plague must have been hard for Aaron to endure. Never knowing if his brother would come back or if he'd fall into the endless sleep himself.

Rose pulled back from Aaron's magic. She had her answer. There was no problem evaluating a Suden at the source. She wasn't sure if she was happy about the result—it seemed the best case. It just meant she needed to go slower with Luc's weapon.

His power was different from anything she'd dealt with before. She had never worked with anyone who possessed that much magic. And the way her magic was drawn to his made it all the more challenging to control her exploration. She tilted her head, considering. Luc wouldn't take this well. He'd still think his magic had hurt her. If anything, it overwhelmed her. It really was her fault. She had felt her exhaustion when she reached for the second scene—but she'd done it anyway. She was enthralled by his magic, and she wasn't sure how to tell him that.

She heard a cough behind her.

"And what do we think we're doing here?" Luc asked. He stood in the doorway, his arms crossing over his chest.

Rose glanced at Aaron, the two sharing a shrug before turning to face the Suden Point.

"I know you're not testing your magic again so soon after passing out while using it..." Luc paused as if to give her a chance to refute his suspicion.

Her mouth curved into a smile, telling him she'd do no such thing.

"Rose," he said, wiping his hand across his face.

Her smile broadened. His gesture was one of her favorites to pull from him. "I needed to understand what happened," she said. She wouldn't hide it from him. Too much of her life had been spent trying to keep secrets that others needed to know.

"Did you learn anything?" He raised an eyebrow at her.

She nodded. "I evaluated Aaron's magic. While I didn't make him a weapon, I know I could. This experience was much more in line with my past evaluations." She shrugged. "Searching your magic was"—words failed her—"different."

"I'll leave you to it," Aaron said as he headed for the door, squeezing past Luc's glare.

"It's not bad, Luc," Rose assured.

He shook his head, ready to disagree.

"It is more power than I'm used to, and my magic wants to..." She hesitated. "Well, it wants to know all of yours—all at once."

"What does that mean?" he asked as he stepped toward her, his body drawn to her words, like her magic was to him. At least it was a mutual addiction.

"I'm usually only learning enough about someone to determine the best weapon." She reached for him. "With you, my magic wants to know more than what weapon to make you. It wants...*everything*."

He couldn't hold back the self-satisfied smirk that tugged at the corner of his lip. "I'm glad your magic and I are in agreement," he said. "But it can't come at the expense of your safety."

Rose let out a breath. It was a start. The sun's more insistent rays caught her eye through the window before she spoke. "Can we continue this conversation later? We should get going. We promised to be back at Norden house early."

Luc's fingers wrapped around her shoulders, trailing movement up and down her arms, reassuring himself that she was okay. "You're really fine?" he asked.

"I am," she said, meeting his gaze. "I won't lie and say it was a normal experience."

"Nor would I believe you if you tried."

"It's something we can work through together," she said.

"Rose..." His hands slipped down to hers, and he entwined them. "I can only imagine what you experienced with my magic. I caught a glimpse of the scene you saw. My power hasn't always been pleasant." He dropped her hands and ran his fingers through his hair. "And it hasn't always reacted as expected. I don't know if you should trust it."

"Why not? Your magic is you, and I know you would never hurt me."

"My power isn't normal, but I've made peace with it," Luc began.

Rose very much doubted that.

"That doesn't mean I give it free rein," he said firmly. "I keep it on a tight leash, but something about you makes it want to slip. I don't think we should risk it."

Rose tilted her head, considering before responding. "It was just overwhelming. I'll go slower next time."

Luc shook his head.

"How you describe your magic and your relationship with it affects you. It's not something to brush aside. I've felt the draw you speak of, but I've never once felt in danger. It wants to protect me, cherish me even, but not harm."

Luc's eyes widened. Had he not registered his magic's recent attention to her? Or had he thought she was unaware?

"But I also felt your disgust in the memory, especially as a child, for what your magic had done. Maybe more importantly—how it made those you care about feel."

Luc opened and closed his mouth—uncharacteristically at a loss for words.

"Let's continue this conversation later," Rose suggested, knowing she'd given him enough to think about. "We really should get to Norden house. I have a seat of power to claim."

CHAPTER FOUR

Power flooded through Rose as she stepped out of the boat and onto Norden soil. The lake water lapped at her feet, her element rising to reach her on the beach. The land accepted her as the Norden Point. It was time to see if everyone else would too.

Three Norden gathered on the property. Her gaze skimmed each of them, eyes wanting to widen in surprise at the last fae in the line of elders. Schooling her features, she stepped forward to greet them. "Meg, Catherine... Samuel." She nodded to each.

Samuel was the elder responsible for testing Norden magic. He knew she should have been named the future Norden Point on that terrible day. Where had he been? Why was he here now?

Meg and Catherine—long-standing advisors to the Norden Point—returned her gesture. Rose glanced at Juliette, the Osten Point, and Carter, the Vesten, also on the beach. Her gaze lifted to the hill before them, on which Norden house sat. Dozens of Norden had gathered to watch the proceeding. This should help her case. Her water magic display likely delighted these same Norden at the Solstice Ball. And they would have also seen her step in at the Refilling Ceremony when Aiden couldn't complete it.

She was glad this would happen with an audience—less chance for the elders to weasel out of any accountability for letting the incorrect Norden Point sit for ten years. The fae courts had kept too much hidden for too long. With Samuel there, though, she had some questions that not everyone needed to hear.

As if anticipating her concern, Juliette spoke. "I'm going to give us a little privacy here to start." The Osten Point's fingers twitched, and Rose sensed wind magic whipping around them. "A sound barrier," she said. "I know this is inherently a Norden discussion, but as Compass Points, we've never experienced anything like this before." Juliette leveled her gaze at the elders. "Rose could complete the Refilling Ceremony, and Aiden, the seated Norden Point, could not. We can't continue to operate under the assumption that Aiden is the Norden Point. And the Compass Points cannot be incomplete, especially with the looming presence of the mist plague." Juliette gave Carter and Luc a moment to voice their own concerns. Instead, both simply nodded at her statement, a show of their support.

Rose wasn't sure what she expected, but the remaining Compass Points being united in this was a good start.

Murmurs ran through the crowd. They must have realized the conversation had started on the beach, and they couldn't hear it. Rose wouldn't push Juliette now, but neither would she have this entire conversation in secrecy. She felt strongly that the Norden fae needed to know more than just the outcome.

"The Compass Points believe that Rose is the true Norden Point. We would see her take the seat." Juliette's voice carried across the metaphorical line that had been drawn in the sand. The Norden elders on one side and the Compass Points on the other. Her eyes narrowed as she said, "It's time to fix this."

Rose inwardly cringed. The Norden elders would not want to admit there was something to fix. Rose was still missing a lot of information, but there was little doubt in her mind that the elders knew Aiden was not the correct Norden Point. There were too many signs. The checks and balances in the Norden Point test would have caught such a scheme. At the very least, Samuel knew she had passed the test. And only one Norden per generation passes. She didn't know his angle—willful ignorance or something more malicious. She wasn't sure she cared.

Rose would become Norden Point.

"Thank you, Juliette." Rose spread her arms to the elders. "As the Compass Points say, Aiden has proven unable to fulfill the duties of the Norden Point. I was."

"It's not that simple," Meg replied.

"Why not?" Carter asked, his head tilting.

"Aiden passed the test." Meg gestured at Rose. "She did not."

Rose didn't miss the sharp dart of her gaze to Samuel and Catherine. Rose had seen enough. She wasn't buying this. Her gaze met Samuel's.

A weight fell on her shoulder as Arie, in his raven form, landed. The small knot in her chest uncoiled at his presence. She wasn't sure what those on the beach had put together about him. Right now, it didn't matter. Right now, he was her best friend—not the Vesten god. And he was offering his silent support.

With Arie's light press on her shoulder and Luc's hand slipping to the small of her back, Rose knew she was different from the girl who'd fled here ten years ago. She was not facing this alone.

"I did pass."

The elders met her words with silence. Samuel's gaze lingered on the Suden Point's hand as it casually rested on her. His eyes lifted, meeting hers. She raised her chin, daring him to deny her. Daring him to call her a liar.

"She did pass," he relented with a heavy sigh.

Catherine and Meg gave Samuel icy stares that might just freeze Compass Lake. The anger in their eyes told Rose everything she needed to know. They were complicit. She wouldn't waste words trying to explain her tragedy to them. It was clear they didn't care.

"What's the problem then?" Rose glared at the elders with

more confidence than she felt. The scent of Luc's magic hit her nose, and the increasingly familiar feeling of his magic wrapping around her made her stand a little straighter. The Norden land below her feet thrummed its approval, sending waves of power through her.

"Why didn't you take the seat if that's true?" Meg asked, feigning ignorance of what she clearly already knew.

They didn't deserve her story, but she wouldn't be denied because she refused to share information. Rose took a deep breath. "The day I passed—the day I should have been recognized as the next Norden Point..." Her words failed her again. Water rimmed her eyes, and she used her element to stop it from trickling into tears. Warmth flooded her, beating back the bone-chilling cold reliving this night brought her. Luc's magic circled more tightly, wrapping her in its protective shield. Her voice was even as she continued. "My family was murdered. My home destroyed. The false Norden Point tried to kill me. He thought he'd succeeded until a few days ago."

If she'd been expecting a sympathetic glance from an elder, she would have been sorely disappointed.

"It's been ten years," Meg continued as if Rose hadn't just relived trauma before her. "You may no longer have...appropriate qualifications." Her gaze lingered on Luc's hand where it touched Rose.

Catherine nodded in agreement. She crossed her arms over her chest and looked away from what she must consider a distasteful display of affection between a Norden and Suden. Never mind that it was between the rightful leaders of each court.

Their reaction to Luc, unfortunately, wasn't a surprise. This scenario had been her biggest fear in acknowledging her feelings for him. The mixing of fae courts was...frowned upon. But Rose had decided they would face this together, as they had plenty of deadlier trials in the short time since they'd met. She wouldn't let the elders dictate who she could be with based on outdated beliefs.

If pure lines from a single fae court were supposed to be the most powerful, how did they explain her? How did they explain her Norden water magic and her Osten wind magic?

She wasn't ready to bring that secret out for all to examine. It was unclear how she had both lines, but that wasn't the point. She was still strong enough to hold the Norden seat. And she had still been taught to hide the duality of her magic because of prejudices like the elders'.

"I guess it wasn't all an act," Juliette said, breaking the silence. Her gaze roamed between Luc and Rose for confirmation of the elders' unspoken accusation. Rose wasn't sure if she was thankful or angry at the conversation being brought to a head.

"I'm not sure that's anyone's business but ours," Luc stated coldly. His jaw clenched, and his magic gave Rose a reassuring squeeze. Meg inadvertently stepped back when his eyes locked on hers. The ground didn't shake, but the thick heft of his magic was potent around them all now.

An inappropriate laugh bubbled up as she considered the deadly glare he gave those around him and the warm embrace in which his magic held her. To Rose, Luc just appeared to be working hard to stop that dangerous red glint from overtaking his irises. But this was the Suden Point they all feared—yet she was cocooned safely in his power. She wouldn't have it any other way.

"How much longer before he really gets angry?" Arie asked into her mind, noting her attention. She couldn't respond to him now, but a small smile crossed her face as she figured another two minutes max— then his eyes would flash red, and they'd be in for a fun display.

"It's most certainly our business," Catherine replied when she realized Meg wouldn't continue. "The Norden Point must focus on what is right for their court. They must protect the ways of the Norden. They cannot have uncertain loyalties."

This was a more interesting argument, at least, Rose thought.

"Is that an official part of the test?" Luc pried, a smirk tilting up the corner of his lip.

Catherine's spine straightened at the challenge. She eyed Luc with more than a little pride. He had trapped her into having to answer in front of the other Compass Points. No matter what she shared, the group included representatives from each fae court. He ensured Catherine was doing more damage, revealing the ways of the Norden ritual with other fae courts, than Rose ever had.

"It is technically accounted for in the second part of the test," Samuel said, stepping back in.

"And you say Rose already passed the test," Luc pressed.

"Yes." Samuel had, interestingly enough, joined team Rose. She wasn't sure what to make of that.

How had Samuel let Aiden claim to have passed the test? It was a surprise to see him today, because she thought him dead. She assumed him to be a casualty of Aiden's deadly ambition. Or was it Aterra's? Not knowing who controlled Aiden's actions still stung.

"It's complicated, Rose, but I do owe you an answer," Samuel said, as if able to see the questions cross her face. "I don't ask forgiveness for my actions but seek to explain them." He paused. "Maybe to give you a warning to not repeat my mistakes."

Meg's lips pursed, and Catherine rolled her eyes as if she knew that Samuel's explanation would ruin any chances they had to contest Rose's claim.

Rose crossed her arms over her chest and waited for him to continue.

"Aiden did take the test, like all Norden. Though I can't quite see it, I am sure his power was mediocre. At least, that was my expectation of him, having seen his magic as a child."

"What do you mean you can't see it?" Rose couldn't help herself. The elder had piqued her interest already. She didn't miss the other Compass Points leaning forward too, listening intently to his story.

"There is a shadow over those specific memories," Samuel said. "A fog that obscures what actually happened and leaves me with a result that, until recently, I believed."

"Explain," she said. "And do it quickly." Luc nodded as he continued to tamp down his power.

"I'm trying, Rose." Her name was like a plea as he twisted his hands together, considering his next words. "Are you familiar with Aterra's artifact?"

Her eyes widened, unable to mask her surprise. This was taking a turn. "What?" Rose asked.

She glanced at Luc, feeling his magic flare. He'd lost his internal struggle, and his eyes flashed red at the elder's words. A smile curled her lip at the accuracy of her guess on how long he'd hold it in.

"Each of the gods left an artifact for their court. A second gift, along with the elemental magic they granted," Samuel said.

Rose sensed the dagger she had hidden in her boot. She had hoped she wouldn't need to use it to claim her seat. Her actions at the Refilling Ceremony should have been proof enough. She shrugged. Her words were casual as she replied, "Yes, I'm aware."

"The Norden have never understood the other fae court's artifacts. However, there were enough rumors, especially at the creation of the courts, about the power of Aterra's ring," Samuel added. His tone was dry, giving no indication he knew his words made Rose's heart race.

Her body went rigid as she waited for more information. The steady weight of Luc's hand found itself on her lower back again.

"It was said to be shaped like a mountain, with an onyx gem placed inside the triangle peak." Rose let her eyes close for just a moment as she pictured where she'd seen that exact ring before. Samuel continued. "The bigger danger is the needle said to snap out of the tip, on the Suden Point's command."

A memory flashed to the fore of her thoughts: The Solstice Ball. Aiden stabbing Luc with his ring.

"We think that if the needle point pierces the skin, it can produce the rumored mind shadow of the Suden." Samuel paused, studying Rose's features. "I see you might already be familiar with the artifact and the power."

Rose stilled. She wouldn't betray Luc's secret—that he wielded mind shadow—but admitting Aiden was wearing the ring didn't seem risky. That was where this conversation had to be going. She nodded. She felt Carter and Juliette's eyes on her as she continued to stare at the Norden elder.

"I won't belabor the details of the power, but my memories of Aiden's test were taken and replaced with those of him passing," Samuel concluded.

Mind shadow was known to cover memories, and she knew from Luc it could also share them. But she hadn't realized it could replace memories with new ones. She must have said as much aloud.

"The memory replacement isn't clean. It's fuzzy for me. I can tell the memory has been tampered with, but it's enough to force the change the wielder wants, especially in the moment. I believe I was struck with the needle when Aiden wanted me to declare him the future Norden Point. In that moment, I sensed he had passed the test. It wasn't until later that I realized it might not be true."

"But you still remember that I passed?" Rose asked.

"Yes, he either wasn't able or didn't think to remove that memory." The elder shrugged. "Maybe he didn't think it would matter since he assumed you dead."

It made sense. But Rose was no longer thinking about what Aiden and Aterra had done to the Norden elder. She was more focused on what Aterra had been trying to accomplish when he stabbed Luc with the needle a few days ago. It was meant for her. What memories had he been trying to replace? And what would it have done to Luc if Arie hadn't been there to help?

"I appreciate the information," Rose said. She wouldn't thank him. He said the memory was fuzzy, which meant, at some point, he knew it was wrong. Yet he still did nothing about it until she made her claim known. He may have helped her move things along with the elders today. He may even be trying to do the right thing now by sharing this information, but she couldn't so easily forgive that he'd let an imposter sit as Norden Point for ten years. The damage was done—to her, her family, and the continent.

She reined in her thoughts as she again registered the Norden fae on the hill before her—her court. She turned to Juliette. "Let it down."

The sound barrier around them fell as Rose spoke. "I won't entertain accusations that I am unfit due to my relationship with the Suden Point." She stood taller as the power flooded her again, the land acknowledging the right of her words, her right to speak before the Norden. She flexed and stretched her fingers, her water magic rippling through her.

She didn't need it, but given the elders' fascination with the godly artifacts, she wanted to use it now. She pulled Aurora's dagger from her boot. It would be another item she carried with her always, just like her compass. "I have claimed Aurora's dagger. I offer it as further proof that I'm the rightful Norden Point. I passed our test, as Elder Samuel can confirm."

Samuel nodded, and the crowd began to murmur, finally hearing the words discussed before them.

Meg and Catherine started to interrupt, realizing they'd lost control. Rose spoke over them. "I don't care about the reasons the elders left this secret buried." She glanced at the elders as she said, "I'm sure you even thought you were doing what was best for the Norden court. The problem is those assumptions were wrong. The power to deny my claim is no longer yours."

Her focus returned to the fae on the hill. "The mist plague is here because of the imbalance on the continent." Juliette and Carter moved closer to Rose and Luc as she ramped up her speech. The Compass Points stood together, uncoerced for the first time in Rose's existence. "We must maintain our own balance to counteract any selfish acts of the gods. The Compass Points, with Aiden, were incapable. With me as Norden Point, we stand a chance."

Rose held out Aurora's dagger again. "I have claimed our goddess's blessing to the first Norden Point. Only one that can claim the position can wield the weapon. I accept the responsibility to find and bring Aiden to justice and will not do it alone." She glanced at the other Compass Points beside her. "I claim my place as the rightful Norden Point." Rose held out her arms again, in a final challenge, and her magic surged, a wall of water erupting in the lake behind her.

The murmurs on the hill shifted to cheers at Rose's display of power.

"You can't just do this," Catherine hissed.

"I can, and I have. Now, if you'll excuse me. The Compass Points and I have some work to do. We have to rid the continent of a plague."

No one stopped her as she walked up the hill and into Norden house.

CHAPTER FIVE

The newly confirmed Compass Points entered the lavish Norden house library. Rich, leather-bound volumes covered the walls. No fire was burning, but the fireplace held ashes from recent use.

Carter strode to the western seat of the circular table. Juliette, to the drink cart. She must have realized that more information was coming, and it wouldn't be good.

Luc sat in his traditional southern seat, and Arie perched on his shoulder.

"Did you get a new familiar, Luc?" Juliette asked, her voice dripping with sarcasm.

"Something like that." He shrugged. Arie's feathers ruffled, and he poked Luc in the face with his wing.

Carter's gaze was fixed on the bird—Rose had seen him watching Arie at the beach meeting as well. How well could Compass Points sense their patron god? She'd never had occasion to think about it.

Rose barely took time to appreciate this as the momentous occasion that it was—her first meeting as Norden Point. She surveyed her new partners in what she knew would be no easy task. "So, how do you want to do this?" she asked, looking at Arie.

"Why don't you two get us started, and I'll add commentary where I feel necessary," Arie spoke into Rose and Luc's minds, the other Compass Points still in the dark about his true identity.

"We're telling them everything?" she asked, choosing her words carefully for those listening.

"Technically, the continent is doomed if you can't figure out how to work together, but I guess it's up to you. The good news is...there's almost no way for the Compass Points to trust each other less than they currently do." The bird flapped its wing into Luc's face again.

Rose gave Arie a look that suggested his motivational skills could use some work.

Carter tracked the interaction. His head moved back and forth as if anticipating that someone—or something—was responding to each of her questions. He knotted his fingers together on the table before him.

"Why don't you start from the beginning," he suggested.

The unease was heavy in the room. Though the Compass Points had stood together against the Norden elders, Arie was right, they were far from trusting each other. Rose understood on some level. Revealing her magic to Luc had been its own struggle, but as Arie also pointed out: They were short on time.

"The distrust among the fae courts is something I'm all too familiar with," Rose said. "I want to start my tenure as Norden Point differently. With that, I think you should know some things."

Looking at Luc, she paused. She wasn't sure how much detail of his side quests for weapons masters he wanted to reveal to the Compass Points. She would tell her story, but she didn't need to tell his. He caught her hesitation and picked up her thread seamlessly.

"*We* think you should know," he echoed.

Rose swore she felt a reassuring squeeze of her hand and the faint brush of his touch slide up both arms as he emphasized they were united. It sent chills down her spine. It was also impossible since Luc was sitting directly across from her, but pine and cinnamon lingered in the air as the warmth left her hand. She smiled as his magic retreated. It would reassure her when he could not.

"I found Rose when searching for a rumored magical weapons master. I was looking for my own solutions to the mist plague when I felt the Compass Points were no longer taking my concerns seriously," Luc continued.

Carter's gaze was mysteriously focused on the books on the wall now. This was off to a good start.

Juliette tapped her fingernails on the large wooden table as she finally took the eastern seat. "We knew that, Luc," she said. "Though I guess we didn't know that's what Rose was when you brought her back. You played your relationship a little too well." Her gaze lingered between them.

"Yes." His eyes met Juliette's. "That's not really what we are discussing."

Juliette's lips set into a thin line. She looked like she would say something, prying further into the alliance created between the Norden and Suden Points through Rose and Luc's not-so-fake romance.

"We're getting off track," Rose said. She did not doubt that the Osten and Vesten Points would worry about such an alliance, especially given the depth of power the Suden Point possessed.

Power was coveted in the fae courts. While those at the table now didn't seem like they would burn the world for more of it, she would never underestimate a Compass Point. It was no accident by which they came to their positions, and she was sure they would do whatever was necessary to maintain them.

"The mist came for the village of Bury the same afternoon that Luc found me. We realized my blades could stop it. They can't reverse the damage already done, but they can be used to fight the mist-born beasts and prevent wielders from succumbing to the mist plague."

"That's the only way I got her to return with me," Luc commented. "When she realized she held the key to averting more loss by the mist, she couldn't ignore my request to return to Compass Lake."

Rose rolled her eyes at Luc. "I'm glad we're calling that a request," she commented before she could think better of it.

Carter looked up from the calming movements of his fingers. His wide eyes indicated that sassing the Suden Point wasn't a regular occurrence.

"We're getting off-topic again," Luc said.

Rose liked seeing him flustered. He was always so annoyingly self-assured.

"So that's how you stopped the mist from entering the Compass Lake Village? With your weapons?" Juliette asked. Her cat-like grin told Rose she would return to the couple's first meeting at a more appropriate time.

"Yes. Though, there's something else you should know," Rose said, looking at the Osten Point. She glanced briefly at Carter too. She was really doubling down on honesty—hopefully, it wouldn't backfire. They didn't have time to worry about secrets among them. They needed to unite against the mist and Aterra. Leading by example was her only move, sharing her secrets and asking for nothing in return. "I also have Osten fae in my lineage."

Juliette assessed her in a new light, her head tilted to the side in contemplation.

"So, I wield both wind and water magic. It's important for this next part."

Juliette gestured for her to continue.

"Aterra is at least partially controlling Aiden. When his eyes are gray, Aterra is in control."

Juliette and Carter looked between Rose and Luc to determine whether this was a joke.

"If you don't mind me asking, how could you know that?" Carter gently questioned.

"Well, first, Aterra told me when we were in the sandstorm on the beach yesterday. And second"—she eyed Arie—"my friend over there"—she gestured to the bird, still on Luc's shoulder—"is Arctos, Lord of Fire."

Juliette laughed. "Luc? He may think highly of himself, but he's no god."

Rose was right to suspect the Vesten Point's attention on the black bird. Carter stared, though not at Luc.

"Not Luc," Carter said. "The bird." He bowed his head slightly.

Juliette reappraised the animal perched on Luc's shoulder.

"Arie has been with me for years, but only recently revealed some critical information about his identity. There is more at stake here than the imbalance of the Compass Points. Having the incorrect Norden Point was a problem, but it was not the only problem. We've been in the middle of a power struggle between the gods for years, and we haven't known it."

Arie nodded on Luc's shoulder.

"After the Covenant, the gods were forbidden from interfering with the Compass Points. Aterra has done the opposite. While there is likely more to that story"—Rose gave Arie a sharp glare—"we must prioritize tracking down Aiden and ensuring that Aterra is banished from his person. We don't know the extent of what Aterra has done, just that Aterra's interference has led to the mist plague on the continent."

"How do you know the mist is related to Aterra's interference?" Juliette asked. "I understand your point that Aterra broke the rules, but he's a god. Who is punishing him if not us? Our positions were created because no one else could hold a god accountable."

"Well, that's where it gets interesting," Rose said. "Have you been around the mist, Juliette?"

"No, I've only seen villages suffering its aftermath."

"And has any of the lingering mist...felt familiar?" Rose asked.

"Just say what you mean," Juliette said, sipping her drink. It was clear she knew she wouldn't like hearing whatever Rose was about to say.

"Well, we believe my magic-infused blades work against the mist plague because I inadvertently infuse my weapons with my wind magic. The mist seems unwilling or unable to hurt its own." Rose looked meaningfully at Juliette. "In this case, its own is strong wind magic. We believe that the mist plague is sent by the Lost God, Zrak, and he's been trying to tell the Compass Points that Aterra is interfering with the balance that he sacrificed himself to preserve."

Juliette's hand tightened on her drink, the glass shattering. The brown liquid seeped across the table. She stared openly at the bird on Luc's shoulder as if she wouldn't believe Rose's claim without a second opinion.

Carter's mouth opened and closed a few times. No words came out.

Arie's beak dipped in assent.

"How?" Juliette asked through clenched teeth. Her hand went to a necklace chain that disappeared beneath her dress.

"We're not sure," Rose said.

Carter finally found his voice. "If he's warning us of Aterra, why is he leaving the Suden worshipping villages alone?"

Juliette seemed to regain a modicum of control. "I thought that was simply a rumor because everyone feared the Suden Point." She gestured to Luc. "Is it really true?"

Rose shrugged. "We don't really know. Luc and I were looking at a map of taken villages, and honestly, it seems like the mist started further north where there happen to be no Aterra-worshipping villages."

Juliette looked thoughtful. "But the first village taken all those years ago was in the northeast?"

What was Juliette thinking? "Yes." Rose nodded slowly. "That's what the Suden records indicate. What about it?"

"Nothing," Juliette said, pulling herself out of whatever thought process she was in. "I think to get the real answer about which villages the mist is attacking and why, we'd need to ask the Lost God himself."

Rose wanted to ask if such a thing were possible. The Osten Point had said at the Solstice Ball that she still worshiped the Lost God. What did that look like? It seemed too personal a question to ask in this setting. Tucking the topic away for later, she said, "I think we should focus on how to stop it."

"And how do you think we do that?" Carter asked.

"We do what the Compass Points were created to do—keep the gods' power in check. We don't know everything he's done, but we know Aterra is out of line. We need to balance the scales." She gestured around the table to emphasize she meant everyone in the room. "We need to go after Aterra. We need to ensure his meddling on the continent is done." Rose looked around the room, a little nervous to ask her next question. "Does anyone know how exactly we stop a god?"

Carter's gaze fell to Arie before responding, as if deferring to the god to answer. Arie remained silent. "I'm not sure it's ever been tested," Carter said. "We've not had this type of situation since before the Covenant was established."

"I was told that our magic would know what to do once we were aware of the situation." Juliette gestured casually. "But as Carter says, none of our predecessors have had to test it."

This wasn't promising, but there was really no choice to be had. "Well, we have to go after Aterra and Aiden and see what our magic can do together as we track them."

Carter interjected quietly. "Isn't this no longer a breach of the Covenant by nature of Aiden no longer being Norden Point? Aterra is no longer breaking the Covenant if he's not interfering with a Compass Point."

"It's a good line of thinking," Luc said. Carter flinched away from his voice, even as it issued a compliment. "Unfortunately, there is more to the story than just the Compass Point interference and the mist plague."

"Of course there is," Juliette said. She leaned forward, her elbows on the edge of the table, her head resting atop her intertwined hands. One could mistake her for serene if they had missed her blatant display of rage moments before.

"Yes, I don't think we fully understand what Aterra has done to disrupt the balance. We know he's been recklessly pursuing the growth of his own power for longer than the mist plague has existed. Inhabiting Aiden is not his only sin here. He is also holding Aurora hostage."

Juliette couldn't hold in a deep chuckle. "I'd call you both liars"—she glanced between Luc and Rose again—"but the things you're saying are too ludicrous even to make up."

"I'm not sure this is funny," Carter replied.

"No. It is not," Juliette said, getting up to get another drink after using her wind to effortlessly sweep the glass from her last one into a neat pile on the table. "How do we pursue this rogue god, then?"

Rose pulled Aurora's compass from beneath her tunic. "This will lead us to what I want most on the continent. I want to stop Aterra more than anything. We can follow it to him."

Juliette stretched her neck, like this might be one revelation too many for the day. "So, let's go through what you need us to do," Juliette said, focusing on action. "We need to find Aiden and Aterra." She gestured with a wave of her hand as she crossed the room. "We must stop a god from further inhabiting a fae's body. Setting aside, we don't know how often he inhabits Aiden or what we would do with Aterra once he's separated..." She lifted the bottle of golden-brown liquid as she continued. "Then, we must determine what else Aterra has done in his quest for power, which at least includes freeing a goddess who has somehow been imprisoned." She glanced at Rose as she poured a little more of the liquid into a new glass. "And finally, we have to convince the Lost God, Zrak—who's been missing for five hundred years—that we corrected the mistakes he's angry about, we've maintained the balance, and he can leave the continent alone and return to being lost?" She moved the glass to her lips and asked, "Did I sum that up correctly?"

"I think you got it all," Arie said aloud.

CHAPTER SIX

"That went as well as could be expected," Luc said as he opened the door to Suden house that evening.

The Compass Points agreed to leave with them. They would follow Aurora's magic compass to find where Aterra and Aiden had fled. Carter and Juliette needed time to settle things at their courts, which Rose and Luc also required. Rose couldn't think of another occurrence when all four fae leaders had left Compass Lake together.

"You're right," Rose said, leaning into Luc as he wrapped an arm around her shoulder. "I just wish there weren't so many unknowns."

"Any bothering you in particular?" he asked.

"I think, more than anything, I'm worried about what we will do when we find them." Rose shrugged. "I believe the compass will lead us to Aterra. From how often we saw Aterra with Aiden in the few days here, I assume they will be together. I know the others said our magic would know what to do, but I can't help but worry about how that will work."

"*For what it's worth, they're right,*" Arie said as he flew in the door before Luc closed it, landing on Rose's shoulder. He spoke to both of them. *"We gave the fae leaders the tools, but the execution—you will need to figure that out together."*

"Well, that's something," Rose said.

"The Compass Points containing a rogue god was Zrak's idea. He said the fae leaders' magic would unite when the time came. I think the time is here—so you should try to test your magic together while you travel." The bird's head swiveled.

"That is not very helpful," Rose replied, and Luc squeezed her shoulder as they headed up the stairs.

"Speaking of which…" Arie started.

"Speaking of you not being helpful?" Rose asked playfully. Arie flicked his wing at her.

"Yes, but you should be more respectful toward me. I'm a god."

Rose rolled her eyes.

"I'm not coming with you," Arie said.

Rose stopped in her tracks on her way up the steps. "What?"

"I'm not coming with you," Arie repeated, apparently taking her question literally.

"Why?"

"I need to find out how Zrak is controlling the mist. I don't even know where he is." Arie ruffled his feathers. He looked uncomfortable. *"It didn't even occur to me to look for him."*

He sounded almost ashamed. She didn't know much about the gods' relationships, but she couldn't imagine it was easy to lose someone you'd existed with since the beginning. "Were you and Zrak close?" she asked.

"We were," Arie said. *"I was devastated when he was chosen. I'm sorry to say that losing him made me selfish. It's hard to learn your time may not be as infinite as you thought."*

That was understandable. Losing someone tended to make the living reflect on their mortality. It must be even stranger for a god who thought mortality wasn't something they'd ever face.

"Now that I know he can connect to the continent somehow, I have to try to find him," Arie said with finality.

It sounded like Arie was carrying some guilt about not realizing this sooner. Rose knew the story of Zrak's sacrifice as well as the next fae. The compass had chosen, and there wasn't anything Arie could have done. Arie was her family, and she wanted him with them to confront Aterra, but she knew he wasn't required. "I get it," she said.

"When will you leave?" Luc asked.

"*I'll leave tonight, but I wonder if I can borrow you, Rose, for a little bit before I do?*" He turned his head to look between the two of them.

"Yeah, of course, Arie," Rose said. "What do you want to do?"

"You two chat," Luc said, heading to the library. "I'll talk to Aaron about anything he needs in my absence."

Arie's voice took on a mischievous tone as he spoke. "*What do you say to some light breaking and entering?*"

※

THE DAYS WERE at their longest, but they waited for the sun to set completely before Arie judged it was time to go. They left the comfort of Suden house, and Rose walked toward the property's western edge. Arie remained in his bird form, sitting on her shoulder, telling her each direction seconds before she needed it.

Luc wasn't with them, but she could feel his power as they walked the property. It trailed them like a secret guard, ready to launch into action should she require it. Rose let it follow them. Luc was likely protective in general over Suden property. His power trailing them was how she knew the moment they approached the edge of his domain. Its potency waned as they stepped toward the property line.

"Arie," she whispered.

"*Keep going, Rose.*"

"Arie," she tried again. "I'm Norden Point now. I can't just let myself on to other Compass Point's properties."

"It wouldn't be breaking and entering if it was somewhere you're allowed to be."

She shook her head, knowing she would regret this decision. As she stepped over the threshold from Suden to Vesten property, she gave a slight wave to Luc's magic. It was silly, but she knew it wouldn't follow them onto Vesten land.

A new feeling took over as she entered Carter's property. Now that she knew, Rose wasn't sure how she'd missed Arie's connection to Vesten magic. The property felt like him. It smelled like the forest floor, trees, and grass. The scent she'd associated with Arie the first night she'd met him. Rose hadn't witnessed Carter's magic yet, but she was sure she'd find familiarity in it too.

"What are we doing here?" she asked, hoping he'd answer her this time.

"I want to give you what help I can. There's something here that we need to collect so you can take it with you."

Rose didn't like the sound of that. "I am not breaking into Vesten house," Rose said flatly. "That would be seen as an act of aggression."

"Give me some credit. We're going to the Burning Garden at the back of the property."

Her shoulders sagged in relief, be it ever so slight. An uninvited walk in the garden was less concerning than letting themselves into the house. Her only question now was what they'd be leaving the garden with.

"We'll want to stop by the shed to grab a shovel."

She couldn't stop her eye-roll.

※

FIRES WERE STILL BLAZING in the Burning Garden as she let herself in. Arie flew next to her, landing on various benches and bushes as she moved. Her shoulder was now occupied by the shovel he'd made her grab.

The garden was a thing of beauty, one she had never seen up

close, even as a child. Flames danced atop columns every few feet. Greenery ran wild, around and between them. The garden was rumored only to bloom flowers resembling fire—an homage to the Vesten's element. Rose tracked the scene: the garden in full bloom, the reds, oranges, and even deep yellow flowers everywhere. It was a lovely tribute to Vesten magic.

"*Over here, Rose,*" Arie called to her from his perch under a large tree with a long drapery of leaves. She parted the wispy branches like a curtain and walked into a shaded area.

"What now?" she asked, searching the cove. Arie sat on a low branch.

"*Start digging,*" he said, gesturing with his wing to a spot next to the trunk.

Rose looked up as if to curse the gods but realized the one she wanted to curse was, in fact, right in front of her. "Are you going to help?" she asked.

Arie flapped his wings, affronted. "*I am helping.*"

"How?" she asked. "You could at least change shape into something with paws."

Arie chuckled. "*I'm here in more of a supervisory role.*"

"This had better be worth it," she growled as she hefted the shovel off her shoulder and started to dig.

"*The real gift is spending time with me before I leave,*" Arie chattered at her as she worked.

"You better hope that's not all that's here, or I might take a swing at you with this." She waved the shovel at him. Her next scoop brought a solid clang as she hit something hard.

"*Here we go,*" Arie preened.

"What is it?" She bent down to unearth a small metal box. Flipping open the lid, she saw a gold coin on deep green pillowed cushioning. "I think we have enough coin for our journey," Rose said sarcastically, picking up the piece of gold. It was surprisingly warm to the touch.

She was about to demand more information from Arie when she heard a rustling of branches on the edge of the garden. Her shoulders tensed as she searched the perimeter for an intruder or, worse, the Vesten Point, but saw nothing.

"*Let's get going, Rose. We've lingered too long.*"

Nodding, Rose pocketed the coin and tried to remove evidence of their activity. "He's definitely going to know we were here," Rose said.

"*That's not really my problem, is it? You're a Compass Point now, Rose. You'll have to think on your feet when he confronts you tomorrow.*"

Rose scowled.

"*I already have second-hand embarrassment just thinking about your response. It's good you have the night to come up with something.*"

She couldn't help her gaze lingering on the bushes as they left the garden. She swore a yellow-green glint flashed in them as she turned to walk back to the safety of Suden house.

"So, this is your artifact? The Burning Coin, right?" She'd put it together as they left. She couldn't sense Vesten magic from it, but she could feel its heat. Rose had been on edge thinking about what she carried the entire walk back.

"Do you want me to give it to Carter?"

"*I want you to study the Vesten magic.*"

Not for the first time, Rose wondered what Arie was up to. "Do you know what you're doing? Not giving this to him will be a major slight, and with you gone, he'll take it out on me." Rose had grown used to trusting the shifter god. But she couldn't even feel the Vesten magic in this—how could she study it? She said as much and added, "I want to unite the Compass Points, not further sow distrust among us."

"*Of course I know what I'm doing. I'm a god. And you'll feel the Vesten power in the coin once you start to understand it.*"

"That's circular logic, Arie."

"*You're already making progress.*" He chuckled.

Rose sighed. It was too late to put it back. She'd have to play it by ear with Carter.

"I think you'll need to know all of the elements to succeed."

She tried to process what that meant. She guessed it tied back to the Compass Points' powers working together. Her weapons-making magic and her dual elements left her uniquely positioned to help with this. She sensed and understood more magic than most.

"This coin is the best representation of the Vesten power I have. Once you understand it, you can give it to Carter."

"You intend for me to give it to him eventually? That won't be awkward at all..." Rose thought about the yellow-green glint in the bushes. She feared the Vesten Point would have a lot of questions for her in the morning.

"Of course I want you to give it to him. It amplifies his power. I'm sure he'll need it. But only when you're ready." Arie paused uncharacteristically. *"I have a favor to ask before you give it back."*

She couldn't help but tense at his words—what else would he ask of her?

"I want you to use the coin as a source to make him a weapon on your journey."

Rose turned her head to stare at the bird on her shoulder. "Is that an official request from a god?" she asked, putting her hands on her hips.

"No, Rose. It's a request from a friend—one who has your best interests in mind. I think you'll need to make weapons for all the Compass Points before this is through, but I leave that up to you. I just wanted you to have the means to evaluate the Vesten magic without being at Compass Lake." He gestured to the coin in her hand. *"This should do it."*

"Fine," she said, feeling its heat in her fingertips. She'd already come to the same conclusion as Arie. Each of the Compass Points would need one of her weapons, but he didn't need to know that. She might have told him if he'd explained his plan before making them steal onto Vesten property. "I'll do what I must to give us our best chance of success."

"Good job pretending you didn't intend to make him a weapon anyway," Arie said, spreading his wings.

Rose hmphed. He knew her too well.

"Now, I do hate to run, but I hate goodbyes more. I'll see you soon, Rose. Be careful."

He didn't give her a chance to respond before he flew off through the trees.

CHAPTER SEVEN

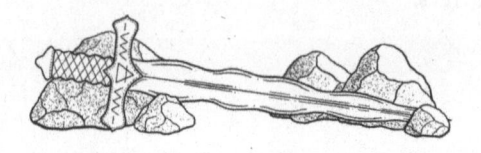

Luc couldn't take his eyes off Rose as they started the slow ascent to the mountain pass from Compass Lake Village. While he held the reins with one hand, his magic bounced a stone gently in the other. His power was behaving this morning, but the day was still young. No matter what she said about just needing to slow down, or her overdoing it—it angered him that his magic caused her to pass out yesterday. He thought his magic was protective of her, especially since their conversation on the beach. Overwhelming and exhausting her was the exact opposite of that. He sighed. It was back to its usual disappointments. His power acted with a mind of its own on occasion, especially where she was involved. He would concentrate even more than usual to keep it from slipping its leash.

The stone bounced in his hand, and he could smell his magic. He was sure Rose could, too, even though she rode ahead. The first time Rose described his magic so succinctly was burned into his memory. He had wanted to marvel at her for how she described it but knew he needed to focus instead on the fact that she *had* described it. Something a half-fae weapons master should not have been able to do. His magic had also liked her description, flexing whenever it could since then, to ensure her awareness of its presence.

How many other fae thought of their power as a separate entity? He shook his head. His magic was a mess.

Winter solstice generally came to mind when he thought of his power. The scent of pine wreaths around the house, and the cinnamon that Andrew added to their mulled wine. He liked to think of this as his power's one good feature. Reminding him of fond memories with Aaron, and later Aaron, Andrew, and the children. Most other associations with his magic were a bit darker.

Watching the scene Rose found yesterday was a harsh reminder of all the memories he'd buried. When he closed his eyes, he could still picture it: the terror on the other children's faces as the ground started to shake. The rage in his heart as he saw cracks form and the ground shift beneath Anthony. Then, the ice-cold fear prickling on his spine and the pounding nausea in his throat when he thought he'd hurt someone. That he'd been happy to do it. He hated remembering that feeling, especially given the other incidents.

The one she found was bad, but it wasn't the last time his magic had taken charge when his emotions were intense. His mind wandered to another event, the first one significant enough to draw the notice of the Suden Point. Within days of the awful incident, Michael had been on his doorstep asking to test him. Even as a child, he understood the test had been a formality. The Suden Point didn't leave Compass Lake to meet just anyone. He said he felt the earth shake all the way up at Suden house and needed to find out where the magic had come from.

Even the older fae, the leader of the Suden court, had shown a little trepidation at meeting him. Luc couldn't ignore that Michael's care and attention finally got him through school, though. Michael had taught him how to hold tight to his magic, if not control it. His guidance stopped the accidents from occurring.

Until Rose.

The archer that shot at Rose on their trip was the first time he'd lost control in ten years. Rose had been in danger, and his magic had buried the archer alive in retaliation. Thankfully, Rose and her hidden depths had saved him from himself. But his power's reaction to her—it was one more thing to worry about. Sometimes, it ran on pure instinct. He *thought* its instinct was to protect her. But his magic ran too deep, too strong, too all-encompassing to let off its leash in one of its single-minded pursuits—no matter how much they both wanted her. Yesterday proved the point.

Even when it seemed hell-bent on protecting her, it was still unpredictable. He shook his head again as the rock bounced in his hand. How could he have miscalculated? She'd passed out from going too deep. It had coaxed her down into its depths and then swallowed her whole, and all he did was watch.

Of course, she wanted to try again. But a magical weapon was not worth her safety. He'd done without for this long. If the mist struck, he could borrow one of hers. He didn't need the amplification one of her weapons would give him. The only problem was, she wouldn't like that response. She would ask again—soon. And denying her was as much a struggle as controlling his power.

His gaze slid back to Rose. When she'd returned from the Vesten gardens last night, she said they hadn't been caught. But if he had to guess based on how Carter was staring daggers into her back... He hoped she had come up with an excuse but knew she hadn't. She was dead set on being honest with the Compass Points—and if she couldn't be honest, she would say nothing. He grabbed the rock from the air as it bounced and closed his fist around it. He was sure that wouldn't go well. Rolling his head, he stretched his neck, readying for the long day of riding ahead.

He moved to spur his horse to catch up with Rose when he felt Juliette drop back to ride beside him.

"A word," she said.

He nodded. "Of course."

"You'll forgive me if I ask a slightly rude question, given the nature of this quest," she started.

He was not sure he would forgive it, but he gestured for her to continue regardless.

"Do you commune with Aterra?"

He squeezed the rock in his fist, grinding it into dust. "What do you mean?"

"I mean the same thing Rose meant when she asked me about my connection to Zrak. Do you have a means of communicating with him?"

An unmistakable rage flooded through him. His eyes flashed red and his magic grew thick in the air. He reined it in. Conceptually, he understood that Compass Points were supposed to commune with their patrons, but to his knowledge, none of them did. Juliette hadn't really answered Rose's question when she'd asked at the Solstice Ball. She had said she still worshiped the Lost God, but what did that really mean? Luc shook his head. Not that he wanted a connection with Aterra at this point. His face must have pinched at the thought, and Juliette held up her hands in a gesture of peace.

"I mean no offense, Luc. I'm merely trying to ascertain if we overlooked a simple solution. I see from your expression that we did not."

"If I had a means of communing with him, don't you think I would have known what he was doing?" Luc asked.

Juliette raised her chin but said nothing.

"Ahh, I see." He let his lip curve into a smirk. "You think I did know."

She moved her horse back into line without further explanation.

Her insinuation that he was in league with Aterra was unfortunate, but not unexpected. He knew Carter and Juliette disliked him. He had thought it was because he opposed their plans when they sided with Aiden—but that was too easy. He should know by now that it always returned to his power. They didn't trust it. It shouldn't surprise him. He didn't even always trust it. He thought back to what Arie told him before he'd left the night before.

The black bird had flown through the open window as he slipped into bed with a book. It was late, but he was waiting up.

"Where's Rose?" he asked as he saw Arie but felt no disturbance walking through the house yet.

"*I left her on the Suden side of the property line. She'll be a few minutes yet.*"

"Which side?" he asked.

The bird shook its beak at him.

"*It's irrelevant. I want to talk to you. Rose asked me about evaluating your magic tonight.*"

He sat up. He wasn't sure he liked Rose talking about his power, but he also wanted to hear what Arie had to say about it.

"*Don't look like that. She didn't tell me it was your magic her questions were about, but I'm a god, not a moron. She was asking if there was such a thing as a fae's power being too overwhelming to understand. If there was a limit to her weapon-making's ability to capture the essence of the wielder's magic.*"

That sounded like Rose. She would assume her passing out was a failure on her part, not a defect of his magic. "What did you tell her?"

"*Your power is strong. I doubt I have to explain that to you.*" He paused, and his head cocked slightly as if listening for something. "*I don't know if her magic has limits, but I think you should let her continue testing them. Your power won't hurt her.*"

Luc caught Arie's phrasing. His power wouldn't hurt her. Arie, too, must think of his magic as a separate entity. Luc shook his head. "I thought the same until this morning," he said bitterly.

"*Your magic this morning didn't hurt her. It overwhelmed her. There is a difference.*"

"What do you mean? She was on the ground, passed out

because of my magic. That seems like hurt to me." Luc swore the bird smirked at him, but surely that wasn't possible with a beak.

"Believe me, she knew she should have stopped this morning. But her magic is drawn to yours as much as yours is drawn to hers. She will just need to learn to go a little slower with the evaluation."

Luc made a noncommittal grunt, but his heart beat a little faster at Arie's words.

"It's not quite the same, but my magic overwhelmed Kenna, the first Vesten Point, in a similar way. I didn't know how to separate various aspects of my power. I gave too much, too quickly, leaving the Vesten with shift and flame. I didn't hurt them, though. I intended to help, and my magic was my intention."

"My power has its own intentions," Luc grumbled. He rarely spoke about it at this level with anyone, but he figured a god was a good place to start.

"I suspect that's because you never quite learned how to tame it. Your power is too tangled up in instances of lost control." Arie gave Luc a knowing look that had Luc wondering how much of his past the god was familiar with. *"I'd even hazard to tell you that because of those incidents, you fear the depth of your magic, though I know you'll reject that."*

Luc bristled at the idea. He didn't fear his power—it was a part of him. He couldn't fear himself. He laughed, realizing he only used this argument when it suited him. His power was part of him, so he couldn't fear it, but it wasn't part of him when it was beyond his control. He knew he needed to sort out his relationship with his magic—soon.

He focused on Arie's first words. They felt truer. He never learned how to tame it. "You're telling me to let her try again?"

"I wouldn't presume to tell you what to do. That is between you and Rose. I'm telling you what we both know: She will ask to try again. And I'm trying to help you understand that you don't have to put her off forever."

Luc pulled his hand across his face as he thought about Arie's words. He smirked. Now Rose was drawing the gesture from him even when not in the room. "Thanks," he said for his apparent godly wisdom. Met with silence, he looked back to where the bird had been perched on the bed—he was already gone.

"So much for goodbye," Luc mumbled as he lay back down to stew on what the Lord of Fire had said, waiting for Rose to return.

CHAPTER EIGHT

Rose was steadfastly ignoring the eyes boring into the back of her head. She wanted to turn to see if Juliette was talking to Luc. She could hear soft voices and feel Luc's magic flaring to life. But only Carter's stare would await her should she turn to check. The Vesten leader rarely made eye contact, but it turned out that, when he did, it made his point.

The feeling of his gaze piercing her skull eased as Carter brought his horse into position next to her. The road had finally widened enough to ride side by side again as they crested the mountain pass. She waited for his words—the accusations she was sure would come. Her gaze raked over the land below them. The main road north and south was barely visible from the top of the mountain. It would be another long half-day before they reached it. She felt for the necklace chain that held the compass beneath her long-sleeved tunic. Where would it lead them from there?

Carter still hadn't said anything. She broke the silence. "Can I help you?"

His eyes narrowed, just as she'd imagined. His whole face pinched either in anger or a detailed evaluation of her person; maybe both. "What is it about you? Why does Lord Arctos choose you?" he asked.

Interesting, Rose thought. This wasn't about the artifact or being on the Vesten property at all. This was about the presence of Arie with her instead of him. "He's my friend," she replied.

"Do you hear yourself? What Compass Point—no, what *fae*—has ever been friends with one of the gods, let alone one who is not their patron?!"

His voice was rising. Rose could see Luc pushing his mount forward, likely unsure, just as she was, of what the Vesten Point would do. She let a hand fall from holding her horse's reins and gestured for Luc to wait. It would do no good to avoid this conversation with Carter if they were meant to build any kind of trust.

"I know it's unique, but aren't all our circumstances?" she asked. "Until a few days ago, he was just Arie to me. He wasn't Lord Arctos. He wasn't the Vesten god. Maybe I had to know him as *just Arie* for a friendship to form." She shook her head. "Honestly, you'll have to ask him why he hid his identity. It's his story to tell, not mine."

"It's hard to do when he immediately disappeared again. Without, I might add, so much as a conversation with me."

"I don't control him."

Carter leaned in and whispered angrily. "You and Lord Arctos were digging on the Vesten grounds last night. What were you looking for? What did you find?"

Rose sighed. Even though she'd had all night to come up with an answer for this, she hadn't. Of course it had been Carter's shifted form in the bushes. Part of her wanted to give him the coin now—say that Lord Arctos might have been wrong in his direction. But another part of her wanted some time with the Vesten artifact to learn whatever it was that Arie thought she could. She wouldn't lie to Carter. Maddening vagueness was her only option.

"I don't know what to tell you. I'm not your enemy. It was Arie's mission—he wanted me to come with him."

Carter assessed her words, his brow pinching impossibly

deeper. "Again, I point out, he is conveniently not here for me to question!"

"Arie does as he wishes. You won't win any favors with him trying to change that."

"You don't think having him with us as we go after a rogue god would be helpful?"

"He was with me for ten years," Rose said. "He had plenty of time to go after Aterra himself. He clearly had his suspicions about the cause of the mist plague. And I am sure he knew something was wrong for far longer than that."

She turned to face Carter, her gaze locking on his. "The thing is, he didn't do anything about it. He found me, the rightful Norden Point. He befriended and supported me and was there with me on a journey to take back what was mine." Rose sighed, wiping her hand against her brow as the sun beat down on them on the mountain pass. At the high elevation, it was hot without the tree cover from the ascending or descending switchbacks. "Arie agreed with our plan. He can't do anything on his own about Aterra. *We* need to do it." She let the statement hang there, willing Carter to understand they were the continent's only hope.

Carter's eyes widened. Particularly as she noted that Arctos couldn't solve all their problems. It may be near blasphemous to him, but it was the truth from Arie's mouth. Rose knew that Carter and Juliette needed to understand it, or they would never succeed.

"It's up to us." She paused. "The gods can't help us. This is why we exist. We can and will stop Aterra."

"Yes, you said that yesterday. I'm still not sure I believe you."

"And that is part of the problem. We know our magics are going to need to work together. I can't imagine that will be easy without trust."

"I might trust you more if you gave a better explanation of why you were on Vesten property. 'The Lord of Fire made me do it' is a little weak."

Rose sighed, acknowledging that he was right—but she had

nothing else to offer him now. She wondered if he could sense the coin in her pocket. It was obviously a source of Vesten magic. But it wasn't exactly...doing anything. Like with fae, it's magic probably needed to be actively in use before others could sense it. The problem was that Arie hadn't told her precisely what it did. It enhanced Vesten power—did that mean only Vesten could activate it?

They had learned quite a bit about what the Suden artifact was capable of yesterday morning. While she had the Norden dagger, she didn't actually know what it did either. It was known to be a symbol only the Norden Point could claim, so she had done so. She hadn't had time to test what additional magic that symbol brought to the wielder. As she considered what she knew and didn't know about the godly artifacts, she wondered what the Lost God had left the Osten. It bothered her that they were riding away from Compass Lake, one of the main sources of information to answer these questions. The libraries at the Compass Points houses would absolutely have held this knowledge. But stopping Aterra was the priority, the artifacts more a curiosity. If their journey took them to Sandrin, they might be able to research there.

Finally, they reached the other side of the mountain pass, which required them to drop back to single file for the descending switchbacks. Maybe it was for the best that there would be little possibility for further conversation today.

CHAPTER NINE

The coin weighed heavily on her the rest of the day. She tried both her wind and water magic to activate it—but was unable to provoke a response. She hoped again that Arie knew what he was doing when he asked her to study the coin before passing it to the Vesten Point.

Part of her doubted he did.

They made camp at the crossroads where she and Luc had stayed on their previous journey from Bury to Compass Lake. Staying on the western road would lead to Sandrin. Heading north would ultimately take them back to Bury. Rose checked her compass. They would be heading south for this journey. She set up her bedroll next to Luc's as she tucked the compass beneath her tunic. Carter and Juliette spread out far away from each other as well as Rose and Luc.

"You didn't come up with a response to the question you knew he was going to ask, huh?" Luc questioned as one side of his lip curled into a smile.

"I couldn't lie to him," Rose replied as she ran her fingers through her hair. "And like I said last night, is it really stealing if the Vesten god told me to take it?" Her tone was wry as she reminded him, "It's his to begin with."

Luc hmphed a laugh, but she could still see the worry lines marking his brow. The concern was evident in his quiet voice as he spread out a blanket. "You seem to be collecting godly artifacts. Do we know what this one does?"

"I was trying to figure that out on today's ride, with no luck. I assume Carter knows, but I can't exactly ask him."

Luc nodded. "While you're right, none could rightly contest you having Arctos's artifact if he gave it to you. He's not here right now. And I'm not sure how Carter will react when he finds out."

"Noted. He said as much this afternoon, and he doesn't even know I have it. He just knew I was on his property with Arie."

"Which, I assume, he didn't care for?" Luc asked, his voice low and teasing again, sending unexpected shivers up her spine. She wished they had more time to enjoy the newness of their relationship before heading off to save the continent.

"You assume correctly," Rose replied, pausing their conversation as Juliette approached.

"You two seem cozy," the Osten Point said, her gaze lingering on the proximity of their sleeping mats.

Rose fought the urge to roll her eyes. It wouldn't help the situation. Instead, she kept her gaze locked on Juliette's.

"We talked about this already. It's a thing. Consider it none of your business."

"While I'm not one to worry much about mixing of fae lines—"

Rose cut her off. "Juliette!"

Juliette held up her hand in a gesture of surrender, as if she hadn't just casually spoken about Rose and Luc procreating. "I find our predecessor's concern on the matter repulsive. I'm saying I agree with you."

"You're also talking about my...relations." Rose's anger had her out of sorts, and she fumbled over her words.

Juliette laughed loudly. "You're a Compass Point now. Who

you share a bed"—her gaze slid to their mats—"or bedroll with is everyone's business."

"We've veered off topic," Luc cut in.

Juliette sighed. "While I have little concern for the courtly legitimacy of any offspring you might have, I am well within my rights to worry about such an alliance between the Norden and Suden Points."

"Ask your question," Rose replied.

"Will the full power of the Suden Point come to the Norden's aid when threatened?" Her gaze rested over Rose's shoulder. "I can see by the flash of red in our dear Suden Point's eyes that it will."

She met Rose's gaze again and continued. "Can we also assume that the mysterious dual magics of the Norden Point will defend the Suden?"

"We get it, Juliette. You don't like that we're united. How about we focus on all four Compass Points uniting instead of me and Luc against you and Carter."

Juliette's laugh echoed through the clearing. "I'll let that pass since you're quite new at this. You really should know better, though. You can't expect us to forget five hundred years of court politics." Her gaze lingered on Luc again, over Rose's shoulder. The mistrust between the Osten and Suden was stronger than most.

"We are supposed to work together!" Rose was exasperated. She was too tired for the politics this conversation required. "That's the whole point of our positions. Only through our combined power can we defeat a god. One or even two of us working together will not be enough to stop whatever Aterra is doing. It has to be all of us."

Juliette assessed Rose evenly. "How do you propose we overcome broken trust and trespasses against our courts?"

That was oddly specific. Rose would need to look into the Compass Point history a little more closely. She couldn't say she had learned of the machinations of the courts in great detail as a child. Regardless, who had wronged whom five hundred years ago wasn't a top concern for her.

"We need to focus on the four of us—on the Compass Points as they stand now. Why don't we start with you and me?" Rose challenged as she gestured to the open meadow behind them.

Juliette's gaze was questioning.

"We need to find out how our magic will work together to stop Aterra. I, for one, don't want our first test to be when we find him. I know it will take time to build enough trust for us all to wield our elements together, but you and I?" Rose gestured between them. "We both have wind—it should be easier."

Arie may have wanted Rose to learn about Carter's power, and she would, but learning about the Osten's seemed just as important. Maybe even more so, given the element also ran through her veins.

She wouldn't waste this opportunity with Juliette to learn. "You speak of alliances. You and I have the most aligned magic—ever—among the Compass Points. Why don't we see if we can do something with it?"

Juliette's eyes glittered at the challenge. "Let's see what you've got," she said as they moved toward the flat meadow behind them. "Show me your wind as we walk."

This had been Rose's idea—she couldn't hesitate now. Reaching for her magic, Rose felt her water respond, rushing toward the surface. She sighed to herself as she tugged at her wind. It was what she would need for this challenge. With the gentle pull, wind burst forth, spiraling around her. The gust wrapped around her body. She smiled, still impressed that it came after so many years of dormancy. Rose flicked her wrist in a snapping motion, sending her power like a cracking whip towards Juliette. It enveloped her, sending her long black hair billowing in the sudden rush.

"Not too bad," Juliette said, a smile forming on her lips. She pushed both hands outward from her hips, readying her own magic. The action seemed defensive in nature—a shield similar to the one Rose had made in her battle with Aterra. A blast of wind swept under her legs. Rose stumbled forward, unprepared for the attack, her arms barely flying out to catch her fall.

She twisted her neck to glare at Juliette from her push-up position.

"Not all wind requires grand hand gestures," Juliette tutted as she looked at her fingernails. "You should have been ready for an attack."

Rose scowled, shoving herself back up. "We're not here to test my magic. We're here to see if we can work together." She traced Juliette's magical scent as she spoke. Sage and citrus. Two smells that hadn't been in the meadow moments ago.

"I think those two things are the same," Juliette replied. She snapped her fingers, and another gust shot beneath Rose's legs.

She was ready this time and jumped the blast, tracking it with her nose.

"You learn quickly. That's good," Juliette said as she readied for another attack. A cyclone came spinning across the distance between them. Its movement was jerky, but now that she knew what she was searching for, Rose could mark its progress.

"This isn't helping," Rose tried again. "You're just testing your magic against mine." She sighed, realizing what she needed to do. She would have to break this standoff. Instead of challenging the cyclone, Rose let herself be sucked into it. Relaxing into Juliette's magic, she let it lift her feet from the ground. Luc groaned loudly from somewhere in the distance, probably at her recklessness. Her body spun in time with the circling wind. She caught a glimpse of Carter watching from somewhere over Luc's shoulder, still keeping his distance from the activities.

The cyclone didn't expel her—that was already good progress. Testing the flexibility of the wind tunneling around her, Rose shot her magic into the storm, matching the cadence of Juliette's.

Their winds spun together, Rose lifting and falling within the storm as it moved. *This.* This was what she'd been looking for. She wasn't sure how this would help to fight Aterra. She didn't think

TANGLED POWER

they had found some weapon to use against him, but she had never used her wind with an Osten fae. She hadn't known what it would feel like—and she loved it.

Juliette slowed her cyclone, setting Rose gently on the ground. "That was risky."

"A lifetime's worth of repressing my wind magic. I can't believe I've never felt something like that before!" A smile lit up Rose's face from ear to ear. She didn't realize what she was saying until the words were out.

Juliette's eyes widened briefly before she wiped the expression from her face—not fast enough for Rose to miss the change. Rose swallowed thickly. She didn't want Juliette's pity. "You may say you don't care about mixing fae lines, but I assure you it's not a common perspective," Rose snapped. "My parents taught me to hide my Osten lineage from a young age. It was the only way they knew to protect me."

"Your wind is very healthy despite your parents' poor choices."

Rose bristled. She wasn't willing to hear a Compass Point speak ill of her dead parents. Her parents had loved and protected her the only way they knew how.

Juliette, seeming to realize Rose was about to explode, explained. "They did you a disservice. That's all I mean. I can never know their experience or why they chose to teach you to hide your wind. I expect it was from a position of fear, as you say—from a desire to keep you safe. I'm only pointing out what you already know. Magic needs to be used to flourish."

Juliette looked around the clearing. She stepped closer to Rose to make this part of the conversation more private. "If rumors are correct, you even suppressed your water magic. I knew it, at least, would still be strong, given your ability to claim the Norden Point seat. I suspect you're also quite powerful with your wind." Rose started to speak, but Juliette interrupted her. "Trust me, I can tell. With both of those powers raging through you, it was dangerous for you to bury them the way you did. No matter how one tries, that kind of power can't be suppressed."

Juliette's glance moved to Luc with her last sentence. Rose wondered how well-known Luc's ascension had been. Had the others known that a Suden child of so much power could not control it in the south?

"It will find a way to make itself known," Juliette finished.

Rose stretched her neck to the side, trying to evaluate her reaction. Her body bristled again at the comment against her parents. At the same time, she understood what Juliette was trying to convey. Arie had said she inadvertently poured her wind into her weapons. Was that her power making itself known?

The Osten Point would have tested all manner of Osten fae, especially over her tenure in the position. She was complimenting Rose's magic while criticizing her parents' fear. Hadn't Rose herself recently questioned why they let her live with such fear for so long? Hadn't she also ultimately thought it the wrong call, considering the continent's state and what she might do to help?

"I'll thank you not to criticize my dead family when you compliment me." Rose wasn't ready to hear anything negative about her family from Juliette, but she wanted to take the peace she seemed to be offering over their shared Osten magic.

Juliette nodded. "Again?"

Rose gave Juliette a come-and-get-it gesture as the smell of sage and citrus rushed toward her.

CHAPTER TEN

Exhaustion settled over Rose as she slumped to the ground by the fire. It was good that her wind was getting to flex, but training with the Osten Point herself might be more than she bargained for. Her water magic rolled through her, like waves begging to crash on the shore. She'd need to let her water have a turn soon. Luc handed her a bowl of the meal he and Carter had prepared.

"So, are we any closer to being ready to confront Aterra?" Carter asked as he scooped a spoonful of stew into his mouth. He had disappeared for a little while as they practiced, going into the forest that abutted the mountains and returning with meat. No surprise that his animal was a hunter, but what kind of shifter was he? It was rude to ask, and he had—unsurprisingly—offered no information.

At least Juliette opened up about what Osten could generally do with their power. It wasn't some big secret, Rose supposed, but it was new information to her.

"We have to start somewhere," Rose echoed what she had told Juliette. "We have to be comfortable enough to use our magic around each other before we face Aterra. That's what Juliette and I are doing." She tensed, waiting for them to yell at her or tell her she wasn't fit for her position because she hadn't laid out an exact plan. Moments passed in silence as everyone continued eating. Rose sighed softly—sometimes, more than half the battle was in her own head.

"You said we go south tomorrow?" Juliette asked.

Rose couldn't believe they would let such a big question go unanswered. What did it matter which direction they went in if they didn't know what to do once they found their quarry? "Yes, south." She couldn't bring herself to voice the more significant concern. The others had said their magic would know what to do when it was needed. Arie agreed. If no one else was worried about it, she would just continue to familiarize herself with each of their powers the only way she knew how.

She swallowed thickly. Taking action was her preference. Even if they assumed their power would work in a given way when it faced Aterra, they needed to test what it was capable of before then. Her shoulders scrunched as she thought about how to approach what she wanted to do. She had to tread carefully. Juliette would be most willing to listen to her, given their work together today. Carter, certainly, still didn't trust her.

"I was thinking," she started. "Though my and Juliette's magics began working together today, I don't know how that will help us, given we're the only ones with overlapping elements."

"It was a happy thought, then," said Juliette dryly.

She focused on the Osten Point. "I just thought...I should try to evaluate your power. To try to understand it outside of how it connects with my own."

"You want to make me a weapon?" Juliette gave her a searching look.

Rose couldn't quite decipher the emotions flitting across Juliette's face. She saw caution, understandably, but there was something else she didn't recognize. Rose tried to sound casual. "Yeah, I do."

"Don't you have to be at the source—at Compass Lake—to really understand? Especially for a Compass Point?"

"I think I can do it here since we share the element. I can use my wind magic as the source."

Juliette seemed intent on objecting as she pointed out, "You don't have a forge."

Rose turned to Carter and Luc. "Could you two help with that?"

Luc nodded immediately, his gaze already searching the area for stones that would be the right size and shape.

"You would make the Osten Point a weapon?" Carter asked, suspicion marking his face as he searched hers.

"I would."

"Why?"

"I think we need all the help we can get for what comes next. And I believe my weapons *will* help." She tried and failed to make eye contact with the Vesten Point. "I also think understanding Juliette's magic will help me learn how our powers might be able to work together."

"What do you mean?"

"What I said before—working side by side for two of the same magic is fine, but it won't help all four of us with different elements. I need to understand her magic enough that my water would know how to work with it, not just my wind." Rose ran a hand through her hair. "The type of evaluation I do on a person's magic when I make them a weapon should help me understand."

Carter appraised Rose before speaking. He must have accepted her words, saying, "I'll help with the forge."

※

LUC FOUND or shaped stones to the size Rose directed. Carter set a fire blazing in the designated space. Grabbing the steel from her saddle bags, her fingers brushed over the blade she started for Luc. The one she was unsure he would let her finish. They hadn't had time to discuss what happened in the Suden workshop. The early days of her new relationship were being stolen. She and Luc should be locked in his room for days without end, having time for only each other. Not roaming the continent chasing after a rogue god. Sure, it was a petty and selfish thought, but that wouldn't stop her from adding it to the list of things she held against Aterra.

Setting aside Luc's blade, she pulled out the extra steel. Packing this had been its own decision—one solidified by her conversation with Arie before he left. This was what she could do to help them face Aterra.

From their practice today, Rose already had some idea of Juliette's magic. Enough so that she already knew twin daggers would suit her. Just as the wind could blow from any direction, multiple blades could support a range of attacks. A satisfied smile crossed her face as she returned to the makeshift forge with the supplies.

"You just happened to bring everything you need with you?" Carter asked, his eyes widening at her preparedness.

"I told you. I knew we would need to make our powers work together. While I'm unsure how to do that, a better understanding of them seems like a reasonable place to start." She pushed her luck as she continued. "The real question was whether you would let me make them."

Juliette may be first, but Carter's present fire fueling the forge had her magic twitching to examine it too. She'd made no progress in understanding the coin on their ride. It sat dormant. Her power drifted toward the Vesten magic, wisps stretching until they danced with the flame. The coin in her pocket flared as her magic met Carter's. Heat connected the artifact and the blaze —would the coin come alive if she set it in the fire Carter created? And how did this connect to the shifter nature of the Vesten?

The Vesten Point's gaze was appraising. Though a step above suspicion, he still seemed far from letting her make him a weapon. There was a reason she focused on Juliette first—their shared Osten line gave them common ground.

Proving her point, Juliette effectively cut off any follow-up questions from Carter when she asked, "What do you need me to do?"

"For now, just stand there." Rose gestured to the space beside the forge. "Do something with your magic. It doesn't have to be an impressive display, just something to ensure your power is present and engaged while I work."

Juliette nodded as she set a tiny cyclone circling at her feet. The now familiar scent of Juliette's magic filled Rose's nostrils as she began her work. Juliette's activity wasn't as taxing as the one Luc had selected, but it wasn't as passive as Aaron's either. That fit with Rose's understanding of Juliette's magic.

Levels of power transcended the courts. A Compass Point of any court would have more power than an average wielder. Rose couldn't help but use this as another point of comparison for Luc's magic too. After their work together today, Rose could tell there was a clear difference between the strength of Juliette's and Luc's magics.

Was anyone on the continent his equal?

Luc's surprise that Rose didn't fear him in their original travels hit her with new meaning. It had to be lonely if everyone saw him as an uncontrollable threat.

Juliette's magic demanded her attention. She shook her head free of thoughts of Luc's power. When she finished his blade—and she would finish his blade—she'd figure it out then.

Rose worked steady strokes against the first of the two daggers. The Vesten fire was excessive, dramatically speeding up the process. She fell into a smooth rhythm as she shaped each of the blades. Swing after swing, her work could be considered repetitive, but she loved it. On the island, she worked in the forge daily. The last few weeks of travel were the longest she had experienced without forging since setting up her workshop at Lake of the Gods. Her fingers gripped the hammer tighter as she realized how much she'd missed this. Time passed, but she lost track as she relished her work. The flame before her was the only light left of the day when she wiped the sweat from her brow, exhaustion taking over again.

"I don't think I can finish these tonight," she said, setting the twin daggers aside to cool.

"No one expected you to," Luc said, coming up behind her, his hand moving up and down her spine. "You did more than enough for today."

Juliette was silent, observing Luc's hands so casually on Rose, but nodded and let the cyclone slip away. "We don't know how long this trip will be anyway, so we can continue tomorrow."

"Sounds good," Rose said. "Thanks, Carter," she added as she turned to the Vesten Point. She had a fool's hope that observing her work with Juliette would warm him to the idea of her making his weapon. His hesitation told her she had a lot more work to do on that front.

He nodded slowly, his gaze tracking her as they returned to the campsite.

Rose pulled the compass from beneath her tunic again. When she lost herself in her work like that, she thought of Mom and desperately wanted to touch the one thing she still had from her. The compass was warm from the forge, and the needle spun as she held it in her palm. Their path hadn't changed. Tomorrow morning, they would continue south.

"We'll ride early," she said as Carter and Juliette went to their separate bed rolls. "If the compass keeps us directly south tomorrow, we will probably hit a village." She couldn't remember their names but knew a few villages were on the southern road.

Rose looked to Luc, as the other two gave no indication they'd heard what she said. He shifted uncomfortably.

"What—"

"You've made great progress," Luc said before she could get her question out.

She reached her hand out to his now that they were alone, intertwining their fingers. "We don't know how much time we have. We need to work together faster." She turned to face him.

He looked like he would speak, but she cut him off. "Will you let me finish your blade?"

"Rose, we just established that you're exhausted, and your forge went to sleep."

"So, you're not saying no because you're afraid your power will hurt me?" Rose was tired. Too tired to dance around her real question.

Luc wiped his hand down his brow. "I'd be lying if I said I wasn't worried," he replied, "but I also acknowledge this is bigger than my worries. I'll do everything possible to ensure my power doesn't hurt you. Arie seemed confident it won't..." His words faded.

"Occasionally, he provides helpful information," Rose teased. She ran her hands down Luc's chest, soaking up the contact. How badly she wanted time alone with him. They'd found their relationship footing just as they were thrown into this mess, with the entire continent depending on their success.

Luc's gaze lingered on her hands as they explored him. "Arie knew that you'd want to evaluate everyone's magic, and that I'd be as much a holdout as the others, though, I'd like to point out, my reasons are clearly different." He scrunched his brow as he attempted to justify them. "Either way." He shook his head, his hands fitting over hers as they stopped moving. "I won't hold you back. We will be a united front in your approach to learning about the Compass Points' powers—about how our magic will work together."

Rose didn't wait for him to finish. She leaned forward eagerly, her lips brushing across his. "I know you wouldn't," she said as they parted. She moved to his cheek and neck as her lips brushed feather-light over every inch of his skin she could access.

His hand wrapped around her waist. "The others could be watching," he murmured, but didn't pull away.

Who was that warning for? He hadn't cared what the others thought. Was he still doubting she wanted to be tied to him this way in their eyes?

"I've already told them where I stand," Rose said. "And they've made up their minds about our...alliance, as Juliette called it." She nipped at his lower lip.

Luc glanced over her shoulder, turning her body slightly as he walked her backward to their joined bedrolls. Rose's tongue began to explore his mouth as his hands cupped her face, repositioning them to give her a better angle. They were all lips and teeth and unable to catch their breath as they savored the first real moments of peace together since Rose became the Norden Point. Luc's magic surrounded them—its signature scent was becoming one of her favorites. Knowing she was safe in his magic, she sank into the kiss as they fell to the bedrolls. She didn't think twice about their landing, knowing the tendrils of his power would sweep them softly to the ground.

Luc trailed kisses down her neck as they tumbled, his magic slowing their descent, and she enjoyed every extra moment. Reaching her fingers to run through his hair, she returned his mouth to hers. His hard length pressed against her belly as he landed on top of her. Her heartbeat raced, wanting nothing more than to wring all the pleasure from this moment that she could—for both of them.

A scream broke through her thoughts. Shifting Luc, she lurched up, scanning the area, listening again for the sound. His body went rigid, his magic sprawling, seeking out the danger.

"Is everything okay?" he asked, as if he couldn't identify a problem.

"You didn't hear that?" she whispered breathlessly, her gaze still searching the surroundings.

He looked genuinely confused. "Hear what?"

"I thought I heard—" Rose cut herself off and stood. Her gaze landed on another figure in the distance, facing the same direction from which she could have sworn she heard the scream. "Give me a second," Rose said as she got up and jogged toward the figure: Juliette.

"Rose?" Juliette asked as she approached.

"Did you hear that scream?"

Juliette sucked in a breath. "I was afraid of this."

"What's going on? Does someone need our help?"

"It's too late to help them. The mist has taken the village south of here."

Her bewilderment must have been written in her features, as Juliette continued without Rose even attempting to put her questions into words.

"The wind carries secrets," Juliette sighed. "It's one of the little-known traits of the Osten's power. The more you strengthen your wind magic, the more I think this gift will come to you. It can be useful, at times." Juliette paused and looked south toward the village. "Other times, it delivers information with which you can do nothing."

"We heard the village being attacked?" Rose asked.

"We heard the desperate cry of a few villagers. Secrets only dance on the wind when there is particular passion behind them."

"Why are you telling me this?"

"Would you have left me alone until you understood? Or would you have barreled in the dark until you found the danger?"

Rose gave Juliette credit. She would not have stopped until she understood what she heard.

"I thought so." Juliette twined her fingers together as if unsure what to do with them. "Your plan to learn about our powers is the best we have. The best method to prevent"—Juliette hesitated, gesturing around her—"something like this from happening again."

"We could have saved them, like we did at Compass Lake."

"We are nowhere near close enough. We'll barely make the village by the end of the day tomorrow. Even riding on the wind as I now believe you did to save Compass Lake Village, you wouldn't have made it. Someone was already screaming. The Nebulus, Zrak's agents, had already attacked. It was too late."

Their gazes locked. It had cost Juliette to say *Zrak's agents*. Rose heard it in the weight of his name on her lips.

CHAPTER ELEVEN

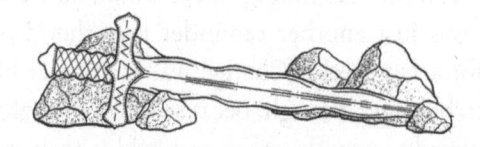

The truth was now apparent. Not that Luc had doubted Rose when she'd returned last night, but it had been hard to process. A wall of shadow encircled the village they approached, just as they had experienced in Bury. And Rose had heard it happen—had heard it a day's ride away. The dark gray mist hanging above the ground was evident even in the late afternoon light.

Luc glanced back at the others, pausing, before coaxing his horse over the mist line. He kept the loaned sword close in case they decided to go in. His gaze lingered on Rose. Solemn and focused, she rode between the other two. Anyone who saw her wouldn't be able to guess she had only been Norden Point for a few days. She carried herself with strength that couldn't be taught. It suited her. His pulse quickened at her approach. Shaking his head, he chastised himself. He was a fae leader, not an adolescent. But he couldn't help his reaction to her, not since first meeting her. Dousing his romantic impulses, he focused on the next part of their journey as they approached.

He was unhappy to still be headed south. He searched the horizon as the sun gave way to night. A pit opened in his stomach, thinking about what lay ahead. The compass would turn them in another direction before the next village, wouldn't it? What would Aterra and Aiden be doing in Loch? Either way, he needed to give Rose a heads up. But it was hard to find time to do so without Carter and Juliette overhearing. Surely, they were ready and eager to tell Rose every awful rumor of what had happened there.

It wasn't as if he were hiding it. He would have told her eventually. This was just another reminder that they'd only known each other for a few weeks. Change was coming at him fast. He couldn't even be angry, though, because it had brought him Rose. The others already knew the story and held it against him. In his heart, he knew Rose wouldn't. But would this finally be what made her look at him with fear? His magic flared from the crevice inside him in disagreement. He hoped it was right.

His gaze locked on Juliette's as the others approached. Her anger was palpable. If the air weren't already thick with the mist plague before them, he'd think her rage was taking shape and poised to choke off his breath. Had she thought Rose wouldn't tell him about the Osten power? Juliette seemed to understand Rose. There was no way she had miscalculated that poorly—no way she thought Rose would keep the information to herself—especially given her goals for the Compass Points.

He didn't even think Rose told him because of their relationship—she told him because she was committed to honesty among the Compass Points. The fae courts' animosity would only end when a better example was given. Rose was committed to being that example. It was one of the many things he admired about her.

Secrets on the wind. Luc ran his fingers through his hair as their horses lined up just outside the village. He couldn't believe that power had been kept a secret of the Osten for so long. It made sense, he supposed. They'd been more secretive than most —they had to be if the rumors from the first Suden were true.

Luc's fingers stretched and flexed as his hand fell back to his side. He knew Juliette held it against him, an event that happened over four hundred years ago when neither of them were even alive.

The first Suden Point had tried to take over Osten house. Michael had spoken of the event with frustration. It tainted the Suden court's reputation. However, Michael didn't hide the fact that the first Suden had thought the Osten Point weak enough to challenge. He'd almost succeeded too. Luc wondered how much of that had to do with their not-quite-Lost God. It wasn't something he had thought too hard about. He had never sensed anything but strength from Juliette. Of course, he knew he had more power, but her magic appeared comparable to Carter's and stronger than Aiden's during their required lake rituals.

He looked ahead at the part of the village just visible beyond the fog line. The mist was heavy in the air, but the bodies of villagers lying on the ground were visible. How much of this had Juliette been aware of? More importantly, how much of it could she have prevented?

She didn't trust him. For gods' sakes, she thought he was in league with Aterra. All the evidence in front of her pointed to Aiden as the now ex-Compass Point to blame, but Juliette still cast doubt on him—on his connection with Aterra.

"Are we going in?" Luc asked, gripping his borrowed sword a little tighter.

"Why should we bother?" Carter asked. His gaze bored into the ground. His disinterest in eye contact never bothered Luc, but this was a new facet. It was as if he was unwilling to look at the village—the humans and fae they were meant to protect—now lost to an unwakeable sleep. He looked...guilty, somehow. Luc must be reading him wrong. The only ones who should feel guilty were Juliette and her Lost God.

"I agree with Carter," Rose said as she pulled her horse alongside Luc's. "What do we expect to find? Sleeping villagers? Us unable to do anything for them?"

Luc didn't have to think too hard about Rose's response. He knew thoughts of Tara and the villagers she'd left behind in Bury were never far from reach. Surely, this brought them to the forefront of her mind, surfacing her own misplaced guilt. He had watched her shoulders tense and her jaw clench this afternoon as they had made it within sight of the village. He was learning to read her. And she was his favorite language.

"Okay," Luc said. His gaze met Rose's. "I think we should ride through on our way, but we don't all have to go." His sympathy was met with a small smile.

"I'll go with you, Luc," Juliette said.

That was unexpected. Before he could respond, Rose was offering Juliette her weapon. "I don't know if you need it, given the strength of your wind, but it's better to go with something we know works than risk it."

And just like that, he was riding through a mist-taken village with the Osten Point.

"She told you," Juliette said. Not a question.

He didn't see much point in lying. He was sure that Rose would tell Carter, too, soon enough. "Yes."

Juliette shook her head in frustration. "Why would she do that?" she muttered to herself.

"I'm not sure you've been paying attention," Luc replied as they rode. The shops were closed, and a few bodies lay spread across the ground. He guessed that made sense. It had been late when Rose heard the scream. Most of the villagers would have already been in their beds.

"What do you mean by that?" Juliette interrupted his assessment.

"It's confusing because you appear to understand her in most things."

"Don't condescend; it's unbecoming."

She was infuriating. "I mean that Rose doesn't want secrets among the fae courts. She wants the Compass Points to trust each other and work together. I'm not telling you anything she hasn't told you herself."

Juliette tilted her head to the side. "She doesn't understand the position we're in. The Osten need every advantage we can get."

"Did you tell her that? Did you tell her why that is?"

Juliette gave Luc an appraising gaze.

"She wasn't raised Osten. Whatever you think is understood by the Osten fae, I assure you, it's new to her. You'll need to trust her with more than simply answering her questions. You'll have to tell her things she doesn't know to ask," Luc said.

"Have you been thinking about what she doesn't know to ask in your history?" Juliette's smile radiated excitement, but the kind you experienced when your enemy just sprung their own trap.

"I—"

Juliette cut him off, uninterested in his response, simply enjoying toying with him. "And why would you point out how to better communicate with Rose—how to gain her trust? You have her exactly where you want her. She's loyal to you above all of us, no matter her lineage."

Luc rubbed his hand down his face. He was happy to let Rose try to have these conversations after the last eight years of Juliette, Carter, and Aiden ignoring or outvoting him. He wasn't sure why he was trying now, except that he wanted to support Rose's efforts. He believed in her ability to win these two to her side. If it were up to him, though, after every time they supported Aiden and blocked Luc's efforts, he'd take more of an I told you so approach.

He let out a deep breath. Rose was right. Throwing Juliette's past in her face wouldn't solve the problem. It had to be all of them together or not at all. He tried again. "I'm not trying to control Rose. I care about her. I care about the humans and fae of this continent that we are sworn to protect."

"Oh, lay off." Juliette flipped her hair over her shoulder. "We all know you have no reason to save the Suden. They've done nothing for you since you came into your power."

Luc shook his head. He was controlling Rose? He hated his court? No wonder everyone thought he was responsible for the mist plague. He was an easy target and did nothing to defend himself from those opinions. He guessed he'd need to start now.

TANGLED POWER 89

"You, more than most, know what I've fought for since taking my position. I argued for a balanced continent, for more magical cooperation between fae and humans. I was in favor of policies that had no material gains for the Suden, and I accepted the duty given to me to investigate the mist plague, putting Suden lives in harm's way because I knew we were best equipped to deal with it."

"I fail to see what this rant proves," Juliette replied.

"I am not the enemy here."

"So, what? I am?" There was a twinkle in Juliette's eyes as she taunted him.

"I'm not above pointing out that you supported Aiden for the last eight years, maybe longer. You can't tell me you didn't know that there was something off about him." So much for not throwing it in her face. He shook his head.

"Knowing something was off and knowing that the Suden god controlled him are two different things. No one could have expected that."

"You didn't need to know that Aterra controlled him to know what he was proposing was wrong!" Luc's temper flared. He was sure his pupils flashed red. He grabbed hold of his magic as it strained on its fraying leash. "You didn't need to know he was a god striving for imbalance to oppose policies and plans that were bad for the continent."

Juliette leveled her gaze at him. "So, what? You're mad that we were mean to you for the last few years?" Her tone was wry. Insulting.

He gritted his teeth. "Don't be difficult. You were complacent in Aiden's stolen reign as Norden Point. You enabled his agenda, knowing it was wrong. I'm trying to point out that I have as much reason to mistrust you as you do me—but I'm trying to give you the benefit of the doubt instead. Why is that so hard to believe?"

"It's hard to believe because it's not done among the fae. Rose may be too newly returned to the courts as an adult to realize that, but you have no such excuse. You can't change five hundred years of history overnight."

"What if history doesn't reflect what we want for the future? Why were the courts so dead set on separation and secrecy to begin with?" Luc didn't even realize the depths of the question. He'd always accepted the behavior as the way things were—never questioning how it came to be that way.

Juliette narrowed her eyes at him. "Power, Luc. Plain and simple. Some courts had it." She gestured with one hand. "And some didn't." She gestured with the other. "Those without wanted it, and those with it wanted more, even at the expense of others."

Luc tilted his head. Here she was, blaming him again for the actions of another fae, hundreds of years ago. The way she explained it, though...had the Osten *been* weaker? Did their god being gone mean that they had less power? Was that true for any of the courts? Rose's power didn't seem diminished even though her goddess was a captive. But Rose was a special case, wasn't she? In fact, why did he assume that Aurora would be her only patron? Did she also draw power from the Lost God? They knew so little about her dual lines.

He turned, his gaze assessing Juliette again. How much of this did she know? What information about Zrak and maybe even Rose was she hiding?

Juliette must have noted a change in his expression. "What?" she asked.

Luc couldn't help his response through clenched teeth. "I realize you are blaming me for the actions of my predecessor. I don't know how to convince you that I am not the same."

"The fae in the position may change, but the nature of the fae does not."

"And are you like your predecessor? You have never struck me as weaker than the rest of the Compass Points."

Juliette scoffed. And he might be reaching, but she didn't correct his assumptions about her predecessor *being* weaker. He looked toward the village limits. They were almost through. He wouldn't ask her more, mostly because he was sure she wouldn't answer. Rose and Carter neared the town's southern gate. It made him feel a little better to know they looked as tense as he felt.

"Let's just meet up with the others," Luc said, spurring his horse forward.

CHAPTER TWELVE

Some unspoken agreement led them all just a bit farther down the southern road. Though they knew that Zrak's agents that brought the mist plague, the Nebulus, were gone—they'd made their mark on the village and left—it was still an eerie thing to be so close to a town of immobile bodies.

"I can start on a meal if you want to try to get some more work in," Luc said as his hand caressed Rose's lower back.

His touch was enough to send heat through her veins. It had her longing for that place of no responsibility—where none of this depended on them.

Making weapons, though, there was no denying that was her charge. The likelihood was high that they would need them soon. Forget about finding and facing Aterra and Aiden. If the mist attacked where they were close enough to do something about it, would Juliette's wind magic be enough to protect her? What about Carter? He had no natural defenses. She sighed, feeling the weight of the Vesten coin in her pocket. One problem at a time.

"Thanks, Luc," she replied as she looked to Carter and Juliette for agreement. "You two in?"

Carter nodded as he drew circles in the sand with his foot.

Juliette gave Rose a searching look. "This is when you'll have to evaluate my magic? Instead of feeling its presence?"

Rose nodded. She thought they had built enough mutual respect that Juliette would let her do this. Yet there was no denying the tension between Juliette and Luc when they had come out of the village. Rose hadn't had a chance to ask him about it, but she was sure it was due to Rose's open communication about Osten secrets.

"What does it entail?" Juliette asked. "I admit I've never had my magic evaluated in such a way. Is it similar to a fae court's test for power?"

Rose understood the comparison. It was something Juliette was familiar with, but Rose couldn't bring herself to reassure her. "The outcome may be similar," Rose started. "The method is quite different. At least in my Norden experience." She took a breath before plunging in. "My magic will test yours, but it's without words or expectations. It's almost like a game. But it isn't about one power winning over the other. It's just the forum in which mine explores. I know that sounds stupid." Rose shrugged. "In a standard evaluation, our magics will behave like this for some time. I'll likely get scents, sounds, and feelings of things you hold dear." Her gaze fell to Luc as she said, "Usually, it's not complete images or scenes. More the essence of the wielder—since that is what I put into the weapon."

Juliette gave Rose a sharp look, clearly paying too much attention to Rose's phrasing as she asked, "What happens in a nonstandard evaluation?"

Luc coughed.

Rose quickly weighed the pros and cons. Juliette deserved to know the stronger the power, apparently, the more chance she had of *seeing* more. "The only Compass Point I've evaluated so far is Luc," Rose said carefully. "I think you'd agree he is a special case."

Juliette nodded, but her eyes didn't leave Rose's, urging her to continue.

"I saw scenes, images, more..." Rose said, unsure how to finish.

"And you think that's because of the strength of his magic?" Juliette asked.

"Why else?"

"You don't think it has anything to do with"—Juliette's lip curled in a smirk as she continued—"your unique connection to him?"

Her cheeks heated. Even as one of them, she was unsure she would ever be comfortable with the Compass Points discussing her personal life. Biting her lip, she returned to Juliette's actual question. This had been on her list of considerations. But with no comparable experience, she didn't know how to weigh its probability. "I can't say for sure."

Juliette glanced between them. Luc's hand had left her back, but his body angled toward her. His eyes narrowed at each of Juliette's questions, deciding if and when he should intervene. He let Rose fight her own battles. She knew his relationship with the other Compass Points was strained. So, she appreciated how much space he gave her to build her own with them. Even if they still thought she was his puppet.

"I'd still like to try if you're up for it." Rose straightened her spine and lifted her chin. She wouldn't let this line of questioning deter her from her purpose. Juliette needed one of her weapons, and Rose would finish the twin daggers she'd started.

"Okay, let's see what happens," Juliette replied, her gaze still assessing but her posture more poised. Had she just been testing Rose? She desperately wanted to know where she stood with Juliette, but she seemed to run hot and cold. They'd trained together and Juliette had shared Osten secrets just yesterday. Not even a day later, she was back to over-analyzing everything Rose was doing and challenging her at every turn. Rose wanted Juliette in her corner. But she wouldn't lay down her pride to do it. Juliette needed to respect her if the fragile trust they were building stood a chance of strengthening.

The three of them moved toward a more open space while Luc cooked. Carter had the forge fire hot before Rose moved to grab the blades from her saddlebags. Juliette met her as she turned back to the workspace.

"I want your word that you'll discuss anything you see with me before you share it with the Suden Point," Juliette said, her voice barely above a whisper.

This was a reasonable request. Juliette wasn't asking her not to tell. She asked for the chance to understand what Rose thought she saw or felt before the rest of the Compass Points knew about it. Rose just wished Juliette didn't feel the need to request this. She hoped it would be assumed that they would discuss what Rose saw. Shaking her head, she couldn't wish things to be different. She needed to put in the work to make them so.

"That's fair."

Juliette dipped her chin. "Good."

The women walked together to the flames Carter tended. His magic sped up Rose's process. Not having to wait for the heat was a godsend. Rose placed the first dagger in the flame as she told Juliette what was next. "I'll need you to do something a little flashier with your magic now. But don't worry if you stop it when you feel my magic starting to mingle with yours. That is normal. I just need yours flaring at the start."

Rose went about her work, and before long, the scent of sage and citrus hit her nose. Juliette's small cyclone was now much bigger. It picked up leaves, dirt, and rocks from the meadow before them as it progressed in its circular movement.

Closing her eyes, Rose worked the dagger's blade. Though short, it would still need to be sharp. She lost herself in the rhythm of smoothing the blade as a spiral of her magic reached for Juliette's.

Her power felt old. Not aged and rotting like what she'd sensed of Aterra's. No, Juliette's had a texture to it, like wrinkles of skin on a human's face. A nuance the fae never had to deal with. This age wasn't a weakness, she thought as her magic prodded further, more like sophistication. It spoke to experience and knowledge that could only be gained through trials. Juliette had put in the work for her position.

Rose's magic tugged on that specific thread. What obstacles had Juliette faced? What had made her such a fearsome Osten Point? She pressed forward with her magic. Determination, perseverance, and justification of any means to achieve her end, these flashes of Juliette flipped through Rose's mind as her magic went deeper.

Luc's magic had been like falling through an endless tunnel. Aaron's had been the wide expanse of a plateau. Juliette's power led her through a locked door disconnected from any structure. The door opened to reveal a descending set of stairs. It wasn't an endless descent like Luc's. She went down them, feeling a flash and a change. It was now cold and a little damp, but Juliette's wind blew past Rose, urging her forward to the paths carved into stone. A cave network.

Instinctively, Rose knew the paths may differ, but they all led to the same place. The Osten fae. They were at the root of this. The Osten needed Juliette. And she did everything to protect them. It drove everything Juliette did. It was different from Luc's care for his court. Different from trying to make herself available and approachable to them. It felt tense and weighty. It was a much tighter bond—a bond bound in blood.

A flash of pain surfaced at her thought. Images flickered before her as her magic searched the cave. Wind sent her forward to an opening at the end of the path—the room all paths connected to. Blood welled on the light brown skin. Juliette's hand gripping into a fist as she spoke words Rose couldn't make out. Drops of deep red falling onto the stone. A strong, penetrating voice echoed in the room.

Where were they? What was she seeing? Rose shook herself free of the sensory overload. What it was didn't matter for the moment. She was forging a blade for Juliette, and whatever this was, it was what she needed.

Knowing and understanding were different. She only had to know to make the blade. This was the center of the storm. It was the heart of Juliette's power and what she did to take care of the Osten fae. Rose sank into the feeling she found in the cave as she pulled her magic back and focused it on the weapon she worked.

Arie's comment made her conscious of it—her wind wrapping around her weapons as she worked them. She leaned into that now. Using her wind as she forged the Osten Point's weapon was fitting.

Reaching for the second dagger, Rose continued to spin her magic around it, focusing on Juliette's blood-deep devotion to the Osten fae as she plunged it into the heat. She created a cyclone of her own wind and weapons master magic, whipping the fire and ash of the forge as she raised and lowered her hammer to the dagger. She didn't overthink the image at the core of Juliette's magic—or what the Osten Point's feelings meant. She didn't need the details to spur the feelings and essence into shape.

The magic may not require it, but the weapons master was undoubtedly intrigued. Her curiosity couldn't be a distraction now. The cold calculation of Juliette's blood falling to stone. Rose's mind circled the image as she worked. Juliette paid the price—the Osten fae were worth the cost.

Emerging from her frenzy, she heard Luc speaking softly behind her. "The food is ready. How long has she been like that?"

The fire was still hot as she opened her eyes. She wiped a dirty arm across her brow and used her wind to cool the dagger. "I think I'm done," Rose said. The blade gleamed in the firelight. The sun had set again during her work.

She flipped the daggers simultaneously, grabbing the sharp blades in her fists with expert ease. Unsure what overcame her, she bowed slightly as she presented them. "For you, Lady Osten."

Juliette's lips curved into a smile as her fingers slid around the hilts. Rose's magic, still awake and tuned to the Osten Point before her, could feel the rightness of the warrior with the daggers. There was a sparkle in Juliette's eye as she raised the blades to an attack position, settling into how they worked with her natural fighting style. "You've outdone yourself, Rose."

Rose was exhausted, but she cocked her hip and smiled anyway. "I'm well aware."

CHAPTER THIRTEEN

Activity emanated from the village they approached. A sigh of relief slipped from Rose's lips—the mist had not been here. Drained from her work on Juliette's daggers the previous night, she was asleep before Luc returned from cleaning up the evening meal. It had not been a restful sleep. Her body clenched, waiting for a warning on the wind she could do nothing about.

Her mind wouldn't stop working over all the things she had to do, all the questions she had yet to answer. The compass continued to lead them after Aterra, but would combined wind magic be enough to stop a god? Unlikely. Was she the only one worried? She resolved to make time today to talk to Luc about it.

The sun hadn't yet set, and they were already at the village. They would have rooms in an inn tonight. She breathed easier, observing the villagers going about their day around them as they walked their horses into the communal stable. The market was winding down. Wooden booths and stalls lined the city square, offering goods that reminded her of Bury.

It was odd. The market didn't make use of the entire square. Patrons and vendors gave a wide berth to a formation in the center. She glanced at the others as they handed off their horses to be groomed and fed. No bewilderment graced their features. There was no hood for an old well or anything she could see. Nor any specific artwork or statue. Whether the Compass Points found it interesting or not, she wanted to investigate. It was so different from the clumsily assembled aisles at Lake of the Gods crowding the entire square.

"Where are we?" Rose whispered to the others. She wasn't as familiar with the southern geography of the continent as she would have liked. Juliette's and Carter's gazes both shifted to Luc. Rose took note since they rarely deferred to him for anything.

"Loch," he replied. His voice was flat and emotionless, but his eyes told a different story. They willed her to understand something. She searched the square again, wondering what he silently desired her to know. Her head shook slowly as she turned back to him.

"The square is so much emptier than Bury," she said. "Remember the chaos of the attempted aisles there?" She tried to make her tone light and playful, but thinking of Bury was hard. And Luc somehow looked even more uncomfortable at her words. His body tensed, prepared for battle.

"Should we head to the inn?" Carter asked.

Rose sighed. She wasn't the only one who found Luc's agitation awkward. As the group walked toward the square, she let her mind wander. The market scents and sounds brought forth more memories of Bury. She tried not to dwell too much on things she couldn't control. That included Tara and the other villagers she'd had to leave behind.

She was doing what she could for them. Finding Aterra and stopping his interference with the balance between the gods and the continent was her number one priority. It was the first step in ensuring the mist plague ceased. They still followed Aurora's compass. It would lead them to the god. She mentally reminded herself of the steps in this plan. She was trying. They were moving as quickly as possible.

Turning to talk to Luc as they walked, Rose was surprised to see he pulled up the hood on his cloak, shielding his face.

"What's that about?" She gestured toward it. He hadn't worn it up when the wind was coolest at the mountain pass or even at midday on their rides, when the sun was at its peak. She tilted her head, watching his eyes shift. Was he nervous? "What's going on?" she whispered, trying not to draw attention from Juliette and Carter.

That was a lost cause, as Juliette's gaze had been locked on the two of them since Rose had asked for the village name.

"I'm sorry, Rose. I'll explain as soon as we're alone," Luc replied.

It was clear he also wanted to avoid having this conversation in front of the others. Rose let it be as they made their way into the market square.

Something drew her forward as they entered. Like a moth to a flame, the avoided area called her. Her magic stretched, desperate to know what it held. Power lingered here. A faint air of familiarity tinged it. She needed to explore. Her feet were moving before she could stop them.

"There's the inn," Carter said behind her.

"Can you make sure Luc and I get a shared room?" Rose said to the group as her attention was drawn elsewhere. Luc wasn't telling her something, but she wouldn't let the others use it to drive a wedge between them. Rose's progress continued, ignoring the others' voices as they planned for the evening. Loch was a small village. She was sure she could find where they were staying. Quick steps led her to the empty center of the square. A need to *know* drove her forward. Confusion hung heavy when she approached her target and peered down.

It was a hole.

A really deep hole by the looks of it—but still a hole.

Rose searched the market again, noticing the whispers and side-eye glances of those still milling about. Her interest must be unusual. She peered down the hole again. The familiarity was striking—a dark, vast tunnel leading to the unknown. Squinting, she tried to find any hint of a bottom—of where this feature would lead.

She was so focused, she missed the sound of footsteps approaching until Juliette was beside her. "You don't know where we are, do you?"

"Clearly not, Juliette. I asked the name of the village just moments ago."

"I don't mean that..." She waved her hand. "You don't know what this village represents, or what this is?"

Rose shook her head, realizing before the words were out of Juliette's mouth why the depth of this tunnel felt familiar—it was Luc's magic.

"Luc is from Loch." Juliette's eyes sparkled with mischief as her words reinforced what Rose was only just putting together.

Of course he was. Rose bit her lip. He said, and his memory proved, that he didn't have fond childhood memories. Living in a village this small, she could imagine everyone would have been in his family's business. Everyone would have questioned his unknown paternal lineage. The hood made more sense to her now, though it was likely a lost cause. He would be recognized here, not as the Suden Point, but as the fae child with too much power.

Her stomach dropped as everything sank in. He would have known yesterday that they were headed here. Why hadn't he mentioned it? She fell asleep before they could talk last night, but he should have woken her to tell her this. To give her a heads up so that Juliette wasn't here, reveling in their lack of communication skills. While she understood he did not want to discuss his past in front of the other Compass Points, he was pushing his luck for plausible reasons not to warn her.

She looked back down into the hole.

"And what is this?" She knew she should go to Luc to get these questions answered now. But the hole called to her in a way she couldn't explain. The question had slipped out. Rose was sure from the feel of the magic and the look in Juliette's eye that it had something to do with Luc—she just didn't know what.

"Maybe I shouldn't be the one to tell you."

"Oh, please," Rose said. "You followed me over here to make sure I knew." Rose was angry that she'd even asked Juliette this question. She needed to find Luc.

"You're no fun." Juliette relented. "Fine. This is the marker of the event that called Michael to Luc." She gestured to the space before them. The hole was wide enough to fall into, and no matter how much she searched, she couldn't find an indication of the bottom.

"How far down does it go?"

"No one knows," Juliette replied. "And no one knows how to close it. Various rumors have been spread about the event that led to its creation. Young Luc let his emotions get away from him. Most say his power exploded and created this hole, this abyss."

"What do you mean, *abyss*? Surely, it has a bottom."

"For nearly twenty years, the courts have been trying to measure its depths. No one has been able to find something that reaches it. Even strong earth wielders like Michael can't sense it. Or so it has been said."

"Twenty years? I would have heard about it," Rose replied. "I would have still been at Compass Lake."

"Would you have heard of Suden gossip, though? You were young and carefree, from what I remember. Many Suden were aware. The Compass Points were also reluctantly told. But it's not like it was general knowledge among the courts."

"So, Luc made this hole to nowhere? That not even other Suden can feel the bottom of? Why?" She cringed at her curiosity. She needed to stop asking questions and find Luc.

Juliette smiled coyly. "Well, that is where we get into salacious gossip."

"You can spare me. I'll ask Luc," Rose replied as she circled the hole. The size made her nervous. She remembered the memory about the playground splitting because he was upset.

Some would say he'd been trying to throw the child who was picking on his brother into a crack in the earth. Was this a similar situation? To her, Luc was so tightly wound. He had such a firm grip on his emotions and reactions. This idea of him losing control felt strange.

He'd been young, though. It was similar to her own childhood experiences when she'd barely realized that she was calling the wind.

"You're not curious about the gossip?" Juliette asked. "You believe Luc will give you a true representation of the situation? Why?" She genuinely didn't understand why Rose wouldn't seek third-party information on this particular event. An event that, in all likelihood, Luc was incentivized to lie about.

"You saw him when we came into town, Juliette," she said, leading them away from the hole. The essence of his magic pulsed there. It was faint, but sure. His scent wasn't present, but the resemblance was still clear. "He's not hiding the fact that something about this place causes him discomfort."

"But he also clearly didn't tell you ahead of time."

Rose put her hands on her waist, stopping them in their tracks. "Why are you so determined to think the worst of him?" She needed this conversation to be over. Juliette was only interested in driving a wedge at this moment. While annoyed, Rose knew the real answers were with Luc.

"Why are you so determined to trust him blindly? As far as I can see, everything he's done for you has only improved his position." She flipped her hair over her shoulder. "He must be one hell of a lover."

Rose fumed but reined in her reply, disappointment softening her tone. "I thought you and I understood each other better than that."

Juliette's eyes widened at the words, vindicating Rose's calm response. Juliette had not expected it. Was she surprised Rose valued the time they spent together and the knowledge she shared? She didn't think she had miscalculated. Even though Juliette was prickly, they had established a kind of relationship, one in which Rose deserved more credit than Juliette was currently granting.

"I guess not," Rose said, the silence building between them, making her fear she was wrong. "Please continue to assume I'm a mindless idiot led by an excellent tumble in the sheets." She turned to walk away, looking for the inn.

"Rose, wait." Juliette's fingers gripped her arm. "You're right. I do respect you more than my words indicated." She averted her gaze as she continued. "It's part of why I'm having difficulty understanding your trust in him. It doesn't make sense with what I know about you."

She gave Juliette a searching look. Nodding, she said, "Can you just accept that if you don't think I'm capable of being manipulated by a pretty face, I must have reason for trusting him?" Juliette wanted a full accounting of why Rose trusted Luc. But Rose wasn't sure the facts would help. Yes, Luc had catered to her demands when he brought her to Compass Lake. He'd sided with her even when he realized her enemy was the Norden Point, and he'd encouraged her to take her place, offering his support for her challenge to Aiden. All of those things individually could be chalked up to Luc making his own life easier.

It was well known that he was working on the mist plague alone. Keeping Rose sequestered went along with that. It was also understood that Luc disagreed with almost everything Aiden did as Norden Point, so supporting someone with a claim to be his replacement wasn't a surprise, even if it had never been done before.

No, her ultimate answer was that her gut trusted Luc. More than that, her magic trusted him. She never feared the power he wielded; she was drawn to it. If she was being honest, her heart trusted Luc too. However, she wasn't willing to look at that too deeply herself, let alone drag it out for Juliette to assess.

After a long pause, Juliette nodded. "I'll try," she said.

That would have to do, as she went to find Luc.

CHAPTER FOURTEEN

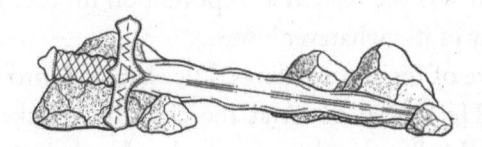

The inn was his only refuge in this godsforsaken village, and he had it in his sights. Carter shuffled behind him, but he was distracted by the hole, like so many others. For a moment, Luc couldn't help but watch. Carter's eyes darted around the depths in a pattern Luc was all too familiar with. He was searching for the bottom. But where others gave up quickly, realizing it didn't exist, Carter's gaze lingered, squinting and focusing on something Luc couldn't perceive.

He left Carter to it. The faster he could get to his room, away from the eyes that trailed him around Loch, the better. It had been foolish to come here. When he realized the compass wouldn't change course, he should have told Rose what was happening and met them on the village outskirts when they were ready to leave. It was unlikely that Aterra was hiding here. They would have been fine without him for a night.

His magic was loath to be away from Rose, though. He was having a hard enough time keeping it in check when she was close. The struggle if they separated might be insurmountable. But he probably should have tried.

No, he had to admit he was a glutton for punishment. Rose

would learn of his past here, and though he'd been too much of a coward to force the conversation ahead of time, he wanted to be available when she learned it. Maybe this was the thing that would change her mind about him. Would she finally stop looking at him with that unquenchable thirst? He was kidding himself—it wasn't only lust that colored her glances at him—nor his at her. It was more. It was the *more* that kept him on his toes and striving to be worthy of it—whatever it was.

Unaware of his surroundings, Luc slammed into someone in the street. He looked down at the child he knocked over. No apology left his lips, but he offered a hand to help him back up. He was Suden, like most in this village.

"Thanks," the fae said, dusting off his trousers as he got to his feet. "You might want to watch..." The child must have glimpsed beneath the hood as his words faltered. "Sorry, sir. That was my mistake." He hurried off, and Luc was unsure what to say if he tried to call him back.

"I wouldn't have let you off so easily," another voice said, crossing Luc's path. "No matter who you are under the hood."

Bold words, Luc thought. Did this second fae already know who he was, or would he be just as surprised as the first?

"You really do owe the child an apology—" The older fae's words cut off. He must not have known to whom he spoke. He did now. Luc was too damn recognizable in this place. This Suden was older, an adult. He was tall, and his skin was brown. Luc looked at him as his words dissolved. There was a fierce pride in his green eyes. He was smart enough to speak more carefully now that he knew who Luc was, but the fire in his gaze said he didn't regret his original words.

"I do," Luc replied. "Unfortunately, he left too quickly. I'd guess he was uninterested in my apology once he realized who I am."

"Are you surprised?" The fae replied wryly.

Luc laughed. The reaction was expected. However, he was delighted by this Suden's commentary on it. "I am not," Luc said, glancing around. The inn was still within reach, but this fae's honesty was refreshing.

"Why are you here?" the ever-impertinent fae asked.

Luc always made himself available to the Suden. And in eight years, no one had spoken to him this way. Members of his court had sought him to ask for things, to make him aware of their concerns—but all with a deference he couldn't overcome. Not when the mark of his power hung so heavy in Loch. "Not many would think it's their business to know what the Suden Point does," he replied.

The fae shrugged. "You're known to make time for the Suden, no matter how much they fear you. I find it unlikely one who does that would kill me for asking a question."

Luc's lip tugged into a smile under his hood. "What's your name?"

"Darren," the fae replied.

"How long have you been in Loch?" Luc asked. He thought he was familiar with all the residents.

"Only since yesterday. I used to live in the village just north of here..." Again, his words cut short. Luc wondered how many taken by the mist plague were those Darren knew and cared for.

"I'm sorry," Luc said and meant it. "I wish we could have been there in time."

Darren shook his head. "All that matters is what you are doing to stop it." His fierce gaze held Luc's again. "Gossip is already spreading through the village that the new Norden Point is leading you all on some journey. Will it stop the mist?" Darren's tough exterior cracked. He was no longer the brash fae who talked back to the Suden Point; worry lines showed on his face, and his fierce gaze fractured.

Luc's eyes held his as he replied. "We're doing everything we can. Correcting the imbalance on the continent, causing the mist plague, is our top priority. We will stop it and return those impacted from their sleeping state."

The fae appraised him, weighing his words. It was clear to Luc he wanted to believe them—he wanted the reassurance they offered. If he knew the stories of Luc's power, hopefully, that was enough to help him believe Luc could deliver.

"I'll hold you to that," Darren said, offering his hand.

Luc shook it. The moment his hand connected with Darren's, his power flared. He pulled it tightly to him, leashing it before it did more harm than good. He tilted his head, seeing Darren in a new light. He had not tested this fae. He didn't have to wonder what the results would be if he did. "I look forward to you visiting me at Compass Lake when this is over." Luc nodded at Darren, whose eyes had widened at the not-quite request from the Suden Point.

※

HER FOOTSTEPS ECHOED down the hallway. He knew it was Rose. Were her footfalls intentionally loud to warn of her arrival? Guess she figured out what Loch was to him, then. She was more than entitled to be furious. He'd made a bad call and could do nothing about it now.

Grovel, maybe.

His magic pushed against his skin. Running from him? Or straining for her? It could be either. Awaiting her judgment, he continued to flip his throwing knife back and forth in his hand, catching first the handle, then the tip of the blade. Each time he grabbed the sharp edge, he called his earth magic to steady it. The game was mind-numbing, but it helped focus his power. He'd been lying on the bed doing this since he made it to the inn.

He hated Loch.

Maybe he should be ashamed that he was hiding from the village—he wasn't. They didn't want to see him, and the feeling was mutual. No, what embarrassed him was that he hadn't shared why he hated it with Rose before they arrived. Juliette had surely told her. She had looked entirely too self-satisfied when he left them in the square. He tossed the knife again, catching the handle, resolving to do better. Rose deserved better.

Their eyes locked as she opened the door. She hadn't even knocked. He liked that—liked that she believed this was her room as much as his. Even though—

"You let Carter get us separate rooms?" she asked, cutting off his thought. She looked far too appealing as her hand moved to her hip, and she closed the door. If only he hadn't been such an idiot, they could talk about how good she looked and what they could do now that they had a bed instead of mats on the ground. This was just further punishment for his stupidity.

"That's what you want to start with?" Luc asked, his eyebrow lifting as he caught the blade's tip on his next toss.

She sniffed the air as he spoke, probably wondering why his magic was so thick here. Her lip curled into a smirk at his words. He couldn't help the breath that escaped his lungs or the way his jaw unclenched. He had hoped she would understand his lack of communication, but her smirk proved it.

He still owed her an apology, though. "Rose—"

She cut him off. "What do you think I should start with, Luc?"

He rubbed his hand down his face, pulling a full smile from her, no matter how hard he saw her try to fight it. "I don't know, maybe why I didn't tell you what Loch means to me?"

Her teasing smile was gone, and her gaze softened. This face was more vulnerable than that of the newly instated Norden Point. He had hurt her, which was the absolute last thing he'd intended.

"And why didn't you?" she asked.

"I'm sorry." He set the knife down and sat up straight, giving her his full attention. His magic reached for her, still trying to slip the leash he kept on it. "I didn't intend to keep it from you. I just kept hoping that the compass would turn us away. That we wouldn't have to come here. Maybe we wouldn't have to deal with this." He gestured faintly to the market square. "Along with everything else."

She walked to the window, crossing her arms in front of her chest as she looked down on the square. "What is it you don't want to deal with?"

"Don't tell me you didn't see the hole," he replied.

"I did." She paused. "What is it to you?"

"Juliette didn't tell you?"

Rose turned to face him, moving back toward the bed, where he sat. She slid onto the edge, one leg folding onto the mattress, leaving space between them. He stared at it. He'd created this space by making her doubt him—making her question why he would keep this information from her.

"I don't want to hear it from Juliette." Her gaze held his. "I want to hear it from"—she gestured to him—"whatever you are to me," she said, her voice growing quiet.

Rose thinking he was an idiot was acceptable, but Rose doubting what she meant to him was not something that could stand. He reached for her hand, and she let him take it. "You are mine." His magic thrummed as the words left his lips. "My partner for as long as you'll have me."

Her gaze fixed on their joined hands. He clasped her tighter than he realized. The uncertainty sketched on her features was more concerning than he wanted to admit.

"I didn't mean to make you doubt me," he said. "Not sharing the story of what happened in Loch had nothing to do with you, and everything to do with me."

"Then please explain. A partner wouldn't carry whatever this is alone." Her tone was even but firm. She was allowing him to do what he should have done days ago.

He considered his power. His claim—that she was his—had appeased it. Especially since she didn't object. A little mind shadow should be manageable without risk to her. "I think it would be best if I showed you this one," he said, offering his other hand so both were joined.

She took it. And the small win he gained with that unquestioned gesture was everything to him. She always trusted his magic. That he trusted it with her, even when he didn't want to, even when it was unpredictable, was something only she would appreciate. He gripped her hands tightly, never wanting to let her go, as he let the shadow of his power sweep over her.

※

"Aaron!" Luc called as he searched the market square. It was packed. The village center was awash in hastily assembled aisles. Merchants of all kinds were here to sell. He heard the soap merchant shout at him as he pulled up the cloth covering his table to look beneath it. Where was Aaron hiding?

Hide and seek in the market was the only good thing about the square being so busy. Luc had been searching for an hour, though. He was beginning to worry. Aaron wouldn't have left him there to go play with the other kids, would he? Maybe Zachary and Edward had shown up and wanted him to join them. They never wanted Luc around. They said he didn't know how to have fun. Luc shook his head. Aaron wouldn't have left the square without telling him.

Tension crept further into his shoulders as he looked under the fruit seller's table. A hand swatted him where he held up the cloth.

"What do you think you're doing?" the seller asked. She sounded angry. Her arms folded squarely over her chest after he dropped the cloth.

"I'm looking for my brother," he said absently, moving to the next stall.

Maybe he didn't know how to have any fun. Hide and seek was supposed to be a simple game. No magic required. He could play without constant focus on keeping his power tamped down.

"Get out of here!" This time, he dodged a broom and snuck

behind one of the sturdier wooden booths to see if Aaron hid behind it.

He ignored the shouts and continued his search. The next aisle was just as packed. There were villagers everywhere, doing their shopping. He narrowly avoided running into someone carrying a large bag of oats.

"Aaron!" Luc called again as he dodged out of the way of passersby.

"Your brother finally ditched you?" a voice asked from behind him. Luc turned to see Anthony with a sneer on his face. "About time. We don't know why he keeps hanging out with you. He would be much better off leaving the bastard fae to fend for himself."

Luc ran a hand through his hair. He didn't have time for this. This fae only ever brought trouble. But he couldn't shake the possibility that Anthony may have seen Aaron. "Have you seen my brother? I'm looking for him."

"Well, that's obvious." Anthony's laugh was unkind. He feigned an attempt to search the market row. "I see him there." He pointed.

Luc turned his head, unable to stop himself.

"Running away from the fatherless fae."

Luc rolled his eyes. Why had he tried? "If you're not going to help, please, just stay out of my way." Luc turned to continue on his path down the aisle.

Anthony jumped in front of him, forcing Luc to stop. "It's my duty to give Aaron as much time to escape you as possible. If he has finally decided to make a run for it, I should support him."

"Get out of my way." Luc held tight to his magic as he tried to shove around Anthony. He almost stumbled, but found he couldn't even do that. His foot was stuck. He tugged hard. It didn't move. Luc turned to glance down at what held it. A small hole had appeared and sucked in his foot. From the smile on Anthony's face, Luc didn't have to wonder whose magic was responsible.

A cold sweat broke out over Luc's brow. He was fine. He took quick breaths but tried to slow them like his mother had taught. "Let me..." Luc struggled to wiggle his foot free. The ground held it tight.

No matter his breathing attempts, he felt his power rising. It did not like to be constrained. It would seek to free his foot by any means necessary if he didn't do something—fast.

"Anthony, this isn't funny," he said quickly. Mentally tightening the leash on his power, he worked to secure it inside his body. Its help was not needed. He could handle this. If only his magic would listen to him.

Anthony's smile was broad, and his eyes were full of malice as he listened to Luc's pleas. "Not so powerful now, are you?" he sneered. "Can't even get your foot out of a simple hole."

Trying again, Luc breathed deeply, closing his eyes and focusing on staying calm. He felt sweat trickle down his spine. This was the wrong time for Anthony to try to assert his dominance. Luc was too frayed. He knew he needed to be calm, but he also needed to keep moving. Aaron was still missing. What if something terrible happened to him?

No—he wouldn't allow the thought to creep in now. Anthony would get bored soon. Picking on Luc should only entertain him for another moment or two, as long as he didn't rise to the bait. Closing his eyes, he held onto his power tighter—just a few more minutes.

"Luc!"

He would know Aaron's voice anywhere—it sounded strained. Luc's eyes opened and darted around the market.

"Luc! I'm here! Don't worry!"

Finally, his gaze latched onto Aaron. He was past the end of the aisle, attempting to fight through a wall of young fae. Luc froze as he watched Aaron struggle to get through the line—to get to him. When Aaron tried to move one way to go around them, they shuffled over, blocking his path. Aaron seemed to realize that

Luc *couldn't* come to him and set off at a run, trying to go straight through the bullies blocking him.

Luc's mind emptied of all self-control the moment the fae in the middle pushed Aaron to the ground. He was slammed backward, his head bouncing against the earth, then his body went still.

Darkness exploded around Luc.

He was sprinting toward Aaron. Those that had been holding his brother fled his approach. Luc knelt before Aaron and pulled him into his arms.

He was breathing. Aaron's chest rose and fell against him.

"Aaron, are you okay? Wake up." Luc shuddered as the adrenaline rushed through his veins. He couldn't even begin to assess how far his power had escaped.

His brother's eyes slowly opened. They were rimmed in tears, quickly widening as he looked over Luc's shoulder. "Luc," Aaron whispered as he shook his head, groggy from his fall. "What happened?"

What did he mean? Aaron's head had hit the ground with a finality Luc would never forget. He had to get to his brother—that was all that had mattered. Unfortunately, the panic in Aaron's gaze told Luc there was more to see.

He slowly turned back to the center of the market. A dark shadow circled the hole where Anthony's magic had held him. No... He set his brother down and stood. Looking from a different angle, it wasn't a shadow. It was a hole—a much bigger hole.

Luc's stomach plummeted. Nausea built in his throat as his gaze searched the chaos. Where were the stalls that had been around him in the center aisle? Where was Anthony?

He was already moving when his brain caught up with him. This couldn't be him. He couldn't have done this. Where was Anthony?

Sinking to his knees, he leaned over the hole and looked down. There was only darkness. A cold sweat broke out on his brow. His body shook. He turned and heaved the contents of his stomach on the ground.

What had he done?

"He... He killed him." One of the fae next to Aaron was pointing and yelling at Luc.

Luc searched again in vain. Where was Anthony?

He hadn't meant to do this.

A crowd started to gather, echoing the same words as the first fae, but giving Luc a wide berth as he crouched by the hole. Aaron was behind Luc in a flash. Though shaky on his feet, he grabbed Luc's arm and tugged him out of the market. They ran all the way home.

※

HIS POWER RECEDED as the memory faded. "It was quickly after that the Suden Point came to call," Luc said, shaking himself free from his past.

Rose's gaze held such compassion. He wondered if she had seen the same scene as him.

"Anthony died," Luc said. "Well, we assume. He fell to wherever the hole leads."

She said nothing.

"He was never found. His family still mourns." He paused. Maybe now she would see him the way the rest of the Compass Points did.

"You didn't mean to do it?" Rose asked quietly.

He shook his head. "That's not the point."

The look she gave him made him realize she would outlast him on this.

Luc grunted and answered her question. "I don't remember doing it. I mean, you felt it. I was trying to get to Aaron. But as you've seen, that wasn't the only time my magic got away from me. It was, however, the last time Loch's villagers were willing to deal with it."

He wiped his hand down his face. "Anthony was the village leader's son. He came to my mother's house that night and tried to arrest me. He said he'd sent for the Suden Point and wanted to have me in custody. Little did he know Michael was on his way before the message was sent. He'd felt my magic when it tore into the abyss, as the villagers say. He showed up the next day—not to arrest me but to name me his successor."

"Neither you nor Michael could close the hole?"

"You're missing the point, Rose. My magic—*I*—killed him."

"I know you believe that. Honestly, I'm sure that's what the continent believes too." She reached for him slowly, giving him time to move away. He held still, barely breathing, while wondering what she would do. She couldn't ignore what he was saying.

Her hand was warm and soft over his. She squeezed it, urging his fist to unclench as she intertwined their fingers. "I'm sorry about what happened. I'm sorry Anthony died. But this certainly isn't going to drive me away, Luc."

His shoulders fell with the breath he let out. How could this be her response?

"Have you tried to close the hole again?" Rose echoed her earlier question, presumably moving their conversation forward. He knew her well enough to recognize and value when she made up her mind on a topic.

Luc shook his head, his power straining toward her, obsessed with her understanding. He tugged it back into place as he replied. "I've tried many times. I'm not sure what I did, but I don't have a way to undo it."

"That makes a lot of sense given the little I could evaluate of your power. Your protectiveness took over—you were working so hard to push it down that when it got free—it erupted."

He met her gaze, squeezing her fingers as he went to pull his hands back, unsure where to go from here. She held his fingers tighter. "Next time, let's please not wait until we're already in the village you grew up in before you share a story that the rest of the Compass Points already know."

Luc raised an eyebrow at her again. "Why are you so calm about this?"

She squeezed his hands again. "I know what it's like not to understand what your magic is capable of—with no one to help you figure it out. I may not have hurt anyone with my wind, but I assure you, I wouldn't have had a way to control it should it have risen to my defense."

He guessed that was true.

"I also know what it's like not to want to talk about something in your past," she said. "I wish you could have shared this with me at the moment of your choosing instead of having to tell me because of this journey."

"Rose," he whispered, "I want you to know everything about me. It's harder than expected to tell you the things I'm not proud of. Things that might make you realize the rest of the continent have reasons for their beliefs about me."

"There are a lot of things I've learned about you since meeting that you shouldn't be proud of." She smiled coyly. "Assuming I couldn't possibly be the weapons master you sought and attacking me in the woods both come to mind."

He rolled his eyes. He wasn't proud of those instances either—but she was already aware of them. They weren't something new he had to explain. She had chosen him despite those failings—how many more could he expose her to before she rethought her decision?

Her face turned serious. "I obviously can't tell you how to feel, but losing control of your magic as a child doesn't make you a monster."

"You know it's more than that," Luc said.

"Yes, a child lost his life. The consequences were tragic. I am sorry it happened that way and that you had so little support with your power. But you learned to control it—maybe not in the healthiest way."

"In that, our childhoods are somewhat similar," he said. "You had no help with your wind, and I had no help with my"—he gestured wildly with both hands— "whatever this is."

She leaned forward and kissed him. It was deep and thorough and stopped far too quickly for his liking. She was already pulling away when he registered her question.

"Now, truly, tell me why we have separate rooms."

CHAPTER FIFTEEN

Rose had a smile on her face as she walked out of Luc's room the following morning. She ran into Carter in the hallway. He gave her a questioning look as Luc pulled the door closed behind them.

"Don't hurt yourself thinking about it, Carter," she said and took satisfaction in a slight blush tinging his cheeks. "I told you I didn't want the extra room. Please respect my decision next time."

Carter coughed and nodded as he headed down the stairs.

Juliette was already down there and had breakfast for them. The inn was nice, but they needed to keep moving. Rose was going to miss having a bed, though. Camping was not her favorite, no matter how frequently she did it.

After a quick breakfast, they headed out to the stables. She couldn't ignore the hole in the center of the square as they passed. It called to her again. Luc's magic was still faint, but its pull was more insistent now that she understood the pain it caused him. Something came over her, stopping her in her tracks. "I think we should try to close the hole," she said.

As soon as the words were out, she knew it needed to happen. It felt right. Her motives were far from pure. Many had tried to close the hole and couldn't. Her magic hummed as she thought of the Compass Points having to use their powers together to do what others couldn't. This town needed closure, literal and figurative. The hole still disrupted their market. The villagers still eyed Luc with disdain.

Fixing it wouldn't heal everyone, but it would blot out the constant reminder. It could also be the scenario the Compass Points needed to test their united magic.

Luc turned, raising an eyebrow at her.

She smiled sheepishly at him. It would have been preferable if she'd spoken to him about this ahead of time. But she hadn't known they'd needed to until now. No taking back her suggestion. The others were just as mystified by her comment. They looked to Luc, like maybe he hadn't fully explained the hole to her.

"I know he's tried. I know Michael has tried. I know all combinations of powerful Suden have tried," she said. "But have the Compass Points ever tried together?"

Luc's lip tugged into a smirk. He knew what she was doing. He wouldn't stop her. "They have not."

"We've had no reason to," Juliette said. "Why would that work?"

"Our united power is meant to balance the gods," Carter said. "Some believe Luc's power would rival a god on the continent today... It's certainly possible."

Juliette realized she was outvoted. Her hands went to her hips, but she moved toward the hole with the others.

"Do you have a plan?" Luc whispered in Rose's ear as they moved. "Or are we winging it?"

"The latter," she whispered, but knew he wouldn't judge her for it. More loudly, she said, "Luc, you should try to pull the hole closed, as I assume you've done before." He nodded in acknowledgment. "Juliette and I will push wind into the ground around the edges to support you." She looked to Carter, unsure what to do with his fire or shifter.

"I'll focus on the bottom. I think I'll be able to tell if it's closing."

Rose noted the certainty in his voice that there *was* a bottom.

"You don't think it's an abyss?" Rose couldn't hold back the question.

He shook his head, but didn't really answer her as he said, "My fire, lighting the darkness, should help loosen the hole's hold over this place."

Luc raised an eyebrow again and met Rose's gaze. She would need to unpack that later, but for now, they had a plan.

She nodded at each of them. "Ready?"

It was still early, but some of the villagers of Loch were already moving through the square. They would be unable to hide this attempt. Insecurity flooded Rose briefly. What if they failed? She shook it off. They needed to try working together before confronting Aterra. Practicing at their campsites would only get them so far. This was a real problem on the continent that needed fixing. They had to try.

The ground shook beneath them as Luc sent his power toward the hole of its own creation. As was becoming a pattern, a tendril of his magic hung back, wrapping around her. She reached for her wind, silently apologizing to her water magic again for its inactivity. But she needed to focus on working with Juliette, and she only knew how to do that through their shared magic at the moment. Juliette's magic circled hers, and they shot together toward the hole. Their power spun as they worked to tighten the circumference.

The heat from Carter's magic flared against her skin even as he directed it into the depths of darkness. He stood closer than the rest of them, his magic pushing into the vast blackness of the tunnel, lighting some of the descent.

Their power may not be a single unit, but working on a common problem felt right. She searched the edges of the hole for signs of movement. Was it getting any smaller? She swore the circle shook and shrunk.

It was a small victory, but they needed more.

They had to push harder. Rose dug into her magic stores. Her power was a lake at her center. Circling the familiar water, she reached for more magic. As she did, a strong wind lifted and guided her around the lake's shore. Tugging again on her power, it flexed, wanting to help but having already given everything she had. She needed *more* to complete this task. Responding to her unspoken demand, the wind deposited her at a door.

What was this? She was deep in her magic, and it was fading fast. She was pouring more than she cared to admit into this endeavor—wanting so badly to succeed. Not just for the victory it would be for the Compass Points to work in collaboration. She wanted Luc to have evidence of such a painful memory wiped away. Rose was about to dive back into her wind and see what was behind the door when shouting startled her.

"What are you doing?" a female yelled. "Stop!" She ran toward the Compass Points. Her voice must have been familiar to Luc because he pulled back his power. The female halted as Luc made eye contact with her. The rage in her eyes was evident, but so was the fear. It must have just crossed her mind that she was interrupting the Suden Point and what that might mean.

"Camilla." Luc nodded at her. His face was blank, reining in whatever he was feeling at the sight of the older fae. His power once again leashed.

Rose stepped forward. This had been her idea, after all. "Is there a problem?" she asked.

"You can't close it." Camilla's eyes tracked to Rose.

"Why not?" Rose asked.

Luc's mouth opened, but Camilla answered first. "My son! My son is down there." Her voice cracked.

Rose let her eyes close, feeling the words—the pain in them—wash over her. This was Anthony's mother. Rose's breakfast roiled in her stomach. Did Camilla think her son would climb back out?

"Why would you try now?" Tears leaked down Camilla's face, and Rose was unsure how to answer, but she knew she needed to. It was a bone-deep assurance from her magic that the Compass Points had to do this.

"I'm the new Norden Point," Rose started. She gestured to the others. "We need a task that requires uniting our powers." That was really all she could say.

Camilla seemed to realize that Rose was giving her more information than she deserved. She looked down at her hands tangled together. "Why?" she asked, her words a whisper.

Rose looked at the others. Their looks indicated that this was her idea, her mess, and she could clean it up however she saw fit. Rose nodded. "I can't begin to imagine your grief, Camilla, but we have to do this. Our power must be united to regain balance on the continent and stop the mist plague."

Camilla let out a breath. She nodded, seeming to acknowledge Rose's words. Still, Camilla gave a lingering glare to the Suden Point as a male caught up to her, wrapping his arms around her shoulders and leading her away.

"Well," Carter said, "whatever you were trying to accomplish, I think you proved our magics *can* do things together that they can't individually." He eyed the hole. Rose did too. It was definitely smaller than when they started.

Rose gave him a soft smile as she reached for Luc's hand and squeezed. He squeezed back. She knew he didn't hold this against her.

"Are we going to try again?" Juliette asked. Rose gave the hole a lingering glance. If she could have opened the door in her power stores, could they have closed it completely? Rose weighed her desire to try again against getting back on the road. She pulled her compass from beneath her tunic. As they'd entered the village yesterday, it had been pointing south.

As she stood south of the hole, it now pointed north.

Her heart sank. She had a feeling she knew what this meant

but needed to test it. Walking to the northern entrance of the square, she looked down at the compass again. It pointed south, directly back at the hole.

At least this made the decision for her. They couldn't continue after Aterra until they closed the hole. Aurora's compass wouldn't allow it.

※

WITH NO OTHER OPTION, they tried to close the hole again. Rose couldn't find the door this time, her mind distracted with worry. The compass directed based on the needs of the wielder. Why now did the compass believe she needed to close the hole more than she needed to find Aterra?

The others didn't seem to hold it against her—but they also didn't have a lot of options. After a few hours, they went back to the inn. Juliette and Luc went to get them a midday meal, leaving Rose sitting at a table in the main dining room with Carter.

Carter had been quiet all morning. She inwardly tensed, waiting for whatever he would say. "I'm sorry for ignoring your request yesterday."

An apology? She had not been expecting that.

"Given the village's reaction to Luc, and the fact that you clearly didn't know what this place was to him, I figured you would want some space." Carter sighed. "I thought I was giving you a reputational peace offering, not offending you." He looked around the room as it filled with villagers also seeking food. "As a new Norden Point, I thought you might want to start with a clean slate with the Suden."

Not quite an apology then. Rose bristled at the assumption but wasn't willing to die on this particular hill. She thought back to Luc's words yesterday. With their fake romantic relationship exposed, she hadn't known what to call them. His phrasing had suited her, though. "Carter." She waited for him to look at her. He did so reluctantly when he realized she wasn't going to continue. "Luc and I are partners until I tell you otherwise. I will forge my own name as Norden Point, and it will be one that stands by the Suden Point, no matter what a particular village thinks of him."

Carter nodded.

Rose wasn't going to linger on the topic. "What was your magic doing with the hole?"

He looked guilty. "Trying to close it, like the rest of you."

"You indicated it had a bottom. It's not an abyss to you."

Carter swallowed. "Do you have a question?"

"What is it to you? What can you see?"

His head tilted, considering her words. "You're quite observant, aren't you?"

He hadn't answered her question. She needed to give him something—a reason to trust her. The Vesten coin was heavy in her pocket. She hadn't had time to study it further, but she suspected it would do her more good with Carter than with her. Maybe it could work as a source to evaluate the Vesten magic while they were away from Compass Lake, but part of her knew she couldn't figure it out on her own. It was a little wild—its heat flaring inconsistently. So very different from the reserved fae before her. But then again, what did she really know about him? "Can you tell me about your magic?" Rose asked.

"Which part?"

"Well," Rose considered, "that's just it. I think I'm confused about the duality of Vesten nature. The shifter and the fire wielder." Rose wasn't sure what to ask, but she knew she was missing something. As her words came out, she realized why. The gold felt hot, like fire. But especially with what she knew of Arie, the fire seemed—maybe not secondary, but still only a part of a Vesten. When she thought of Arie, she thought of the shapeshifter. She hadn't known he had fire magic until a few days ago.

Carter chuckled to himself. "It's an insightful question. No wonder they say you're such a powerful weapon-maker. The two parts of the Vesten power are related. I'm guessing some part of your magic struggles to understand that."

"What do you mean?" she pressed.

He shrugged. "When Lord Arctos gave his magic to create the Vesten, they were both fire wielders and shapeshifters. Like the other gods, he was only trying to give them a bit of his elemental magic, but for him, these two things were literally the same. They couldn't be separated." He shrugged again. "The fire may appear a magic of its own, but the heat—it's a fundamental part of the shift. Some say it starts the shift. I don't think the Vesten god could have given us one without the other."

Rose was stunned. She couldn't believe she hadn't put that together. If flame and shift were one, how was she supposed to get the coin to do anything? She couldn't shift. Whatever it did, she was confident it needed to be in a shifter's hands to work.

Carter cut off her train of thought. "Though I guess you may know differently." His gaze was appraising, cautious again after what he'd shared.

"Arie and I didn't talk about our magic until a few days ago. It was an unspoken rule of our friendship. I don't have some secret knowledge of your Vesten ways." She paused, trying to get him to meet her gaze again. He stubbornly refused. "I'd like to learn."

He was receptive to the ask, if maybe surprised by it. His eyes widened briefly, still looking around the room, but he began to explain. "The fire starts the shift. And then, once in a shifted form, I liken it to an animal's heartbeat as they hunt their prey. Nothing is like being in my animal skin, but it feels close when I use my fire in my fae form. I don't have an answer for you that could be found in an educational text. I can only tell you they are part of the same cycle to me. I feel most alive when I use them together."

She nodded at his explanation. It was similar to what she had come to expect. Magic was never simple or straightforward to explain.

She had never seen Arie's fire, but she'd felt the flame of his existence when he'd momentarily inhabited her as they fought off Aterra. He had been in an animal form, and frankly, that was still all she knew of him. But the heat that ran through him when they shared space was synonymous with *life*.

"Most alive..." She repeated his words, thinking about what they meant. "That makes sense. Both the animal form and the fire are uninhibited life."

"Well." Carter's gaze shifted. "Uninhibited life might be a stretch, but our power certainly focuses on understanding and appreciating existence."

She couldn't quite grasp the meaning between his words. Something was still missing. But she'd learned more from this conversation than she ever would from the coin. In this, she knew that Arie had been wrong, and she needed to find a way to course correct with Carter. He may have been evasive, but he still gave her new information about Vesten magic.

Her magic wanted to explore his—if he'd let her. "I'd like to try to evaluate your magic a little more since we have time. I'm unsure if I have enough connection to the Vesten magic to make you a weapon while we're away from Vesten house." He met her gaze without hesitation this time, shock evident in the stretch of his features. She surprised him a bit more as she pulled the coin from her pocket and held it out. "But I'd like to try."

"Try what—what's this?"

"It's yours. Arie wanted me to borrow it, to use it as a source, to help make you a weapon on this trip."

"Mine?" His mouth moved as he seemed to be sorting through memories. "The coin was what you found? You stole this from Vesten house?" Carter's eyes widened impossibly further.

"Is it stealing when the Vesten god hands it to you? I think it's his, after all."

Carter looked down at it, then back to Rose. He didn't seem to have an argument against that. But he also still looked stunned to be holding it. "Why are you giving it to me now?"

"I think he might have been wrong in this." Rose smiled to

herself, momentarily wishing Arie were here to hear her. "I think...I can learn more about the Vesten magic from you, not from the artifact. I'm giving it to you as a peace offering, hoping these conversations might continue."

"And if I don't want them to?" Carter's eyes narrowed.

"Then they don't. All I can say is that Arie wanted you to have a magic weapon, and I'd like to try to make you one."

CHAPTER SIXTEEN

Carter disappeared for most of the afternoon. They spent the remainder of the day resting their magic. Rose's wind was tired from the morning, her water eager to take over, but she didn't think that was what this task required. She didn't know if she'd be up for trying to close the hole again this afternoon.

"So, we're just going to sit in this village?" Juliette asked.

Rose could understand her frustration. But she didn't know what to say. "I'm sorry. I don't know what else we can do. We could continue to head south, but without the compass to guide us, we'd just continue to the southern sea."

Juliette crossed her arms over her chest. "Should we return to Compass Lake?"

"I think we can give it another day," Luc said.

"We don't have time to waste," Juliette pressed.

This was the first time Rose really saw another Compass Point's sense of urgency about the mist plague. She wasn't exactly happy to see it, but it helped to know she wasn't the only one worrying about it. "I understand," Rose said. "Let's go find Carter. We can try again now."

They didn't have to go far, as Carter walked back into the inn.

He made a beeline for where they sat in the middle of the large dining room. Rose was a little surprised as he met her gaze directly. "I want you to try to make me a weapon."

Rose looked to Luc at her side and across the table at Juliette. "We were just about to find you and try the hole again."

"No." Carter shook his head. "I think we're all too tired for that this afternoon. But your weapon master magic has a different reservoir, doesn't it?"

She tilted her head from side to side. "Not exactly. All of my magic shares the same core, they just pull on it a little differently. But I can give it a try."

This appeased Carter. "Then let's go. I found a forge we can use on the edge of the village."

"You think this is the best use of our time?" Juliette asked.

"I do." Carter sounded the surest Rose had ever heard him.

"Why?"

"I know we've all been worried about what our magic will do together when we actually find Aterra. Don't look at me like that, Juliette. I said we all felt that way. But we're each too stubborn to acknowledge it—except Rose, of course." He nodded toward her. His energy was contagious. It was such a turn from what she was used to. "I think I discovered something that will help me contribute."

"Carter," Rose asked, "what did the coin do?" She needed to understand what had happened wherever he'd been before she agreed to work on his weapon.

The old Carter returned with her question. He looked around the room, considering what to share. He sat down next to Juliette, across from Rose and Luc, his voice no more than a whisper. "Similar to what the Norden elder shared about the Suden artifact, the Vesten artifact enhances the power of the wielder. I'm not sure what it would do for another shifter, but for me, it allows me to reach a shifter form I've not been able to grasp in some time."

"You have more than one form?" Rose asked.

"Shhh, Rose, please." He held up his hands as if trying to stop her words. "Not exactly. It is hard to explain. It is the same form that I usually take, but my form hasn't been seen among shifters in hundreds of years. And it has...unique gifts. My ability to access those gifts has been intermittent. The coin, so far as I can tell, gives me unrestricted access to them."

Rose couldn't help but smile along with the Vesten Point as he spoke. He had a childlike wonder about him now. She wanted to ask more questions but understood he had shared all he currently would. "What does that have to do with making you a weapon?"

"Well," he said. "Considering this unlocks a part of my magic I've struggled with for years, I want to know if you'll be able to see it, sense it."

"You want me to know what it is?"

He shook his head. "From what I understood of your work with Juliette, you won't necessarily see what it is, but you'll instead get flashes associated with it. I know it's a lot to ask, but I just need to know if it's really with me now."

This was what Rose had wanted. She wanted Carter to trust her—wanted him to let her evaluate his magic. She wouldn't argue with his conditions. Glancing at Juliette and Luc, she asked, "Any objections?"

With no objections, Carter led them to the forge. He'd already spoken with the owner and had been granted time for their use. With all the change they'd experienced that day, her hands were eager for a familiar task.

"Do you think you can keep the forge lit while I explore your magic?" Rose asked.

"For a while, of course," he replied. He looked side to side. "Will I need to be in my shifted form for this?"

Rose was silent for a moment. Would he need to be? She hadn't made a weapon for a Vesten. If Mom had, Rose couldn't remember any of the specifics. "I think we should try without first. If it's working, I should be able to feel the shifter within you. And whatever other magic you think you've found."

Carter nodded. His gaze locked on the flames before him as he asked, "Will you be able to tell what it is?"

He seemed so confident before, but she guessed it was becoming more real. "I'm not sure. I've never made a weapon for a Vesten before. Is it a problem?"

"No, I suppose it's not," he replied.

Juliette and Luc joined them, each sitting on the periphery of the workshop. Carter wasted no time starting the fire as she joined him at the forge.

Heat warmed her face as she contemplated the weapon she would make Carter. She really didn't know what it would be yet. Her eyes closed as she wrapped her hand around her hammer. Hopefully, the repetitive activity would calm her mind. She sought the comfort of the tool raising and lowering. The peace of an action she knew she excelled at.

Lost in her work, she jumped as something warmed her left palm—the one not holding the hammer. Part of her wanted to recoil from the surprise of the heat but realized quickly what it was. Carter had placed Arie's artifact there. It felt different. He'd done something to activate it—something she'd been unable to.

Eyes still closed, she smiled to herself. She was glad Arie had made them take this coin, though she would never tell him. He was still wrong about when to give it to Carter. But she'd be more than happy to tell him that when he returned. As much as she understood his decision to go—to try to find his friend—she missed him.

Chocolate and sandalwood filled her nostrils. Carter's magical scent didn't fill the air around him when he called it. It was more like a slow seep into the area. The fire had burned for minutes, and his magic fanned the flame. The scent of his magic grew, just like the fire itself. It started as a spark before burning hot and fast. Once she smelled it, though, she couldn't miss it.

Opening her eyes, she stared at the flame. Getting past her

own fire trauma was not part of this journey. A Vesten had not controlled the flame that took her home and nearly her life. She instead thought of bonfires on the Norden beach as a child. She thought about reading in front of the fire with Arie curled up in cat form. She imagined the fires that heated her forge, connecting her to Mom through their love of making weaponry.

Finally, she let her magic reach toward the flame—toward its connection to the Vesten Point beside her. Before sinking into the heart of it, she instinctively felt the connection to life that Carter had mentioned but had yet to explain.

The flame gave life to the shifter. She couldn't help but sense the opposite as well. The fire ended the shifter's existence as the Vesten went back to their fae form. It was a cycle of life and death. Well, that wasn't quite right. What had he said before about the Vesten having an interest in existence? The shifter didn't die—it could be brought to existence again at the fae's command. Maybe it was similar to how most humans and fae on the continent believed in an afterlife. That felt closer. The cycle of shift and flame didn't feel like death—an end—so much as a constant connection to new beginnings.

Maybe the Vesten connected to whatever was beyond death on the continent.

Rose was confused by this part of her exploration. She really hadn't even made it to the heart of his magic—too distracted by this tangent. One would imagine she had more experience thinking about the afterlife given the loss of her family, but for her, it hurt too much to look too closely.

She took a deep breath as she pulled her magic back. Meeting Carter's eyes, she noted his quickly darted away. "I think that's enough for tonight," she said.

"How'd it go?" he asked hesitantly.

She wondered how many of his secrets she had begun to unearth and how much more uncomfortable that would make him. "I got caught up in a cycle thinking about the new beginnings between flame and shift, shift and flame," she said. She expected him to be disappointed. She thought she'd failed with the fragile trust he'd offered her—but when she looked, his smile burned brighter than the forge.

※

THEY HAD an audience the next morning as they walked into the market square. Word had spread that the Compass Points were here, and they were trying to close the hole. Rose nervously tugged on her compass chain, checking to see where it led. Unmistakably, it set her on the path she was currently on, heading straight for the center of the square.

In her heart, Rose knew the compass direction wouldn't change. She still felt this was the right thing to do. It exercised their power together. It healed old wounds. And it just might be a new start for Luc and his relationship with his magic.

Luc squeezed her hand as they made it to the center, pulling her from her thoughts. At least he'd stopped wearing his cloak hood up while they walked through the village. Not that there was ever a possibility of hiding their presence.

"Are we trying anything different than yesterday?" she asked as they came to a stop before the hole.

"I think the roles are the same, but we might know a bit more about what we're doing," Carter said. He still seemed energized from whatever her magic evaluation had told him the night before. Honestly, it was a bit of a failure to her, but it seemed to be exactly what he was looking for.

"Alright, everyone to their places then."

Luc stood before the hole. Rose could already feel him gathering his power. He would focus it on pulling the hole closed. Carter stood next to him, a fire lit in the palm of his hand, ready to toss it into the abyss. Juliette and Rose stood a little to the side, where they could send their wind circling the hole, helping to tighten its circumference.

Wind rushed from Rose to the hole. Juliette's stream encased hers, following the same path. The feeling of rightness from yesterday snuck back into Rose's mind. The tighter Juliette's wind stream circled around hers, the more something in her said they were getting closer. Rose glanced at the hole. She saw Carter's fire lighting up the darkness of its depths. Luc was throwing off so much earth magic, she thought he might be trying to move mountains. Or maybe move the village of Loch away from the hole and call it a solved problem.

She didn't know how long they would last, using this much magic. Rose closed her eyes, diving into her power, searching for the door she found yesterday. Finding the lake, her power reserve, was easy. Using this much wind magic meant that the gust blowing across the lake was also present. She let it sweep her away. It had led her to the door yesterday.

The wind blew and billowed, carrying her around the lake, but didn't seem to have a final destination. Rose opened her eyes, searching Loch's market square again as the Compass Points used their magic in tandem. Luc never seemed to run out of power, but Rose could feel hers waning already. The hole seemed to suck her magic into it without letting it do anything. Carter didn't appear to tire, but the newly returned coin probably had something to do with that. She wondered how Juliette was faring.

At the thought of Juliette, the wind guiding Rose around the lake of power inside her, tugged her back to it. Not one to ignore signs, Rose closed her eyes and let the magic lead. The wind blew across the lake, and back to the familiar door she saw yesterday. Unwilling to let another interruption stop this exploration, she flung open the door. Though no house, no path, was attached to the door in her center, peering through the opening revealed a set of steps. It was remarkably similar to the way she'd explored Juliette's magic when she made the daggers. She searched around the door before going through. There was still no building attached that would indicate where the stairs led. The door was almost like a portal to another place. She shrugged and followed the magic down a set of steps.

She didn't make it far before being met with a powerful burst of wind. It funneled toward her like a cyclone, billowing past and back across her lake. The door, an opening to a new power reserve. Her wind needed the boost, and the power funneling through the door was more than willing to oblige.

Rose opened her eyes again as the encasing wind Juliette had been providing thinned. The overall stream size didn't change, though. More wind power pushed through Rose's initial blast. Luc grunted in surprise as the circumference of the hole shrank. Each of the Compass Points seemed able to feel the change, pushing their elements with a final boost.

"It's working," Carter said.

The hole continued to get smaller until, finally, it closed.

CHAPTER SEVENTEEN

Their accomplishment wasn't met with cheers. A child had still lost his life. The history of the village and hole would never be easy. Rose's magic hummed their success, though. It had absolutely been the right thing to do.

The villagers gave the Compass Points a wide berth, and as they left the square, Rose noticed no one was eager to walk to the center. It would certainly take time to believe this was a real change, but her magic told her it was—and that it was a necessary step in unifying the Compass Point's power.

"We should probably get out of here and let the village determine what this means for them, right?" Rose asked as they walked back to the inn.

"I agree," Juliette said. A question in her gaze gave Rose pause. Was she not happy about their success?

"I'm more than happy to pack up and go," Luc said.

"Maybe you should check the compass before we get too excited, Rose," Carter added.

That was a great point. She pulled the compass out a little nervously. Would it lead them away from the village now that they had accomplished their goal? The needle spun, and hope fluttered in her chest.

"South," she said. "It wants us to head south."

They packed and left the village through the southern gate. After riding a few hours south, the compass changed course. A barely visible western trail crept into view. It appeared unmaintained, likely to be a challenge for their horses, even single file. But the compass was intent in its direction.

"It points this way," Rose gestured to the tree-covered path.

"Well." Carter shrugged. "At least it's not sending us back to Loch."

"It was unlikely we'd stay on the southern road forever," Juliette added.

They turned the horses, dropping to a single file column in an effort to fit. Rose fidgeted as they slowly followed the trail. Though Rose was sure they'd done the right thing staying in Loch, guilt still gnawed at her for the delay. She had an idea of how they might help make some of it up in their travel—while also exercising her wind.

"I have an idea," Rose said, glancing at Juliette.

Juliette's answering smile was warm. "And that is..."

Rose was thankful that Juliette was willing to get straight to business. "What if we combine our wind to speed our progress on the trail?"

"Are you trying to pull my wind through your magic again?" Her comment gathered everyone's attention.

Rose was a little surprised. Was that what had happened in Loch? "I'm not sure. I don't really know how that happened—if that's what happened."

"I think you pulled my power into yours."

"And...are you okay with that? I can't say I know how to make it happen again."

She assessed Rose's response—her answer must not have been wanting as Juliette replied, "I'm ready if you are."

Rose didn't need more encouragement, calling her wind and wrapping it around the four Compass Points and their horses. Her magic heeded her call and sought out the space between the horses' hooves and the ground, pushing the two further apart every time they took a step. Her wind snuck into the gaps, pressing further, changing their gentle trot to a canter as she moved them forward at a faster clip.

The smell of sage and citrus surrounded her as more wind magic matched her wind's pattern. Juliette's element wrapped around hers, encouraging it into the spaces it sought—bolstering her magic and speed.

Moving two horses down a mountainside was the most that Rose had accomplished. Now, she pushed four horses and riders across the ground. Even though this was reasonably flat land, she wasn't sure about her limits. She had been exhausted the last few nights after such consistent use and weapon-making.

As she rode, she dove into her store of power. That was, after all, how she'd started whatever she'd done with Juliette in Loch. The wind blew across her lake, but it didn't lead her to a door. It didn't lead her anywhere. Her power didn't lag as much as she anticipated, though. With Juliette's power lifting hers, the strain lessened. It was nice to share the burden with her; two carrying a heavy load instead of one. Again, *this* felt right. This had to be part of what uniting the Compass Points looked like. She turned her head to smile at Juliette, enjoying the blending of their power. Returning her grin, Juliette's wind wrapped tighter with hers, pushing the horses forward faster.

※

THE EVENING MEAL WAS QUIET. Carter could still be found toying with the Vesten artifact. Rose was sure he hadn't let it out of his sight since she'd returned it to him. Luc stared into the fire. They hadn't had time to talk privately that afternoon, but Rose was sure he had thoughts on the hole closing in Loch. Rose broke the silence.

"I couldn't find the connection with Juliette again."

"Don't beat yourself up about it," Juliette said. "Our power interacting as we did today is still good practice." Juliette's gaze lingered on each of the Compass Points as she shifted the topic of conversation. "I think I already know the answer based on my prior conversation with Luc, but...does no one else commune with their god?"

"What makes you say that?" Carter bristled.

"Well, for you—the fact that you didn't recognize Lord Arctos until he revealed himself."

Carter's whole face flushed, and he stared down into his bowl.

"I do not, but I think we all expected that answer given why we're here," Rose said, trying to draw the attention from Carter.

"And I already told you my answer," Luc said.

Juliette took another spoonful of her stew before she continued. She looked pointedly at Rose as if to tell her she was trying—asking Rose to notice her effort to work with the other Compass Points, especially Luc. "I'll admit, I was least sure of Luc. Given the rumors of his power, I imagine Aterra would have noticed."

"What do you mean?" Rose asked, doing her part to encourage Juliette's conversation.

"She means that she thinks I'm in league with Aterra," Luc grumbled as he lifted his spoonful of stew to his mouth. Rose glared at him. He was right, but he wasn't helping.

Juliette had no qualms admitting her line of thought, either. "I did. But that is because of a tradition between Compass Point and patron, of which the rest of you seem unaware. It almost makes me question its validity."

"What tradition?" Luc asked.

"I can only describe it as a sharing of power—a connection between Compass Point and their god that helps to strengthen both."

"I've never heard of such a thing," Luc said, his brow pinched. "That's why you thought I communed with Aterra? You think I'm sharing his power?"

Juliette nodded. "It was one of my theories for your unprecedented strength. That somehow Aterra found you early and started communing with you in this manner even before you were Suden Point."

Rose's eyes widened. It hadn't occurred to her that others would have theories to explain Luc's power. It probably should have.

"I've not seen or heard from Aterra. Ever," Luc added.

"Do you know if Michael communed with him? Did he pass down any information about the connection to you?"

"If he did, he didn't tell me, or he didn't put it anywhere obvious. The only thing he passed down was the knowledge of the Suden artifact. I didn't need it because I already wield the power of mind shadow."

Heat flared in Rose's chest as she realized Luc was making his own peace offering to Juliette. Offering her more information than she requested in this exchange.

Juliette's brow raised, she, too, taking notice of the gesture. "Carter?" His name was a question on Juliette's lips.

"No, though the Vesten don't tell the histories so much as they make the new Vesten Point read them. I'll admit, I've not completed my study of the Vesten histories. The knowledge you mention could be in there somewhere."

"Weren't you a scholar?" Juliette asked.

Carter flushed again. "Only the Vesten Point and select scholars can read these works."

"Interesting. Where are the histories kept?"

"In Sandrin," Carter replied. "And they can't be taken from the Vesten stronghold there. It's quite inconvenient, especially for a new Vesten Point who needs to spend time at Compass Lake."

"And made even more difficult to find time with the mist plague's growing threat," Rose added. The Compass Points hadn't wanted to be far from their seats of power. She bet it had been challenging for Carter to spend significant time reading in Sandrin.

"So, what does the connection entail?" Luc asked.

Hot, dripping blood fell onto the cold gray stone. A male

voice echoed around her. Rose's mind immediately flashed to what she'd seen when forging Juliette's blades. It made her think she had an idea of what the ritual entailed. Juliette's gaze locked on hers as if she waited for Rose to make the connection. Rose tilted her head, acknowledging that it was Juliette's information to share.

"For me, it's a blood ritual," Juliette said quietly as if daring the others to judge her for such a practice. The fae courts were so enamored with their elements and the purity of those lines that any other magic was looked down upon. Blood magic, in particular, was something only used by magic-wielding humans. Juliette would do anything necessary to protect the members of her court. It didn't surprise Rose that she would use methods of magic other fae leaders would reject. "I'm unsure if it would be the same for each fae court or if others would have different ways, like with the ways we test for power."

"I can't believe that none of the other fae courts know or talk about this," Rose said. She considered her next words carefully, not wanting to offend Juliette. "Do you think it has anything to do with your patron's sacrifice?"

Juliette nodded. "I believe that is why I *have* to do it." She paused. "I'm not quite sure if the other gods are unaware or uninterested." She paused again. Rose could see by the way she swallowed and straightened her spine that she was carefully considering her next words. "I can tell that most of you don't know or don't believe that the Osten court was weakened with Zrak's sacrifice. But knowledge from my predecessors assures me this was the case." She looked pointedly at Luc.

"I can only explain that the consistency of my ritual with Zrak lessens the impact of his sacrifice. By offering my blood and mixing it with Zrak's in a sacred location, I am able to strengthen Zrak enough that he, in turn, continues to strengthen the Osten." She stopped. Rose didn't dare interrupt. She was afraid anything she might say would stop Juliette's words completely. "I can only describe it as a balance, similar to what we're entrusted to keep for the continent. I can sense when the balance between my power and Zrak's is at risk, and that's when I perform the ritual."

Rose's gaze met Juliette's. Rose offered a soft smile as she said, "Thank you for telling us." This conversation brought forth more questions than answers, but Rose knew the effort and trust shown tonight was unprecedented. It was the first time she had seen the fae courts sharing information without requirement. If they could do this, maybe the continent wasn't doomed.

✳

"You're certainly satisfied with yourself," Luc said as his arm snaked around her. Rose was on her side on their joined bedrolls, her back to him, admittedly thinking of the progress they had made that evening as a group. For once, it wasn't just her magic, and it wasn't just her compass. They'd used their power together to close the hole. They had each shared things about their courts and magic that were previously unknown to the others. This was a win for the Compass Points.

"I am," Rose said as the scent of Luc's magic wrapped around her with his arm. Between the comforting smell, her tunic raised in her relaxation, and his fingers grazing lightly over the skin of her stomach, suddenly, she wasn't so satisfied anymore. Her body craved a different kind of satisfaction—one only Luc could give her.

She leaned back into him. His body went taut next to her as if he sensed the change in her mood but was unsure what to do with it. "We don't exactly have privacy, Rose," he whispered, his lips teasing the skin behind her ear as he spoke. He trailed gentle kisses down her neck, seeing what she'd do with his comment.

"We can be quiet," she replied, scooting back further into him. Luc needed no more encouragement. His right hand continued to trace a path across the skin on her stomach, teasing her as it slid up her ribs and the side of her breast. She let her head fall back onto his shoulder at just his touch. This—this was what she needed.

Luc had been so uncomfortable in Loch. Here, under the stars, they were both a little freer. Luc was free from his past, and Rose from the weight of this journey. She knew she shouldn't take so much of the responsibility on her shoulders, but she couldn't help it. They needed magical blades—she was the weapons-maker. They needed to find Aterra—she had Aurora's compass to guide them. Things just worked out that she was the required leader of their efforts. Not simply because of the things she could bring but because she was the one the Compass Points had decided they would trust—if only a little bit. That, more than the skills she brought, weighed heavy on her.

She may not have had time to say this to Luc, but his action showed his awareness. He did what he could to share her burden or make things easier. He took care of the campsite necessities while she forged, gave her space to talk to the other Compass Points without him, and was there whenever she wanted to collapse into him. She wanted—no, *needed*—that now.

His lips took full advantage of her neck as she rolled back. Her body, usually so tightly wound, sprawled open—giving him more access. He greedily took it. His fingers moved deftly under her tunic as his mouth left a blazing trail along her skin.

Her breath grew ragged when his hand slipped under the waistband of her leggings. She moaned as his fingers continued their progress to her center. He circled and teased her. She glanced over her shoulder and caught the self-satisfied smirk on his face.

"I'm not sure you're capable of being quiet." His mouth was again at her ear. His words were innocent, his actions anything but. Rose made a strangled sound as his finger dipped inside her. She was aching with need now.

"So impatient," he said, slipping in another finger. Her hips rushed to meet him, to quicken his pace. She was burning up as he stretched her. Taking his time, unwilling to cater to her eager demands. Leaning back, further into him, she dragged her tongue along the side of his neck.

"That's not playing fair." His words were rough. She felt a power unrelated to magic at her effect on him. She was glad it wasn't only her. This connection between them strengthened every day. She wanted him, all of him, even the power he seemed so unsure of.

"Luc," her voice was breathy as she all but begged him to give her what she needed.

"I've got you, Rose," he replied as his fingers circled and stroked, building her pleasure. Her eyes closed, and her body tightened like a bowstring aimed and ready. Luc's fingers moved faster, his thumb finally granting her the friction she sought. He tilted her body to him, capturing her moan with a kiss as she found her release.

Her tongue teased his, her teeth catching his lip like a lifeline. He held her as the waves of pleasure crashed through her body.

She rolled over to face him—her hands reaching for him beneath the blankets.

"Ah, ah, ah," Luc said, sliding away but leaning forward for another breathtaking kiss. "I made no such promise of silence. I'll wait for the next inn before we continue."

She smiled softly, raising her hands above the blanket to prove her innocence.

"No one here believes that act, Rose." His returning smile was wicked. His hand cupped her cheek. "I didn't say it earlier, but I should have. I'm in awe of your progress with the Compass Points. I know you carry more responsibility on this journey than you should. But remember, you don't have to carry it all alone." His lips pressed to the corner of her mouth. "I see your progress—it's the most cooperation among us in my tenure—probably in the Compass Points' existence. Don't give up."

Rose's body, already soft from release, went to jelly at his words. She wouldn't have given up—even if she'd been failing—

but she was content to hear her progress was noted. She hoped they all realized the trust they were building in time to put it to use.

CHAPTER EIGHTEEN

The path grew wilder and more untamed the further they traveled. Given how fast she and Juliette had moved them yesterday, Rose wasn't sure how much more land there was before they hit water.

"Is there anything out here?" Carter voiced what they were all wondering. He'd disappeared for a bit this morning, leaving his horse and going into the trees to shift. Whatever power the coin had given his shifter, Carter seemed eager to keep testing it.

"Did you see anything when you scouted ahead?" she asked.

Carter shook his head. "Though the path does end, or at least, it's too overgrown to continue. We'll need to walk the horses shortly."

She held the compass in her palm again, watching the needle hold fast, guiding them west. Walking the horses would slow them down, but this was leading them to Aterra. What other option did they have?

Another day passed. Walking the horses was slow, but the compass's direction was clear. Rose sucked in a breath as a landmark finally came into view.

A cabin. It was tiny—no more than one room. A small,

wooden structure with a fireplace if the chimney was any indication.

The surrounding landscape was breathtaking. Whoever lived here had known what they were doing when picking the location. It was right on the edge of the continent. This wasn't a seashore where the water gracefully rolled onto the sandy beach. This jagged cliff plummeted into dark ocean water—a rugged and stunning view for whomever spent their time here. Rose wondered what the owner had been hiding from. This wasn't the warmth of a home, but it gave her a sense of safety, that no one could find her.

She held up her hand to stop the others. Smoke rolled out of the chimney. Glancing at the compass a final time, she announced this as their destination. Her mind started racing with all the questions she'd put off. Would Aiden be in there with Aterra? Would she be able to do what needed to be done to stop Aiden if he was there? Or would she pause again, wondering how many of his actions were his own? She still had no answers, and she hated it.

"It looks like someone is still here," Rose said.

"How do we approach this?" Luc asked.

"Do we know if Aiden is in there too?" Carter added.

"Does it matter?" Juliette said.

"Aterra is definitely there," Rose said, looking at the compass again. "We have to be ready to do what is necessary if Aiden is in there too."

She was convinced the Suden god wasn't always with Aiden. The gray eyes had started showing up in her childhood friend increasingly as they aged. This was the indicator so far as Rose could guess. She wanted to believe Aiden was himself when his eyes were blue—that the rest of their friendship had been real.

"If Aiden is there, his eyes will undoubtedly be gray, which means Aterra is possessing him," Rose said mostly to herself. The Compass Points nodded in understanding.

"How will we know it's Aterra if he's not inhabiting Aiden?" Carter asked.

"The compass is leading us to Aterra. He is the one I blame. He is in there. Whatever form we find—it's him." It was an interesting question, though. They had proof that Aterra wasn't inhabiting Aiden at times—but what did he do the rest of the time? Did he roam the continent in another form? Maybe they were about to find out.

"What is the plan, though? We think closing a magical hole in Loch translates to capturing a god?" Juliette asked.

"It was clear our magics rose to the challenge of closing the hole together," Rose said. "Your predecessors told you the Compass Points' power would unite when needed. There's no greater need for the continent than stopping Aterra."

"We try what we did in Loch again?" Luc asked.

The Compass Points made a quick plan, focusing on combining Rose and Juliette's wind once more, with the others leveraging their elements to support them and prevent Aterra's escape. Positioning themselves, they approached the only door into the cabin.

The group burst through the door, and Rose's gaze searched the room. She had been right—it was pretty cozy inside. The bed was unmade. A fire was burning, and an overstuffed wingback chair was beside it. And standing by the mantle, his back to them...

"Aiden," Rose said on instinct. His appearance was too familiar to call him anything else, though she knew she'd see gray eyes when he turned around. She lifted her hands to call her magic, her water rushing to the surface.

"Not quite," came Aterra's reply as he faced them. He didn't even bother using Aiden's voice anymore.

Heat flared behind her as Carter's palm filled with a ball of fire.

"Cute, but I don't think that will stop me," Aterra replied.

"The Compass Points find you in violation of the Covenant," Rose said, stepping forward. "You are threatening the balance of the continent. Remove yourself from Aiden so we can restore it."

The god laughed. "It's far too late for that," he replied.

Luc stepped alongside her, and Aterra's eyes locked on him. He appraised Luc's features in much the same way Rose had when she first met him. She wasn't sure what was happening, nor did Luc, if his pinched gaze was any indication. The scent of pine and cinnamon swirled in the room as his magic readied. Rose couldn't help but wonder if that had been what Aterra was provoking. She didn't care for the slow smile that crept over Aterra's features as he finished his assessment, and Luc's power flared.

"We should put that power to better use," Aterra said.

Rose's water shot forth on its own—as unhappy as she was with the god's attention to Luc. A hiss tore through the room as Carter's fire joined her water in the onslaught. Aterra raised a piece of earth to block their elemental streams. This hadn't been the plan.

Rose switched her water for wind. Seeking, wrapping, binding Aterra—her wind moved with a voracity she hadn't yet experienced. Her wind pushed through the earth barrier he attempted. Juliette's magic joined hers, coming together to hold the god. Their winds, used to working together, lashed in tandem, creating tighter circles, getting closer and closer to his skin.

Carter shot ball after ball of flame at the god, ensuring he was distracted as the winds worked. Luc's earth seemed to split, part of it holding the ground beneath them in place and the other part joining Carter to lob distracting attacks. Rose wasn't sure how long they could hold him. He fought hard—pushing back their power. Reaching deep, Rose sent everything she had at him. Her wind had grown in strength, but she knew she couldn't hold this long. She dove into the heart of her magic. This time the wind billowing across her internal lake led her straight to the door.

Aterra in Aiden's body flexed his magic, as he had on the beach, pushing back the wind barrier circling closer.

Rose opened the door, and like before, a storm of wind power billowed into her. She pulled more of it through the opening, funneling the power into her own, binding the god tighter as he fought for freedom.

Juliette's wind stream didn't just thin this time. It disappeared. The Osten Point shot Rose a questioning look but held fast with her support. While Juliette's wind ceased to wrap around Rose's, it undeniably strengthened Rose's stream.

Their winds had merged, Rose pulling Juliette's magic through the open door at the heart of her power.

Aterra's magic flexed against them again. Rose didn't have time to examine what was happening. She clenched tighter to the gust swirling around him. The merged wind snapped closer. She was wielding Juliette's power. It was strong and much more refined than her own. This joining might be enough as their wind inched closer to his skin...

Her plan shattered.

Aterra flexed his magic a final time, and to Rose's horror, the wind trap they had spun snapped like a twig being stepped on. Aterra broke the hold they'd worked so hard to secure.

The earth shook around them. Cracks formed beneath Rose's feet. Aterra was going to escape again. She turned to Luc, whose gaze pinched, his brow furrowed as he focused all of his magic on the ground. She grabbed Luc's hand, wishing she could share her power with him but knowing they had no time for her to explain it. She squeezed tightly as he tried, in vain, to hold the cracks together.

The most prominent slit went right through the center of the cabin. It split just wide enough for Aterra to hop in as he had at Compass Lake. Before he stepped into the crack he'd created, it snapped back together, thinly blocking his escape.

Rose's gaze shot from the ground to Luc as the only explanation. Was Luc fighting Aterra's earth magic with his own?

Aterra's smile was feral, and his sole focus was on the Suden Point. Luc's power pulsed around them. The room was thick with his magic. The scent and feel overwhelmed Rose as he held Aterra's escape route closed. Luc's eyes widened as he realized what he was doing. The earth shook again beneath them, and his attention returned to the god.

Aterra raised his palms together and made a show of separating them. This time, Luc's magic couldn't hold back the chasm he created. Rose tried to shoot wind and water across the crack like a sheet of ice, preventing Aterra from jumping in, but he plummeted right past it, his magic taking him deeper and deeper into the earth.

CHAPTER NINETEEN

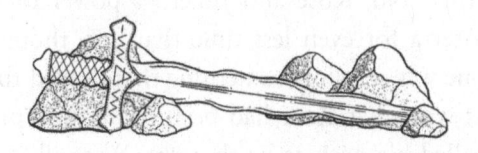

"Well, that went spectacularly terribly," Juliette said. That was an understatement. But he didn't particularly want to discuss it with the others. He wanted to discuss it with Rose. The one person he knew wouldn't judge him for what they'd all just witnessed.

He held a god. His power—unaided—had momentarily rivaled Aterra's.

Their attempt to contain Aterra had been a joke. They were woefully unprepared, and yet, *something* had happened. He wished he understood it. His magic flared, and he pulled it tight. He needed to clear his head.

"I agree. I'm going to set up camp." He didn't wait to hear anyone's objections as he walked toward the opening in the trees where they'd left the horses. Running his fingers through his hair, he replayed the battle in his head.

As he got further from the others, he let his magic unfurl. It should feel depleted from what he did in the cabin, but it seemed invigorated. Unleashed, his power lifted rocks and leaves, anything not rooted in the ground. He wasn't sure what to make of it.

The Compass Points were supposed to be able to overcome a god—but as a group—not an individual. His mind returned to what Juliette had said about the communion between a Compass Point and their patron. Was she right? Was there something connecting him and Aterra? He didn't want a connection to the god disrupting the balance. He wanted to stop him and return to his new life with Rose.

How had he held Aterra without the others? Were the others capable of this? No, Rose and Juliette's power together barely contained Aterra for even less time than his, though, whatever they had done was certainly something that needed further exploration. That was what Rose had been trying to reproduce since Loch. He rolled his neck as he thought. Were all their elements able to merge like that? Or only like elements?

How could so much be unknown about connections between Compass Points and how they were supposed to fulfill their purpose? The connection between a Compass Point and their patron drew his attention back. If Juliette communed with Zrak in that way, was it possible for the rest of them?

In the moments his power had held Aterra, the Suden god's gaze had locked on him as if he'd expected it. The moment tugged on a memory, one Luc couldn't quite reach.

He stood on the cliff's edge. He hadn't realized he had wandered so far from the horses. Seeing the stark, deadly overlook made him reach for his magic. The large, jagged rocks below felt like clumps of sand he could crush between two fingers. He was far past believing that his power was normal, even for a Compass Point, but he envied Rose's weapons-making ability at this moment. He would like to evaluate someone else's magic, just for some reassurance that there were others with power as deep as his.

"Your magic is not normal, but you already know that." Rose's voice was soft as she approached.

She'd extricated herself from the others. Somehow, knowing that was exactly what he needed. He didn't say anything as she continued her progress toward him. Standing on her toes, she wrapped her arms around his chest and rested her head on his shoulder so that her front was flush with his back. Wordlessly, he slouched to make the position more comfortable for her. They breathed together, silently staring at the waves crashing against the unforgiving cliffs.

Finally, he turned to her, unsure what he'd say. "I held him."

Rose nodded. "You did." She paused. "Do you know how?"

A chill rushed up his spine as the memory came forth. "Do you remember the scene I shared with you about my first Compass Point meeting?"

Rose nodded. This was the memory that had evaded him earlier.

"I want to show you another part...after the meeting." He paused. "It was always a little odd, but it was the one time I know I saw Aiden with the gray eyes, and they looked at me just like they did today."

Rose took Luc's outstretched hands, and his mind shadow pulled her along as he remembered his first time alone with the ex-Norden Point.

※

THE VESTEN and Osten Points left the room immediately. Luc didn't linger on purpose, but he hadn't rushed to leave like the others. He organized his notes and papers, his gaze roaming the room, unexpectedly meeting the Norden Point's.

"Congratulations on your first meeting," Aiden said.

Luc nodded, unsure how to respond, given their interaction.

"You'll get the hang of it quickly."

"I'm not sure about that," Luc said carefully. He didn't want to make enemies, but he wouldn't cave to the Norden Point like the others seemed to. It was then Luc noted a flash as the Norden Point's eyes turned gray. Hadn't his eyes been blue?

"Who are your parents?" the Norden Point asked. He studied Luc like he hadn't just spent the last few hours in a room with him.

Luc's brow furrowed. He didn't get this question so directly anymore. Most were aware by now that his father was unknown. "I figured the Compass Points would already be well informed on that gossip," he replied coldly.

"Humor me."

"Rebecca of Loch is my mother, and my father is unknown."

"Finally," Luc swore the Norden Point whispered, but the slow smile that spread across his pale face made Luc uncomfortable.

"As I said," Luc replied. "Expect my rebuttal to the fund reallocation proposal shortly." He held the gray-eyed gaze for another moment before exiting the room.

※

LUC PULLED THEM BACK, his hands still clasped to Rose's.

"That was the only time you saw them?" Rose asked.

"I think so...." Luc paused. "I can't say that I studied Aiden's eyes with any frequency. That scene sticks out because I saw the change happen. And the way he looked at me then. It was so similar to how Aterra looked at me today."

"What do you think it means?" Rose asked.

"I don't know what to say except that I think my power matches his." Luc shrugged off the massive statement. He was doing everything he could to downplay the insanity of his words. She would see through that, though. She didn't respond, letting him process his thoughts and continue.

"Do you ever wonder what he's done to try to disrupt the balance?" Luc asked.

"Aterra? You mean besides taking Aurora hostage and interfering with a Compass Point?" she said. "What else do you think he did?"

"I don't know. I suspect those are simply steps on a path that seeks to increase his own power. But I can't figure out how they fit. I just can't imagine a god would risk it all to bully the Compass Points. There has to be more."

She tilted her head, evaluating his words and where his thought process was leading.

Luc continued, "You know how the Compass Points and the fae came to be. Aterra was the only one who didn't think the gods owed the continent anything. Yet, he had to follow the compass scheme because he couldn't overrule the other gods." Luc shook his head again. "I'm sure the first thing he did once the fae had been created and the Covenant was made was to find a way to ensure he never had to do something like that again. I bet he searched for a way to overpower the others next time, should it come to that."

Rose scrunched her nose. "That makes sense, but I'm not sure we can know that. It also doesn't get us closer to understanding what he would have done to pursue more power. How does a god increase their power?"

"If there is a connection between gods and Compass Points, then maybe the action is simple—make sure you have a powerful Suden Point in place..." Luc trailed off.

Her eyes widened briefly as he knew she heard what he wasn't saying.

Luc pulled his hand down his face. "I don't know." Maybe if he kept repeating that, he would find a different response. "What am I supposed to do? It wasn't all of us working together—it was just me. And even that was only successful for seconds."

Rose took his hand. She had a crooked smile on her face as she replied. "Didn't you tell me last night that you wished I didn't have to carry so much alone? That you supported me? Let me do the same for you. That's what partners are for."

The laugh lines on her face calmed him somehow. "That doesn't sound like me." He shook his head.

"You're wonderful, Luc. I'm a big fan." Her smile grew wide. "But not even I think you alone are meant to save us. We need to figure out how we unite our magics—across elements. I do not doubt your messy power is required for our success."

How did she do that? With so few words, she supported him

and teased him for the self-importance of his thoughts. She didn't just soothe him. His magic calmed with her words. It was no longer restless and eager for use. He was able to regain his usual hold on it. He would never know how he got so lucky as to find her. She was exactly what he needed, what he wanted—always.

His lip curled into a wry grin. He saw Rose's eyes light up before he even spoke. Apparently, she could read him as well as he could read her. "What would I do without you to put me in my place?"

"Probably brood over here for another few hours," she said.

His hands covered his heart, as if her words stabbed him there. "Maybe we want to talk about the attributes of mine of which you are a fan? It would help my crumbling ego."

She playfully shoved his shoulder. He caught her hand and wrapped it around his neck. Her fingers didn't need encouragement as they laced themselves in his hair. He stepped into her space. He wanted nothing between them but knew this wasn't the time. "Thank you." He pressed his lips to the edge of hers, then felt them curve at the contact. Her face turned, and her mouth sought his as she returned a lingering kiss.

It took all his self-restraint to step back. He watched as her eyes danced at his movement.

"Tease," she said.

He would get lost in her for days if he could. His smirk was back as he shook his head slowly. "We should go learn how to unify our magic, right?" He knew the correct answer was to return to camp, but he didn't want to.

She laced her fingers in his as they left the natural meeting point of the deadly cliffs and mighty ocean.

✳

"So, what's next?" Carter asked as they were back within earshot of the others. Luc didn't understand the Vesten Point.

Sometimes, he seemed so afraid of his own shadow, and others, he was ready to persevere.

"We are not going to ignore whatever happened with Luc's magic," Juliette said, bringing her hands to her hips. Only yesterday, she had been warming up to him. His inadvertent display of power must have put her back on her guard.

"There's nothing to say," Luc replied. "I don't know what happened. It was so short a time. I don't think it's a key piece to our strategy. It seems more relevant to focus on whatever you and Rose did."

Juliette pursed her lips and looked at Rose. "What do you think?"

This was new. Juliette had been in her position the longest. She'd held her own against a whole separate set of Compass Points. He'd never seen her proactively defer to another.

"I think the scale of Luc's power will be important in whatever we're meant to do." Rose's gaze darted to Luc. "But I don't think he is meant to do it alone. We need to figure out how to merge our magics, like you and I did."

"But you and Juliette wield the same element. Do you think we could do that with other elements?" Carter cut in.

"We need to find out," Rose said. "The more I think about it, the more it seems like what we're missing. No matter what we saw with Luc's power today, it's unreasonable to think one of us could hold a god. There has to be some way to unify our powers. This is the second time Juliette and I found a way to do that, even if it was through shared elements. We would be foolish not to explore that further."

Carter looked thoughtful.

Rose glanced down at the compass as she tugged it from beneath her tunic. "We could always follow the compass again," she said, reading it. "It's pointing north. At least Aterra doesn't know that's how we found him." Rose shrugged.

"It seems fruitless to follow him again if we know we can't stop him," Juliette said. "We should find some way to test your theories before we pursue him. As you say, we are clearly on to something."

"We weren't able to get it to happen again while we were pushing the horses. I'm not sure what the key is that allows me to reach for your magic in the first place."

"I think I have to open my power to you while you're reaching for it. I can't be using it on my own."

"Well, that's new," Carter said.

"You saw how my wind stream dissipated as Rose pulled my magic. I still think we're missing something though," Juliette added.

"What do you mean?" Rose asked.

"I would have ceded my magic to you when we tried to push the horses. I was waiting for your tug, like in Loch. But I never felt it."

Rose nodded and looked to Carter. Luc wondered what she was thinking. It was like he could hear her mind working. He didn't have to wait long.

"Carter, do you think there is anything in the Vesten histories that could help us? I know you said you didn't get through much of them, but they seem an important source." Luc loved watching her like this. She relentlessly thought through an option once an idea started forming in her mind. "Would you be willing to let us all read them?"

Carter seemed understandably apprehensive. These were texts that he wasn't even allowed to read when he was a scholar. Only select scholars and the Vesten Point could see them. Luc thought she'd maybe finally asked too much of him. But then his hand reached into his pants pocket, no doubt grasping the coin, and he nodded.

Luc covered his smirk. Rose had won him over more than he'd realized by giving him the Vesten artifact.

"We have pretty comprehensive journals from Kenna," Carter said. "She was the original Vesten Point."

"Sandrin, then?" Rose asked. "I think we're on the right path with our powers working together, but I think we need to find a way to do more of what my and Juliette's wind did. I'm hoping we can find more detail on how this is supposed to work in texts from the time of the Covenant. They couldn't have left us this blind on how to achieve our purpose." She let out a tired breath. "And if we don't find anything, we practice what Juliette and I have been doing to keep our powers familiar with each other."

"It also keeps us moving north," Luc added. "Even if we don't learn anything, we're still following Aterra's trail."

Her shoulders sagged just a little at his comment, like all she needed were those few words of support. She looked at the others. "Any objections?"

"Well, that, at least, sounds like the start of a plan," Juliette said, "if still a bad one."

"I started reading Kenna's works when I became Vesten Point," Carter said, scratching his brow. "She seemed particularly interested in the Compass Points' powers, likely because they were so unknown and everyone was still adjusting to existence."

"Do you think they will have any information about the connection between a god and their Compass Point?" Luc asked.

All eyes fell on him. He arched an eyebrow. "You were all thinking it," Luc said wryly as he waited for Carter's response.

"It's possible," Carter started. "I can't guarantee her journals have what we need, but I agree with Juliette. It's worth looking into before we chase after Aterra again. We need something to be different before another confrontation."

"It sounds like the best plan we have," Rose said. "Let's get going."

Luc knew Carter was cautioning him not to get his hopes up, that he didn't know what was in these journals. But Luc realized he had his own goal. Rose's assessment was correct. He wasn't intended to save the continent alone, but there had to be a reason his power was different. It should be able to do something that could help them. If he could hold a god, even for a moment, what else could he do?

TANGLED POWER

CHAPTER TWENTY

There was no path now as the Compass Points rode their horses slowly through the forest. Occasionally, they would encounter a hiking trail or path they could use, but most days, they made their own way.

Rose and Juliette took the opportunity to speed up the trip north whenever possible. They practiced their magic together, spinning their wind around the Compass Points and their horses' feet to push everyone forward faster. But Rose still couldn't find the door connecting her to Juliette in her magic stores. Even when they practiced at their campsites, and Juliette readied herself for Rose's approach, the wind blowing across her internal lake of power led her nowhere. Juliette was right. They were missing something.

She couldn't help but feel like they were flailing in their efforts. They had a plan—they were going to Sandrin to try to learn more about their powers and how they were meant to unite before attempting to confront Aterra again—but was that enough? The continent was still slowly falling to the mist plague, and its leaders were going to read books.

When not practicing her wind, Rose tried to understand Carter's magic. The Vesten Point had just come back from a run in his shifter form. His hair was extra shaggy as he pulled his shirt over his head, coming out of a thicker patch of trees near their campsite.

Rose, Luc, and Juliette were already around the campfire eating. Carter filled a bowl before sitting at his customary spot around the fire. It was funny to her how Carter tended to sit at the western point and Juliette always at the eastern. She and Luc seemed to take turns sitting at northern or southern points. They always sat next to each other, though, so they ruined the appearance of each Compass Point sitting at their cardinal direction around the fire. She liked that they brought change to this group. It was good for them.

In her more dramatic moments, she worried about how none of it would matter if they couldn't stop Aterra when they found him. The weight of the problem sat heavily on her chest. Combining their magic had to be the answer, but did she have time to keep learning the others' powers before their next encounter with Aterra? She didn't know if her exhaustion was from magic use or the days of travel, but she was too tired to act like she knew what to do next.

"I know we're going to Sandrin to try to learn more, but does anyone have ideas on what else we should try to fight Aterra? I don't feel like we're doing enough." Her fingers instinctively reached for the compass beneath her tunic.

She felt the three other Compass Points look at her. Luc pulled his hand across his face and spoke up first. He was quick to respond. Too quick, as if he'd been looking for an opportunity to talk about this, and she'd handed it to him on a silver platter.

"I think we all owe you an apology, Rose." He glared at the other Compass Points. "It's okay not to know, and our next step is to try the Vesten archives to learn more." He spread out his hands, gesturing to the three of them. "It's not like we know either. Frankly, we have been at this job longer than you, so we shouldn't let you carry all the weight of figuring this out." His gaze met and held each of the other two Compass Points—a silent reprimand for taking advantage of Rose's tendency to carry the weight of the continent on her shoulders. "I know we've made you feel you had to come up with the answers for fighting Aterra, and it isn't okay. You've been the fastest to understand all of this." He gestured generally to everything around them. "But we forget that you are newer to the power of the Compass Points than we are."

Rose let out a breath. She hadn't realized how much she'd needed to hear those words, though they were met with silence from the other two.

The scent of pine and cinnamon started to build, overpowering the smell of their food in her nose. Rose looked at Luc, and to her surprise, so did Juliette and Carter.

Carter coughed into his hand. "Yes, well, we're sorry for making you feel like you have to carry the burden alone. We're going with the best plan we have."

Rose stared at Carter, dumbstruck.

In her peripheral vision, she saw Juliette's bowl of food shake. Juliette held it steady with both hands and glared at Luc.

"We'll help you brainstorm to have more ideas ready after Sandrin," Juliette said. No apology, but even the help offered made her feel it wasn't up to her alone to solve this.

Rose looked at Luc, who wore a self-satisfied smirk. The scent of his magic eased, letting the smells of the stew and fire fill the space again, but tendrils of it still seemed to wrap around Rose where she sat. She laughed to herself as she realized that he'd created mini earth shakes for each of them until they offered an apology of some kind. Her insides warmed at the consideration, and her shoulders sagged with relief as a little of her stress abated.

She'd been carrying the burden of finding out how to make their powers work together. This was different than what she'd chastised Luc about only days ago. He thought his power alone could solve the problem. Rose thought she was responsible for finding a way to unify the Compass Point's magic. Both were incorrect. She could lean on the Compass Points—they would all work on the problem together in Sandrin.

A thrill ran through her at the weight lifting. They would help her—though she'd continue to do what she could to ready them the only way she knew how. "Can I try to further evaluate your magic?" she asked Carter.

Luc shook his head at her, a fond smile curving his lip like maybe she'd missed the point of his speech. Ignoring his look, she wondered if it would be easier to learn about Carter's magic the closer he was to having shifted.

Carter shrugged his consent.

She didn't wait for him to move closer or for them to build a forge before she sent her magic searching. The repetitive movements helped but weren't required. Last time, she hadn't even made it to the heart of his magic—she'd been too distracted by life and death. They could go back to a forge when she was sure she could get to the heart of him.

A light, curling wisp of her magic stretched toward Carter. It circled him—just barely sinking into his skin—feeling for the recent shifter form. Even on the surface, she recognized the inconstant affection, the indelicate grace of not entirely giving your full attention to those around you, and the uncanny ability to see what others could not. She thought of Arie's black cat form. All the times he licked his paws instead of looking at her when she spoke. The way his head tilted when she saw nothing new in the room. Whatever Carter was, it felt feline.

She pulled her magic back. While still distracted with information about his shifted form, she made it a little further, and she was satisfied for tonight with what she found. At least it connected to something she understood, something about Arie she could relate to.

"What?" Carter asked. "Are you stopping?"

"Yeah, I made it past the surface cycle of life and death. I got a little bit about your shifted form. I think to go deeper, I want a forge again—but we don't have to set one up tonight."

Carter reached in his pocket. She was sure the coin was there. "Do you have an idea of what kind of weapon you'll make?"

Rose smiled. That was a question she did have an answer for. She had already been thinking about the duality of the Vesten nature—Flame and Shift—but the concept of existence, the cycle of life and death, had thrown her at first. The more she thought about it, the more the weapon came perfectly to mind. "How do you feel about a double-headed ax?"

Carter's lip tugged up at the corner, a smile starting.

"And I think we'll need a central spike on it, to help show off that third piece of your nature—the one I'm still trying to figure out. But like I've said, knowing and understanding are different. I know it's there, and that should be enough for the weapon."

At that, his smile was instant. Maybe she was finally figuring out the Vesten Point.

※

THE NORTHERN EDGE of the forest was in sight. Rose was so excited to break through the tree line as it came into view that she missed the signs. It was midday. The sun should have been high in the sky, but it was suddenly dark. Peppermint broke through the familiar smell of the forest around them. What little trail was available could no longer be seen as the mist unfurled, thick and heavy. In the lead, Rose immediately grabbed her sword and sent her wind to push the others back.

"The mist is here!" she yelled.

She hopped off her horse and held her weapon at the ready. She hoped that Luc would get Carter somewhere safe. Luc had her spare weapon, and Juliette had her daggers. Carter would be unprotected.

As if answering her unspoken thoughts, Juliette appeared beside her. "Luc is taking Carter east."

"Good," Rose said, moving into a defensive position next to the Osten Point.

Juliette didn't have her weapons ready, though. Rose spared a glance as Juliette held one of her daggers in her hand. With the other, she reached for a cord that hung around her neck. She pulled a small vial from beneath her dress, filled with a thick, dark liquid that could only be blood. There was no time to react as Juliette's dagger pricked her fingertip. The Osten Point let her blood well on her skin before mixing a few drops from the vial with hers. The scent of Juliette's magic filled their space, but another smell she recognized became stronger—peppermint.

"Juliette," Rose started.

"Later," she replied, tucking the vial back beneath her dress. She turned her hand over and let the mixture of two bloods fall to the ground. "Zrak!" Her voice was strong, powerful. It was that of the Osten leader who protected her court for a generation.

They stood silently—waiting.

No words came, but neither did the Nebulus. Rose's eyes darted around them as Juliette continued her ritual. Rose did not doubt this was the ritual she'd mentioned—this was how she communed with her patron. It was clear Juliette had done this many times in her tenure as Osten Point. Her movements were too practiced. Her voice was too steady for this to be anything but a regular part of her duties.

Juliette let a few more drops of blood fall to the ground as she called the Lost God again. "Zrak! I need answers. Why are you doing this?"

No response came, but Rose was sure the mist was starting to dissipate. She wasn't sure how far north the haze stretched. There were homes between the forest's edge and Sandrin. She hoped their story would not be the same as the southern village. At that thought, she tried to call her wind. She didn't know how to ask for secrets—she only received the one by accident. She wanted to send her wind forth, searching for sounds. But she heard nothing.

Confident that the mist had fully cleared around them, she looked to Juliette. "Do you think it took any of the homes north of here?"

"I didn't hear any cries for help if that's what you hoped to catch with your wind," she replied. "We likely won't know until we get there, though."

"Juliette, what you did... That didn't look like the ritual you described. You said it had to happen in a sacred place. And the flashes I saw while forging for you, they made it sound like..." Rose wasn't sure how to phrase this.

"Spit it out, Rose."

"They made it seem like Zrak is there with you when you do it. Like you talk to him."

Juliette studied Rose and finally nodded. "You're right. This was a blunt-force attempt that will likely cost me. You deserve to know, as it's why I left Aiden unchallenged as Norden Point when I knew he was unfit."

Rose sucked in a breath. She had yet to ask Juliette about that directly. She felt the fierce need to protect—the blood—when making the daggers, but she couldn't connect those to specific events or reasons to leave a false Norden Point in place.

"Zrak may have saved the continent when he came up with his plan for the Covenant," she started. "But he damned the Osten fae in the process, as I've said."

Biting the inside of her lip to hold her questions, Rose waited for what came next.

"It is a fact myself and my predecessors have had to deal with. When Zrak sacrificed himself, he took the Osten fae's connection to their magic with him."

Rose couldn't stop herself. "But as Luc pointed out, your wind is powerful. The full ritual sustains you?"

Juliette's smirk attempted to hide her pain. Rose knew enough now to see through the mask. She saw the Osten leader protecting her court. "Yes. It's powerful because the dampened connection is sustained regularly. There is a portal in the Osten house that takes me to the place where I perform the ritual. I do it regularly."

Rose couldn't stop her gaze from roaming back to Juliette's

finger. How many scars did Juliette bear for the blood price to sustain the Osten magic?

Juliette followed her gaze and nodded. "The Osten Points have had to manage the balance of our power this way since a few years after the Covenant, when we realized our magic was fading."

"And the vial?" Rose asked.

"Zrak's artifact. I'm told he made four glass vials before he departed, filling them with some essence of the remaining gods' magic. His—he filled with his blood—knowing what his court would need to do once he was gone." She pulled the vial back from beneath her dress. "It has always magically refilled."

"When it gets to the bottom?" Rose asked, looking at the half-empty vial.

"Usually before then. But we have time before I panic about it. One problem at a time, Rose."

She nodded. "Do you know where Zrak is?"

"The portal in Osten house takes me to caves on the eastern shore. They hold a wild magic. Zrak describes it as a thinning between planes. I can't cross it, and neither can Zrak, as far as I can tell, but we can communicate briefly when he's been strengthened."

Rose opened her mouth and closed it. Another plane sounded like the afterlife—going beyond the veil. To her, that meant death. But Zrak clearly wasn't *dead*.

Of course, this would connect to what she still didn't understand about Carter's magic.

Juliette continued before Rose could figure out what question to ask. "Aiden, well, in hindsight, it makes sense that it was Aterra—he knew what I was doing. More importantly, he knew where I went, and he threatened to destroy the caves." Juliette looked away, unable to meet Rose's gaze. "I'm ashamed to say I put my court's magic before the continent's health."

She took a deep breath and let Juliette continue.

"I'm not sure how much you know about the initial fae courts. I know you've heard me make mention of it to Luc. They were power-hungry. The first Suden Point realized our situation and tried to destroy us—to claim Osten house as his own. Judging by Luc's response to my accusation, I am unsure that Suden Point actually understood the nature of the Osten weakness." Juliette sighed. "It is irrelevant, though. After that, the Osten Points have been tasked with never letting anyone learn of our situation. Everything I did was to preserve that legacy."

"Juliette," Rose said quietly, hoping to pull her gaze. Slowly, so slowly, Juliette's head turned. Her face was set. A cool mask in place, ready for Rose's judgment. "I'm familiar with doing what needs to be done to survive. I'd never judge you for it." She chose her words carefully as she continued. "I don't know much about the original fae courts, but my parents' fear of reactions to a mixed lineage was real. It wasn't something they questioned, only something they knew. I understand how that deep-rooted knowledge can lead one to make difficult decisions."

"Touché," Juliette said, wiping a tear from her eye. "I see I understand your parents more than I hoped to."

Rose smirked. "We make tough decisions to protect those we love."

CHAPTER TWENTY-ONE

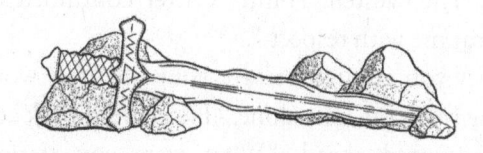

Every instinct told him to turn around. For once, he and his magic agreed. They both wanted to be with Rose as the mist swirled around their feet. One look at Carter made it clear that was not an option. Carter needed to get out of there—fast. He had no wind-born weapon to help protect him against Zrak's agents. Luc's concerns didn't seem high on Carter's priority list as he stood frozen next to him. Carter wasn't looking at the ground where the mist started to build. Instead, his gaze was fixed to the treetops, darting from branch to branch.

"Why are they gathering?" Carter mumbled to himself.

"What—" Luc started but changed his mind. They had already taken too long. Luc couldn't wait for Carter to pull it together. He grabbed for his earth magic. Its response was immediate, even though both he and his magic would rather be elsewhere. A burst of power swept Carter off his feet and floated him above the ground, similar to how Luc usually played with his nephews. He tugged on his magic until it moved Carter away from the mist.

"What the—" Carter shouted. Now that he was floating above the ground, Carter regained focus. He thrashed like a cat in water as he tried to right himself to stand on two feet. His gaze, though, still lingered on the treetops as he struggled. Luc decided he was still too unfocused to be trusted. The thousand-yard stare, aimed at whatever he saw up there, distracted him from saving himself.

"Don't fight it," Luc said. "I'll let you down when we're clear of the mist."

"I. Am. The. Vesten. Point." Carter continued to struggle. "You will treat me with respect."

"I respect you enough to save your life. You wouldn't have made it away from the mist alone." He glanced back at the Vesten Point as he jogged ahead. "What were you staring at? You mumbled something about gathering?"

Carter's gaze met Luc's and widened as panic set in again. "What did you see?"

"Now you sound like Rose," Luc murmured as he wiped his hand down his face. Before sharing with him the nature of her dual magic lines, Rose had always been worried he saw something about her magic that would give her away. It made him wonder what magic Carter was hiding. Rose had better be okay. He knew she could take care of herself, but who knew if her weapons were a guaranteed solution against the mist. They'd worked so far to fight against the Nebulus, but what if one got around her blade? Depending on how many of Zrak's agents came with this particular mist attack, Rose and Juliette could be outnumbered.

He couldn't think of that now. "I didn't see anything other than you staring upward." He'd get Carter far enough away to be safe and then return to Rose. "What were you looking at?" he tried again. He might as well attempt to learn something from this unexpected one-on-one time with the Vesten Point.

"Nothing." Carter's eyes darted around even more than usual.

Luc laughed. "No one is buying that answer. I need to get you outside the mist radius. You have time to explain why you froze."

"I didn't freeze." Carter crossed his arms petulantly over his chest as he lay horizontally in the air, Luc continuing to tug him along.

"You're not fooling anyone. But I suppose you can keep your secret if it helps you." He looked back at Carter as he jogged through the trees.

"Thank you, Luc."

Thank you for what? Leaving him alone? For not bugging him about whatever he was hiding? It was no problem for him. He was used to the fae courts keeping secrets from each other. It was Rose who was the idealist. It was a unique feeling to realize that he had begun to embody the energy she was trying to spread among them. Her ideas were contagious like that. They spoke of a world he wanted to be a part of—with her.

Now, he worried that his power's similarity to Aterra's might take that future from him. Would Rose's support of him dampen her ability to align with the others? He saw the way Juliette looked at him. No matter the strides they made sitting around the campfire in the evenings, he knew she didn't trust him, and she wondered why Rose did. He would keep trying as long as it took, though. He was thankful for every damn day with Rose—even in the middle of this mess.

"Luc." Carter's voice broke into his thoughts. Panic tinged the edges of his call.

"Yes." Luc risked a glance behind him as he continued to jog. The mist was following them.

"Let me down. I think we need to move a bit faster." Carter's head was tilted back as he watched the mist catch up to them. Luc noted his gaze still darted between the mist hanging on the ground and something higher up. "No, a lot faster."

Shit. Luc's magic dropped Carter, and they both took off in a sprint. They put distance between themselves and the dark mist threatening to envelop them. Carter, more familiar with running through the trees, kept turning his head and calling out their progress.

"We've got some good distance now. Wait—it looks like it's retreating." He paused, slowing down, and mumbling to himself. "Why are more coming?"

Luc stopped and turned. Carter was right. The mist wasn't just retreating—it seemed to dissipate, just as it had whenever he and Rose cleared an area of Nebulus in their past battles. He scratched his head as he tried to imagine what was happening. He let out a breath as he concluded Rose and Juliette must have won their battle. He gestured to Carter as he went to investigate. "Stay there," he directed.

"Wait—" Carter called.

Luc paused mid-step and turned to face Carter. The Vesten Point's gaze was roaming all around them as if there was an audience that only he could see. His gaze wandered similarly to the way it had around the hole Luc had created in Loch. "Carter..."

Carter's head tilted. "Okay, you can go check."

Luc shook his head. Maybe he'd been spending too much time on the road with the Vesten Point. Especially if he was noticing this much about him. Moving back through the haphazard trail he'd just cut through the trees, Luc saw no sign of the mist. "Carter, I think you can join me."

Carter was beside him in no time. "What happened?"

"Rose and Juliette must have held off the Nebulus."

"Hmm."

Luc started to walk back. Carter put his hand on his arm, turning Luc to face him. "Thank you for taking control of the situation back there. You were right. I did freeze."

"No problem. We're on the same team."

"You are the last I'd expected to hear say that."

Luc met Carter's eyes. "Whatever Aiden, or Aterra, had on you...I'm sure it wasn't an easy decision. We all have our limits. I suspect Aterra found yours."

Carter nodded.

"Don't beat yourself up too much for it. A literal god was blackmailing you."

"You sound so casual about it, Luc," Carter said as they started walking again. He seemed eager to continue the conversation but not to have to look at Luc while they had it. Luc shrugged and met Carter's pace.

"You're not the one I'm mad at."

"What, you're mad at Aterra?"

"Well...yeah," Luc said. He paused. If he wanted Carter to be honest with him, he might as well take Rose's tactic and try it himself. "But I'm also mad at myself."

Carter's head turned toward Luc as he kept walking. "Why is that?"

Luc sighed. "I told myself that everyone was just looking for someone to blame, and I was an easy target when they talked about how the mist plague wasn't attacking Aterra's villages. I never thought that it could be a real pointer to the problem we were facing. I'm angry that I couldn't do more to protect the taken villages. I'm angry I tried to scare someone I thought was a village shop girl into putting me in contact with a magical weapon master as my one path to success."

"You lost me there."

"It's a long story, but suffice it to say, I was flailing in trying to figure out what was happening on the continent. I was desperately working to save those who fear me and blame me... And maybe they're not even that wrong."

This territory was way too vulnerable for Luc's comfort. He was the one who couldn't look at Carter now as he said these words. They weren't exactly secrets. The secret was that Luc acknowledged them. He thought about them, even when he gave the appearance of shrugging them all off. Rose was the only person who seemed to realize that they might bother him. It was one of the many reasons he—his magic flared in his chest as he stumbled over the thought. He grabbed his shirt, trying to make room for him to breathe. He hadn't fully acknowledged his feelings yet, but his magic was aggressively on board.

Carter didn't seem to notice as he charged on in the conversation. "I can see spirits," Carter blurted out. "Especially those at the threshold of the veil."

Thoughts about his feelings for Rose left his mind as he turned to face Carter. They both stopped in their tracks. "Come again?" The threshold of the veil? As in, those about to go beyond the veil? Were they talking about *seeing* the afterlife?

"You heard me," Carter said, then he reiterated. "I can see spirits. It's an incredibly rare gift in the Vesten court—connected with a shifter form that's all but extinct. We only have a record of one or two others with the power, and no one else alive can take the form. Aterra knew, and that's what Aiden held over me."

Luc shook his head, trying to collect his thoughts. "That's unexpected. Though your conversations with Rose make a bit more sense." Then he added, "Why is it such a bad thing if others know?"

Carter gave him a look that said he already knew the answer. "Yes, I think Rose is close to understanding, though I'll just tell her now that I've told you. But besides the perils you are all too familiar with regarding uncanny demonstrations of power, the more pertinent issue has to do with the form I take. If certain entities knew about it—my life would be in danger. Even more so now with the extra power from the Vesten artifact."

"I see." Luc wanted desperately to pry into the shifter form Carter took, but he sensed the Vesten Point didn't want to share more on that topic. He pursued a different line of questioning. "You see spirits around the mist, then?" Luc paused. "There were spirits in the woods as the mist appeared?"

Carter nodded. "The mist tends to carry spirits everywhere I've seen it. I don't know enough to understand if they're victims of the mist plague or...something else." Carter's words were careful.

"You think those impacted by the mist are dead?" Luc asked. He thought of Tara's body when they'd found her in Bury. Her breath had still risen and fallen in her chest. She couldn't be dead. Maybe this was another reason it was good Carter's ability wasn't widely known.

"I'm not sure," he said honestly. "Spirits can be disassociated from a body, but the person may not be dead. Existence is much more than the binary of life and death. I don't think we'll know for sure until we rid the continent of the mist." He shrugged. "This was weird, though. Here, more spirits arrived as the mist dissipated. It's why I asked you to wait. I've never seen that before," Carter said as they finally broke through the tree line. "They seemed harmless, but they flooded in from beyond the veil somehow with that mist—maybe with the Nebulus?"

That didn't make sense. Rose and Juliette should have been fighting the Nebulus as soon as he and Carter started running. He wondered at Carter's comment but lost his train of thought as he let out a deep breath—Rose was in his sights again. His power pushed against him to get to her.

Carter reached for his arm before he could rush forward. "There's something else you should know."

Luc turned back to Carter, his face much more concerned than it had been in the forest. "What?"

"The hole in Loch? Spirits gathered there too."

Luc reeled. Of course. That's what Carter had been looking at.

"I can't determine if they were passing beyond the veil there—I don't think they were—but spirits were gathered there at least *thinking* it was a place they could pass through."

Luc nodded. "Thanks for telling me, Carter." He shook his head as he refocused on Rose. She was safe. Now, he smiled wryly, thinking about her motto for this trip. Treat the Compass Points as you want to interact with them in the future, not the past you've experienced. Halfheartedly, he rolled his eyes as he thought how unbearable she would be when he told her she had been right.

CHAPTER TWENTY-TWO

Sandrin was alive around them, abuzz with activity as they entered. Rose hadn't realized how nervous she'd been that it, too, had been impacted by the mist plague while they traveled. It had been over a week. She wasn't sure what news they had missed once they'd left Loch. Being back in a city brought other creature comforts like books to choose from, easy access to a forge, and, of course, a bed.

The forest floor hadn't been as accommodating to her new relationship as she would have liked. Even with the discomforts, the thrill of waking up next to Luc every morning wasn't waning. What little time they had alone left her breathing easier. His steady support grounded her in a way she'd never before experienced.

Luc caught her staring, and she quickly turned her attention back to the city. She wasn't embarrassed—she just wasn't one to gush over her feelings. They would have time to figure out their communication style. They would have time to be together after Aterra was dealt with. The pull she felt toward him was only growing stronger. It was a physical force at times, encompassing all her senses—even her magic.

They wasted no time heading straight for the Vesten Quarter.

It was funny that they called it that. The Norden Quarter, the Suden—it implied that the city was divided neatly among the four fae courts. It was clear that this naming convention was created by the fae given its complete disregard for the fact that humans also lived here. Sandrin was a city run by humans. The fae courts only held a few buildings in each respective section of the city.

Her mind roamed to what Luc had learned of Carter's magic. Spirits—Carter could see spirits. Luc unraveling Carter's mysteries was a surprise. Not so much the secret itself—that fit perfectly. No, the interesting part was that Luc had been the one to pull the information from the hesitant Vesten Point.

She bit her lip as they rode. Would she have figured it out without Luc's breakthrough? It didn't matter, she guessed. She knew it now, and it felt like exactly what she had been missing. If flame and shift were two sides of the same coin, life and death—existence—was the cycle on which they connected. She may not have known precisely what was missing in her evaluation of the Vesten Point's magic, but she had been right that there was a third piece, like the spike she wanted to use to sit between the double-headed ax she would make him.

The Vesten library loomed before them. They needed to conduct their research quickly while continuing to practice uniting their power. With Carter, the Compass Points were instantly recognized and ushered through private halls into a large open room filled with books and shelves. He led them with an expertise that spoke to years working in the stacks before assuming his position as a Compass Point.

"Will the Vesten elders be unhappy that you shared these histories?" Rose couldn't help but ask as they walked. The library staff had been cautious noting the fae leaders, but were eager to please the Vesten Point by letting them through. They were certainly unaware of what texts the group intended to read.

"I find this to be the perfect situation in which we should ask forgiveness later, instead of permission." Carter shrugged.

Guiding them to a specific corner, Carter let his finger brush along multiple spines before pulling a handful of well-worn journals down. "Here they are," he said, handing volumes to each of them.

"You don't know which one we should read?" Rose asked.

Carter shook his head. "It will be faster if we each start reading one and share any interesting passages. These five cover Kenna's tenure as Vesten Point. That is where we should start if we're looking for information about the Covenant."

Rose took her volume, sat on the floor, her back against a shelf, and carefully leafed through the pages.

"You trust us to read these documents?" Juliette asked. A variation on Rose's line of questioning, but an important difference. Carter's actions indicated a new level of conviction in the goal to unite the Compass Points. One Rose wasn't sure Juliette had yet reached.

"I think I'll take a page out of Rose and Luc's book." Carter shrugged again as he flipped through the pages himself.

Juliette eyed Luc suspiciously before taking the volume she was given and going to find a chair.

"Shall we reconvene in a few hours and discuss any pertinent entries?" Carter asked.

"Sounds like a plan," Rose said, barely looking up as she started reading.

※

Five Days After the Covenant

THE GODS WERE *clear in their direction, but I felt I was the only one who heard them. The others would have surely objected otherwise. Today was the Lake Refilling Ceremony. It was only days since the Covenant, the day of our creation, and this ceremony would cement our relationship with our makers. The gods and fae leaders gathered at the newly formed Compass Lake. A ritual was* performed with the elements. For this first ceremony, the gods took our places. Aurora shot the lake water like a geyser into the sky, and Aterra, Zrak, and Lord Arctos used their earth, wind, and fire elements to reinvigorate the lakebed. From here out, the fae leaders, the Compass Points, would be expected to take these actions as our commitment to the Covenant.

"This is what you will do once a year to honor the gift we bestow upon you," Zrak said. "In addition to a piece of our magic, we also grant each of you an artifact to carry on this continent. They are amplifiers of our power, given to show our favor and assist you as leaders."

"What are these tokens?" the Suden Point asked.

Lord Aterra stepped forward and handed a ring to the Suden Point. It was shaped like a triangle, with a dark onyx stone as the centerpiece.

Lord Arctos stepped toward me, placing a coin in my hand.

Lady Aurora stepped toward the Norden Point and placed a dagger in his.

Lord Zrak stepped toward the Osten Point and handed her an empty vial.

We all said our thanks, though I suspect none of us knew precisely what these artifacts were for. What else were we supposed to do? All I could think about was finding somewhere to establish my court—far from Compass Lake. I would travel here once a year if needed for the ceremony, but I wouldn't be tied to these other fae while they figured out their powers.

"I hear your whispers, each of the fae leaders amongst their court," Zrak continued. "You mean to leave this area. You mean to establish territories for your courts and rule over them, fighting any who seek to enter the land you claim." Zrak had looked to Aurora and Lord Arctos. "That is not the continent we would have."

I held my breath. We had all heard the whispers. Lord Zrak was not long for this world. He would make his sacrifice any day now. It may not be the continent he would have, but it would be the one he got.

"You are made to serve the continent together. Not to build walls and go to war to claim territories from one another," Aurora said as she stepped forward. "You must remember: The Covenant obligates you with responsibility as much as us." She gave a solemn nod and gestured to the lake. "You will live here." Her voice rang loud and clear.

I bristled immediately. I couldn't help it. The lake was too small for four fae to establish their territories.

As if reading my thoughts, Lord Arctos spoke. "You will not need space. You will not have your own domain over which to rule. You will each be granted your cardinal direction position on the lake. That is the only place on the continent that each of the four fae courts should consider their own."

"Where will we live?" I asked timidly. We hadn't been presented with many opportunities to question our creators.

"The fae will spread far and wide across the continent. They will live among the humans—intermingled—in villages and cities."

The Compass Points looked uneasily amongst ourselves. I had spent the last few days planning the Vesten's moves—planning what place we could call our own on this continent. Members of my court had roamed on our behalf and found a wild forest on the continent's western edge. We were planning to make it our own. It was defensible. It was beautiful. Why wouldn't Lord Arctos want this for us?

"Why would you keep us together in this way?" the Suden Point asked, echoing my thoughts.

Zrak answered. "Your purpose is to hold us in balance. Should the need arise..." Zrak looked at his fellow gods. His gaze lingered on each of them. "You would need to hold one of us that may seek to unbalance the continent accountable."

And how are we supposed to control a god, I wondered. It seemed an impossible task, even for four gods-gifted fae.

"You will wonder how you can achieve that," Zrak continued. "But that is why you must all be here at Compass Lake. To uphold *your task, you must work together. The powers we bestow you with must intertwine—a bond that strengthens and does not break. They must be as united as the water in the lake, unable to tell which drop has touched which shoreline."* Zrak looked at each fae leader. *"Lest you think you can ignore us, we will never be far from you. Your power is connected to the lake. The land here will be your seat of power—this is where you will be strongest."* He paused. *"And we'll know if you weaken,"* he added as an aside. *"You cannot allow walls to be built nor battles to be fought among the courts. If you do, all will be lost when the time comes."*

※

THIS WAS EXACTLY what Rose had been looking for. No, it wasn't a list of steps they needed to take to capture Aterra, but the imagery was clear. Rose could tell that their individual powers were stronger when they were using them around each other. This was evidenced by the fact that they had made progress on closing the hole in Loch together, *before* Rose had inadvertently pulled Juliette's magic. How many times had Luc said he tried to close it himself? It wasn't until their magic was working side by side that any movement occurred. Each of their magics had been strengthened simply by the fact that all four Compass Points were wielding their element.

Zrak painted a picture here where all the Compass Points' elements were as merged as Rose and Juliette's shared wind. Their power should be so tangled together that it would be impossible to tell which element had come from which wielder.

CHAPTER TWENTY-THREE

A Year After the Covenant

I CAN'T BELIEVE *they forced us into such close quarters. I can see the Norden Point as we work on our respective houses. If our power is strengthened here, if all four of us are to live on this lake, we'll see who can make the most intimidating fortress.*

I've already covered the ground in seedlings. We'll have a forest on our property—a remnant of the one we wanted to claim. Whatever I must deal with living so near these other fae leaders, I'll ensure my successors will not. I will give them a cover under which to hide—woods to roam. Keeping our additional gift of shifting a secret was a lost cause. Just last week, the Suden Point saw my brother coming out of his bear form. He was so angry, raging that Lord Arctos snuck us a second gift. That he somehow cheated the power balance. It proves how little he understands the connection between our element and our animal. Two sides of the same coin, like Lord Arctos's gift to us.

The worst offense is still having to come together for the

Refilling Ceremony. The Summer Solstice brings us together every year. We honor the gods like we were told. Not that we've seen much of them since the first Ceremony.

Zrak, at least, has an excuse, though I think the Osten may feel his absence more than we realize. The Osten Point is resilient, but her wind feels faint as it blows around my fire during the Ceremony. I think it will get the job done, but I wonder if the others notice. We've lived in relative peace, but weakness, if sensed on either of her borders, would bring trouble.

Lord Arctos is rarely here. When he comes, it is only with Aurora. The Norden goddess is more eager to visit her court, at least. She makes herself available to ensure its success. She even stopped by my property with Lord Arctos. I'll admit, she asks about the strangest things. A few weeks ago, she questioned me about the trees I was planting.

"Kenna, this will be a lovely forest. But do you think it will discourage visits from your Norden and Suden neighbors?"

"That's the point, my lady," I gently reminded her.

She shared a look with Lord Arctos then, her hand clasping his.

"How will you fulfill your duty to the continent if you don't know or understand your neighbors?" she asked.

"Begging your pardon, but if you focus on not doing anything to disrupt the balance, then maybe I won't have to worry about working with my neighbors." It got quite hot then, like the ground beneath me was burning, though I saw no flame. I looked up, and fire danced in Lord Arctos's eye before his lady squeezed his hand tight enough to douse it.

"Have you at least seen Aterra here to visit the Suden Point?" Lord Arctos asked.

"I must have seen him a few weeks back. He doesn't come often, and he doesn't stay. I think I overheard the Suden in the Compass Lake Village saying he was spending more time in the southern villages. A good many Suden left the lake to live elsewhere. I even heard they started establishing villages of their own."

"Villages of their own?" Aurora asked.

"Yes, per your request, they'll let in any humans that wants to come, of course. But instead of living in a village filled with humans, they decided to build a village for themselves."

I saw Lord Arctos running his hand through his hair, pushing it back in disarray. I'm not sure what he was so upset about.

※

One Hundred and Fifty Years After the Covenant

TODAY IS my last day as Vesten Point. I'm passing the torch, if you will. I've made some mistakes and will share my learnings here for future generations since they no longer do me any good. Nicholas has more taste for politics than me. I focused on defending our court, establishing our borders at Compass Lake, and giving us space to thrive.

Then, we started meeting regularly as Compass Points.

The annual Ceremony was no longer enough as the number of fae grew and spread out. They needed help to live in harmony with the humans. While none of the gods instructed us, we all knew this fell within our remit of maintaining balance on the continent. We would hold a god in check should it ever come to it, but more often, we were to ensure humans and fae lived together peacefully.

These meetings brought as many headaches as solutions. I had to bring more Vesten into positions of power within my court to manage the duties. Nicholas was one such appointment.

In addition to his duties, he came to me with ideas on securing our position among the courts. We needed to have information to trade, information of value to the other Compass Points. Nicholas didn't think that open war and conquering territories was the only way to gain position among the fae courts. He formed a group of Vesten who traveled the continent and sought information from villages or lands more heavily inhabited by the other fae.

The Osten—no surprise—did not stray far from Compass Lake. However, they don't seem to need to leave the lake to learn of the goings on of the continent. The Osten Point is always more informed than I expect. She must have done something to enhance her power. I rarely notice a lapse at the Ceremonies. And they proved they could hold off attacks from the Suden Point. No one will ever admit to it, but I know the Suden Point tried to take Osten house. Nicholas may patrol the continent, but my knowledge of what goes on at the lake is absolute. I've been best at keeping my shifter form a secret. No one notices a black bird sitting outside an open window or flying around the lake at night.

The Norden are an uninteresting lot. Many have established themselves up north. They did much the same that the Suden did years ago and made Norden-filled villages near the human ones. They never barred humans from entrance, but it's funny when the humans and the fae have their own space; they don't mix often.

The Suden. Well, it's not the Suden themselves who are interesting, but their god. The only good thing from Nicholas's prowling the continent is hearing what Aterra has been up to. He has been seen more than any other god among his fae. I guess Lord Arctos and Aurora are able to entertain each other—Aterra only has the Suden. Reports indicate that he is more familiar with some Suden than one might think proper. I can't imagine that is a good idea, but I also can't fault an immortal being for much.

Nicholas, armed with his spies and his secrets, has found a way to lift himself up. He found out the other courts have a test for power, each one different. He convinced the Vesten that we needed one too. It should be no surprise that the test he designed, and he happened to take, ensured he was the strongest Vesten on the continent.

I leave you with this. Trust no one when you are in power, or you will find yourself not in power for long.

※

THE COMPASS POINTS assembled the most critical entries. The sun was setting, and they hadn't finished reading, but they had plenty to discuss.

Rose's entries from the first Refilling Ceremony, and sometime a year later, were particularly enlightening.

Luc had found the entry from Kenna's last day as Vesten Point. The entry left him more contemplative than Rose cared for.

"So Zrak at least seemed right about how we would be lost if we continued with our seclusion," Carter said. "What do you think about what he says here?" Carter pointed to the page:

"To uphold your task, you must work together. The powers we bestow you with must intertwine—a bond that strengthens and does not break. They must be as united as the water in the lake, unable to tell which drop has touched which shoreline."

"You think this means more than the same elements working together as you and Juliette have?" he asked.

Rose nodded. "I can't imagine that the gods would have considered a situation where two Compass Points had the same element. It has to mean that what we've done with our wind is possible with all the elements."

"Saying it must be true and doing it are still two different things," Juliette said cautiously.

"I agree." Rose nodded. "It helps to read that it's possible, though. I was also thinking about something we might have overlooked."

"Don't keep us waiting," Juliette said.

"All of these pieces—working together, intertwining, uniting —they speak of the power of all four Compass Points. This might be obvious, but I think we each have to use our elements at the same time."

"We were using our elements together in Loch when you pulled power from Juliette," Luc noted, catching her train of thought.

"Exactly, and when we faced Aterra." She looked at Luc and

shrugged. "It would also explain why I couldn't find the connection when we were using our wind to push the horses."

"It makes sense..." Juliette said thoughtfully.

"I think we should call it for today." Rose stretched and twisted her body from the hours spent sitting on the floor. "We can put it to the test tomorrow."

CHAPTER TWENTY-FOUR

The heat from the forge slowly started to fan her face. It was so different from the makeshift forges she'd used on the road. Rose had stayed in the Suden quarter of Sandrin with Luc last night. Luc had offered to follow her to the Norden quarter, but she was too tired to introduce herself there and find accommodations. Luc's already established residence was much easier. The sun had risen all too quickly, though, and with it, their responsibilities.

Working at the forge in the military school was a dream Rose had let die before it had even been voiced. The workspace was immaculate. It was well used, the most used among the Compass Point armories. Once the second generation of Compass Points had emerged, the game was more about politics than open physical confrontations, or so they had learned yesterday in their reading. It made sense, though, that the Compass Points had assigned things like military responsibilities to the Suden court.

Rose never dreamed she would be able to make a weapon here. A Norden working in a Suden forge was not an aspiration to be shared. Today was different. She brought change to the fae courts as she sank into her role as Norden Point—she also brought change in this small, selfish desire. And it felt good.

A cough sounded behind her, and she turned. "Carter, thanks for coming so early." She smiled warmly. She was glad it had been Luc who'd pried free Carter's secrets. Juliette was always so wary of Luc—his motivations and power—it was nice to see Carter overcome those concerns and share something of himself.

"It's not every day a Vesten receives an invitation to the military school. As a former scholar, honestly, I was intrigued."

Seeing him yesterday in the library, it fit. He probably would have been happy to live a quiet life as a scholar, just as Rose would have been content to live her life as a reclusive weapons-maker. Destiny had other ideas for the Compass Points.

"Feel free to look around. Luc saw to it that we won't be disturbed."

Carter glanced at the forge. "Don't you need me to get started?"

She laughed. "I have to wait for this forge to heat up the old-fashioned way. Then we can get to work. It's almost ready."

Rose swore Carter's cheeks flushed at the compliment to his flame. He busied himself wandering around the spacious room, looking at projects in progress and those finished waiting for use.

"It's kind of silly when you think about it."

"What?" Carter asked, his fingers carefully running down the length of a broadsword.

"I mean, this—this room, these weapons—are the heart of the continent's defense strategy." She lifted her arms, gesturing to the racks of weapons around them. "Yet, it seems quite useless against what we face."

"We'll find and stop Aterra. Think of everything we learned yesterday."

"I admit, it gave me hope, and my hope had previously started waning. It should be easy enough to replicate what Juliette and I did if the key really is all our elements being used at once. The problem is a different one. In Loch, and when we fought Aterra, I didn't sense any connections to your power, or Luc's, like I did

Juliette's. And that part—is one line in a journal enough to ensure it works?"

"Well..." Carter paused. "You've taken your turn giving us all hope and trying to bring us together on this journey. As Luc chastised us the other night—you don't have to do this alone. Maybe it's time for the rest of us to convince you it can be done."

Rose smiled in a way she was sure didn't meet her eyes. Another idea she appreciated even as she was unsure of its practicality. "I think the fire is ready. Let's get started."

Carter moved to the space to her right, similar to the position she and Juliette had taken as Rose forged her daggers.

"Just use a bit of your fire. It doesn't have to be strong, just active while I forge the ax head and spike."

"What about my other powers?" Carter asked.

"Both your shifter essence and connection to the cycle of existence hit my magic in the face before I even started the traditional evaluation. I think we'll be fine."

"Do you need this?" Carter reached into his pocket and pulled out the coin.

Rose shook her head. "You hold on to it. It should make your power clearer."

Carter nodded and called a flame to his palm. His eyes glowed the yellow-green she'd seen in the Burning Garden as they focused on the fire dancing along his skin. Rose wasn't sure she had ever seen him look more like a predator.

The familiar rise and fall of her hammer was fast with this project. She'd started the ax head earlier this morning. The spear tip, she would borrow from the Suden forge. That freed her now to focus on harnessing Carter's unique magic.

Chocolate and sandalwood filled the room. The scent of his element wasn't enough, though. His flame was only a part of his power. What she'd learned about his shifter form came to the forefront of her mind. Unable to grasp it, the elusive nature fitting with her feline guess, was good enough.

Rose sent spirals of her magic toward him. It wrapped around

Carter, seeking, sinking into his skin. Her power chased to the heart of the Vesten leader. She was unsurprised to find a campsite setting at the heart of his magic. A forest of trees so thick she was already lost. A small opening held a large willow tree. It's draping branches pushed aside to show a bedroll beneath it and a fire just outside the perimeter of its branches. Carter's core of magic was peaceful—solitary.

To Arie, she knew the shifting was freeing. He had a human form, but she had never seen it. He was comfortable when he could blend in and go unnoticed by others, who were not suspecting an animal with his kind of intelligence. It felt similar with Carter—Kenna's journals indicated the same.

Her mind roamed over all the information they'd learned from Kenna's journals, lingering on a piece they hadn't yet discussed. Zrak said their power would be strongest at Compass Lake and that the gods would feel if they weakened. Did this allude to the connection between a god and the fae leader that Juliette described?

Rose pushed her thoughts to the magic before her. Carter's magic was so different from the others, but so uniquely him. The strong yet sweet smell of his power balanced the heavy weight he carried. Seeing spirits, a constant connection to the cycle of life and death, to the existence of all on the continent. It was an honor, but she was also sure it was its own burden. They hadn't even gotten to the part where she asked if he had to do anything to help the spirits find their way beyond the veil.

In the heart of Carter's magic, the quiet of his campsite, Rose readied for the flashes, the feelings—but nothing came. That was an answer itself. The heart of Carter's magic was solace from the world around him. It was escape from the weight of his power. While a weapon wasn't ideal for that desire of his magic, in their situation, it was necessary. The spike between the ax heads would have to act as a pointer. As the Vesten leader, he could steer his court, and hopefully, the continent, to this quiet solace he craved.

She had her connections as she made the final few swings of

her hammer, the ax head gleaming in the firelight. "Give me a little more magic," Rose said as she spared a glance at Carter.

"No problem." The small flame in his palm spread up his arm. The fire danced over his skin and clothes, leaving the fire wielder unharmed.

Her magic sealed the Vesten's essence, with Carter's specific talents, into the metal. She sent blasts of icy wind and cooling water around the ax heads. It was nice to be in the Suden forge for this, since his ax required some assembly. She reached for the wooden handle and the spike she had picked out, fitting them into place. This would be a finished project before they left the forge today. Pushing a little more of her wind around the ax, she nodded with satisfaction. The Vesten Point would have his defense against the mist plague.

The heat died down. Carter let go of his element. His eyes focused on her as she worked on the finishing touches.

"This should do it," she said as she flipped the handle toward him. "Now Luc won't have to drag you away from any other mist attacks we encounter."

Carter flushed. "Thank you."

"I should thank you for the opportunity," Rose said. "It isn't every day that I evaluate three powers so unique but so combined in a single person."

"I'm sure we could say the same about being evaluated by the weapons master from Lake of the Gods." Carter smiled back as he hoisted his ax over his shoulder, and they left the forge together.

CHAPTER TWENTY-FIVE

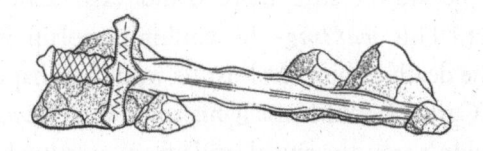

Luc ran into Rose and Carter as they were leaving the workshop.

"Thanks for letting us use the space," Carter said, his ax still proudly resting on his shoulder.

"Glad you put it to good use," Luc replied. Turning to Rose, he asked, "Do you have time before we meet the others?"

"We'll catch up with you later, Carter." Rose waved.

"Actually, wait," Luc said. "If we're going to test our magic, shouldn't we do it in a less confined space?" He looked between Carter and Rose. "I know Rose wouldn't want to damage any of those pretty books in the library."

Rose smirked at him and then looked thoughtful. "What do you suggest?"

He gestured behind him. "We can use the training grounds here."

Carter was contemplative. "Sure, I'll let Juliette know, and we'll meet you back here in a few hours?" Luc nodded, and Carter left.

"Round two already?" Rose's smile was a challenge and a request.

Luc's magic flared at her suggestion. He didn't even mind his power slip—he agreed with it—but a corner of his mind still thought about his magic's response to Rose. It was said that other relationships paled in comparison to the demands of bound fae. If that was true, he wondered how those bound got anything done. He spent so much time keeping his magic in check when around Rose. Being bound was an impossibility, given their court affiliations—but he wasn't sure there could exist another level of wanting her. This *wanting*—he couldn't explain it. Surely, it would be the death of him. At least he would die happy—or exist happily, as Carter would insist if his spirit went beyond the veil. Still, he couldn't stop the sinful smile from crossing his face as he replied, "I'm going to need you to hold that thought."

The heat in Rose's eyes had him rethinking the necessity of his request. He shook his head. He wanted to show her this before the others arrived. "I want you to see something." Rose let him lead her down the hall and into the training grounds. "This won't be as exciting as the breaking and entering trip you took us on last time we were in Sandrin. And we already know there is no prize to be found...but I want to show you anyway."

The wide-open space seemed to captivate her. It was a unique setup in the southernmost part of the city. He could fit the entire military in this one space when needed. It was a large, rectangular area with little to recommend it. A low stone wall surrounding the training grounds held a fighting ring and a host of more familiar practice equipment. His military held regular sparring and practice sessions here. While Rose and Carter had worked, Luc had talked to his generals to see if they could clear the grounds for the day.

"What Suden secrets are we learning today?"

Luc laughed. She was closer to the mark than she realized. "Any you want, Rose. You need only ask." He took her hand. "But the journal entries made me think of this."

Rose's answering smile was brief and authentic—one that he would do anything to see more often. He turned around to face her and, leaning in, gave her an all-too-quick kiss. Her tongue teased the seam of his lips as he stepped back and reminded himself they had work to do.

As they walked across the field, he started a slightly different conversation. "I know you'll want the Compass Points to practice merging their magic today. Assuming the key we've been missing is all our elements being used together." She'd already confirmed as much by letting him change the location of the meeting to give them more space.

Rose's gaze searched his face questioningly. "Is that a problem?" she asked.

"No, of course not. It's the right next step." He ran a hand down his face. "I just know I should be the one who volunteers to try with you."

Rose's head tilted to the side, but they kept walking.

"We already know you and Juliette can merge your powers when needed. It might be interesting to test if you could merge your water with her wind when you pull it, but it's more important to prove that two elements with no connection can meet and intertwine. That takes trust. We haven't discussed the details of your experiment with Juliette, but *someone* must be in control when magics connect that way. Someone must be directing the joined power."

He saw recognition flash in Rose's eyes as she nodded. "You don't think any other pair of Compass Points will have the trust required to cede control," she stated as a fact, not a question.

Nodding, he continued. "Carter and Juliette, no way, Carter and you..." He tilted his head from side to side. "Maybe."

"What about you and Carter?" she asked.

"If it's me and anyone, Rose, it will be me and you. There is no one I trust more, and as much as you want to put the politics of the Compass Points behind us, we shouldn't discount what a display like this says."

Sometimes, Luc wished he weren't so aware of the perceptions of others. He wished he wasn't always calculating what a display would mean or what others would read into a specific action. His brain couldn't ignore the statement the first cross-element merger would make.

She stopped walking and turned to him. "I'm confused," she said. "Of course I'd pick you—but why do you look like you'd rather not do this?"

"My power is..."

"Vast?" Rose offered.

"Dangerous," he said.

"Luc." She took his hands and stepped into his space. Her hands moved quickly from his, up his arms and wrapping around his neck. She didn't press her body against his, but it was a near thing. He could feel the inches between them—wanting to close the small gap she left there with every part of him.

"Your power won't hurt me. It's not dangerous. It's you. I don't think it wise to continue to think of it as an entity apart."

"What if I don't want it as a part of me?" Luc whispered.

Rose's smile was gentle as if she suspected that was the case, but maybe she hadn't expected him to admit it so freely. He wouldn't have—to anyone else.

"I don't think that's a choice we get to make. Just like we don't get to choose who brings us into this world. But once we're here, we can make the time and the gifts our own."

Her words were so damn calming. When did she obtain this new power over him? One that had nothing to do with magic? He knew it was somewhere between putting him flat on his back with a shoulder roll and saving him from doing something idiotic with the archer who'd attacked them on their journey from Lake of the Gods.

He leaned his forehead against hers, so they shared breaths. "I want to believe that. All that you said. I also want to be prepared for..." He lifted his head back, shaking it. "Worse outcomes."

She shook her head. He saw the moment she decided not to fight him on it. She must have known she couldn't convince him to change his mind.

"How do we prepare for those?"

"I'm so glad that you asked." He offered her his arm, and she hooked hers through it as they walked to the southern part of the wall around the training ground. "I thought we could let my magic out a little before the others got here. I can try to tire it out a bit."

Rose nodded. "I'm more than happy to watch." She hopped up on the wall to sit as he rolled up his sleeves. He couldn't help the self-satisfied grunt as her eyes raked over each new piece of exposed skin on his arm. He was back at her side in a second, his lips crashing into hers.

She laughed as she kissed him back. "To my knowledge, this doesn't use your element."

His lip curled into what he believed to be her favorite smirk as he straightened. "We should test that."

Her eyes lit with interest.

"Actually, before I get too distracted, I did say I wanted to show you something." He took her hand and tugged her as she jumped off the wall to meet him. They walked together to its outside perimeter. "We already know the ring is not here, but there is a hiding place on these grounds for the Suden artifact."

Rose stopped walking, her motion pulling Luc to a halt since their hands were linked. "You've known where it was for eight years? Why have you never tried to collect it?"

"Other than the fact that we know it's not there?" he replied as her face scrunched in thought.

"You didn't know it was missing before, did you?" She was curious. He could hear it in her words. He liked that. He wanted to read every one of her tells. Her curiosity was warranted. She'd chased down the item that showed her claim to the Norden seat. Why would he leave something like that to the chance someone else could find it?

"It's not something I needed." He shrugged. "My claim was not only uncontested but some would say thrust upon me before my time, due to the sheer force of my magic's presence on the continent."

"Well, when you put it that way..." Rose's lip curved into a smirk of her own. Her smile faltered as she continued, "The Suden Point just tells their successor where the ring is? You don't try to collect it together? Or better yet, why didn't Michael have it?"

They bent down at a specific section of the brick wall. "The ring amplifies all Suden power—not just the element. As we heard from Samuel, it's best amplification is for mind shadow. Michael had strong feelings about that ability. He didn't want it. Wearing the ring grants it, regardless of whether it's an ability the Suden Point already possesses." Luc shrugged. "We didn't go check it together. He simply told me where it was, and I was happy to assume it was still there—as did he. In my defense, I can't say I anticipated Aterra being on the continent and coming to claim it himself." His earth magic shook a brick free of its place, falling to the ground. Luc reached into the vacated hole, his hand returning empty.

"No surprise there," Rose said.

"I'm a little surprised by how well Aiden can wield it," Luc said, thinking back to their encounter with it at the Solstice Ball and Samuel's claims about Aiden's test.

"I assumed he could only use it when Aterra was inhabiting him." Rose shrugged. "His eyes were definitely gray when he stabbed you at the ball."

"Do you ever think about what memories he was trying to take from you?" Luc asked quietly.

"I did when Samuel first mentioned what happened to him, but I haven't given it a lot of thought. Honestly, I've not given Aiden a lot of thought in this whole mess. I'm not exactly sure what I'll see if I examine it too closely."

"You don't want him to be responsible." It was a statement, not a question. Luc knew that Rose wanted some semblance of her childhood friendship to have been real. "At least by the ball, he'd given up on trying to kill you," Luc said, trying to lighten her mood. He knew she would have to come to this conclusion on her own—likely whenever they found Aiden again.

Rose opened and closed her mouth. She finally settled on replying with, "You say that like taking my memories is better?"

"Of course not. I'll end him for considering either." Luc's tone was calm, but he meant every word.

He and Rose didn't talk much about what they would do to Aiden when they stopped Aterra. He wanted Rose to have time and space to decide what to do about him. No one could say for sure how much of what Aiden did was his choice and how much was Aterra controlling him. Ultimately, he made a wrong decision to align with the god, but if Rose was correct, he had done that when he was little more than a child. Luc wouldn't blame Aiden for the unthinkable scope of one poor decision, but he would undoubtedly condemn Aterra.

Rose's hand wrapped around his and squeezed. "Thanks for showing me this."

"Anytime." He stood from the crouched position by the wall. "Ready to watch me let off a little steam before the others arrive?" He took her hand as they went back to the inside of the low stone wall, wanting her calming presence.

"I have one more question," she said.

"Ask it."

"Are you ready to let me evaluate your power again? I need to finish your sword."

Luc ran his hand down his face. To be fair, he'd known this was coming. She was out of other Compass Points to make weapons for. "Rose..."

"I've figured out how to work with larger powers. I was tired working on Juliette and Carter's weapons, but I finished them. I think I'm ready for yours."

"I'm just scared my magic will hurt you again. Let me think about it—it's not like you'll be able to start it today while we're practicing with the others."

She nodded. As he turned to head to the field, she tugged him to her. "You're going to try to merge magic with me today? No matter how much power you think you let off?"

He wouldn't let the opportunity to show such a solid united front pass them by. It would also be a good test for his magic. "I will." His magic sagged in relief at his words. Hopefully, that meant it wanted to work with Rose, that it would behave and not overwhelm her again.

His power sprawled across the field in dense tendrils as it lifted everything it touched off the earth. His power was still a bit of a mystery. They'd barely found tidbits of information in the Vesten journals about a connection between the fae leaders and their patrons. What had Zrak said? The gods would know if their power weakened—if they spent too much time away from the lake. He suspected the other gods might not have known the extent to which that balance of power could be manipulated.

Aterra must have figured it out—given how he threatened Juliette and the Osten fae. Her ritual proved a fae court leader could share their power with their god. Of course, she did it with the goal of her god returning that power to the Osten court, but surely that wasn't a requirement. As Juliette had said, with power, someone was always willing to abuse it to take more. Aterra had already proven he didn't care about the balance on the continent. Luc would bet anything he was more than happy to also abuse the balance of power between a Compass Point and their patron.

The Suden god's plan was clear, at least to Luc. Kenna said Aterra walked the continent more than most. He was *closer* to the Suden than seemed appropriate. Luc didn't have to think too hard about what that meant.

Aterra sought to *create* his own Suden Point. A Suden sired by the god would have power significant enough to strengthen his own. Luc's power flared around the training grounds. He looked down at his hands—hands that wielded a strength of earth magic that terrified many. There was no question in his mind whether Aterra had been successful.

He just wondered what he was willing to do about it.

CHAPTER TWENTY-SIX

Rose let her mind wander as she watched Luc flex his magic. The tendrils sprawled across the field. They threw, dug, and filled—exercising all the classic Suden moves. His magic didn't feel any less potent to her senses. He even exercised moves more unique to his magic. He lifted Rose and himself, using the earth as an anchor and pushing them away from it. She could watch him endlessly, and part of her wondered if that would truly be needed to exhaust it. He'd been at this for an hour, and his power hadn't dampened.

She sighed as he threw another boulder. He didn't trust his magic.

This was a foreign concept to Rose. Trusting her water magic was the same as trusting herself. She may have been taught to hide her wind, but even it, she trusted. She always described her wind as there to help her—to topple the item off the high shelf that she couldn't reach—or push her higher and farther on a swing. It was tricky to wrap her head around Luc's position. How could you distrust something that was so wholly connected to you?

Juliette and Carter walked in at the northern entrance. They saw Luc in the center of the grounds and headed toward him.

Carter's gaze searched the training grounds as if anticipating an attack. Juliette's, though less obvious, was certainly cautious.

Rose wanted to laugh at what they read yesterday. How the gods thought they could force cooperation by making the Compass Points live together at the lake. She couldn't imagine what the gods had been thinking trying to trap the four fae leaders together like that. It had taken a literal continent-threatening event to unite them. And they'd only started to trust each other after leaving the lake.

"Come on in," Luc called. He spread his arms. "This is a much safer place to test our powers together than in a library filled with priceless books, right?"

"Thanks again, Luc," Carter replied.

"We're certainly going all in on this sharing among Compass Points thing, aren't we?" Juliette added. Her tone was wry, but she was present, and she understood what they were there to do. She didn't oppose it, and that was good enough for Rose.

"So," Rose started. She might as well confirm everyone was okay with this once more. Not that they had any other options. "We all agree that we need to join elements? We all need to use our elements together to attempt what Juliette and I did to unite our wind?"

They each nodded. Luc's magic flared and circled Rose. It called to her like no other power she had experienced before. She didn't have to keep her magic leashed like Luc did, but she certainly felt a pull toward him—and she didn't fight it.

"We should start by using our elements and ensuring I can see the door to Juliette's magic." Rose shrugged. She expected the first part to work. It was a simple thing they had missed but made all the sense in the world, given the gods' goal. "But assuming that works, we should try to pair differing elements."

"I'll do it with Rose if she's willing," Luc said before anyone else could volunteer.

No matter what he said or thought about his magic, Rose

wanted this. She trusted him and his power—completely. She knew they were one and the same whether he liked it or not.

"Of course," she replied.

Carter seemed to expect nothing less. Juliette crossed her arms over her chest as if she wished there were another option, but she was unwilling to propose an alternative.

Rose hopped down from her perch and strode toward the center of the grounds. Juliette and Carter leaned against the wall where she'd sat.

"I'm very glad we picked this location instead of the library. I'd hate to have disrupted or ruined the books," Rose murmured to Luc.

His smile was sinful again as he replied. "We are avoiding ruining them with our magic display. But, if you're interested in breaking in there later tonight, I could be persuaded to disrupt the books in other ways."

Rose's face warmed at his taunt. "Play your cards right."

"Less verbal foreplay, more magic merging," Juliette called from the sidelines.

Carter coughed into his hand.

"Okay, let's do the simple test first. Is everyone ready with their element?" Rose felt each Compass Point power come alive. Earth, fire, wind, and water—her water would finally get its chance to play. "I'm going to search for the connection to Juliette," she said as she dove into her store of magic. Her internal lake was full, and the increasingly familiar wind blew across it. Even while calling her water, Rose didn't have to follow the wind far to find the door. It was as easy as walking to a friend's house. "I've got it."

"That was fast," Juliette commented.

"It's a lot easier now that I know what I'm looking for."

"What does that mean for finding connections to the others?" Juliette asked as she let her wind die down.

"I suppose that is what we need to test." Rose looked at Luc.

"It took multiple tries to familiarize myself with the connection to Juliette's magic while using the same element. I might need a little longer to find a connection to yours."

Luc nodded.

Rose laughed a little, nervous herself. "Ready?"

"With you? Always." His smile was sinful as he raised his hands.

The sand in the opposite corner of the field started to lift. Coalescing into a spinning storm, it swirled its way over to them. Fire and wind flared over by the wall where Carter and Juliette stood.

"Well, that works." Rose called her water again. All four elements active. She suspected their shared wind made it easier for Rose to find Juliette's door. But Luc and Rose shared something deeper than an element. The core of their magics reached for each other at every opportunity. She didn't want to say this in front of the others, in case she was wrong, but she didn't think she'd have a problem finding a connection to Luc.

She closed her eyes and quickly found the lake at the center of her power. Observing the lake's perimeter, she wasn't sure exactly what she was looking for. Luc's power was falling through a dark tunnel the one time she'd evaluated him—is that what she'd find? She felt him here, felt his magic reaching for hers. She only needed to find the source and open it.

No new doors or other connection points surrounded the lake. But she felt him nevertheless. It had to be close. She stared into the lake's depths, thinking where else she could look. A slow smile crossed her face as she found her answer.

The lake was deeper than usual. A dark pit in the center where it was previously a deep blue. Luc wasn't on the periphery of her power, he was a part of it. She dove into the lake without hesitation, needing to find a way to open the connection. Reaching the pit, the darkness didn't seem to have an ending, an echo of the hole in Loch. There was no door to open, nothing to unlock. She wasn't sure what the tunnel needed from her to allow power through.

Rose did the only thing she could, and threw herself from the comfort of her lake into the pit. She plummeted like the first time she fell through Luc's magic. But she didn't fall through his tunnel of memories. His power only needed her to cross the threshold willingly, to prove she wanted its connection. It held her at the precipice between their magics as Luc's power flowed around her, overflowing her lake.

Rose opened her eyes, the sandstorm Luc had created still dancing across the training field. Power burst forth, echoing the first thing she'd seen. A spinning funnel of elements moved to meet Luc's. Rose's funnel was earth and water, the twisting forces of their elements intertwined and flowing through her.

Luc's smile was pride mixed with caution. He hadn't doubted Rose either. He was as much aware of their magic's connection as she was. Luc didn't drop his sandstorm, but he let her spinning mix of elements consume it, leading the merged elements left and then right across the field.

Their shared power was hers to control.

Pushing their connection, Rose wanted to see what else they could do. Luc's power was bottomless as she flung herself further into the pit in her lake. No longer hovering between the powers, she wholly submerged herself into Luc's.

The flashing images on the tunnel walls were back—moments, scenes, episodes of his life flying by as she fell. She opened her eyes, and instead of plummeting further into Luc's magic, she was back on the training ground, floating above the field. She looked down and saw Juliette, Carter, and Luc staring up at her, their eyes wide. What was she—

She was plummeting again. Not through magic, but literally toward the solid ground. Unable to grasp what was happening, she didn't even think to call her wind. Luc stepped beneath her, raising his arms and magic to catch her. As he safely tucked Rose into his chest, she looked up at him. His brow furrowed, and his lips pressed tight together.

"That was fun," she said.

His eyebrow lifted. His mouth opened like he was about to tell her how much the opposite of fun that was. This did not bode well for her getting another opportunity to work on his weapon. But before he could say anything, a black bird flew onto the field.

"Never fear. Lord Arctos is here," Arie said into Luc and Rose's minds as he perched himself on the wall next to Carter and Juliette.

That was enough to break Luc from whatever he was about to say regarding Rose's fall. "He did *not* just say that," he murmured to Rose.

She couldn't cover her laugh.

"There's no need to be more *disrespectful. I'm back, and I have news. Gather round, Compass Points."*

Luc set Rose down with a look that said they would continue the conversation later. They walked to where Arie had landed.

"Welcome back, Lord Arctos," Carter said formally.

"I'll speak to everyone, shall I?" Arie said into the minds of all the Compass Points as his bird head swiveled.

"Did you find Zrak?" Rose asked.

That caught Juliette's attention. Her spine straightened as she waited for Arie's answer.

"I located him, but we weren't able to speak. I'm not sure how to get to him."

"Where is he?" Luc asked.

"If you would stop interrupting and just let me tell you, we would all find out a lot sooner, wouldn't we?" Arie said.

Carter's mouth hung open as he watched the conversation. He must still be uncomfortable with such a casual exchange with Lord Arctos.

"Well, don't leave us in suspense now," Rose drawled.

The black bird peered down its beak at her, looking as imperious as an animal could. *"Zrak is beyond the veil."*

Rose felt her lip curl up in a wry smile. "I think we knew that, actually. Though it's good validation that you agree." She winked at him.

Arie bristled, looking unconvinced that they might have solved this without him. *"How?"*

"Well..." Rose looked between Juliette and Carter, trying to decide whose secrets to spill first. Inspired by his patron's appearance, Carter seemed inclined to his divulgence.

"I can see spirits."

Juliette, more reluctantly, added her own confession. "I commune with Zrak. His artifact contains his blood, and I use it to strengthen him so that he may strengthen the Osten fae in return."

Arie's head swiveled between the two, unsure who to focus on.

"The key is both of these pieces of information together, though," Rose said.

"Explain yourself."

"Carter saw spirits gathering when the mist met us coming out of the woods south of Sandrin. He's seen them every time the mist comes." She glanced at Carter for his confirming nod. "But this time was heavier—there were more." Her gaze moved to Juliette. "This was when you did the incomplete version of your ritual. I don't think we can discount the fact that, though not complete, Zrak heard your call, and the Nebulus didn't come. Whatever your connection, it was strong enough to thin the veil between planes—at least momentarily—so he could hear you. But that also allowed spirits access to the continent from beyond."

The Compass Points pondered this idea.

"The timing works out," Luc added. "Does that mean Juliette's act is what thins the veil?"

"I don't think it's the act so much as the connection to Zrak," Rose said.

"The ritual calls him to me and strengthens his power. While he uses that to strengthen the Osten fae, he may also be using it to thin the veil and send the mist." Juliette didn't look happy as she said it. "Outside of the forest, that was the first time I did the ritual anywhere other than the caves." She paused, considering. "Zrak said the caves already held a wild sort of magic, and that made our connection easier to maintain. I'm not attuned to the veil like Carter is. I'm not sure I would have come to that conclusion on my own."

Arie swiveled to face Juliette, his head tilting as she spoke about wild magic. Then he turned back to Carter. *"You've all been running around with these powers for years and not done anything with them?"* he asked, incredulous.

"You are hardly one to talk, Arie." Rose glared at him. "We spent ten years hiding on an island."

"I see your point." The bird nipped at his feathers as if he couldn't be bothered to pay attention to this conversation any longer.

"Do you think we can get Zrak back?" Juliette asked.

Arie's head tilted to the other side. *"I don't think it should be your primary concern. But yes, I do think it's possible."* He changed the topic. *"What were you all doing when I arrived? Why was Rose falling from the sky?"*

"We were trying to use our elemental magics together—combining our power to deal with Aterra," Juliette answered.

"Very good," Arie said.

"But that's what we're supposed to do?" Rose pressed. "Merge our powers?"

"Only the Compass Points can decide how to complete their goal. You should continue on that path if you've found something that worked. Though, why were you falling?"

Rose looked to Luc, whose hand was rubbing over his face. "I think Rose found her way back into the core of my power. It may have given her too much too fast—again."

"Luc." Rose turned to face him, ensuring he made eye contact and acknowledged her words. "I reached for more power. I pulled —it only did what I asked." Her words were firm. Direct. "This was my mistake, again." She smirked as she echoed his words. "One of many I'm sure we'll make as we figure this out. It had nothing to do with your power overwhelming me."

Luc opened his mouth to respond as Arie cut him off. *"Sounds like progress to me. What's next?"*

CHAPTER TWENTY-SEVEN

After practicing, they went to the Vesten Library together, to do a bit more reading. In an unexpected show of unity, the Compass Points also had dinner together in the Vesten hall. Carter's father, Gabriel, hosted them. He was so different from his son. He had a warm, welcoming persona. He had joined them in the afternoon, letting himself into their private library and making his own introductions. If Carter had feline aloofness, Gabriel had all the warmth and acceptance of a canine pack. And whether they liked it or not, he treated the visiting fae leaders as part of his pack—shepherding them off to dinner when he deemed they had worked too long.

"Have you been to Sandrin before, Rose?" Gabriel asked as he passed her a platter of meat.

"Yes, Luc and I visited before the Summer Solstice Ceremony, though, I admit, that was my first time here. I'd always wanted to come."

"Well, I hope you get to explore a little." He smiled cheerfully. "How about you, Juliette? Do you get to Sandrin often?"

Rose glanced at the others. They each seemed confused in their own way. Carter's confusion was most certainly rooted in embarrassment. He clearly hadn't told his father what they were doing here or the urgency of their journey. Juliette, on the other hand, wore a bemused expression. Rose suspected it had been a while since anyone had tried quite so hard and so genuinely to draw her into a conversation.

"I do not," she replied. "My duties keep me at Compass Lake."

Even Luc, who had been in a mood since they practiced merging powers, could barely hold back a smile as he watched Gabriel energetically interrogate each of them.

"Carter, you don't come home enough." He waved a hand in a dismissive gesture. "Though I suppose I tell you that all the time."

Rose wasn't sure she had ever seen Carter flush so deeply. She lifted her napkin to hide her smile.

"The Suden Point." Gabriel turned next to Luc. Here was the only indication that Gabriel might be more nervous than he appeared. He bowed his head and shoulders slightly as he addressed Luc and couldn't bring himself to address him by name. "You, of course, need no introduction to the city. How are you finding your stay? You visit quite often, do you not?"

"I do." Luc dipped his head back. "We appreciate the meal," he offered. "We've had nothing but stew on our travels."

"And where have you been?" Gabriel asked as he passed the roasted vegetables to Rose.

Everyone turned to Carter. "I told you, Dad, we can't talk too much about it. We've been traveling in an effort to stop the mist plague."

"Oh yes, of course," Gabriel said as he drank his wine. "I expect the four of you together will be able to stop it."

Rose would swear that he was goading them, but his enthusiasm was genuine. The pride he held in his eyes for his son wasn't that which could be faked. "We're certainly working on it," she chimed in.

"Actually, Dad, maybe you can help us," Carter said. He glanced around the table briefly to see if anyone would stop his questioning. No one did. "Are you aware of any texts we have about the relationship between Compass Point and their patron god?"

While Arie had said he wouldn't join them, Rose was unsurprised to feel what could only be a cat brush against her legs under the table. "*What is he asking about?*" Arie asked her.

Rose shook her head. There was no way she could respond without alerting everyone he was here. She gently kicked him, trying to usher him out from under the table to make his presence known. "*No,*" he said, holding his ground. "*This is much more interesting. Do you think the patron god's power is tied to their Compass Point? Tap your foot once for yes and twice for no.*"

Rose tapped her foot once.

Gabriel looked up. Rose got the impression he was going through a mental index of all the reference books in his archive to see if he could give his son any pointers. He looked disheartened when his gaze returned to the table. "Have you tried Kenna's journals?"

"*And you think this because Juliette can boost Zrak's power?*"

Rose tapped her foot once. She heard but didn't track Carter's reply to his father.

"*But...*" Rose felt Arie mentally hesitate. "*She only boosts his power when she feels the Osten fae magic waning...is that it? And then with the boost, Zrak can strengthen the Osten...*"

He'd gotten there all on his own. Rose tapped her foot once. At least this answered whether Arie knew about it.

"*I know you'll call me an idiot, but I hadn't put that together. I knew Zrak's artifact was a vial, but I assure you, it didn't have his blood in it when he gifted it to the first Osten Point. He always had too many plans going for his own good.*"

"Rose?" Luc nudged her with his elbow, bringing her back to the conversation at the table.

"I'm sorry, what was the question?" The others all stared at her. Her diverted attention hadn't gone unnoticed.

"Just if there was anything in Kenna's first journal about the shared power." Carter eyed her suspiciously. He couldn't possibly know she was secretly talking to the Vesten god, could he?

"Oh, well, there was what we discussed about Compass Lake being where we are strongest and the gods knowing if we left—presumably, that means they'd know if our power weakened." She gestured vaguely. "It could be a simple threat to get the firsts to do what they wanted."

"Or it could have meant we would weaken if you did." Arie paused. *"Kenna never tested me on that. Neither did Nicholas. They stayed at the lake... Juliette's ritual requires a mixture of her and Zrak's blood?"*

Rose tapped her foot once, desperately trying to keep both conversations straight.

"We should leave soon," Arie said to her. *"If this is true, I think Aterra's plans are worse than I realized."*

"When do you leave?" Gabriel asked Carter. The conversation must have moved on, though she missed any conclusion from her point.

"Have you and Luc talked about what this could mean?"

Rose froze. A feeling like a pit opening in her stomach overtook her. What part of this would she have talked to Luc about specifically? She tapped her foot twice and glanced at Luc. She was worried about many things for Luc, but nothing tied to the power of the gods. If Arie was worried about him, they needed to get going, and she needed to find out why.

"I think we should leave tomorrow," Rose said, interrupting whatever response Carter would give.

"Rose?" Juliette said her name like a question. Luc, it appeared, had glanced under the table and made some assumptions about why she was acting so scattered.

"I think we need to continue our journey," she said.

"But we haven't really begun to practice with everyone," Carter said. "We don't know if this will work..."

"I know," Rose looked at Juliette. "I think some of the things we learned today add urgency to our journey. We'll have to continue to practice as we travel." Pieces of information were sliding together in Rose's mind. If the gods knew when the Compass Points weakened, it would stand to reason they knew when they strengthened. That was what Luc had been getting at—how Aterra would strengthen himself.

Juliette's hand went to her necklace as she took a final bite of her meal. "If that's the case, I think I should excuse myself to get some rest." With a last glance at Rose, she added, "We leave early?"

Rose nodded. "We should get going too, Luc." She looked at Gabriel. "Thank you so much for the hospitality. I apologize that we weren't able to be more enjoyable company."

Gabriel demurred. "You were wonderful. Come back any time."

It would damage the trust they had built with Carter to leave so abruptly, but if Arie was worried about Luc, Rose would risk Carter's anger.

Luc had been thinking a lot about his magic since their confrontation with Aterra. She just hadn't fully realized the conclusions he had come to.

※

"TELL ME EVERYTHING," Arie said, including Luc in the conversation, as Rose closed the door to his quarters behind them.

"I don't know what else to tell you," she said.

"Were you making her tap yes or no responses through dinner?" Luc asked, his eyes dancing with mirth.

Rose glared at him.

"*Of course. It seems you all omitted some details about Juliette's secret this afternoon.*"

"How so?" Luc asked.

"*You didn't indicate your suspicions that the power sharing could apply to all Compass Points and their patrons. Given what he* had planned to do, I assumed it was something Zrak set up for himself."

"I mean...we don't know for sure. It's a question." Luc considered. "The fact that you know nothing about it lends itself to being Zrak-specific."

"Why don't you tell us why you think it applies to other gods," Arie said, jumping up on the bed so that his yellow-green eyes could stare unblinkingly at Luc more easily.

Luc glanced at Rose, then back at Arie.

This was going to be it. Whatever Luc had concluded about his magic—about Aterra—Arie had also. Rose was anxious to hear it. It felt like a weight settling over them.

"What if Aterra plans to use me in the same way?" Luc said.

Rose tilted her head. Use Luc in the same way that Zrak was using Juliette? Why would that matter? Luc would never be a willing participant. And Aterra wasn't in a position where his magic needed to be strengthened for the Suden fae. She said as much aloud.

"It requires a mixing of blood, Luc. Yours and his. And Rose has a point... It would be hard to get you to complete that ritual without your knowledge."

"What if our blood is already mixed? What if I'm Aterra's son?" Luc asked.

This was what he'd been brooding over for days? She considered what they'd read the day prior—Aterra's too-close relations with the Suden.

Arie's tail flicked back and forth as the seconds passed.

Rose couldn't refute the idea, though she felt they lacked proof. "Say you're right, which I still don't think we can confirm." She paused. "Still, say you're Aterra's son. You have his blood in you. Wouldn't you still have to complete a ritual to be useful to him? To boost his power in some way?"

Luc pulled his hand down his face. "I guess," he said. "Juliette has the vial, the artifact left by Zrak. Maybe I need the ring? The

Suden artifact? But we assume he already has that, so it's not a stretch to think he planned to slip it on me."

Taking Luc's hand, Rose squeezed it and stared at Arie. "Anything to add, Lord Arctos?" She couldn't help her sarcasm. She had hoped that one of the gods would have more information for them.

"*I don't think Luc's assumptions are incoherent...but I honestly can't say for sure. There was so much about the creation of the fae courts that we didn't discuss. I trusted Zrak knew what he was doing.*"

"Maybe there is one way to test it," Rose said. Arie and Luc turned to look at her. "What if we have you test it, Arie? You and Carter?" She paused as the pieces clicked together in her mind. "We have your artifact, you, and the Vesten Point. Why don't we see if he can share his power with you? If it works for any god, even one not weakened through sacrifice?"

Arie licked his paw.

"It would be a bit of a gamble," Luc said, staring intently at Arie. "Could Carter trust Arie wouldn't abuse the power given to him if it worked?"

"*I take offense to that.*" Arie continued to lick his paw and wipe his head with it. "*But Luc's not wrong. It's a huge ask. And I haven't exactly done anything to gain Carter's trust.*"

"He knows that you asked me to make him a weapon. I told him when I gave him the coin. So, I may have helped you there." Rose stepped forward and patted Arie on the head. "Though, if you want to do this, you'll have to ask him yourself. But he knows you were looking out for him. That has to be a good place to start."

CHAPTER TWENTY-EIGHT

Rose pulled out her compass as the group readied to leave early the following morning. Carter glared at her as he secured his saddlebags while she filled Arie in on their first experience tracking Aterra.

"*I can't believe he was at my cabin!*" Arie said.

"Your cabin?"

"*Yes—you were there. It's not like there were others around to get confused about. My cabin is on the western edge of the continent. It was where I went to be alone—to hide away from everything.*"

Rose lifted her hand to cover a small smile as she thought of Aterra in Aiden's body, standing possessively in front of the fire when they burst in. "I think you might have to fight him for it."

"*This is not funny.*"

"I would generally agree—a rogue god upsetting the continent's balance isn't funny—but somehow, him hiding out at your all-Arie alone-time cabin is kind of entertaining."

Arie flew away from her as she looked down at the compass again to establish where they were going. Hopefully, he was going to talk to Carter. Someone needed to explain why they'd left dinner so abruptly and what they now needed to ask of him. She didn't think it should come from her.

"It's pointing northeast," she said as Luc approached. "And, yes, that was my fault he flew away, but in my defense, it was funny."

"You're in a good mood," Luc said as he wrapped an arm around her waist.

"It's good to have him back." She tracked Arie's flight as he landed on Carter's shoulder. Good. "Even if he doesn't have all the answers, having him with us is comforting." Her face must have shown her concern as she glanced at Luc.

"I'm fine," he said.

She wasn't sure about that. He had convinced himself he was Aterra's son—birthed to strengthen Aterra's power to a level that the Compass Points or other gods couldn't control. "Don't carry it alone," she said. He needed to work through some things independently, and she trusted him to discuss them when he was ready.

He changed the topic. "Didn't we have questions for him while traveling? I can't think of any of them now that he's here, though," Luc said.

"That reminds me, I did have one." She looked at Arie. "Arie, I'm sorry. Can I borrow you for another moment?"

Reluctantly, the bird flew back to her. *"This had better be important."*

"I think it is, but I don't think you'll like it," she said as they finished saddling their horses and mounted. Her voice was loud enough for the others to hear, though she paused as she figured out how to ask Arie such a sensitive question.

"Do you know..." She considered her words carefully. Arie hadn't shown much of the pain he carried during their time together, but she knew this topic would hurt. "Do you know what happened to Aurora?" she asked, taking a direct approach.

Startled, Arie flapped his wings, the left tip brushing her face. *"What's this about?"* he said only to her.

Rose looked at Luc. She caught his nod and decided it was

safe to share even if the Compass Points were listening. "We were talking more about Aterra's artifact."

"*Ahh,*" Arie said. "*You wondered how long Aterra has had it? And what else he might have done with it?*"

"Pretty much."

"*What made you think he used it on Aurora?*"

Rose shrugged. "When I realized that Aterra's artifact was the ring he used to stab Luc at the Solstice Ball. It wasn't the first time you'd encountered it. You knew what it was. The method of his attack confirmed for you that it was Aterra inhabiting Aiden's body."

Arie ruffled his feathers. "*Unfortunately, you're right.*"

"What happened?" she asked.

"*I'm not sure I could bring myself to tell you,*" Arie said. "*I think that I could show you, though.*"

"Show me? You don't have mind shadow..." Rose meant it as a statement, but she couldn't help that it sounded like a question by the end. What did she know about what the Vesten god was capable of?

"*You're right. I don't have the Suden gift, but I think I could focus enough on a memory that you would see it if you tried to evaluate my power. This is a strong one for me. There are few times I felt like I failed to protect those I loved. Once when Zrak sacrificed himself for the continent, and again when Aterra took Aurora. They've left their mark on my magic.*"

"You want me to evaluate you?" Rose wasn't sure she understood. "The only time I've seen full scenes like that while making a weapon was for Luc." She glanced at him as he got on his horse. "I thought I only saw his memories because of his power."

"*I can't be sure. And if this doesn't work, I'm sure Luc could see it, but I'd like you to try. I think you saw scenes while evaluating his magic because of its strength and how much those individual scenes make his magic what it is today. I think it would be good for you to test this theory.*"

She had enough trouble evaluating Luc's power—she wasn't

sure she was ready for a god's. But would Arie recommend something he didn't think she was capable of? She didn't think so. "Okay. Just to be clear, do you want me to make you a weapon?" Rose asked as they started their ride. She knew academically that he had a human form, but she was so unused to the concept, she couldn't imagine him with a sword.

"*I don't want you to make me a weapon. I want you to want to make me one. It would be a nice token of our friendship. Think of it as a violent friendship bracelet.*"

Rose snorted a laugh as they rode out of Sandrin.

※

THEY TOOK the same road east that intersected with the northern route—the one she, Luc, and Arie had traveled together before. This trip turned out to be a big circle of the southern part of the continent. Aurora's compass still guided them. It started to shift north as they came upon the crossroads. They stopped for the night, a half day's ride from the turn that would lead them to Bury. Instinctively, she knew the road and the journey they would be taking—Arie seemed to know as well.

"We're going back to Lake of the Gods," Rose said as they set up camp for the evening.

"*You didn't even have to see the memory?*"

"I was guessing. You're just confirming. I still need to know why. What happened?"

"Do you need me to help with a makeshift forge?" Carter asked as they settled the campsite.

"*I am the Lord of Flame,*" Arie said haughtily to all of them. "*I am sure I can handle it.*"

Rose rolled her eyes. So much for Arie and Carter bonding. The Vesten Point, dismissed, walked back toward the campfire to help Luc and Juliette with the meal. She unsaddled some of the steel she'd taken from the Suden forge. "Do you need me to explain what to do?"

"No, but I do think Luc should be over here."

"He's helping prepare the meal. Why do you want him here?"

"I assume he hasn't let you further evaluate his magic?"

"You assume correctly," Rose said, crossing her arms over her chest.

"I think it would help him to watch this."

"You think you throw off that much magic, Arie?" She cocked her hip to the side and put a hand on it. It was all bravado because she was undoubtedly nervous to search Arie's power. "If I don't pass out from the magic of a god, how could I pass out from the magic of a powerful Suden?"

Rose understood conceptually, but she was afraid this might backfire. If she couldn't handle Arie's power, wouldn't that solidify Luc's point?

"Powerful Suden indeed," Arie said. "I see you're nervous. Don't be. You can do this."

Her gaze shifted away from her work setting up the forge to Arie. "You haven't seen how tired I've been after finishing the weapons for the Osten and Vesten Points."

"Ah, but you finished them. That's my point. You have more strength than you know."

Not wanting to talk about this further without Luc present, Rose called him over. "Can you watch us? Arie asked that you join."

Luc shrugged. "Sure."

"Alright, let's get started."

They didn't have to wait long with the Vesten god fanning the flame of the makeshift forge. The fire burned so hot Rose wasn't sure she could stand close enough to work. "Could we tone it down a little, oh Lord of Flame?"

Luc coughed to cover what she was sure was a laugh.

"*Hmph*," Arie said as he pulled back the heat.

Rose sank into her magic. She was getting faster. In this case, she wasn't sure if it was the strength of Arie's power or that she had been using her abilities regularly for the last few weeks.

She felt the flame and reached for it with her power as she fell into the rhythm, working the metal before her. Her ethereal magic sprawled around them. With Luc and Arie present, it seemed unsure of where to go. The pull from Luc was always strong. But he hadn't agreed to be evaluated—Arie had. Rose sent her magic spiraling toward the black bird. His magic smelled of the forest floor and summer rain. It was like a run through the woods on a hot day, ending with a dive into a cool pond.

Fire flared around her—maybe not a cool pond, but relaxing into a hot spring. That suited the heat of his magic better.

Her magic sank into Arie's bird form, searching for the heart of his power. Flames guided her forward. They were warm but not hot—she could walk through this fire and not burn. It kept her on track, pushing her toward a goal, a memory.

She finally arrived at an immense fire, though she stood in a hallway of flame already. Carter's magic may have been a cozy campfire in the woods, but Arie's inferno could only loosely be labeled as a bonfire. It was huge and untamed. It spat and hissed as it sent sparks in all directions. One landed in her palm.

The fire touched her skin, but she knew she was safe.

She peered at the spark. It didn't go out once it touched her. It kept flaring. A scene played out in the dying light's yellows, reds, and oranges. Rose blew on it, coaxing it to burn brighter. The flame expanded, bringing the scene to life.

✴

THREE STONE TABLES sat in the depths of a mountain cavern.

A test for each remaining god to claim the vial, holding their magic, atop them.

Aterra's failure...the results more devastating than Zrak had led Arie to believe. A mountain explosion—a volcanic eruption from wild and unbalanced magic. Flashes of red cascaded—Arie and Aurora barely made it out of the cavern as it filled. Aterra, as usual, slipping away beneath the earth...

Later. The scene flashed to something new.

Arie shook his head as he and Aurora arrived at the crater that used to be Mount Bury. No matter how often they returned to it, it always looked sad. Jagged features dotted the crater's bottom. A single larger formation reached up in the center. This must be the external representation of the cavern in the heart of the mountain.

"I can't believe the test failed so spectacularly," he said.

"I don't know if we can consider it a failure. It did point out that one of us was striving for imbalance. That is what Zrak intended."

"I guess..." Arie started.

"We can't give up." Aurora took his hand and squeezed it. "I know you're disheartened that we haven't been able to find Aterra, but we can't stop looking."

Arie nodded, though he wasn't sure he agreed. If Aterra didn't want to be found, he wouldn't be found. Arie wasn't sure what they could do about it. He would follow Aurora anywhere, though, and she knew it. "Humans and fae used to come from all over the continent to the temple atop Mount Bury. What have we done to it?"

Aurora conceded the point. "I'm not sure we could have expected such a violent explosion from the test."

"Is there nothing we can do to make this better? Aterra would be the one—" He cut himself off at the thought. Aterra's earth magic would have been precisely what they needed to clean up this mess. Too bad he was also the one who'd caused it.

Contemplating his words, Aurora searched the crater. She seemed to find what she was looking for as she said, "I think I can do something." She stepped away from him and focused on whatever she had identified.

Arie peered into it with her, trying to see what she was looking at. Ah, he saw some water droplets. Barely. A mountain spring must have found its way into the bottom of the barren and desolate crater.

She called her water. Aurora was calm and commanding as

she drew more than droplets from the springs beneath the mountain. They stood on the crater's edge, and the water filled the empty basin before Arie's eyes, covering all of the rock features.

"Almost..." she murmured to herself as she worked. She opened her eyes, her gaze falling on the lake she'd created. It was deep blue and beautiful—a marvel.

"It's missing something," she said. Closing her eyes again, she pushed the water away from a section of the lake. As the water moved, the large rock formation became visible. Arie understood what she was doing—exposing an island. The water rushed around the newly excavated land, the small hill its distinguishing feature.

"I think that's much better," Aurora said.

Arie took a deep breath. The mountain air smelled a bit fresher already, with the lake water covering all manner of their sins. "I agree." His hand slipped into Aurora's, their fingers intertwining. They'd admitted their feelings for each other long ago. It was a comfort to have her strength when he started to worry about the continent's future.

Zrak was gone.

He had planned for so much, but in hindsight, Arie realized he'd told them too little.

From the test, they knew Aterra had done something to unbalance the continent—trying to bring himself more power—though they couldn't confirm how. As Zrak had warned, it was already too late when they proved he was disrupting the balance.

The Compass Points, the fae leaders they had created, were supposed to stop him, but they were more isolated than ever, each court pettier than the next. How could they be the continent's salvation? No, it was up to Arie and Aurora to do something.

"Well, isn't this a horrible picture?" a deep voice drawled behind them.

Turning, Arie saw Aterra walking the crater's edge. "Where have you been?"

"Surprised I wasn't destroyed in that explosion you caused?"

The Suden god looked at his cuticles like he had no care in the world.

"That's not quite how—"

"No matter," Aterra cut him off. "I'm sorry to disappoint. I've been looking for you." His gaze moved to Aurora.

The hair on Arie's arms stood on end. He didn't like wherever this was going.

"We've been looking for you too," Aurora said, stepping toward Aterra. "We need to discuss the results of the test."

Aterra waved away her comment, stepping closer to her. "Zrak wasn't thinking clearly when he set that up. He didn't know what he was doing."

"That's not—" Arie tried to interrupt. He'd been there when Zrak had created the test. He'd known exactly what he was doing. Aterra ignored him, moving closer still to Aurora.

Arie was increasingly uncomfortable with Aterra's proximity. Aurora was a goddess, though. She could hold her own.

"The test did what it was supposed to," Aurora continued. "It exposed that you've created an imbalance. You need to come clean about what you've done so that we can work to rectify it."

"Isn't that what your precious fae are supposed to do? Let them worry about the imbalance. That was the plan, after all."

Aurora sucked in a breath, and her eyes narrowed. "You agreed to the plan. Submit yourself to the Compass Points if that's what you prefer. We need to take care of this before things get worse. We've already seen a village taken by a dark mist in the north. Whatever you've done, it needs to stop."

"What have you done?" Arie asked, curious if Aterra would answer.

His gaze narrowed at Arie as he inched ever closer toward Aurora. He was too close to her. Arie knew it—a cold shiver ran down his spine. Aurora also seemed to realize it a second too late.

Aterra struck, his hand snaking out to her wrist.

Arie moved. He didn't know what Aterra intended. He couldn't physically hold Aurora—she was too strong. But that didn't mean he could just grab her. To Arie's shock, Aurora slumped into Aterra's grip. A slim needle sticking out of a large onyx ring on his finger drew Arie's attention, the tip sliding out of Aurora's arm.

"What did you do?" Arie yelled as he reached for Aurora.

Aurora straightened as she stood. "I'm fine, Arctos." Her voice sent another chill down his spine.

"Aurora?" he asked. She hadn't called him Arctos in hundreds of years.

Aurora was already moving past him, her hand braced on Aterra's arm as they walked toward the water's edge of the lake Aurora had created.

"Aurora, what are you..." Arie trailed them. He only had seconds to figure out what was going on. He couldn't formulate words. He didn't know what to ask. Aurora appeared to be walking of her own volition. She couldn't *want* to do whatever this was, could she? Should he stop her? He knew he was too late when Aurora stepped into the water. She used the same ring to prick Aterra's finger. Blood dripped from it to the lake, the water seeming to seal where it fell, rippling out across the water.

Then, she and Aterra disappeared beneath the surface, leaving no trace.

Arie ran after them, only to ricochet off an invisible barrier, the magic throwing him flat on his back on the crater's ridge, preventing him from following.

※

ROSE WAS FLUNG from the memory. She stumbled back from the forge into Luc's waiting arms.

"Rose?" her name was a question as he caught her.

"I'm fine," she said, her fingers moving to her temple, then to her face. She felt tear tracks on her cheeks like she'd been crying. Her gaze shifted to Arie, who still sat perched on the edge of the forge. As a bird, his face was so hard to read. She was too distracted by what she'd learned to examine his appearance. He did have a human form, though.

"Arie?" she asked.

"Yes. That's how I knew what had happened to Luc at the Solstice Ball. The same ring, the same action, took Aurora from me. Even though it appeared to be of her own free will." Arie spoke into both of their minds, although Luc still worked to piece together what he was hearing. He hadn't watched the scene by the lake like Rose had.

"But then..." She was trying to sort through what the scene meant—what memory had Aterra created for Aurora? What memories had he changed to make her think going into the lake with him was a good idea?

"We can only guess." Arie ruffled his feathers. "He must have created a memory that made her believe she needed to go in and seal it off from anyone else using Aterra's blood."

"I can't say I've tested those attributes of mind shadow, but I do think that would be possible with what I understand of the power," Luc said.

"Well, we confirmed something helpful from this horrible memory," Rose said, straightening herself. "We're definitely headed back to Lake of the Gods." Her gaze fell heavy on Luc, suddenly glad the others were at the campfire preparing the meal. "And if Aterra's blood sealed the lake..."

His brow furrowed as he replied. "Maybe it can open it as well."

CHAPTER TWENTY-NINE

"We should at least use this time to strategize," Carter said as they rode toward the crossroads. They would head north to Lake of the Gods. Arie perched on his shoulder. She hoped he had asked Carter about the power-sharing they wanted to try. They needed to confirm their suspicion before arriving at Lake of the Gods.

"What exactly are we strategizing about?" Luc asked.

"What magic combination should we try next?"

Juliette's gaze roamed between the Compass Points, finally landing on Rose.

"What do you think, Juliette?" Rose asked, drawing her into the conversation.

"We proved the Compass Points can share power across elements." Her gaze danced between Rose and Luc. "Maybe even more so than we originally thought."

"What does that mean?" Luc's voice was defensive. Rose wondered if Luc and Juliette's distrust of one another would ever wane.

"Rose could reach into your power source." Juliette narrowed her eyes at him. "It means exactly what we all should fear. We're not only sharing the magic we choose to wield, we're sharing the essence of our power. Are we allowing anyone with whom we merge elements to tap into that?" She looked to Rose.

It was a good question. "I think..." Rose considered her response. "I think we can decide who leads. Who has the opportunity to control the merged magic and the ability to dive into each of our powers." Rose scratched the side of her head. "I can't know for sure since it has only been two powers merging each time. But I certainly had to search for the connection to each of you—and how I ultimately gained access was slightly different for each."

Juliette looked thoughtful.

"Our connection was very formal, Juliette. I opened a locked door, and I imagine I could only do that because your power let me." She paused, wondering what this information would mean to the others. "Luc ceded power to me. His tunnel of magic was more of an open reservoir for my own lake of power. I had only to say I was in need, and it shared," she concluded, glancing at him.

He nodded as Juliette asked, "He did?" She must have immediately realized how her question sounded as she tried to hide her disbelief.

Luc had not missed it. "Juliette, I'm not trying to steal the other Compass Points' power. I'm not sure if you've noticed, but I have plenty of my own. Of course I let Rose lead. I insist, if we're to get anywhere in this attempt, that she is the one who leads us all."

Juliette appraised him as if she didn't know what to make of the statement, proving no matter how much progress they made as a unit, Juliette thought of Luc with distrust first, always.

Rose couldn't quite figure out the picture of Luc that Juliette held. She understood Juliette's protective instinct of the Osten and their magic. She was the sole connection to maintaining an even level of power with the other fae courts due to Zrak's sacrifice. It must be a heavy weight. But did she really expect Luc was plotting to steal her power? Did she think the same of Carter?

All Rose had ever known of Luc was the depths of his magic. And after she saw that, she noticed his hesitancy with it. She didn't expect Juliette to see his reluctance, but she thought everyone at Compass Lake knew the enormity of his power. Why would he need more?

"Those with power rarely take more because they need it," Juliette said. "They take it because they want it. They take it because no one can stop them."

Aterra was a perfect example, Rose thought. He was a god. What did he need more power for? He didn't need it—he wanted it.

She turned to Luc, whose face had gone contemplative. "I don't know how to convince you that's not what I want." He raised his hands in a gesture of surrender.

Carter, who'd been observing the conversation, stepped in. "I think we should try to merge all four of our elements. Let's let Rose lead."

While not a shock to Rose, given Luc and Juliette's conversation, she was a little surprised Carter was the one to suggest it. She didn't object. As the newcomer and one heavily wronged by Aterra, she seemed least likely to subvert their attempt to overpower him.

Juliette nodded, though she didn't say anything. Her gaze returned to the road as the compass directed them north.

"If that's what we want to try, it would be helpful if I could spend some time on today's ride trying to find the connection to your magic, Carter," Rose said. "That way, we can practice all together at camp."

Carter nodded as he looked at the others. "Is everyone able to use their element for a little bit while we ride?"

Rose smelled each of their elements flare to life. She closed her eyes immediately to start the search. Her internal lake of power was full, and she barely glanced to see Luc's dark tunnel still open on the lakebed. She didn't need to visually confirm it—she could feel it there, ready to answer her call. It may be her imagination, but his power seemed more stable since they'd established this connection.

Leaving the lake, she followed the wind to Juliette's door. It was getting easier every time she found it. She was sure she could knock, and it would open, but this wasn't what she was here to find. What was she here to find? She thought about Carter and his magic. The duality of shift and flame, the connection of the cycle of existence. What would represent the complexity of his magic? How would she connect to it?

As if brought forth by her thought, a large tree appeared on the western shore of her lake. It stood taller than those around it. She recognized it as a match of the tree under which the Vesten coin had been buried. Long, thin, draping branches covered with leaves parted to allow her entrance into a secluded spot. As she walked to the trunk, the weeping branches started swaying. Stopping her forward progress, she waited to see what it would do. The tree burst into flames around her. It burned hot and fast, incinerating the willow. The fire didn't burn her, but as it extinguished, only the ashes of the tree remained.

So much for this being the connection point to Carter. She turned to continue searching when, all too quickly, a new sprout poked through the ashes. Was a new tree growing before her eyes? It grew large and broad, just as it had been, but this time, with a tunnel through the trunk. She could see from one side of the tree to the other. She peered into the opening, wondering if she should try to walk through. As she examined it, she saw a shadow-like fabric billowing in the non-existent wind.

Sending her own breeze through the tunnel, the rippling fabric was tousled even further, but it didn't blow away, even though it had no anchor. Rose reached her hand through the opening, still a little unsure about walking through it herself. Her hand seemed enough; as she pulled it back, a small animal came through. A black cat—so similar to a form she was used to seeing Arie in.

As soon as the feline crossed through the tunnel, Carter's power flooded in.

Rose's eyes shot open, her smile wide as she locked gazes with the Vesten Point. "I found it."

※

IT WAS one thing to talk strategy and another to put it into practice. Rose knew they needed to do the latter when they made camp. Theory would get them nowhere when they found Aterra—they needed to be ready. It was another two-day ride to Lake of the Gods. They were running out of time to prepare.

Once they arrived, another host of problems would greet them. Like how to access the lake or where it would lead. She also needed Arie to test their other theory with Carter so they could be more certain of their conclusions. If power-sharing worked between Compass Point and patron god, outside of balancing Zrak's sacrifice, she felt confident they understood Aterra's plan. If not, they might be back to square one.

"Want to give this a try?" Rose asked once they set up camp.

"I'm game," Carter said, walking away from his bed roll.

Luc and Juliette stared evenly at each other for a moment. "I will try with Rose in control. I'll stop if anyone else attempts to guide our shared magic," Juliette said.

Luc nodded his agreement.

Arie came to land on Rose's shoulder. *"Tough crowd."*

Rose rolled her eyes at him and mumbled, "Not helpful," under her breath.

"So, now that you can find each of our powers, do you know what you'll do with them?" Juliette asked.

"I think a unified stream sounds easiest to visualize. I'm not sure I'd be able to wield each one individually," Rose said.

Juliette didn't seem to object.

"Okay. I will try to aim our powers at the cluster of trees over there." She pointed. "If all goes according to plan, we should be able to knock them down." Her voice elevated at the end like a question, unsure of her overall goal. She just knew their powers needed to work together. No one objected, so Rose closed her eyes and slipped down to her internal lake to open their connections.

She didn't have to dive into the water this time to alert Luc's magic that she needed it. She only nodded in its general direction, and the connection opened. Carter's tree, now that it had cycled through its life and death, stood with the weeping branches parted so the tunnel through its trunk was visible. She reached in through the hole, passing the billowing shadow fabric to make the connection, welcoming the animal that came through. It was still feline, but much larger. Rose wasn't familiar with the species, but she felt the power flowing between them. She shrugged and moved on.

Her wind led her to Juliette's door. Rose knocked. The door didn't seem ready to open. She knocked again with no response.

Opening her eyes, she tracked the sharp hissing sound as flames met water. She smelled the familiar chocolate and sandalwood of Carter's power as his fire and her water intertwined before them. She glanced behind her to see what Juliette and Luc were doing. The connection with Luc's magic was there, but it seemed to be waiting for something before it sent its element into her and Carter's joined stream.

It was a standoff. Neither moved. Rose wasn't sure which would be better—for Luc to go first or Juliette. She bet Luc wasn't sure either and was trying to let Juliette decide. Instead, Juliette averted her eyes, ignoring him. Luc shook his head as he released his power. His element poured into her lake, and the ground broke around them, sending rocks and debris flying into Carter and Rose's merged stream of power.

She glanced again at Juliette. Thinking it might be a goodwill gesture, Rose tested her control. She felt the elements tightening around each other as she sought to steer them. Pushing the stream slightly to the left and back to the right, she turned again to Juliette to ensure she was watching.

Juliette rolled her eyes at Rose's blatant display and stepped forward with the others. The smell of sage and citrus strengthened as she felt the door inside her burst open. The wind rushed through her, but it was moving too fast. Instead of uniting with the others, the wind struck through the center and broke them apart to make room for itself.

Even with the control she displayed, Rose couldn't hold all four elements together with the force of Juliette's wind. The streams diverged, and the Compass Points pulled back their powers.

"What was that, Juliette?" Carter turned to her, his hands rising to his hips.

Juliette's eyes were wide. That at least told Rose that whatever had happened wasn't intentional.

"Leave it, Carter," Rose said. If Juliette hadn't been in control of that, the last thing they needed to do was verbally attack her while her emotions were already heightened.

"No." Juliette shook her head. "No, it's his right to ask," she acknowledged. "I don't know, Carter. I think I lost control." Her gaze darted quickly to Luc.

"Don't look at me," Luc said, raising his hands in defense.

"I'm not blaming you," Juliette said, surprising herself. "What did it feel like when Rose reached for too much of your magic?"

"But I didn't—" Rose started.

"No, Rose, I'm not blaming you either," Juliette straightened, trying again to explain herself. "I am just wondering what it feels like to have lost control of too much power in this situation. Luc, you're the only one I know that's experienced it."

Luc's shoulders slumped a little, but Rose saw him recognize the value in the question. Juliette was asking for him to explain some part of his magic. She was willing to listen, and Luc seemed resolved to answer, no matter how challenging the answer might be.

CHAPTER THIRTY

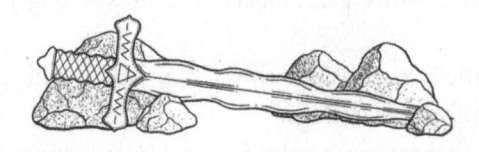

Frustrated as he was by Juliette's constant distrust, he would be a fool to pass up this opportunity. The only real question was, how did he explain losing control? The Compass Points knew of his childhood. Juliette never let him entirely forget it. They knew he could lose control, volcanically, earth-shatteringly, but they also knew of the leash he kept on his powers.

He looked at Rose, and his magic strained toward her, even as he thought about the iron grip under which he held it. She was the one person he'd lost control in front of twice in almost as many weeks, and she still hadn't feared him. Didn't fear him. By all counts, she found his lapse somehow endearing. He shook his head. It didn't have to make sense to him. He just had to accept it.

Juliette was another matter. Juliette would publicly flog him for any perceived wrongdoing. Juliette would believe the worst in him until there was no other option but to deem him not horrible. What could he even say to her to illustrate what she'd likely experienced?

"You know what? Forget it—" Juliette started.

"Wait." He held up a hand. "I'm trying to think of an answer. You must realize it's not an easy thing to describe."

That paused Juliette's retreat. She waited, arms folded over her chest.

"Did you call your magic any differently than you normally do?" Luc asked.

Juliette shook her head. "I called it the same, but its response was quite different."

"Were you"—his gaze locked on hers—"angry when you called it?"

She seemed to consider this. "No, but I will acknowledge other uncomfortable feelings."

Luc felt that response in his bones. It was never a single feeling that could be easily identified but a collection of emotions that built up to discomfort. Luc thought of the memory he'd shared with Rose. Thinking his brother was missing, seeing his brother held against his will—no matter how much he tried to convince himself that Aaron wasn't in danger—a collection of emotions shook through his body the same way he shook the earth. How could he ask Juliette to name just one? "Understood," he said. "Let's focus on that."

Juliette nodded cautiously. Rose had moved closer to his side. Her stance was unsure, like she knew he spoke of something difficult for him, but she wouldn't interrupt this time between him and Juliette by reaching out and taking his hand. Her hand stretched toward his in some internal struggle, then fell to her side as she cocked her hip toward him, getting as close as she could without interrupting—wanting him to know she was within reach.

He couldn't catch his breath as he unraveled the thought. He had someone who cared about him beyond his brother now—Rose cared for him—deeply enough to stand with him against the other Compass Points. Did Juliette have the same? Her body language told him any further questions about herself, her magic, or her life, would be unwelcome. He would have to share something of himself and hope she made the connection.

"I remember one of my big explosions as a kid. It was never

just one thing. It was a single drop of water that made a cup overflow. The kids at our village school picked on my brother, telling him his dad was a pushover, that my mom was unfaithful. Then, when I came to defend him, they told him I was an abomination and that standing too close to me would contaminate him." Luc wiped his hand down his face. He hated thinking about these stupid memories—the idiotic things children said.

"It wasn't just that I was mad at them for saying these things or confused about why Aaron was still standing there, listening. I wasn't even worried that some of it might be true. It was the utter lack of control over the situation. Nothing I could do or say would change those kids' minds. And the worst part was what they were saying had absolutely no impact on their lives. Our parents' relationship didn't mean anything to them. My unnaturalness wasn't their problem."

Luc stopped, though he had just been warming up to his rant. Rose's hand had slipped into his, somewhere around "unnatural." He looked down at their linked fingers, and his magic thrummed through his body. Unsurprisingly, Juliette's focus was also on Rose when he looked back up.

"I'm sorry," Rose said, not letting go. "I didn't mean to interrupt."

Luc could read her well enough to know she was only half sorry. Sorry her action stopped the conversation, sorry it brought his rant to a standstill, but not sorry that she showed him her support.

"I don't think she's really sorry," Arie's voice was in his head, and from Rose's eye-roll, he was sure the exact words echoed in hers too.

She squeezed tighter.

"What I'm trying to say," Luc said, "is that it feels like you can't do anything right. Anything you do makes the situation worse or at least more complicated. Everything, even your own actions, is out of your control." He paused. "And I don't envy anyone who feels that."

Silence fell as Luc finished. Was what he had said enough? He hadn't told her how to regain control, but for him, just knowing someone else struggled as he did helped. The worst thing for him as a kid had been realizing no one else lost it like he did—realizing how different he was.

Juliette nodded and said, "I think we should try again."

No one objected. The Compass Points retook their positions, Rose leading as she quickly made the internal connections. Her stream of water shot forward to the collection of trees. Luc's earth magic joined her, lifting debris and spinning around her water again. Carter's flame followed. Mixing with the others, its heat sent steam circling the combined stream.

This time, it appeared Juliette found a more graceful entry. Rose whipped Juliette's wind around the steam, tamping it back down into the pillar of elements blasting across the grass. Juliette's wind didn't break their flow. It bound them, tightening their connection, pressing them deeper together.

Rose exhaled shakily at his side. Luc glanced at her and realized that they were doing it.

She had been right. Of course she had been right. They could do this.

The Compass Points could unify their power. They found the connections to channel enough magic to challenge a god.

Rose moved their stream of elements to the left and the right. Luc felt his magic split, no longer only flowing through Rose, but another tendril circled her as she worked. He didn't pull it back or try to control it. He understood its intention and, for once, approved. It wrapped around her, encouraging her and supporting her.

She relaxed into his power as it surrounded her, giving their streams a final push against the trees she'd pointed out earlier. Their magic split a single trunk into a collection of woodchips, exploding at the force of their combined power.

They'd done it. She had done it. They would have never made it this far without her. He couldn't hold back his magic as it swept her to him, his arms already waiting to catch her. He and his magic were more in sync regarding her. It liked the internal connection it held to Rose's lake of power. He liked it too. His eyes met hers as he thought of the perfect way to celebrate this win with her. "Should we do another makeshift forge tonight?" he asked.

Rose's stare turned suspicious, likely wondering if he was really offering what she thought he was. He nodded, and her smile lit up her entire face. She could explore his power again. She could make him a weapon.

"Yes, I think we should," she replied.

※

WITH CARTER'S fire fueling the forge, Rose went to grab Luc's sword from her saddle bag. He still had a bad feeling about this, but with one look at Rose, at her excitement and desire to do this for him, he was powerless to stop her. He wanted her. He needed her, and his power was in stark agreement. Rose evaluated Arie's magic yesterday—a literal god—she could handle whatever his power was. He trusted that she knew what she was doing. He so badly wanted to believe Arie when he said Luc's magic wouldn't hurt Rose.

Rose wasted no time getting started. "I don't smell any pine or cinnamon, Luc," she called as she went to work with her hammer.

Luc didn't need to be told twice. His magic was already reaching for her. It was funny to him that she focused so much on the scent of his power. Though he was one to talk. The rosewood and vanilla scent of her magic made him forget how to breathe. He inhaled deeply, trying to take in every inch of her. The smell was all-consuming to his senses—perfectly representative of the strength and peace she brought him.

He focused on his magic, redirecting it to break a nearby rock into tiny pieces. Mentally, he sliced one sliver of the rock off after the other, as easy as a warm knife slicing through butter.

"I won't even begin to comment on what that activity says about you," Rose said as she closed her eyes, and he felt her magic surround him.

"It means that I'm precise in my control," Luc commented, letting his hand fall palm up.

"Hmph," Rose said, not opening her eyes. "More like a unique way to de-stress, which requires your full attention."

Luc folded his arms across his chest and kept slicing with his mind. He got a little rush each time he targeted and sliced off a particular rock section. She might have a point. "I'd be more than happy to give you my full attention," he replied instead, his lip curving into a smirk he knew she wouldn't see.

Carter coughed politely, indicating he was still within hearing distance. He backed up, trying to give them space but staying close enough to keep the fire hot. His green eyes danced in the firelight, though. Luc swore there was amusement in them. A flap of wings out of the corner of his eyes told him Arie had also joined them. He sat comfortably on Carter's shoulder, watching the Vesten Point fan his flame while he oversaw the experiment.

Hopefully, Arie and Carter would be up next for a magical test.

"Okay," Rose continued. "I'm going back in."

Luc wasn't sure he was ready but took another clean slice off the rock and said, "On your mark."

Rose's magic danced along his skin. It was almost as familiar to him as his own. He couldn't remember a time before he understood her magic, though in reality, that time was mere weeks ago. Her magic brought its own balance to Luc. Even as it twisted and skittered along every part of him, he knew he had nothing to fear. He relaxed into it, and her power sank into him, as if his shoulders falling was the permission it needed to make itself more welcome in his body.

Her magic swan dived into his chest cavity, burrowing into his very being. Unsure of what to expect next, he held still. Last time, she said she had been falling down a tunnel to the core of his magic.

He cut one more thin slice off the rock before a memory emerged. He knew he and Rose were watching it together.

※

HE WAS STILL uncertain about his role with the Suden Point. After Michael first came to him, they met regularly. Michael insisted on coming to Loch instead of asking Luc's family to bring him to Compass Lake.

Luc was okay with that. It was already understood in Loch that he was odd, maybe even unnatural. Michael coming to see him only solidified what they already thought. He couldn't imagine what it would be like at Compass Lake, where the courts would watch his every move. There was no need to subject himself to that kind of scrutiny.

Michael sat in his stepfather's office. When he visited, he stayed at the local inn but used the extra room Aaron's father had at their house. His stepfather worked as a magical farming strategist. On the days Michael was there, he arranged to teach in the fields. Luc thought his stepfather enjoyed his job. At least he was always excited to tell Aaron and Luc about his work with humans and other Suden, to develop new sustainable agriculture methods.

On the other end of the spectrum, Michael did not appear to like his work. He was constantly rubbing his temples or putting his forehead in his hands on the desk when he thought no one was watching. But Luc watched keenly, knowing Michael's job would be his someday.

"This will all be your problem soon enough," Michael said to Luc as he ran his fingers through his hair.

Luc didn't know how to respond. "Yes, sir."

"Don't you want to know what the problem is?" Michael asked.

"I'm not sure it's relevant, sir."

"We've talked about this. You should call me Michael when it's just us."

"Yes, si—I mean Michael," Luc said as his cheeks flushed with his mistake.

"I think it is relevant for you to know, by the way. It's relevant for you to know that your court and the other fae leaders will question your decisions at every turn." He sighed heavily. "It's relevant for you to know that many will try to use you for your influence and power. You will want to believe they are interested in you, but the hard truth is, most won't be." Michael tilted his head, considering Luc. "In your case, given the gossip about your power, you may have a separate set of problems. You will scare others. And fae don't always act rationally when they're scared. Especially if it's not a feeling they experience often."

"Are other fae afraid of you?" Luc asked. He knew his power was different, but he also thought there was something about the Suden Point position that made others wary.

"Not in the same way they will be of you." He ran his fingers through his short hair again. He had brown skin and black hair. He looked about forty, but that meant nothing in the world of the fae courts. Luc gathered that he'd been in this position for over two hundred years. His hand gestures, his fingers at his temples, or his hands through his hair, were the only evidence of his age. They were the only signs of stress, showing the weight that he carried.

"What problem are you dealing with today?" Luc asked. He needed to prove that he was more than his magic. He would be worthy of this position in other ways.

"How much do you know about the creation of the fae courts?" Michael asked.

Luc shook his head. He didn't know much beyond the fact that the gods created them to preserve balance. It never occurred to him that he'd need to learn more.

"I am the second Suden Point in the court's nearly five-hundred-year history. It will be my duty to tell you some of the mistakes of my predecessor, as well as my own."

Luc knew better than to ask what they were. He let Michael share what he wanted in his own time.

Michael nodded his approval. "When the courts were created, and after Zrak sacrificed himself, the balance of the magic was rumored to be somewhat unsteady. I have no idea whether that was true, but I know that my predecessor took it as an opportunity to try to overtake the Osten court. I guess it was either them or the Vesten as our neighbors on Compass Lake." Michael sighed. "He tried to subjugate the Osten Point, and while he failed, barely, it has given the Suden Point a bit of a legacy."

Nodding, Luc considered this. A failed coup would not be ideal for any leader. He couldn't imagine the damage it did. He was about to ask another question when there was a knock on the door.

"Who is it?" Michael asked.

"Rebecca, sir," Luc's mom replied without opening the door.

Michael gestured for Luc to get behind the couch so his mother wouldn't see him when she stepped into the room. Luc didn't question the order. He hid, and Michael invited his mother in.

"Thank you for seeing me, Michael." She searched the room, clearly deciding it was just the two of them. "I wondered if we could talk about Luc."

Michael gestured for her to continue.

"I just wonder if it would make sense for him to stay with you more permanently at Compass Lake?"

Michael's head shifted slightly, the only indication this was an unexpected inquiry. "You would be so eager to see your son away from home? In such an unfriendly place?"

His mother must have noticed her mistake as her eyes widened. "I-I—" she stammered, but Michael cut her off.

"Speak plainly."

"He doesn't fit here."

The words hit Luc like a punch to the gut, knocking the breath from his lungs.

To assume this was one thing, to hear kids taunt it was another, but to listen to his mother state it was something else entirely. He shouldn't be here. He shouldn't hear this. Why had Michael made him stay?

Michael's eyes narrowed, and his lips flattened into a straight line. Maybe he hadn't anticipated this conversation. Perhaps he regretted Luc being here for it. Michael seemed to choose his words carefully, considering what was appropriate in front of all present.

His mother had no such discernment. "He scares the villagers. And they react poorly. Loch hasn't been the same since that child died! Part of me knows it's not his fault, but he also does nothing to stop it. It's like he enjoys their fear."

Luc froze. He knew that using his power made others go away. Lately, when he was in a situation where his control was fraying, he let his magic scare away the bullies. He didn't realize his mother had noticed. But this way, he didn't lose control... No one actually got hurt, not like with... He still couldn't think about the hole without guilt swallowing him.

"I don't think being here is good for him," she said.

"Good for him or for you?" Michael asked harshly.

His magic squirmed. He wanted to defend his mother, say that of course it wasn't good for her if he was gone. That no matter what he did, she'd always have a place for him here. Her words cut off his train of thought—

"Both!" Her voice rose. Luc could see her shoulders sag after the word came out.

Michael looked at the ceiling as he let out a long breath. "Fine. He can't come to Compass Lake, but we can start him at the Suden military academy in Sandrin. It's a few years earlier than I intended, but at least they'll want him there." Michael choked on the last thought as if he hadn't intended to say it aloud. His gaze darted to where Luc hid.

Rebecca's gaze followed, finally recognizing the shock of black hair barely visible behind the couch. Her hand covered her mouth, and she fled the room.

※

THE MEMORY ENDED, and Luc opened his eyes. He was staring into Rose's. She waited for his acknowledgment and then wrapped her arms around him. He looked over her shoulder. She had made quite a bit of progress on the sword now cooling beside the fire.

CHAPTER THIRTY-ONE

Rose couldn't decide if she was wildly excited that she'd been able to dive back into Luc's magic without issue or if she was heartbroken on his behalf over what she'd seen. She understood power like his didn't make childhood easy, but she thought, from the way he was with Aaron, that his family had been supportive throughout. The scene she'd seen last night told another story. Maybe his mother thought she was supporting him in the only way she knew how—by getting him away. Or perhaps she was overwhelmed by his power. No wonder Luc's expression had been so complicated when he first told her about his mother's passing.

"It's okay, Rose." Luc rode beside her. He must have been watching her thoughts swirl for a while before interrupting.

She looked at him. "I was just trying to see things from her perspective." Rose shrugged.

Luc's eyes widened in surprise. "I'm not sure I was expecting that."

Rose smiled. He probably expected her to be boiling with rage. "I may still land on anger. Please don't commit me to an emotion just yet," she replied.

"I think I expressed my opinions on the matter yesterday. It's never just one thing."

Rose reached out her hand for his. "I am sorry you had to leave home so young."

He squeezed her hand, letting it fall quickly since they were both on horseback. "I think it was right for me. I'm unsure about her reasons, but the fae were more accepting of me at the military academy. I'm sure it was because they saw my power as an asset, but...it was still a nice change."

The Suden there would have started with a healthier amount of fear and respect for Luc. She could see how that would be preferable to kids who grew up with him and were used to getting away with bullying him. Not sure there was a correct answer, she set the thoughts aside. "I'm happy with the progress we made on your weapon yesterday," she said, changing topics. "I think I only need one more session."

Luc nodded. "Are you..." He hesitated. "Are you ready to be back at Lake of the Gods?"

Arie landed on Rose's shoulder speaking to both her and Luc. *"I'd like to know that, too. About both of you."*

Rose gave Arie a sidelong glance. "I'm fine. It's Luc we should worry about." She glared at the bird. "If you would prove the power share goes both ways ahead of time, maybe we would be more prepared."

"Don't get mad at me because you're scared for your"—he waved his wing at Luc, batting Rose's face in the process—*"whatever he is. Your connection has grown stronger in the short time I've been gone."* Arie noted.

Rose agreed, but how could Arie know that simply by looking at them? "What does that mean?" she asked.

"Have you even asked Carter yet?" Luc cut off Rose's line of questioning. She didn't miss the suspicious look Arie gave to Luc.

Arie flew over to Carter's shoulder, effectively cutting off Rose and Luc from his conversation.

"How are you handling being back here?" Luc asked.

"Fine." She shrugged. The village of Bury loomed before them. She said she'd been ready for it but wasn't sure that was true. It didn't matter that she had saved the villagers of Compass Lake or helped save other villages in their travels. Her failure here lingered. If she tried to get more information from Luc at the market, would she have believed her weapons were vital to defending against the mist plague? Would it have helped Tara if she had one of Rose's magical weapons with her?

She urged her horse forward into the mist that still hung over Bury. Luc still had a borrowed weapon, and everyone else had protection. There was no need to hesitate. Her gaze roamed down the path that led to the barn on the outskirts of town. That was where Tara had been waiting for Rose when the mist plague struck. She shook her head. Going to see her sleeping form would do her no good. It would only delay them.

She watched Luc open his mouth—likely to ask if she wanted to see Tara—and close it just as quickly as she'd resolved herself forward. Her shoulders straightened, and her gaze returned to the path before them.

"Carter, I wonder if I could ask something of you." Arie's voice spoke to the entire group as they trekked slowly out of the village and onto the crater trail.

His enthusiastic nod gave him away. The Vesten Point was far too eager for his patron's attention. Rose stretched her neck from side to side as she considered what she was about to do.

"We'd like to test something. I'll be honest: I don't know what will happen, and it will be a considerable risk to you."

Rose smiled. She shouldn't have worried about Arie. Of course he would lay it all out for the Vesten Point. Arie wasn't a power-hungry god or one who dismissed the needs of those around him. He wouldn't try to use Carter to further his own power permanently. Arie would help them get the proof they needed to confirm Aterra's plan—before sending Luc into the Lake of the Gods. Assuming he could even access it.

"I can do whatever you need, Lord Arctos," Carter said.

"I think you should get all the facts before agreeing," Rose said.

"She's right," Arie said. "We want to test the bond between Compass Point and patron god. From Juliette's ritual with Zrak, we understand that blood has to be shared. If the test is successful, it will enhance my power. I, in turn, can pass that on to the Vesten fae, or I can keep it for myself."

"That's quite a hypothesis. We would prove whether all Compass Points and patrons have the connection Juliette described?"

"You weren't aware of it, Arctos?" Juliette asked. She'd been listening intently. She seemed so sure it applied to everyone.

"We never discussed it. We went through many details before creating the fae and in the weeks after. Zrak, especially, prepared me for all manner of contingencies. I'm not sure how well you know him through your connection..." Arie paused as if waiting for the Osten Point to fill in his gap.

She didn't.

"Well, he was—is," Arie corrected, "a planner. He had plans for everything and told them to the god he thought most likely to need them. In most cases, that was me." Arie ruffled his feathers. "I can't imagine him leaving this loophole without telling us."

"Maybe you don't know the Osten god as well as you thought you did," Juliette replied coolly.

Arie bristled again. "That may be true, which is why I propose this test."

"Why are you so intent on testing this now?" Juliette's eyes scanned Arie, Rose, and Luc. She noted as Rose's gaze trailed to Luc.

Carter ignored Juliette's question, asking one of his own. "So, you don't know if it will work, but do you think it will?"

"I am not sure. I want to think it won't—but I fear it will."

"I'll do it."

"Are you sure?" Rose asked. "We don't know what the outcome will be. Arie could become the next Aterra—seeking his own power and bringing further imbalance to the continent."

"*I—*"

"Ahhh," Juliette cut off Arie's outrage. "You are testing this to see if this is what Aterra has planned for the Suden Point? You think...what? That he will take all of Luc's power for himself?"

Rose bit her lip. They hadn't told Juliette and Carter about Luc's specific hypothesis. Rose told herself they didn't need to share it until it was confirmed—it was still just suspicion. But with Juliette asking so blatantly about it, she couldn't evade answering.

"I think it's more than that, Juliette," Luc said. "I think he made me precisely because of how power can transfer between god and Compass Point."

Juliette sucked in a breath. "Made you..."

Rose saw the pieces slide into place, the time Aterra spent among the Suden that Kenna deemed inappropriate. Luc's unexplained power and lack of paternal claim.

Luc nodded at Juliette's unspoken conclusion. "We'll be at the lake soon enough. If I am Aterra's blood, I should be able to access it." He paused. "But after that, I'd like to know what he could do with me before heading straight toward him."

"I said I'll do it," Carter cut in again. He glared at Juliette, stopping her from giving a sarcastic reply. He turned his head back to Arie on his shoulder. "May I have some of your blood for the ritual?"

※

THEY WOULD DO the test once they got to Rose's island. Rose hadn't missed Juliette's talk of wild magic in the cave where she met Zrak.

Arie latched onto it as well. "*If wild magic is required, there is nowhere better than the center of Lake of the Gods.*"

"The center of the lake?" Carter asked. They were on the

crater trail, headed toward the lake's edge. "The island? I thought the lake had a magical barrier."

Rose smiled. "Our path is just ahead."

"The lake is just ahead," Carter said, jumping off his horse as the trail grew narrower.

Juliette's gaze lingered on Rose before looking out to the lake, landing on the island.

It didn't surprise Rose that she'd figured it out—she had experience with this mode of transit, after all. "I have a portal just ahead that will take us to the island. That's where I lived."

Carter's eyes widened, but he didn't object.

She first took them through in groups of two. This was the most fae that had been on the island. She wasn't sure she liked the feeling. It was her space—hers and Arie's. While she had been intrigued by Luc investigating her home, she had no such interest in Carter and Juliette's assessment.

They gave it to her anyway.

"This is unique," Carter said.

Juliette snorted. "It's impressive," she said. "Not that we expect anything less from you at this point."

"Where are we going to do this? Do we need anything else besides blood and wild magic?" Carter asked, his gaze darting between Juliette and Rose.

"Juliette has the Osten Artifact when she does it. I'm not sure if that is a requirement."

Carter reached into his pocket. As Rose suspected, the coin was never far from him. "I have the Vesten artifact."

"Then it is your blood, Arctos's blood, and your will," Juliette said.

"What about my will?"

"You have to be a willing participant in this. I don't know what form it will take for you, but you will feel it in your magic. You'll have to cede some of your strength to Arctos."

"What?" Rose glanced at Juliette.

Juliette nodded. "It's not just strengthening the god's power, it's weakening your own—for a time." She looked around at the others. "We should all know—better than others—that magic seeks balance. If we give power to a god, that power must come from somewhere."

What Juliette said made perfect sense. It was heartbreaking to Rose in a new way. Had Aterra created Luc to destroy him? To drain his power? Rose couldn't imagine the result going well for the Compass Point if too much magic was given.

"Let's stop guessing and try," Carter said as if understanding the silence that met Juliette's statement. "Lord Arctos, would you allow me some of your blood?"

Arie transformed into a black cat and quickly nicked his paw, smearing drops of his blood into Carter's open palm. Carter didn't hesitate as he cut himself in return, allowing their blood to mix. He placed the coin in the same palm and closed his fist.

"Now I will it?" he asked, looking at Juliette.

"You'll know in a moment," she replied, stepping back.

Carter's body jolted. His knees buckled, hitting the ground. Rose moved toward him, but Juliette grabbed her arm and held her back. "He won't have control of this the first time. We should give him space."

Rose didn't have time to reply as fire erupted from Carter's hands. In some last-minute instinct, he seemed to force the flame skyward.

The black cat's tail flicked. It paused mid-swing, the only indication that something might be wrong. Rose tried to get to him. Power flared around them. This wasn't right.

Arie's hackles rose, his hair standing on end as he grew before their eyes. Formerly a small cat, his size now matched a bear. But this animal was still wholly feline. Dark brown fur was striped with deep red as it shook itself in its new shape.

"A veil beast," Juliette said, shock evident in her hushed tone. "But they're extinct."

Its tail swished back and forth as it stalked around the

Compass Points. The movement of the beast's tail seemed to count the moments before the predator struck.

"Arie," Rose called, still held in place by Juliette's grasp. The feline looked familiar. It was similar to the animal she saw when she made the internal connection to Carter's magic.

"Carter?" Luc called. The Vesten Point's pillar of fire was still burning hot.

Arie, in the new animal form, snarled, showing more teeth than Rose preferred, exposing elongated canines perfect for tearing into flesh.

"Carter!" Luc tried again. Carter's magic didn't falter at the call. If anything, he seemed to be pouring more magic into it.

"He is funneling too much of his magic into Lord Arctos," Juliette said. "We need to get him to cut it off."

The ground beneath Carter shook as Luc took action. Carter tipped from his knees, catching himself with his hands in the dirt. This distraction broke him free of the exchange. The giant feline beast gave pause, his tail halting mid flick.

"Arie?" Rose asked cautiously.

"*Yes, yes, I'm here,*" he said as he sat back on his hind legs and seemed to shake off the magic, like a cat shaking off drops of water. Rose felt the power Arie shook off as it made a beeline for Carter. The Vesten Point seemed to stretch and flex as he reabsorbed it. Arie shrank down to the small black cat he started as and began casually licking his paw. The action was so at odds with the beast previously before her, she couldn't help but laugh.

"Everyone okay?" Luc asked.

A chorus of nods answered him, though no one seemed ready to put the experiment into words yet.

"Is a veil beast the same as a veil cat—the animal responsible for ferrying spirits beyond the veil? I thought those were myths," Rose asked.

"You should know by now that most myths are rooted in some kind of reality." Carter gestured to the necklace chain that held her compass. "But yes, they're the same. While definitely feline, most found veil cat too tame a name. So, most know the animal as a veil beast."

"Juliette, did you say they were extinct?"

Juliette nodded. "I believe the Lady of the Veil killed them all in an attempt to more tightly control her plane."

"So why did Arie turn into one?"

Arie in cat form glanced at Carter, his yellow-green eyes piercing. Rose could have sworn he smirked before going back to licking his paws.

"I guess it was the boost of power," Carter said cagily. His gaze darted to the ground. Rose was sure he wasn't telling the whole truth, but she wouldn't push it. They had proven what they needed. The sharing of power could be done between any of the Compass Point-patron pairings.

They knew Aterra's plan.

The group went their separate ways momentarily as they tried to collect their thoughts. Rose followed Luc as he meandered to the lake's edge.

"Luc," she called.

He stopped and turned. His hands were behind his back, almost as if he'd been hoping to sneak away but got caught.

She put her hands on her hips but didn't say a word.

He sighed. "Now that we know that worked, I just thought, maybe, I could get to the lake's edge and test the next part without"—he gestured around—"everyone watching."

She couldn't fault him for that. "I'm not sure I'll let you sneak away until we finish this sword. I'll feel better knowing you have it."

"I'll feel better having it with me." His power circled her as he spoke. She was sure his magic would be pleased to have a part of hers with him. It seemed to caress her skin in unspoken agreement.

"Let's see if the others are settled. I'll tell them we need a little time to finish your weapon, and then we can find Aterra and end this."

CHAPTER THIRTY-TWO

"This session should finish it—any final worries about what I'll see?" Rose asked as they entered her workshop. She didn't realize how much she'd missed it until they were there.

The large, open room carved out of the inside of a hill on the island was where she had made her home—and stayed connected to Mom after losing her. Her gaze roamed to the most prominent piece in the room: the forge. The fire was already burning hot. Arie had started it for them once he had collected himself. He didn't need to stay close to keep the flame going.

"I've got nothing to hide from you, Rose," Luc said, stepping toward her. "I've only ever been worried about your safety." He stretched his fingers as if he were looking at the power in them. "You, and I guess my magic, have convinced me you'll be safe." He paused. "Is there anything you're afraid to see?"

She gave that question the eye-roll it deserved.

"I see." His laugh was low and soft, sending sparks through her entire body, though she hadn't touched him yet.

"You aren't worried about finishing this without being at Suden house?" he asked.

"Not with you." They didn't even have the Suden artifact to

use, like she'd used the Vesten coin with Carter. She smiled softly. She knew she didn't need it. "Making magical weapons is all about understanding a wielder's magic. Most of the time, that can only be done when the magic is interacting with the source." She shook her head slowly. "I've seen your magic at the source. But honestly, I've come to understand it more each day we've traveled together." She paused before asking her next question. Her magic reached for his, even as she pondered it. "What did Arie mean when he said our connection had strengthened?"

Luc glanced away before returning to her, his gaze penetrating. "Do you feel it?" His voice was quiet, not its usual asserting tone. Whatever he was asking—it meant something to him.

"Feel a connection between us?" she asked. "Of course." She moved closer to him, invading his space and cupping his cheek. The urge to touch him was so strong.

"What does it feel like?" he asked.

She didn't hesitate. "You're the first thing I sense when I walk into a room. Your magic behaves like an extension of myself at times, considering my needs before I even think of them." She thought of the workshop and how it had held her as she worked. She thought of more playful events, catching them as they fell to the ground in each other's arms because she was too impatient to take her lips from his. Her pulse spiked as the memory of that night flooded into her mind. Luc must have been thinking of it too. A tendril of his magic snaked around her.

"Sorry," he whispered, stepping away from her touch, pulling his magic with him.

She shook her head and reached for him again. Pausing before her hand touched his skin, waiting for the nod he gave her.

"My magic has never been like this with anyone before. It's not even this protective of Aaron and the children."

Rose felt it wrap around her again as their hands reconnected, pulling their bodies flush together. "What does mine feel like to you?" she asked.

"It's less insistent," his lip twitched, and his power flared at his word choice. "But no less present." His head tilted. "You must have restrained yourself quite a bit to keep from asking me daily if you could evaluate my magic. Because I felt your desire to do so constantly."

"I'm sorry." Rose flushed. She had wanted to evaluate his power, but she had respected his need to figure out his relationship with it before throwing herself back into the mix.

"Don't be," he replied. "Your magic's reaction to my power was not something I'm used to. Fear, uncertainty, and caution are more the norm. It was good for me to see your undiluted desire for my magic." He paused. "I don't think you've ever feared it."

"Not for a second."

He reached for her then, his hand cupping the back of her neck, as he pressed his lips to hers. Softly, at first. A slow exploration of everything they were to each other.

He hadn't exactly answered her question about their connection. Maybe he didn't know. Whatever was between them was strong, the feeling soul-deep. It harkened back to romance stories and bound fae—while impossible for them, the idea of a perfect match, a bond between powers, was a dream she had kept tucked away. He adjusted his grip to coax a better angle for the kiss as his tongue swept in. Heat swirled through her as she nipped at his lip.

This—what she had with Luc—was better than any dream. He kissed her again, leaving no time to catch her breath as their magic swirled around them. Her hands wrapped around his neck, running through his hair. His fingers skidded down her side, clasping her hip and pulling them tighter.

He broke the kiss, leaving her heart pounding and her body longing for more. His smile was soft, one he saved only for her. His words were not—they cut through the haze and the growing smell of pine and cinnamon as his magic spread through the room. "I love you, Rose."

The words felt natural, as if he'd whispered them to her a hundred times before—maybe he had. He had with every time his magic lent her strength. Every time he handled the more mundane tasks of their trip to give her a chance with Juliette. Every time he held her as they drifted off to sleep under the stars.

"I love you too." The words were right as they slipped from her lips. Her gaze held his. He looked inexplicably surprised at her response before his lips turned up into a smile that lit the room brighter than any forge fire. His voice was decadent, reminding her of their first meeting as he leaned forward again.

"I'm glad to hear it." His easy confidence returned as his hand cupped the side of her face and brought his lips back to hers.

This kiss wasn't searching—it was claiming. It was scorching as their tongues tangled, deepening their connection with every stroke. They'd done this before, but he explored her like this was uncharted territory. Perhaps it was.

Their magic spread through the workshop, echoing their movements, intertwining in something deeper than an evaluation. She sucked in a breath as she felt their power sink together, unaided.

She broke the kiss momentarily, her focus on magic reminding her why they were here. A weapon—she needed to finish his weapon. She could multitask. "I am going to do the final evaluation on your magic." Her mouth brushed his again. She swore she heard him growl as her teeth tugged at his bottom lip. "But don't stop this." She gestured between them. "It'll help." She winked at him as she pressed another kiss to his lips.

He understood the assignment as his lips moved from hers to her neck, nipping and sucking every inch of skin he could find. She held in a moan as his lips found that spot behind her ear.

Her magic wrapped tightly around his body, pressing them further together, sinking under his skin. His power rushed to follow. This exploration was more a formality than a necessity. She already knew the answer—she understood his magic like her own. Experiencing it with Luc, though, she couldn't pass that up. His power took the lead and pulled her through the familiar tunnel. Scenes flashed by her as she fell, familiar faces now, Aaron,

Michael, his mom and stepfather—her. Fearlessly, she went further toward the heart of his power.

Time passed. Beyond the scenes of his life, she fell into a darkness like none she'd experienced. It was a comforting unknown. Here, his magic finally stopped, asking her to spread her power and feel him—all of him.

Her eyes fluttered, and she whispered, "I found it," as she felt his lips brush hers in the present reality.

Closing her eyes tightly again, she sank back to where their magics knit together in the darkness. His power was no mystery. It was insistent and could be overwhelming, but it cared for its own. Luc was the same. He could intimidate, and he could terrify. But he was searching for something *softer*. A place where he didn't have to. His magic could create safety if given the chance, and he fought to secure it for himself and those he loved.

And she was one of those he loved.

As he was one of hers.

Her breath caught with a swell of emotion that overcame her as she concluded her evaluation.

She kept her eyes closed and stepped away from him in the workshop, pulling her magic back. It seemed to return to her through her internal lake of power instead of his tunnel. She didn't have time to consider what this meant as she poured her feelings and understanding into the blade before her. She knew what Luc needed—she'd known all along. It was the part of him that she'd been drawn to.

A weapon that could help him create that safe space for his loved ones. He was a weapon—his power was a weapon. This blade would amplify his intention to not have to be—to find another path.

She lost track of time as she worked.

He moved toward her. His steps faltered as she took a final swing, pushing the last pieces of power into his weapon. She felt his arms cage her from behind, his body staying carefully out of danger.

She leaned into his strength and the rich smell of his magic still floating throughout the forge. It surrounded her. She sealed the essence of it into the blade and carefully cooled it with her magic. The heat in his gaze set her senses on fire. The moment the sword was out of her hands, Luc's mouth was back on hers.

Their magics' newfound intimacy was apparent in their kiss. His tongue slid over hers, and their power circled every point at which they made a physical connection. Luc's hands ran down her body. His magic followed, leaving a current that felt like a physical thing in its wake.

Rose yanked him towards her, needing no distance between them like there was no distance between their magic now. The connection was something she never thought possible, something she couldn't put words to. Deepening their kiss, their magic swept again around them. Rose had the good sense to walk Luc backward, moving away from the fire. Her lips didn't leave his longer than necessary to open her eyes and ensure they didn't crash into anything in the workshop.

Her wind swept around them, clearing a corner of the shop, and weapons flew off the wall as she pressed Luc against it. Hot and demanding, his mouth trailed down her neck again, distracting her as he spun them, her back now pressed against the mountain cavern. She didn't mind as his hands slipped under her shirt to tug it over her head. His lips found her exposed breasts. He worshiped her, his mouth sucking as his tongue teased her peaked nipple. She leaned back, her fingers running through his hair, pulling him closer.

His mouth moved across her skin, and she reached for him. She groaned when she realized he was still clothed. She needed less between them—nothing between them. Their magic swirled in agreement with her unspoken thought.

"I need you," she said. "Now." Their entangled limbs rushed to finish undressing, another moan slipping from her as his fingers caressed her flesh. "Luc," she cried as two fingers eagerly plunged inside her—her body more than ready for him. Her voice was unrecognizable as she urged him on.

"You certainly don't have to beg, Rose," he said with a wicked smile. He chuckled as his magic lifted her from the ground. His hands moved to grip her waist, her legs wrapped around his torso, and he brought them together.

She gasped as their bodies joined, the rightness of their physical connection more than she could take. His power held her, allowing his hands to roam as he set a steady pace.

His magic was everywhere, along with his hands, teeth, and lips. His power—an additional whisper over her bare skin—caressed her as they moved together. She sank into the thick essence of it around her, trusting herself to its hold. The grip of her legs loosened around Luc's waist as she angled her hips. He had her exactly where he wanted her, his fingers teasing that bundle of nerves as he thrust into her. Each stroke had her body tightening—her pleasure building. He caught her moan of release with his lips in another claiming kiss. Her toes uncurling, her body softening was all he needed. His fingers tightened again on her waist as he followed her over the edge.

CHAPTER THIRTY-THREE

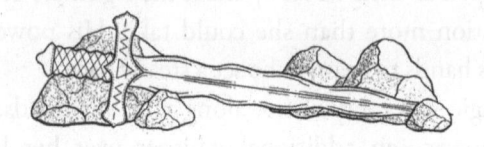

Luc wasn't surprised to find Carter, Arie, and Juliette waiting by the water after they emerged from the workshop.

So much for testing this without everyone watching.

He tucked his chin and strode forward. No one would get the satisfaction of seeing him hesitate. The sword Rose made was still warm at his hip. The familiarity of his magic radiated through the steel.

He touched the sword hilt reverently. Her magic still lingered on it. He might like that most of all. It wasn't so much a surprise as a confirmation of what he knew. He'd learned not to underestimate her—and he hadn't—but he was sure their *bond* had driven her power to new heights.

It shouldn't be possible—but there it was.

His finger caressed the sword hilt again as he walked. As much as he didn't want to admit it, he was glad to have this weapon for the battle that was sure to come. No matter what he was to Aterra, or Aterra's plans for him, he wanted his power to be a weapon the Compass Points could wield. The way the sword pulsed with a mix of his and Rose's magic would only make that easier.

His magic reached toward the lake as his steps brought him closer to the island beach. As if it knew what this test would prove. Rosewood and vanilla hit his nose. Her magic reached for his. Her magic had just had him—all of him. His lip twitched in satisfaction as he realized it wanted more.

Her fingers intertwined with his, slowing his progress. He should have known Rose would be exactly where he needed her. She tugged him back, stopping his trek to the water. He got a minute to breathe without Carter, Juliette, and Arie staring at him and wondering if he was nervous. He turned to face her, and noted the sly smile lighting her face. She was most breathtaking when mischievous.

"Have you thought about what you will do if it works?" she asked. Her voice was low, loud enough only for him.

He shook his head. He was usually very thorough, but this had him out of sorts. He had given up wondering who his father was at the age of ten—convincing himself that his past no longer mattered when his future clearly held the position of Suden Point. He had been an idiot. And he was still suppressing his emotional turmoil now.

Thankfully, Rose knew it too.

"I thought not." She took a deep breath. "We're searching for something in the lake that can lead you elsewhere. It might be an entrance to a structure, but it could also be a portal. Let's not rule anything out."

Luc nodded. His gaze roamed to her lips as she spoke. He wanted to kiss them again, even though they still held a faint imprint of his teeth.

"I'm going to keep the water away from your head when you dive in, so you can breathe. This will last through anything except a portal. If you get transported away from the lake, my magic won't hold. Think about that before diving into the unknown."

Luc couldn't stop the crooked grin from crossing his face. She was worried about him. Of course she would be. This was a scenario she wasn't great with. She had to wait on the shore while he went exploring. She much preferred to do things for herself.

"Are you going to be okay?" he finally asked.

"I think I'm supposed to ask you that," she said.

"We both know it's harder to wait than to be the one with the next assignment."

"I'll be fine." She glanced at the others. "Just make sure you come back as soon as you can."

They were no longer speaking in hypotheticals. It wasn't about what would happen if this worked. This would work—his blood would work—and he had to find where Aterra had taken Aurora before returning to her.

He nodded again. "I should go. One more check of the compass?"

She tugged the chain out and held the compass in her palm. It spun in a slow circle, not holding a final direction. "I don't know what that means regarding where Aterra is." She shrugged. "I'm no longer sure finding him is what I want most. I want you to do what you need to and return to me so we can end this together."

Luc squeezed her hand.

"Find a way to bring us to whatever you discover." She let out a breath.

Maybe this pause was for her as much as it was for him.

"Did I give you enough time to catch your breath?" She winked at him.

His lips turned up into a smirk as he replied, "I'm going to say this was for both of us."

They walked hand in hand to the beach. Luc turned and gave Rose an all-too-brief kiss before stepping past the invisible barrier. His boot was wet from the lake before it even occurred to him that he should take it off. But that was just a tangent his brain was taking him down to avoid the main event.

He had stepped into the Lake of the Gods.

He was Aterra's son.

His sword belt slung low on his waist, heavy with its prize, but he took off his cloak, boots, and top layer. With a final glance at Rose, he dove into the Lake of the Gods. Rose's magic wrapped around his head, pushing the water far enough back to give him space to breathe. A cool wind brushed his mouth as her wind magic provided fresh air for his bubble. He sucked in another breath as he kicked deeper into the lake.

Her magic felt like an extension of his own. There was no hesitation in his strokes—he knew her power would keep him breathing. Was this what she felt about his magic? How could she when it was inherited from the god who had brought only devastation to her life? The god who had killed her family, who had tried to kill her? He shook his head as he swam further down.

She didn't see him that way. His actions were his own, she had told him. He just needed to believe it.

He would do nothing to help Aterra further imbalance the continent. They had proved that a Compass Point could strengthen their patron, but only with the artifact, their blood, wild magic, and, importantly, their will. Luc was Aterra's blood; he proved it by passing the Lake's barrier, which meant their blood was already joined. The Lake of the Gods housed a wild magic like Juliette described, and Aterra had the Suden ring, his artifact. But Luc would never give his power voluntarily.

The thought made him sick—that Aterra had created him to make his power greater. If that was the case, why had he done so little to pursue Luc since he came into his power? That didn't sit well with him. He remembered the scene he shared with Rose—the first time he met Aterra—he seemed to have nothing but patience. An unshakeable belief that they would put Luc's power to better use—eventually. Maybe that was the timeline of gods. Luc had existed for thirty years, but Aterra had been planning this for hundreds.

He pushed the thoughts from his mind as he swam. The

bottom of the lake was almost in sight. He wanted to search it and work his way back up.

Dark thoughts crept back in as his gaze roamed what he could only describe as an underwater mountain with Rose's island sitting atop it. Was he even supposed to be Suden Point? He only existed because Aterra sought to disrupt the balance. Was there someone else on the continent with a more normal but respectable Suden power? Michael had retired early because his power had been so great. While Michael had said he wasn't angry about that, Luc was never really sure. Most in power weren't so happy to be pushed aside. But his claim was undeniable.

He thought of the Suden he met in Loch, the one whom the mist had displaced—Darren. His earth magic had been strong. How many others like him existed in Luc's generation?

A new ache in his arms reminded him of how long he had been swimming. He moved toward the bottom of the underwater mountain. As far as he could see, it was the lake's only feature below the surface. It was jagged, with dark areas that could easily be tunnels or holes holding portals. He would have to investigate each of them. If he were Aterra, he would hide an entrance to a prison somewhere in there. It provided plenty of natural cover, and from what he gathered of Arie's story—there was once a cavern in the heart of Mount Bury—if any of it still existed, it would be inside this feature.

He kicked closer to the mountain, poking his head into every crevice. His earth magic sprawled, searching for any weak points or tunnels with hidden depths. It found something. A hole large enough to swim into. The tunnel narrowed, giving him less room to maneuver, but he knew this was what he was looking for.

The tunnel veered up, and he followed. His head finally breached the water. The cavern walls were dark, but his eyes locked on the shape of a door directly before him.

He shook himself dry as he walked across wet sand to the entrance. The wild magic of this place settled over him. His power flared, and his leash, no matter how tight, couldn't contain it with the area's influence. The air felt thin around him. This had to be the place Arie had shown Rose—big magic, explosive magic, was enacted here—the ramifications were palpable. What would Carter see here? Lore was unclear about where and how spirits passed beyond the veil. That was part of its mystery. But the connection here to something other was intense.

The hair on the back of his neck tingled as he reached for the door handle. A momentary hesitation had him wondering if this was what Rose feared—would this door be a portal through which she'd be unable to follow? He dismissed the thought as soon as it surfaced. Aterra wouldn't go anywhere else. He would get a perverse feeling of power from being precisely beneath where Arctos had settled with Rose.

Gripping the handle, he twisted it open.

CHAPTER THIRTY-FOUR

"*He'll be fine.*" Arie landed on her shoulder. She wasn't sure how much time had passed since Luc disappeared below the water. Hours? More? That pit in her stomach widened as she considered everything that could have gone wrong.

They hadn't talked about how long he would search. Or what he would do if he found something. Had he been portaled away? They didn't have a way to go after him if he didn't return. She breathed deeply, grounding herself. This had been their only option. He was the only one who could search the lake. She clenched her fists at her side as she reminded herself that she trusted his judgment. She latched on to Arie's reassuring weight on her shoulder as she released another breath.

A splash tore her eyes from their thousand-yard stare at the point where Luc had disappeared. A dark head of hair broke the water's surface. Tension left her body, her fingers stretching. Luc was back.

"*I told you,*" Arie said as she swatted him away. She ran to the lake's edge, almost forgetting the invisible barrier. Luc stepped onto the beach before she hit it and caught her in his arms.

"You're okay," she whispered into his neck.

"*No Aurora?*" Arie asked, his disappointment evident. He must have spoken to them all as Luc responded.

"I found her, but I couldn't bring her with me," Luc said, breathless from his swim. "I think I need your help to break into her prison."

"Well, how do you expect to manage that?" Juliette asked, wandering back to the shore.

"Aurora. She gave me a way. She told me what Aterra does to bring others down there."

"Others?" Rose asked. "Who else is down there?"

"Aiden, of course," Juliette answered for Luc.

Luc nodded. "Aiden was there."

"Okay," Rose said, still unsure how she was supposed to feel about her childhood best friend. He was responsible for the death of her family, of those she held dear. She would never forgive him for it. His selfishness had put the continent at risk, allowing Aterra unprecedented access to control the inner workings of fae and humans.

Yet, how much choice did he have after his initial childhood mistake? Weeks of sorting through these feelings hadn't brought her clarity. She would have to go with her gut when she saw him.

As if reading her jumbled thoughts, Luc said, "We can leave him there. Aterra isn't possessing him—or he wasn't when I saw him."

Rose shrugged. It was all she could do for the moment.

"*What did Aurora tell you?*" Arie asked, his focus clear.

Luc looked at Rose. "Do you have Aurora's dagger with you?"

She nodded. She always had it on her person. She reached into her boot to retrieve it and then handed it to him. There was no time for her to object as he slashed it across his palm. He hissed at the pain, wincing as blood beaded to the surface of the cut.

"What are you—" Rose tried to ask, but Luc had already

started dabbing his blood with his index finger and held it out to her mouth.

"You have got to be kidding me," Rose said.

"I assure you, I'm not," Luc replied, offering her his finger again.

She closed her eyes and licked it. He moved to each of the other Compass Points, offering a drop of his blood. "If you have even a little of my blood in you, the barrier will let you in."

"I'm glad someone else is dabbling in human magic," Juliette said, unphased, as her tongue snaked out to collect the drop. Carter did not look pleased but must have realized he had little option. It was Arie who hesitated. Arie, who, moments ago, would do anything to get back to his love.

"*You want me to consume Aterra's blood?*" His disgust was apparent.

Rose hadn't thought of it like that. Though, they hadn't addressed the unassailable fact of Luc's lineage since he returned. It seemed too easy to have asked Arie to let it go, to let them take care of the threat and not waste time on Luc's parentage.

"Do you want to see Aurora or not?" Luc asked, nonplussed.

Rose lifted her hand to cover the smile that crept over her face. It was as if Luc had had that line ready and waiting for Arie's objection.

"*She told you to say that, didn't she?*" Arie said flatly as his tongue flicked out from his beak.

Luc's smirk was answer enough.

"Are you planning to swim as a bird?" Rose asked.

"*I'll take care of myself,*" he said, ruffling his feathers.

"Alright then, are we all ready?" Luc asked.

"Do you mind, uh"—Carter glanced around, uncertainly—"at least telling us what to expect? Where will we swim? What will we need to do? Will we even be able to communicate when we're down there?"

"Oh, right," Luc said. "Funny story." He looked between Rose and Arie. "There is an underwater mountain just below this island that leads into a cavern in Mount Bury." His gaze stayed on Arie. "If I had to guess from what you told us, and what Rose described, it is the cavern where you, Aurora, and Aterra took your original test."

That did not sound like a funny story to Rose. By the flap of Arie's wings, he didn't think it was funny either.

"*Right below us?*" Arie asked. "*We've been on top of them this whole time?*"

Luc nodded. "Just head straight down. Follow me, and I'll lead us to the entrance. Once we're in the heart of the mountain, we'll be able to speak freely."

Rose took a shaky breath. They had been so close to Aterra's lair all these years. Her gaze was drawn to Arie as she thought how close he had been to Aurora—unable to reach her. Her chest tightened imagining his pain.

Arie didn't say a word. He leapt off the shore, turning himself into a large fish and splashing into the water. Luc's blood—Aterra's blood—did the trick. The Compass Points moved past the barrier. With a final shrug at Carter and Juliette, Rose dove into the deep blue waters of the Lake of the Gods.

※

UNSURPRISING FOR A POWERFUL NORDEN, Rose had loved the water since she was a child. Swimming in Compass Lake on a hot day had always been her refuge. It had broken her heart when she and Arie established themselves at Lake of the Gods but could not touch the water.

She was making up for it now.

Rose wrapped her magic around each of them, giving them space and air to breathe so they could easily dive. Each stroke took her further below the surface, her power sinking into the natural, wild magic of the Lake of the Gods. The water was so dark and deep that it was difficult to see anything ahead. Luc had been right, though. They swam toward her island and then went straight down.

Luc led them to the tunnel. It narrowed around her as she swam through it, her head breaching the surface on the other side. Her heart beat rapidly from their pace. She tread water as she surveyed Luc, Carter, and Juliette heading for the shore.

Her breath caught at a face that she didn't recognize. Beige skin, shoulder-length blond hair, and ageless green eyes that looked like a forest. She knew who it was before he spoke.

"Hello, Rose," Arie said. She did a double take as his lips moved and sound came out. The voice she was so used to hearing in her head. He jumped out of the water and landed on the beach. His long-sleeved shirt was pushed up to his elbows, and his dark pants were sopping wet.

"Arie?" She couldn't help the question in her voice, though she *knew* it was him.

He nodded.

"About time," Luc said as he stalked up the beach.

Words failed Carter as he met the Lord of Flame in human form.

"You clean up well, Arctos," Juliette said as she sent her wind whipping around each of them to dry their clothes. One would never know if she was serious or mocking. Regardless, Arie's smile lit up the room.

"We need to keep moving," Luc said, returning reality to this unique reunion.

Rose agreed. No one knew how long they would have before Aterra found them. Luc said he had avoided Aterra in his exploration, but that could change at any moment. They needed to free Aurora.

"Lead the way," Rose said, gesturing Luc forward.

They walked through the tunnels, attempting to be quiet. They preferred to have time to free Aurora before dealing with the Suden god. Speed in this part of their task was their goal.

Luc took them down a winding set of paths, all sloping

slightly deeper into the underwater mountain. Finally, they opened into a vast cavern. Rose could only describe this as the heart of the mountain. This was the room she had seen in flashes of Arie's memories. Three vials, a test, an explosion. It had all happened here. Rock formations grew from both the cavern floor and ceiling. Instead of a set of tables in the center from Arie's memories, the far wall from their entrance held multiple pathways leading to other tunnel-like corridors.

How much power was needed to reshape this area into something livable? That part of Arie's memory had been shrouded in fire—not his flame, but a volcanic explosion. It must have been Aterra's earth element that cleared this cavern out and made it usable after.

Instead of a cool, damp cave, steam broke through cracks in the floor as they walked toward the tunnels. The magma must not be buried all that deep, its heat seeping into the open room. What was the likelihood of this volcano exploding again? Did they have to worry about natural disasters down here as well as godly ones?

The only thing to do was to keep moving. Rose marveled at Luc's sure steps through this maze. How had he known which one to take the first time? Now, his journey seemed relatively quick, given all the wrong turns he could have taken.

Her spine straightened as it occurred to her that she hadn't clarified one point of his story. He had returned *too* quickly. There was no way he had found the right path on his own.

Luc seemed to note the shift in her step. "He's not as much a prisoner down here as you think," he said.

She paused to make eye contact with Arie, still an unfamiliar action. He blinked, his head tilting, mirroring the familiar gestures of his bird form. She was not going to like what they found at the end of this pathway.

THE SMALLER CAVE they walked into could be a family room. At least it was decorated with some living furniture—something that looked like a chair, a few stone tables, and personal items strewn about.

"What is this?" Juliette asked, looking around.

She was right to ask. The room didn't look plushly appointed enough to belong to a god. However, it was no prisoner's room.

Before Luc could clarify, a door across the room opened, and Aiden stepped through. Not much of a prisoner, indeed.

"The Compass Points have arrived," Aiden said mockingly.

The glare Rose shot at Luc could freeze the depths of Lake of the Gods. "Luc?" she asked, a question clear in her tone.

He stepped towards her, his hands raised in surrender. "I know you're still not sure what to believe about his actions. I didn't want you to overthink it on the way down here." Luc turned to look at Aiden. His gaze slowly returned to Rose.

"We can end this now," Luc said. "I can take care of him, for everything he did to you—your family. Just say the word."

"You idiot," Arie said to Luc, realizing what he intended. He rubbed his temples and looked at Rose.

It took Rose another moment. Aiden wasn't a prisoner. Luc was offering to kill him. It was sweet in a weird way. The weight of Aurora's dagger was heavy in her boot. She'd missed her chance last time. She had hesitated when the moment was critical, and then Aiden and Aterra had escaped.

If she suspected correctly, though, Aiden had helped Luc through the cavern tunnels—that was the only way Luc would have made it back to the shore so quickly. When Aterra wasn't controlling Aiden, he didn't appear to be trying to destroy the continent.

"What's he talking about, Luc?" Aiden asked. "Aren't you going to free Aurora?" He looked concerned as his gaze moved across each Compass Point, finally landing on Arie. "Who are you?" he asked, his imperious tone returned.

She searched Aiden's face as he spoke, looking for the friend she grew up with. How much of this was his fault? The only way to know for sure was to ask.

"What are you doing, Aiden?" she asked, her brow pinching as she tried to stare into his being—to understand his choices. How would she know if he was as corrupted as Aterra? Or if he was a prisoner of his own childhood decisions?

He looked away. "Luc burst in and said you were here to free Aurora. If that's what you're here to do, move quickly. Aterra could arrive at any moment." His eyes finally met hers. "If you're here to kill me, let's get on with it." He lifted his hand in a half-hearted come-and-get-it gesture, as if he couldn't muster the energy for villainous banter before a fight.

Rose cocked her head to the side, her gaze still searching. Her heart conflicted. She stepped forward. No one said a word as she moved close enough to strike. Aiden's blue eyes didn't leave hers. He didn't prepare to defend himself, to fight. Killing him wasn't justice. No matter what he had done to her. "You chose this, didn't you?" she asked. It was the question she'd wondered about since returning to Compass Lake.

His shoulders stiffened, and his lip curled in a sneer. "Of course I did, Rose."

But she knew him. As much as she wished she didn't sometimes, she knew this look—that curl of his lip. He used the same one when he pretended his father's words didn't wound, when Rose's parents asked if he needed to be home for dinner and he said no one would notice his absence.

"I saw the gray eyes the first time I met you," she said.

He blinked. His face softened.

"How long before that?"

"A few years," he said with a shrug.

"Before you had any friends," Rose said, finally knowing the truth.

"He said he was my friend." Aiden's voice was so quiet. She almost missed it. She knew the words, though. She had suspected them since she realized something was inhabiting Aiden's body.

"I know," Rose said. "I don't forgive you for those decisions and what they cost me." She shuddered.

She turned to look at Luc. "Neither will we kill him." She wouldn't do it, and she wouldn't let Luc do it. They would take him back to Compass Lake to face a Norden trial for his actions.

If Aiden's actions with Luc earlier were any indication, he wanted out of Aterra's control too. Aterra was the problem—one they would deal with as soon as they freed Aurora.

CHAPTER THIRTY-FIVE

Decision made, Rose walked through the next door—the one Aiden had come through. This room wasn't what she pictured. A cell with metal bars stood in the corner, and someone was behind them. Though disheveled, she could only be one being. Her skin was golden brown, and her tangled hair was black as night—she was the Norden goddess, Aurora.

"This looks too easy," Rose said, mostly to herself as she looked around. No barred cage could hold a goddess. What was she missing?

"Are you the Norden Point?" an exhausted voice came from the sparse bed against the wall in the cell.

"I am." Rose nodded as the others filed in behind her. "These are the rest of the Compass Points, though I believe you already met Luc." Her gaze fastened on the cell door. "We don't have a lot of time. Do you know—"

She lost Aurora's attention the moment Arie walked through the door. Silence filled the room as the Compass Points realized their irrelevance in this reunion. Aurora's entire person lit up when she locked eyes with him. It was a light brighter than Arie's biggest flame. And it was entirely for him.

"Arie," Aurora whispered.

He was on his knees at the metal bars instantly, reaching his hand through...

An explosion shook the room.

Arie's human form flew backward from where he knelt. His body arced backward and crashed next to the door they had just entered.

"Well," Aiden said smugly. "I tried to warn him."

Rose needn't have worried. It was a cage to hold a god, not kill one. Arie sat up and glared at Aiden.

"You should have said it louder," Arie grumbled, rubbing the back of his head.

"It wouldn't have stopped you," Luc said.

Arie had a glare for Luc as well. Turning back to Aiden, he asked, "What magic holds her? Tell us how to get her out."

"I can speak for myself, love," Aurora said. "The magic that holds me here is Aterra's and the amplification of the wild magic in this place."

"The wild..." Arie couldn't even finish his curse. He seemed enraged that a natural power helped Aterra. "I still don't understand. The magic of this place...the amplification—it shouldn't take sides in this," he said instead of stringing together a sentence of curses. His face still looked like he would prefer that route.

"And it hasn't, Arie." She looked at him so patiently. "You know as well as I. It latches on to one magic at a time."

Aiden gestured to the cell that was holding her, ignoring her words. "It certainly looks like it has."

Arie glared at him. He scratched his head as he stood. "When I was here with Zrak. The wild magic only affected me. And when we took the test, it clearly latched on to Aterra."

"We always thought its wildness was drawn to the most volatile magic," Aurora said.

Arie balled his fists at his sides in frustration.

"The why doesn't really matter." She shrugged. "The wild magic still supports Aterra. And I can't escape while his magic holds me here."

"Let's move on to how we can get past it then, shall we?" Juliette asked.

"Shouldn't Aterra's magic be able to get you out?" Rose said.

"Yes," Aurora replied, her eyes darting to Luc. "But I don't think the Suden Point alone is enough." She tilted her head.

Luc took over the conversation, taking a step forward. "Is there a key?"

Rose's gaze searched the room, her eyes landing on Aiden. "I think the best key would be the one on Aiden's finger."

The Compass Points and two gods turned to Aiden. He looked down at his hand. The gold triangle ring with the onyx center was still on his middle finger. "This ring?"

Rose couldn't believe she'd missed it earlier. Of course he would be wearing it.

"Yes, Aterra's artifact on the continent. This could strengthen Luc enough to break the lock."

Aiden, to his credit, didn't hesitate. He pulled the ring off and handed it to Luc. Rose noted the lack of objection from the other Compass Points. If they weren't pressed for time, she'd take a moment to enjoy it. Only days ago, Juliette would certainly have objected, loudly, to offering Luc more power. He seemed to earn more of their trust by coming clean about his suspicions of his lineage.

"Won't me putting it on strengthen Aterra?" Luc asked.

"We've proved it depends on your choices once wearing it," Arie said.

Luc shook off the comment. His shoulders straightened as he resigned himself to whatever happened next. Slipping the ring on his finger, he stepped toward the cell.

A chill swept through the room.

"What do we have here?" came a cold and ageless voice from Aiden's body. His eyes flashed gray as he spoke. Aterra had arrived.

✳

"Aiden, you disappoint me," Aterra said. This sounded odd coming from Aiden's lips. "Just leading our guests to the one room in the heart of the mountain where we happen to be keeping a goddess as a long-term guest. Tsk, tsk."

Rose rolled her eyes at the phrasing, but her mind worked quickly behind them. They needed more time. Luc needed a chance to get Aurora out. He knew what to try. He just needed to be able to get to the cell lock. Unfortunately, the only thing she could think of to give Luc time was to attack Aterra—as the Compass Points. That, however, also required Luc's magic.

His power spun a tight circle around her as she thought. A protective bubble ready to defend. He had more than proved his power could do two things at once. She would have to trust that. She would also try old-fashioned distraction first, to see how long it bought them.

"Why him, Aterra?" Rose challenged since Aiden was saying nothing to defend himself. Could he speak while he was inhabited?

"He is irrelevant," Aterra said, his power pulsing as it flooded into the room. The ground shook, and steam rose through the created cracks. This room was too small to fight the earth god. He could wipe them all out with one well-placed quake. The only positive was that he had worked so hard to create Luc. Surely, he wouldn't wipe him out of existence so easily. When the steam cleared and she could see again, another being stood beside Aiden. His olive-colored skin, dark hair, and sharp features looked so much like Luc that she couldn't believe Arie hadn't questioned Luc's parentage sooner.

Aiden opened and closed his mouth next to the god of earth. When was the last time he had seen the god instead of being inhabited? Aterra's true gray gaze evaluated every person in the room, lingering longest on Luc.

"Ready to put that power to better use?" he asked.

Luc glared at his father. "You already have one puppet. I'm not sure why you need another."

"He had power, though not enough," Aterra responded, sounding bored. "He was desperate for attention and validation. And he was in a prime position to take the Norden seat and overrun the other Compass Points."

Carter and Juliette blanched at the statement, though it seemed accurate from where Rose stood, though Aterra failed to mention that included blackmailing each of them with secrets of their courts—secrets only godly power could unearth.

"What did you even get out of it?" she asked as Luc's hand palmed the dagger in hers. She needed to keep Aterra talking and focused on her. He pulled back on the blade, and she didn't hear a hiss of pain as he wordlessly added his blood—Aterra's blood—to the Suden artifact on his finger.

"Isn't it obvious? The continent's imbalance. A prime seat to watch the show. The best position to see if my plans for further power proved successful." Aterra's gaze fell again on Luc.

His body tensed next to her and angled slightly toward the cell that held Aurora. His power thrummed through the room like Aterra's had moments earlier. Except his magic's scent was infinitely more comforting than that of the god's decrepit forest. Luc seemed intent on hurling the artifact into the lock. His earth magic would guide the needle point of the ring to enter the lock mechanism.

She hoped it worked. If Aterra got his hands on the artifact with Luc's freely given blood on it… She didn't want to wonder if that counted as Luc giving his will.

"But you didn't even tell Luc your plan," Rose challenged, drawing Aterra's attention again. "How could you gain the power you sought if you didn't ask for it?"

"He wasn't ready." Aterra glanced at Aiden. "And this one was serving his purpose well enough."

Rose rolled her eyes.

"Aiden was well positioned to further the imbalance in a different way," Aterra continued. "Through the affairs of fae and humans." He paused to glare at Arie. "And imagine my delight when I realized using Aiden also displaced the rightful Norden Point for Aurora, further depreciating her power." He flashed a feral grin.

Arie's control snapped, and he lunged at Aterra.

The Suden god must have been waiting for Arie's attack, intentionally provoking him. Aterra didn't even move as he tossed Arie, much the same as touching the metal bars around Aurora's cage had. Arie's human form once again flew across the room. This wasn't going well for him.

"What do you hope to gain here?" Luc's cold voice broke in. "We know where you are. The Compass Points are here to stop you, to do our duty, and to rein in the imbalance you've created. You've lost. Why can't we all acknowledge that?"

"I acknowledge nothing. You still have so much to learn, but I can teach you."

Rose side-stepped in front of Luc, putting herself between him and Aterra's stare. "He's not yours." Her voice was steadier than she felt, and her magic hummed in agreement.

"Some might debate that point, but to address the Suden Point's question, you may know where I am." He glared at Arie as he started to pick himself up off the floor. "But stopping me is another story. The Compass Points are incapable of holding a god. You are Zrak's failed experiment. There is nothing left for the continent but another Flood."

Rose startled at that. Aterra wanted to destroy the continent again? She thought this was about power.

"No one wins with another Flood, Aterra," Arie said, spitting blood from his mouth as he stood.

"That's what you think. With a cleansing Flood of all the magic on the continent and with the strength of my Suden Point, I would be the uncontested power. We could start again without the requirement of balance."

Rose had only moments to finalize her strategy. Carter and Juliette's gazes were locked on her. She had their attention, and she would use it. They would unite their magic for an attack.

"You're right, Aterra. The Compass Points haven't proven they could keep a god in check. But you had your hand in that too, didn't you?"

She let out a breath as she readied to strike at Aterra. As each element made itself known, she dipped down to her lake of magic to open the channels. Luc's gaze kept darting toward the cell in the corner of the room. Rose could feel his magic rising, preparing to throw the ring and guide it into place.

A familiar voice in her head offered precisely what she needed. His appearance may have changed, but at least this was the same. "*Luc, throw me the artifact, then do what you need to do.*"

Luc dipped his head next to her. Arie spoke to them both, taking on the problem of freeing Aurora so that she and Luc could focus on Aterra.

"You ensured the Compass Points were too weak, too divided to stand against you. Well, that ended with Aiden's term as Norden Point."

Luc tossed the ring to Arie, and that was her cue. She wanted to pray for luck to some higher power, but looking around this room, she didn't like her options. All the gods were on her shit list. The Compass Points were the only option to defend the balance.

Earth, wind, water, and fire flared in the small room. Reproducing their successful pattern, Rose shot a stream of the elements, layering them around one another, straight at Aterra. The strength sent by the most powerful fae on the continent. This had to work.

Her body shook as their magic raged through her. They had all listened to Aterra's plan—the destruction of their way of life, of their continent. She thought the power that flowed through her during their tests had been substantial, but it paled compared to what surged in her now. Their magic *wanted* to defend the continent.

She wanted to let it.

In the seconds it took the Compass Points to send her their

magic, Rose smelled the dreadful, older scent—Aterra's considerable magic was rising.

The ground shook, the earth splitting below them, sending each Compass Point flailing for balance. The shaking and splitting floor was only his opening move. Rose felt the earth rattle and break on her left, where Carter and Juliette stood. Turning quickly, she heard Luc's shout. He jumped clear of the collapsing ground and onto a stalagmite that he shot up from the cave floor.

Their joined magic faded as Juliette held herself and the others up with her wind, and Luc built a plateau for them through the wreckage. The other Compass Points' magic left her as they used it to defend themselves. Unlike Luc, they couldn't do two things at once with their power.

This would be problematic. Aterra would spend his energy making sure they were defending against his magic instead of attacking with theirs. Red lava bubbled up through the cracks Aterra forced into the earth. Apparently, the volcano below them wasn't exactly dormant—one more thing to worry about as this battle escalated.

Luc lifted himself with his earth magic as Aterra attempted to impale him with jagged rock spikes from the floor.

This was not going to work. Rose had only taken a single shot at Aterra in the seconds she led the magic of all four Compass Points, and he'd defended. She sent a blast of wind at Aterra in her frustration as she tried fruitlessly to distract him, to bring his attention back towards her.

The telltale creak of unused metal joints swinging open indicated things might be going their way. Arie must have been able to free Aurora.

Now that he wasn't distracted, Arie sent a stream of lava boiling and bubbling around the ground where Aterra stood, encircling him and drawing his focus, if only for moments. He gave the Compass Points a second to regroup.

"We have to get to the heart of the mountain," Rose yelled. The Compass Points joined her, running for the door. They would never win against him here. His power was too absolute in the confined space. He could destroy everything on which they stood in one swoop. They needed to be able to spread out to make themselves more challenging targets.

They sprinted down the hallway with Aiden in tow, returning to the initial cavern, the heart of the mountain, a room Rose knew from her journey through Arie's memories was where this all began for Aurora, Aterra, and Arie.

In seconds, they split up, each spreading as far as they could, positioning themselves by the other various hallways that led out of the main cavern before Aterra came crashing through the hallway behind them.

It was incorrect to say that he used the hallway. More accurately, Arie and Aurora seemed to have thrown him through the wall, his earth magic helping to break apart the tunnel and guide him through it as rock burst from the new hole his body formed.

Arie and Aurora were right behind him. As soon as Aterra landed, he spun his fist, creating a sandstorm. The crushed rock, silt, and sand flying through the cavern made it difficult for them to aim.

Rose was determined to try. The Compass Points were with her, sending their power back through the open connections. The elements layered to strike.

She hadn't released the stream when the tunnel cracked. "Arie, look out!" But her warning was too late as the hallway fell on top of him and Aurora.

She sucked in a breath. No tunnel collapse could kill a god. Arie and Aurora would be fine—if a little delayed in assisting in this battle. She hadn't counted on their help anyway. Her own magic rose again and snaked around the power gathering within her. She rolled her neck. The Compass Points had to do this alone.

She would make this one count.

CHAPTER THIRTY-SIX

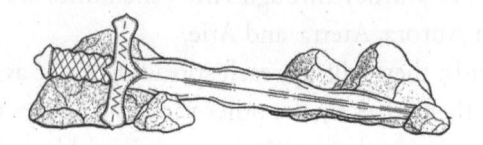

The earth danced beneath him with power before it started to shake. Aterra was the god of earth and aided by the wild magic in this place. Luc's one accomplishment so far was that Aterra no longer had his artifact. Maybe it wasn't great that Arie, who had it, just had a tunnel collapse on top of him. But at least Aterra couldn't use it.

Rose's glance went upward. Luc would bet anything she was thinking about the village of Bury somewhere above them. If their magic was too strong, if an explosion like the one that had happened in this place so many years ago erupted, the village wouldn't make it. The villagers and Tara, still taken by the mist plague, wouldn't even be able to evacuate. They would need to be careful about how they won this battle. But he was committed to them winning—no matter the personal cost.

Luc funneled magic to Rose while taking a separate shot at Aterra. Using his signature move, he tore a hole in the ground below his opponent.

"That won't do you much good." Aterra taunted. "That power came from me. I know everything it can do." He took the distraction Luc offered, hovering above the hole.

"I'm more than happy to keep trying." Luc rose himself and

looked down the hole—he couldn't help but compare it to his abyss in Loch. Definitely not as devastating as that one, but something about the magic here—the *thinning* he felt when he first arrived—he knew he could do better.

Rose made eye contact with him. He dropped to the ground and nodded to her as he sent her more magic for their combined onslaught. His magic, already thick around them, grew heavier. It wrapped protectively around Rose as she pulled their powers together seamlessly. He used to think she was used to his magic—used to directing it—but he knew it was more than that now. Luc felt the power build in the stream as she pulled in Carter and Juliette's elements. Rose whipped the stream of earth, wind, fire, and water at Aterra.

She aimed to knock Aterra back—possibly trap him in the other half of the tunnel he had collapsed. If she could block him into a corner, maybe he wouldn't be able to see them well enough to attack.

Aterra barely stumbled at the onslaught of magic.

Luc had an idea, but it would not be particularly easy to communicate. Rose wiped the sweat from her face. Her furrowed brow told him that she wasn't sure what to try next. Aterra retaliated, sending a rolling wave of rock and stone toward Rose. She barely had time to lift herself with her wind to get out of the way.

"I've got an idea," Luc yelled, hoping her wind magic would catch his words and bring them to her.

It did, as she replied, "I'm all ears." She lifted herself above another earth shake.

"We'll try the old-fashioned way," Luc said as he reached for the blade strapped to his back. Rose laughed. He understood the sentiment. This was a life-or-death situation, well beyond their ordinary dealings, and she likely hadn't even thought to grab a weapon—he hadn't. But he had a sword, magically imbued by the best weapons master on the continent. Rose grabbed her weapon from the back sheath she wore, and Luc moved to her side, as they positioned themselves to face off against Aterra.

Luc lost sight of Aiden. He must've been staying out of the way. Luc could mostly determine where Carter and Juliette were positioned along the cavern. Far enough from each other that one earthquake wouldn't collapse the ground between them both. Getting into this room and spreading out had been a good idea. It was too bad it hadn't slowed Aterra. He was relentless—tailoring attacks to each Compass Point simultaneously.

"You are proving to be quite a disappointment," Aterra said as he shook the ground below Rose and Luc. He was not trying to kill them, only ensuring their magic was distracted in defensive measures. Luc steadied them both as he approached Rose. He knew what this was. Aterra was testing his magic.

Heat flared from the left as Carter and Juliette tried to help with a fanned flame. Aterra appeared to have no problem stopping the wind and fire, building a stone wall blocking the elements on the side they attacked.

He was boxing them in again, forcing them into a smaller space where his control of the earth controlled the battleground.

"Did she even like you? Or did you demand her submission?" Luc spit out.

The disdain in his voice pulled Aterra's attention back to his son. Good. Luc was angry, no matter how much he pretended not to be. He was angry for himself, and no matter where he and his mother had stood, he was angry on her behalf. Had she even known what she was doing? Or did Aterra use his artifact on her?

These wounds were old and deep, but this was likely his only chance to get his questions answered. Plus, his backup plan could only benefit from his heightened emotions—that's when his power was most volatile. He let himself sink into the anger.

His mother had met more than unfriendliness from the fae community over Luc's father disappearing. Bound fae were impossibly rare, and life partners weren't always common, but it was unheard of for a fae parent to disappear from the child's life completely. Their village blamed his mother. And when he was older and his power more apparent, they blamed him. Luc could never escape the shadow of whoever passed their magic to him, and neither could his mother.

He had a chance to reckon with Aterra now. He would take it for both of them.

"How dare you," Aterra spat.

Luc didn't need a real answer as he lunged across the cavern toward Aterra, bringing a wave of rock and stone with him as he moved.

Aterra created a shield of the earth to meet Luc's blow. Rock exploded in all directions as they clashed. Luc shielded himself, levitating through the backlash. He glanced at Rose to ensure she was covered. Her wind circled, protecting her, but Luc also felt a strand of his power lying in wait. His magic wouldn't stray from her in such a precarious situation.

"She wanted me." He scoffed. "And every time I returned, she was more than eager." Aterra's words drew his focus back to the god before him.

Luc didn't know if that was true—part of him hoped it was—he didn't want to imagine his mother's choices being taken from her. Anger flowed through Luc's attacks, his magic becoming more reckless with each onslaught of earth and stone. Aterra, however, wasn't going on the offensive against him. He was only defending.

Luc was happy that Rose didn't immediately join in. He knew his attacks weren't productive, but they felt good. He shook his head slightly as he sent another rock hurling at Aterra. His gaze marked the boulder's path but caught on the black bird flying into the cavern. He must have transformed into something small enough to get through the debris. Arie dropping onto Luc's shoulder was the reminder he needed.

They had to defeat Aterra together—all four of them.

"*I'm assuming you had a better plan than simply wailing on dear old dad here?*" Arie asked as Luc put some space between himself and Aterra.

"Yes," he whispered. "Tell the others to send their magic to

Rose again, but we need to let her *take*, not just use what we're offering. She'll understand—tell her to do what she did with me in Sandrin."

Arie nodded and uncurled his talons, dropping the onyx ring into Luc's hand as he mentally passed the message to the others. Luc slipped the ring on his finger. He would take every advantage he could get against Aterra. His well of magic never felt empty, but somehow, the ring made it instantly overflow. Power shook through him as the natural amplification took hold.

Arie said nothing about the ring or the power pulsing around them as he replied, "*They're ready.*"

Luc sensed it before he saw it. Before Rose had a chance to reach for her power, he felt a wave of magic crashing. A literal wave, as the rocks that Aterra had dropped to block the tunnel rolled and washed away. A surge of water crashed them forward, and steam hissed as it slipped into the cracks where the magma lurked below the cave floor.

Aurora stepped through the rubble, looking regal, though she'd certainly been through hell. "You and I have unfinished business," she said to Aterra.

The list of those who had a bone to pick with Aterra was growing long.

Luc looked back and forth between Aurora and Aterra. He wanted to let Aurora take her shots—there was no question she deserved them—but Arie had been pretty clear before they left Compass Lake. It wasn't a god or goddess who could subdue Aterra. It was only going to be the Compass Points.

They had to do what they were made to do.

"You were in the way. You needed to be taken off the board."

"It's never your fault, is it?" Aiden said as he erupted from where he had been hiding, near the water entrance behind Rose and Luc.

"You are just doing what you must—what needs to be done. You're a god! Take some responsibility for your own plan!" Aiden yelled. "No one made you do anything. You chose this."

The room stood in silence at Aiden's outburst. He had been cooped up with Aterra for too long. Given the impact of his actions, Luc couldn't bring himself to feel sorry for Aiden, but he could recognize that this was him picking a different path now.

Aiden stalked up beside Luc as he raged at Aterra. Luc didn't think twice as he handed off his blade to Aiden stomping forward, water erupting from the cracks in the floor as he passed. Aiden had made poor choices, but he, too, was entitled to a reckoning with Aterra.

Aiden, whose Norden mother and father only saw him as a means to an end. Aiden, who had been alone and vulnerable as a child and whom Aterra had preyed on for his own means. Luc knew this wouldn't solve their problems, but as with Aurora, Luc had difficulty saying he didn't deserve his revenge. If nothing else, it would give the Compass Points needed moments to send Rose their power. To let her *take* more of it.

A wave erupted beneath Aiden as he took the offered sword, propelling him across the cavern as he lobbed himself at Aterra.

CHAPTER THIRTY-SEVEN

Aterra didn't repel Aiden's attack.

An unfamiliar power rose with Aiden's wave. A strength Rose could only assume was godly. She suspected the Norden goddess assisted Aiden's approach. The Suden god also appeared too shocked by Aiden's actions. And as Aiden's wave rolled him forward, his arms outstretched, both gripping the hilt of Luc's sword, he met no resistance. With all of his momentum and magic with him for this attack, he drove the blade down through Aterra's shoulder.

Aiden's face shifted as the weapon in his hand sank into godly flesh. It went from pure vengeance—a rage Rose knew she had felt on her own face before—to terror. He clearly hadn't expected the blow to land. Caught off guard by his actions, Rose realized too late that this was a distraction, giving them time to ready the Compass Points' magic.

Juliette and Carter also lost their focus, their eyes locked on the fae they knew to be cruel and selfish, the one who had blackmailed them over the years to get his way. She recognized then that they were as conflicted as she had been about Aiden. They hadn't known how much of what happened was his responsibility versus Aterra's control. Rose hoped this action would bring them the same peace she had found earlier. Unfortunately, they were too invested in what this action would bring to realize Rose needed their power—now.

She turned to Luc. Though he had as much cause as the others to be distracted, his eyes were locked on hers. She had seen Arie land on his shoulder and watched him slip the Suden ring on his finger. The smell of pine and cinnamon grew in the cavern, though it had already been incredibly potent. Luc sent his magic spiraling at Aterra to support Aiden's attack, but as he did, he opened up his great chasm of magic to Rose. As Arie had instructed, she reached for it through the tunnel at the bottom of her lake, pulling from the darkness that was his power—letting it fill her. Luc was a part of her, flooding her from her toes, out to each fingertip. She couldn't help the full-body roll as the magic connected. It felt right—more than right. Their magic more than unified—bound in a way she'd never experienced. Luc's power was an onslaught, but one she was more than capable of handling. He didn't moderate the channel between them—she had full access to all of him.

Wind and fire quickly joined Luc's magic inside her. Juliette's door burst off its hinges, and the opening in Carter's tree was unguarded by a veil beast. They no longer only pushed their magic into her. They offered their power so she could take what was needed.

If Rose and Luc's power was bound as a single force inside of her, Juliette and Carter's elements circled tightly. All four elements united in a coil of strength, ready to burst. Luc pushed more magic to her, urging her to take. The depth of his power called to her, even as it seamlessly fed her own.

Caught up with the Compass Point power building, she had only a moment to realize Aterra had struck back against Aiden. In what amounted to a godly-sized backhand, Aterra swatted Aiden away. He had no prepared defense, and his body flailed as he was thrown across the cavern. Aterra plucked the sword from his shoulder and cast it away.

Rose saw too late that Aterra hadn't only hit him, he'd pulled a sharp piece of rock from the cavern to stab him as he tossed him aside. Aterra's aim was true, as an earth wielder's would be. Rose's whole body pinched as she heard Aiden's scream. Arie burst into action, landing at Aiden's side in human form. She knew his healing powers firsthand—but she was unsure it would be enough.

Aurora was the only one who seemed undistracted by Aiden's actions. She layered her own attack, sending wave after wave crashing into Aterra. Rose swore the goddess nodded at her, indicating it was her turn to strike.

She couldn't worry about what would happen to Aiden now. They needed to finish this. They wouldn't waste the time that Aiden and Aurora had bought. Rose took a deep breath and aimed the magic spiraling inside her—the power of the four Compass Points—directly at Aterra.

Luc wasn't where he had been in the cavern. She felt through the channel for him, the Suden child whose father walked out on him. The Suden Point who was blamed for all of Aterra's wrongdoing. The strong fae who didn't let any of this stop him from being the male he wanted to be. She couldn't see him but knew he was with her—his magic flared as a reminder.

All of Aterra's wrongs hadn't changed Luc's course. Just as the list of grievances she held against Aterra hadn't changed hers. Aterra had taken her only friend from her. He killed her family. He all but banished her and stole her place as Norden Point. He made her path more difficult, but ultimately, she drew strength from the pain she'd experienced.

This path had brought her Arie and Tara's friendship. This path had put her on a collision course with the Suden Point. She couldn't imagine what type of relationship they would have if they had met in a Compass Point meeting instead of her dismissal at the market booth and a scuffle in the woods.

Her path wasn't easy, and it had been filled with grief, but it had made her who she was.

The Compass Points' magic flowed as she thrust out her hands, melding wind, water, fire, and earth together to create a single flowing channel—instead of four tangled streams. She wasn't sure what to call the result, but the elements swirled and mixed to build a solid attack as they shot across the chasm toward Aterra.

Still distracted from Aurora's attacks and flinging Aiden across the heart of the mountain, Aterra wasn't prepared for what hit him. The vortex slammed into his chest. He couldn't find purchase with his earth magic to hold himself in place as he had before. He stumbled backward.

Rose pushed her advantage—taking a step toward him across the cavern. Aterra stumbled again. Rose continued. She let out a small sigh with each step she took as she saw Aterra fall further.

Luc remained out of sight, but his magic pulsed as she reached for more. She funneled more of their connected power forward alongside the fire and wind magic pouring into her.

A plan formed in Rose's mind as she took another step. Aurora had cleared the collapsed tunnel when she burst free. She would have to walk Aterra right into the cage that could hold a god. Could the now empty cell contain Aterra if she got him there?

A step.

Another step.

One more.

The Compass Point's power pulsed through her. They'd moved across the cavern. Each step cost Rose, though. Her magic lagged, and her knee buckled as she tried for another. She didn't think she could continue.

"Just hold on," she swore she heard, whether a secret on the wind or a whisper from Luc's tendril of power that circled her, she didn't know. Her eyes widened to search again for the magic's bearer as it tightened its grip on her, steadying her stance.

Aterra hadn't found a way to repel her. Her gaze remained locked on him, focusing their power, while she did what the voice asked. She held him where he stood—no longer sure she could reach the cage. Even with the reassuring strength of Luc's magic, another step was beyond her. Aterra flicked his fingers and flailed his arms desperately, trying to call to his amplified power to fight the Compass Points' attack.

"What are you doing to me?" Aterra shouted as he stood his ground but could not escape her hold. Sweat dripped down her brow as the magic she commanded strained to hold him in place.

"Just a little bit more." The whisper was at her ear again, and more of Luc's magic flooded her senses.

"We're reminding you that gods don't like prisons!" Rose yelled as she tried to lift her foot for another step. Meeting too much resistance, she let her foot fall back to the ground. The earth around her caught and stabilized her—additional support from the Suden Point's power. "The only way to teach you this lesson seems to be for you to experience it yourself." He was still held—contained—even if it wasn't the cage she had hoped to put him in. He couldn't escape the combined power that locked him in place. She didn't know her endgame. She only knew she had to hold him here—just a little longer.

"You can't contain me! I'm more powerful than all of you!" Aterra bellowed.

He was panicking now. His magic pushed back against the unified power she wielded. He seemed to realize he had no escape. His eyes darted around the heart of the mountain, searching for a solution.

"I think we might finally be your match," Rose said, her voice struggling. She thrust her arms out again to help physically keep the magic stream in place. She had him—but she was losing her hold.

An influx of power flowed through her. Carter and Juliette seemed to dig deeper into their power stores and thrust more magic through their connection. Her spine straightened as she reached for what each of them offered.

Breathing deeply from the exertion, Rose lifted her foot,

successfully taking another step forward. "You see, Aterra, you meant to destroy, abandon, and weaken us, but we chose differently than what you destined us for."

Aterra tried to lift himself from the ground, making himself a moving target. He flailed as his heels rose and fell, restricted from their usual movement. Rose, keeping the stream of power barreling toward him, lifted herself with an extra burst of Luc's magic. She aimed their unified stream at a downward angle, pushing Aterra into the earth he usually commanded. His foot sank into the ground below him. Luc's magic was warm and supportive, like a quick squeeze through intertwined fingers. He would never let her do this alone.

"You seek only to sow chaos and destruction. You seek to elevate yourself above the other gods. But we will leave this continent better than we found it. We will protect the humans and fae living here. We will restore the balance—no matter the price."

Rose took another deep breath and sent a final push of the power she stewarded forward. Aterra's body folded in on itself as the unified magic hit him like a punch to the stomach.

As his body unfurled, she realized it hadn't been only the punch of magic that had kept him in place. Luc stood behind the Suden god, and even from her vantage point, she could see the ring on his finger had the needle point outstretched—piercing Aterra's neck.

"You idiots. You can't contain me here," Aterra ground out, though he stumbled as the magic of his artifact used against him overtook his body.

The ground below them shook, Aterra's earth magic taking root. The ripples in the cavern floor didn't make it far, though. Aterra's power momentarily muted.

Unsure what Luc was doing, she caught his eye, and he winked at her. He seemed to have a plan, at least. She pushed one more burst of the Compass Points' magic at Aterra, anchoring him where he stood to give Luc another moment.

His magical blade appeared in his right hand. He must have

collected it while she marched Aterra across the floor. She loosened her hold on Aterra, ceding Luc's magic back to him at his request. Would her magically forged weapon be enough to kill a god? She didn't think so—but she wasn't sure what else Luc would do.

"Forgive me, Rose. I know you'll come for me." Luc's gaze met hers as the whisper reached her.

Horror flooded her, her stomach plummeting, as he found another path.

CHAPTER THIRTY-EIGHT

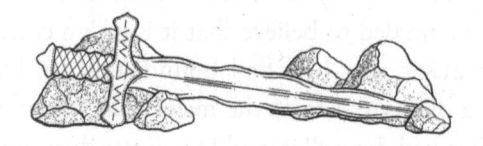

He knew this was the right path when Rose had reached for more of his power. It had never been about connecting and directing their magic in concert. The price to hold a god was always going to be higher. It was about the Compass Points trusting each other enough to give unbridled access to their power. Access to the depths of one's magic was a risk—one that could be easily abused—but one he had already taken with Rose. He'd suspected on the Suden beach, the evening after her initial fight with Aterra, that there was more to the way their magics intertwined—he just hadn't been ready to face it with how he felt about his own power. After their experience in her workshop and the way their magic had come together with their bodies, he had no doubt that they were bound.

It wasn't a conscious choice that fae made; it was a soul-deep connection—magics finding their perfect match. A binding couldn't be controlled, but it also didn't happen without the consent of all parties. Luc had opened himself up to Rose in every way he knew how, and he was astounded to realize she had done the same with him.

She chose him too.

Their connection was unprecedented. Fae could only be

bound with those of the same court—but nothing about Rose and Luc's connection had been normal. Nothing about Rose and Luc themselves followed traditional paths.

He'd tested their bond, talking to her through his magic during the battle. Bound fae's power connected on a different level—sharing everything. Rose was everything he needed. He just hadn't realized the totality of what that meant. He needed to trust his power—he needed to believe that it wasn't a curse. It was his uncommon magic that hers had bound itself to. Her love had shown him a different side to the magic that sent most running. And his power had done all it could to ensure they could keep her.

His attention returned to the battle. His chest constricted as his gaze found Rose, the one who had managed to bring them all together. The only one they would all trust with their magic. The one he couldn't live without. They wouldn't have stood a chance without her. She had brought forth their ability to hold Aterra. But no one had a plan for what to do with him now that he was restrained. The Compass Points couldn't stand in this cavern, holding him forever.

He knew what he had to do. He hoped Rose would forgive him.

She pulled on his magic, taking what she needed. More of his power strained to go to her. It was drawn to her the same way he was, like the beach waiting for the ocean's tide. He knew, academically, that his magic was him. They were not distinct entities. It was just one of the ways he had been taught to control his power. If it was a separate entity—he could leash it. But the reality was that he was only leashing himself.

His power strained toward the one who didn't require that of him or his magic.

The pull didn't slow him down. He knew he had to keep moving. He fed Rose a steady stream of his element as he let his magic off its leash. They had more to do while Rose trapped Aterra.

A spiral of magic drifted toward Rose, steadying her as she marched. It braced her and met her steps with the earth. It supported her physically while Luc couldn't.

He ran to where Aiden lay with Arie, in human form, already at work, Aurora had joined him. Luc had sucked in a breath as he saw the rock sliver's placement. Shaking his head, he knew he couldn't dwell on Aiden's fate. There were bigger things at stake. Aiden had made his choice, and in Luc's opinion, it had been a decent one. Luc had come to retrieve his sword. He would need it for this next part.

Bending to pick up the magically forged weapon, he gave Arie a brief nod. He assessed his blade—and felt a further amplification of his power glide through it. He hadn't had enough time to marvel at what Rose had done. But he could feel his magic's connection to the weapon—could feel how it amplified his natural tendencies and instincts.

He thought of the hole in Loch, a hole he'd made on raw emotion alone. This time, he had two amplifiers and a lot more to lose. With a final glance at Rose, he reassured himself that this would work.

It was then Arie glanced up from his work to nod at Luc. The earth shook under them as Aterra fought back against Rose and the magic of the Compass Points' hold.

"Do you know what you're doing?"

"Of course not, Arie," he replied.

Arie shook his head. "Be careful."

"She'll get me back." He paused, unsure Rose would realize what their connection meant. He needed someone to explain it to her. "We're bound," he added.

Arie gave him a soft smile of acknowledgment followed by a look that indicated he wouldn't spend time trying to make Luc find another option. Arie was the one person who had as much faith in Rose as Luc did. He knew, probably better than Luc, what she was capable of. It was unclear how Arie guessed his plan, but Luc was oddly reassured that the Vesten god didn't try to stop him.

His plan hinged on the fact that Rose could do anything she put her mind to. And Luc accepted that she would put her full attention to retrieving him—if only to scream at him for what he was about to do. He'd take it gladly if it meant they were together and this was over. While hating the danger this plan put her in, they didn't have a lot of options.

The Compass Points held a god, but they had nowhere to put him.

Luc did.

Rose would have doubts—of course she would. That's why she didn't get a say in this part. For all that she knew how strong and capable she was, Rose still saw limits to her capabilities. Luc did not. He wished there was another way. He really did. But they were in this cavern, where, five hundred years ago, Zrak had put a contingency plan in place—one that was ultimately needed. Luc was only doing the same. Aterra needed more than just momentary containment, and Zrak had already proved the best location to hold a god to preserve the balance.

It was time to take Aterra to it.

Aurora's compass had served them well in finding Aterra and leading them to this final battle, but maybe it had chosen poorly when it first decided which god would make a sacrifice. What if Aterra had been the one to sacrifice himself? Wouldn't Arie, Aurora, and Zrak have been better able to preserve the balance on the continent? This was the crux of Luc's plan. They needed three gods on the continent. He simply wanted to change which three.

The earth shook again as Luc glanced at Rose. She was tired. He could see it from where he stood. But she was so strong. Her dark brown hair, tied back for most of their journey, flew free as she fought for a few more steps. She was trying to back Aterra into the prison where he had held Aurora. Luc believed she could get him there if she wanted to, but he didn't think it would keep him for long. Whether Luc willingly shared his power, the fact that he existed and was the Suden Point already strengthened the Suden god's magic. Aterra needed separation from the continent for what he'd done—a price needed to be paid for the imbalance he created. Luc would ensure that Aterra alone bore the cost of his actions.

He looked down at the ring he'd slipped on his finger. It was gaudy as hell—a large gold triangle shape with an onyx stone carved to fit inside. He let a drop of his magic run over the onyx stone, and the familiar needle popped out.

Shaking his head again, he laughed a little at the fact that this needle, this weapon, had been used against him. In some ways, he was glad it had. It meant he knew that even someone with strong earth magic wasn't immune to the strike. The impact would be different, but it would do *something*.

With others, like Aurora or the Norden elder, Samuel, it acted like limited mind control, overwriting what they thought they knew and inserting a new story. For a strong earth magic wielder, it was less about mind control and more about his body being at war with itself. Two powerful earth magics fighting inside a single host. It had felt like a poison ravaging his body. He hoped it felt the same to Aterra. It would buy Luc a few moments.

His steps took him across the cavern to Aterra's side. Aterra—his father. Luc shook his head again. That would need further examination at a more convenient time—just then was not it. Rose still held Aterra in place. No matter how he raged—he couldn't break free. She must have realized that Luc was doing *something*. Though she never would have stopped if she'd known what would come next. He let go of the doubt. She would understand. He believed that, as he stabbed Aterra's neck with the needle tip.

"What the—"

Luc could only guess that Aterra was feeling the flow of foreign magic ripping through his veins. He only had moments to focus his power and get them to the more permanent holding place he had in mind.

"I need my magic back," he sent to Rose through their bond. He had plenty to spare, but he needed every advantage and amplification to make this work.

Rose nodded, her face wrought with exhaustion and confusion, as she released the Compass Points' unified power. Her trust in him was absolute enough to free the god they had contained.

Luc's magic rushed back to him then, like a returning friend. Power flooded through him, and he tunneled down deeper into the vast reservoir within himself. He lifted the blade Rose made him and let his magic sprawl. It searched for weakness or thinness in the earth's natural barriers. Carter had said the hole in Loch wasn't just a void of darkness. It was a hole to somewhere, or *almost* somewhere. Luc had come dangerously close as a child to tearing a hole through planes of existence.

This place was too filled with wild magic not to already have a small crack for him to pry into. His magic found an opening in the cavern's center, where he could imagine Zrak had set up the test for corrupted power. The god's magic had left its mark, exposing a sliver of a break between this plane and one beyond. Luc ran to it, his magic pulling Aterra along behind him. His power gathering around and within him as he ran. With no hesitation, his last step was a wild lunge fueled by the depth of his power as he thrust the sword, amplifying his strength, into the sliver between planes.

The sword cut, just like he knew it would. It slid through the world like a knife through fabric, the tear like a drape of cloth billowing in the wind. What lay beyond, he'd find out shortly. He sliced deeper as the crack fought to close itself. This was no longer just a thinning between planes—it was a break. A hole big enough for someone to go through. Two someones if everything went according to plan.

The continent and the next plane fought to close the gap connecting them. Part of the natural balance between planes was this separation. That was fine with him. He didn't want Aterra to have an escape route. He only needed this to work once.

Aterra's eyes snapped open as his body fought off the internal magical attack. Luc was prepared, though. He already had his arms around Aterra and was diving headfirst through the opening he'd created.

"What are you—" Aterra couldn't complete the sentence.

Darkness enclosed them as they fell beyond the veil, the crack Luc created neatly knitting itself closed behind them.

CHAPTER THIRTY-NINE

A piercing scream filled Rose's ears as she fell to her knees. It took her too long to realize it was her own. Her eyes widened at the impossibility of what unfolded in front of her. Luc had thrown himself and Aterra into a hole he'd created between planes. Rose didn't have to imagine where it led. Luc had taken Aterra beyond the veil.

She gasped for breath, her magic straining to follow. The crack Luc had created disappeared before Rose could process what he was doing. She had no time to react. Wetness dripped on her hand, and she belatedly realized tears were streaming down her face.

Luc was beyond the veil now.

Luc was beyond the veil—where Zrak had banished himself. He had taken Aterra and flung himself into the unknown. His magic and its scent vacated the cavern. Emptiness crept in without its presence.

How had he known that would work? Rose closed her eyes as she tried to give herself a moment of grief before she started sketching plans in her mind. She couldn't stop her brain from calculating, from thinking through options.

She would get him back.

Arms circled around her, and though she was still unused to his human form, Arie's essence was inexplicably recognizable. She knew it was him without even looking.

"I'm sure you're going to tell me it was the only option," Rose said, wiping her tears with the back of her hand.

Arie shrugged. "It was his choice—and it was probably the best one you had."

Rose nodded. Grief and practicality fought at the forefront of her thoughts. Carter could see spirits—maybe he could communicate through them. And Juliette communed with Zrak—he was also beyond the veil, wasn't he? She had to be able to find a way to get to Luc.

"Do you think I can get him back?" She choked on the final word. A bottomless pit opened in her stomach. She had just found him. She wanted a life with him. No was not an acceptable answer.

"I, like Luc, believe you capable of anything, Rose." He paused, letting that sink in. "I *know* you will get him back."

Rose shook her head, giving up and letting her tears fall. She knew she had other things to do. She couldn't wallow in this yet. The mist plague still ravaged the continent. They needed to find a way to restore those impacted. Logically, all of this could only be done by finding a way to communicate with Zrak, if not bring him back directly.

"You..." She hesitated. "You think he's okay, right? He's not a god. What if the rules of being beyond the veil differ for him." She rushed the last sentence.

"I know we didn't have time to dwell on it, but he's a demigod, Rose. We may have never had one before, but godly power runs through his veins. If Zrak is able to be retrieved, then I believe Luc is too."

Rose released a deep sigh. A hiccup undermined its dramatic effect, and she laughed a little to herself.

"You're a mess, dear," Arie said, though she could hear the smile in his voice.

"I'll get him back."

Arie squeezed her shoulder tighter in acknowledgment.

✳

Arie ushered Rose to where Aiden lay sprawled on the ground. Aurora, Carter, and Juliette stood somberly around a too-still body.

"There was nothing I could do," Arie said. "I'm sorry. Aterra's magic struck true."

Rose heard the words and added them to the list of feelings she would deal with later. She would have appreciated closure between them, but those were never the cards they were dealt. The decision she'd made about him when they found him in the cavern stood. She knew it was Aterra who had been the one to kill her family, to start the fire, to change the course of her life.

She knelt next to Aiden's body and whispered a Norden prayer over him. "Safe waters, my friend," she finished as she looked up at the other Compass Points and gods in the room.

Inexplicably, they seemed to be waiting for her. Whether that was looking for her direction or trying to give her space to sort through the riot of emotion she was feeling, she didn't know, but she was ready to face whatever was next.

"This changes nothing," she started.

Juliette laughed. "This changes everything."

Rose tilted her head. Sure, in some ways, it did, but not in the part that mattered. "We needed to talk to Zrak to stop the mist plague. We discussed getting him back from beyond the veil anyway. Now we have to retrieve Zrak and Luc."

Juliette's face sobered. "We can do the ritual properly. We can try to talk to Zrak." She hesitated. "How will we find Luc, though? My connection with Zrak draws him to the ritual location. We don't have anything like that for Luc."

Rose's head was already shaking with each of her words. She didn't want to hear them, but each was relevant. She wanted to scream at Juliette and tell her to find a solution. Maybe offer a helpful suggestion instead of shooting everything down and crushing Rose's single hope. But she also knew that wasn't fair. Concern lines etched Juliette's face—her tone held a gentleness not often heard from the Osten Point. She didn't relish delivering this difficult news. She was trying to be realistic.

Rose put her head in her hands. No one spoke as she sorted through her emotions. Luc's magic had spoken to her during the battle—she was sure of it. It hit her on a level that was deeper than the whispers on the wind. Even now, she felt his magic missing like a phantom limb. That had to mean something. She made eye contact with Arie—about to voice the incomplete thought about the connection she and Luc shared.

"I might be able to help with that," Carter said, responding to Juliette's question. He stepped forward before Rose could speak. All eyes locked on him as he continued. He seemed to finger the Vesten coin in his pocket. "Spirits always need to move between this plane and the next."

Rose thought of the snarling animal Arie had turned into when they tested the power-sharing ritual. If a veil beast could ferry souls beyond the veil, on some level, it meant travel was possible. She tilted her head, appraising Carter. He'd known more about the beast than he let on. He met her gaze, and his head shook almost imperceptibly.

"Some of the more transient spirits can help get a message across."

Rose was too exhausted to try to figure out what that meant. It was something. Rose wouldn't discount Carter's offer. They could start with that while she considered how Luc's magic had supported her during the fight—and what the limits of their connection might be. Maybe her bond with Luc's magic would be closer to the link between Zrak and Juliette. Bound fae of differing courts didn't exist—but there was something between her and Luc's power. She would figure out what it was. Emotionally exhausted, her gaze roamed the cavern. She couldn't do anything about it right now.

"Thanks, Carter," she said, too many thoughts running through her head. "We will make multiple plans." Her gaze returned to Juliette. "But we will get him back."

✳

ARIE AND AURORA performed Aiden's funeral rites under the mountain. Some would say the ritual performed by the Norden goddess was more than Aiden deserved. Rose thought it was right after what he had done in the end.

"We shouldn't linger," Rose said after observing the ritual.

The others nodded.

"Where are we going next?" Carter asked, looking between Rose and Juliette. "I know the goal—to get Luc back—but I don't think we've discussed the how."

"We need to go back to Compass Lake," Juliette said.

Rose took a moment to smile. She forgot for a second that Luc had sacrificed himself. She forgot that she might not get him back. She took a moment to appreciate how easily Carter and Juliette prepared to use the secrets of their courts to help her. It was a massive milestone for the Compass Points. She wished Luc were here to share it with her.

And just like that, her thoughts returned to the fae she loved and the plans she would form to save him.

Aurora and Arie exchanged conspiratorial glances as they headed out of the mountain cavern the same way they had come.

"What?" Rose asked Arie when she walked beside him.

"What, what?" Arie replied.

"Are you and Aurora coming with us?" she asked. Rose was sure they would want some time to themselves, but no matter how much this problem needed to be solved by the Compass Points, Rose didn't think the gods were off the hook this time.

Zrak may have made most of the plans for the Covenant, but as she'd learned from Arie's memories—he entrusted critical pieces of information to the remaining gods. Arie and Aurora might not realize the value of what they knew. Rose was determined to figure it out.

Selfishly, Rose also wanted to ask Arie about her connection with Luc. He understood more about godly power. Maybe Luc's ability to communicate with her through his magic was part of his demigod nature. She didn't think that was something the other Compass Points would be able to answer.

"We'll meet you back at Compass Lake," Arie said.

Rose wanted so badly to tease him about his newly reunited lover, but the thought only reminded her of the pit in her stomach. And the feeling of watching Luc throw himself beyond the veil with Aterra. She couldn't bring herself to tease. She was just glad that Arie got this second chance with Aurora.

"Sounds good," she said.

She was thankful for the push Arie had given her. Arie's regret over lost time with Aurora had helped Rose admit her feelings for Luc. Now, with Luc beyond her reach, she couldn't even imagine the scale of regret she'd feel if she hadn't acted when she did. If she hadn't told him she loved him when she did. She would hold every moment they had together close.

But she would also fight for the future they both dreamed of. A future of balance for the continent and those on it. Luc knew her and knew what she was capable of—he would have factored that into his plans. His belief in her and his grounding support was a craving she never quite sated. The scent of his power no longer lingered in the cavern. Her hands clenched into fists at her side, and she wanted to flood the space with water for allowing that smell to leave.

A thickness settled in the air around her—calming her. It didn't hold the familiar scent she craved, but it *felt* familiar nonetheless. It made a sound, she thought. Almost like a whisper on the wind, she swore the words "*You'll find me, my love*" echoed through her thoughts. She searched their surroundings before they dove back into the waters of Lake of the Gods. No one was there—no one had spoken to her. She knew better, though. She felt it. There was something inexplicable between them.

She would do anything necessary to get him back.

Want more of Rose, Luc, and Arie? Get news about releases, bonus scenes, and more. Go to https://www.jillianwitt.com/subscribe or scan the QR code to join.

If you loved Tangled Power, please consider leaving a review on your favorite platform.
I love hearing from readers! Keep in touch:

jillianwitt.com

instagram.com/mythandmagicbookclub
tiktok.com/@mythandmagicbookclub

ACKNOWLEDGMENTS

I was overwhelmed by the love given by readers to Compass Points. I'm so thankful for it and I hope Tangled Power finds a special place in your book shelves as well. I know it has mine.

I want to thank Ian and Loki, for listening to the endless worldbuilding and plotting. Loki is lucky he's a dog and doesn't understand what I'm saying. Ian had no such luck, but he persevered.

A special thank you to Rebecca, without whose gentle but poignant feedback, this book wouldn't have become the beautiful story it is today. Thank you to Josh and Katie, your thorough review is always needed. Thank you to my biggest fan, my mom, and your constant love of spreading Rose & Luc's story far and wide.

Milton Keynes UK
Ingram Content Group UK Ltd.
UKHW040840140624
443986UK00005B/16/J